MAKING
BELIEVE

MAKING BELIEVE

JOHN LEGGETT

Houghton Mifflin Company · Boston

1986

4/1986
Am. Lit.

Library of Congress Cataloging in Publication Data

Leggett, John, date
Making believe.

I. Title.
PS3562.E38M3   1986   813'.54   85-21917
ISBN 0-395-39412-0

Printed in the United States of America

V   10 9 8 7 6 5 4 3 2 1

FOR CONNIE

MAKING
BELIEVE

1

THE ramparts of the General Theological Seminary ring the block at Ninth Avenue and Twenty-first Street, just below Manhattan's waist, making an evangelical stronghold in the midst of the city's vast urgencies and agonies. In the Close—Chelsea Square, as it is called—the light is sober on the brightest days.

In 1959, my final year there, I took Horace McVity's popular course, Contemporary Theology, which met three mornings a week in the Sherred Hall lecture room. Tiers of one-armed, yellow oak chairs rose toward a gallery of dusty plaster busts. From their niches at the back, Augustine, Erasmus, Luther, and Calvin looked down upon us and the semicircular stage with its dark table and turret podium.

As gray city light fell through tall, gothic windows, it became lavender, spiritual. The continuous din of truck drives and bleating taxi horns from the traffic on Ninth Avenue was muted, soothing as summer rain on a tight roof.

It was here I had my first glimpse of Royal Train. He was a few minutes late to class. McVity was arranging his notes and taking our measure when Roy strode through the door. Oblivious of the professor's questioning gaze, Roy made for a seat in the first row.

He was slim, well over six feet. His upright bearing, the flash of impertinence in his brown eyes, and a Harris tweed jacket gave him a notably independent air, which I took as disdain for the rest of us in our chinos and short-sleeved shirts.

Later, when I looked up from my scribbling, I noticed that Roy was taking no notes. He was first to question and even to dispute the benign McVity's conclusions. He seemed to be testing the boundless professorial patience, overturning the orderly course of instruction to reveal any cant that might have crept into it over the years.

When McVity inquired about his preparation for seminary, a question that had formed in all our minds, Roy replied that he had served in the Navy and taught at law school.

Roy's probing, his refusal to acknowledge a square foot of sacred ground, began to produce groans from his fellow students, but Horace McVity, who had put in twenty years as Shreve Professor of Biblical Studies and seen everything in the way of seminarian, was unflustered. His rumpled, preoccupied face actually brightened at the sight of Roy's waving hand.

I however saw a provoker, a mischief maker, a tower of self-consciousness, and was offended by all three. I couldn't imagine why he had come to General Seminary. So far as I could see, there was nothing remotely spiritual, even serious, about him.

In late October Roy brought one lecture to a halt over the conflicting evidence in the Gospel accounts of the Resurrection. He cross-examined McVity as though he bore a responsibility for the discrepancies, and finally astonished the class by saying, "I don't see how, in this century, we can be expected to swallow the idea."

"To swallow what idea, Mr. Train?" McVity asked patiently.

"The Resurrection."

Silence in the hall was followed by a humming like the swarming of hornets. McVity ran the fingers of both hands through his mane of fine white hair. "That's the cornerstone of Christian belief, Mr. Train, the conquest over death."

With a shake of his head, Roy dismissed nineteen centuries of Western civilization. "In the first place the evidence is hearsay and in the second it is in conflict. Each disciple saw something different. That's a pretty wobbly cornerstone."

It was my voice that burst forth now and I recognized an irascible edge of my father's in it. "Come on, Train!" I cried. "You're wrecking this class. There are certain givens here, certain beliefs that all Christians share. We accept them in an act of faith. It transcends your courtroom logic."

Roy turned in his front-row seat to find me in the last and to look at me with interest. "I understand that," he said coolly. "I'm asking whether it's historical fact or myth we're to take on faith. That's an important difference and I want to be clear on it. If it's myth I'm being asked to buy, I want to know where it came from, whose it is."

A wave of grumbling swept the lecture hall. In front of me Alvin Bender shouted, "What do you mean, *whose* it is?" Bender's round, pumpkin face was menacing and he hefted his New Testament as though he might hurl it at Roy's head.

The voice of our outspoken fundamentalist, tall, sallow Richard Meach, shouted, "If you don't believe in the Gospels, Train, what are you doing here?"

Roy was leaning over the back of his seat, watching the growing mutiny with a certain satisfaction. "I'm meeting God." Smiling now, he glanced at his watch. "We've got an appointment here."

There were unforgiving growls and some laughter too. Horace McVity, who had been watching Roy's side show with habitual forbearance, cleared his throat and reclaimed his lecture.

"This is all useful, I think," he said, "reminding us not to make too many assumptions—but if you'll be patient with us, Mr. Train, perhaps it will become apparent to you that what can be perceived with our eyes and confirmed by a reputable historian is less important to our belief than what we perceive with our instincts and confirm with our spirit."

This was a reprimand, and I watched Roy's response reveal itself in his face, which had turned thoughtful. "Yes," he said, "I hope . . . I expect it will."

As McVity resumed, Roy sat with his chin on his fist. He gazed not at McVity but at a map of Paul's Mediterranean journeys hanging on the wall. Now he produced a small notebook and from time to time wrote swiftly in it.

The refectory, in Hoffman Hall, a gothic building at the west end of the Close, was a replica of Queen's commons at Oxford, with furlongs of stained glass and carved oak soaring up two stories over the cafeteria service counter and the dozen tables, long ones except for a single round one at the far corner of the hall. It was here we took our meals and gabbled about everything that concerned us.

Would Brooklyn survive without the Dodgers? Could Eisenhower learn how to pronounce *nuclear*? Was Lowry's redheaded girl friend dating other guys? At twenty-four I was still a virgin, unsure of myself with young women, but many of the others had girls whom they saw on weekends.

The round table at which George Suter, Alvin Bender, Richard Meach, Bob Morse, Frank Le Page, and Ted Fenno usually gathered was the liveliest. They were mostly devout fellows, proud as any apprentices of their learning, scattering the names of German philosophers, Greek thinkers, and Hebrew prophets about like rice at a wedding.

As the pudding dishes were scraped and the coffee cups drained, the talk got around to such professional fine points as what Martin Buber had meant about revelation and H. R. Niebuhr by radical monotheism. The blaze of argument was as regular as the chiming of the quarter hours.

Roy avoided such debate. At lunch he would take his tray to a quiet table and open a book. At supper we rarely saw him at all. His room was below mine in Edson Hall, and I had an occasional glimpse of him there studying or changing his clothes, or in the library during the evening hours. But I never saw him at Compline, the last required evening service, and I wondered what he did with himself.

After the McVity lecture and its Resurrection controversy, Roy joined me on the way to lunch, saying, "That was good, your turning us on to faith. I thought there was some ordinance against bringing it up." Seizing my arm, he said, "But it's no problem for you, is it, Soames? I mean, no bullshit. You *do* believe?"

I could not be sure if the sparkle in his eye was a concentrate of facetiousness or curiosity, but I gave him a sincere answer: "Yes."

"And the doubts?"

We walked along silently for a moment. "Well, I'd be a fool not to have doubts," I said, "but the more fool to reject God because of them."

"Ah-h." He appraised me as if trying to guess my weight. "I envy you that."

When we had filled our trays at the counter, Roy came along with me to the round table, and his sitting down among his adversaries from McVity's class produced an exchange of glances. The need now was for initiation.

Meach began it asking, "Where was it you taught law school, Train? Here in the city?"

With all eyes upon him, Roy replied, "No. The Midwest."

"One of the big ones?" Fenno asked. "Michigan?"

Roy said, "A pretty big one."

"You don't want to tell us which?" Alvin Bender asked.

Roy broke a roll and buttered it. He beamed at Bender. "It was another life," he said.

This brought a prolonged silence, broken at last by George Suter, who said, "My brother dropped out of law school last year. He feels law is getting too specialized, too much of a rat race, the way they work you in these big firms. This huge specter of never making the letterhead."

"It wasn't that," Roy said, spooning up his soup. "I was disillusioned by law itself . . . by the way it's practiced."

"How is that?" Meach asked.

"Too empirical." He smiled at Meach. "Not enough myth. I missed the myth."

There was some laughter, and when it subsided Suter said, "But you were objecting to myth this morning, Train. Is that just in Scripture?"

"You misunderstood me," Roy said. "There's a difference in myths. You need quality control. A meter is helpful—a bogus meter."

Meach stretched his long neck. "Are you saying that some of our biblical myths are bogus?"

"A good myth tells a truth. It gives allegorical shape to an idea that's already in our consciousness. It doesn't manipulate us."

"Like what?" Meach asked sharply. "A for-instance."

Roy shrugged. "What do you make of the Ascension? It's all Luke's testimony. He's the only one who claims Christ actually took off from the Mount of Olives. It gets better too; the second time he tells it, in Acts, he adds the welcoming clouds and talking angels. It occurs to me that he elaborated on the story because the other disciples had their doubts about it. *I* sure do."

"It's Scripture, Train." The fundamentalist note in Meach's voice was carrying it above the babble in the refectory. "God's word. You *don't* doubt it."

"No kidding?" Roy asked Meach. "You mean it's never occurred to you that Luke simply made up the Ascension, a spectacle that would amaze his audience and maybe hook them on this new sect he was touting? Or if some creative monk added the trumpets and blinding light?"

Meach groaned. "You're making a joke of it."

Although Roy was clearly enjoying himself, he said, "No, I'm not. Let me ask you this, Meach. If I were to tell you that there had been a backup at the George Washington Bridge this morning that went all the way to Hohokus, so in order to get to class on time I prayed for God's help, and lo, the Hudson River parted and I drove across on the riverbed, would you believe it?"

"Of course not."

"Because you didn't see it? Because I'm a notorious liar?"

"Because it's not the word of God."

"Are you sure?" When he got no reply, Roy balled his paper napkin and dropped it on his tray. "You're right, Meach. I didn't come that way and mine are not the words of God, but you've got to watch out. Got to be particularly leery of anybody who claims to speak for Him."

6

Roy left us jauntily, as though glad enough to have been included at the round table today but leaving no doubt that he was going his own way.

He was pegged as an eccentric, impossibly prepared for seminary but amusing. It was as if he were a clownish skater with a performance, arabesques on ice as thin as paper, worth watching. No one wanted to be too close when it gave way.

Looking back on our seminary experience of twenty-five years ago, I can see Roy's path as already marked, unswerving, and his rejoicing in its deviation. At the time, though, I was simply intrigued by the contrast he made in our midst, in particular by my own uncertainty. You would not, today, take me for an ambitious soul, not with these ears muffled by years of patient listening, these eyes gone watery with the flow of understanding. Still, I now know that I was one.

An ungainly, pathetically dreamy preacher's boy, I prized my ambition as others did their fielder's mitts. I slept with it under my pillow and carried it around in a pants pocket, where I could touch it when I chose, feel it glow at bleak moments on the playground or at the supper table.

Held in my hands, it became a key to the houses on Summit Street where I felt unwelcome, places like the Singletons', with its library and flower garden.

When I was fourteen it became a musical note, a wafer of an eighth note with flying flag. I must have encountered that note in the hymns I'd liked, "A Mighty Fortress" and "Immortal, Invisible," a thousand times but failed to recognize it until I heard it in Paul Whiteman's recording of "Rhapsody in Blue." It was at Danny Singleton's house, incidentally, on that big Capehart. From that moment I was a tank filling with music.

For two years I tried with a forty-dollar clarinet to share my gift for music with family and neighbors. They were tolerant.

When I was eighteen my ambition took shape as a ticket out of Elkhart, Indiana. Elkhart was all I had known, but I suspected it deceived its young people by convincing them it was a world like any other and offered every opportunity within the twenty miles of its limits. Then, when you least expected it, maybe when you were struggling with the clasp on a girl's brassiere, Elkhart caught you, shanghaied you into a lifetime of service to State Farm Insurance or Ajax Pest Control.

I did not doubt my pocket amulet. I thought it would carry me wherever I chose to go, that with it I was a boy Houdini who could slip out of any leg iron, any chain gang a merchant society could contrive. I presumed the qualities, the professional talent, intelligence, energy for escape. I had heard them breathing and felt they would waken, so many sleeping princesses, on cue.

I cannot recall any single dramatic moment of revelation, but while studying at the Juilliard School of Music in New York I learned I would never be that *Wunderkind,* never enjoy a triumphal return to Elkhart. My piano teacher, Mrs. Stilsom, and my much-daunted mother would not be smiling and nodding I-told-you-so's at the back of the auditorium while I led the high school orchestra in the William Tell Overture.

No one said a word, but I read it clearly in the eyes of Arnold Shaw, kindest of my Juilliard teachers. It was an opacity that said, I'm not the one to tell you, Ethan. You must tell yourself and the answer is in your having to ask for it.

I read it too in the evasive eyes of Molly Ross and Joe Arnstein when I offered myself for the Lexington Chamber Group. It was a familiar despair, which I had known from an Indiana schoolyard and from the start.

We must all come to terms with our inadequacies, the nose too big, the heart too small, the ear unsure of pitch. And how easily that stifling disappointment turns to jealousy. *Schadenfreude* is how the German musicians say it, a corrosion of heart that makes it sting from someone else's achievement and rejoice in someone else's misfortune; the closer the victim, the more exquisite the sensation. A spreading malignancy, it devours the whole spirit, making us believe we have failed at *life.*

There are generous spirits who can turn their disappointment into charity, failed poets who man the artistic soup kitchens of the world. They are saints and they are few.

But there is a third, a middle way, which seems to be mine. Transference. It is how I explain the relationship that grew between myself and Roy Train.

*   *   *

I suspected he was neither clown nor fool but a serious man who had to come at problems in his own way. As the year wore on, he was no less outspoken. Roy encountered the Gnostic movement for the first time in Church History 107, the Early Fathers, which was taught by Percy Morrison (*Origins of Our Faith* and *The Five Ways of Thomas*).

Roy was taken with Gnostic cosmology, in particular the concept of a Creation by rebellious archangels. He continuously interrupted Morrison's lecture to inquire about the details.

Halted for the third time, Professor Morrison said, "Well, it is fascinating, Mr. Train, and I think you will enjoy further reading in it, but I'm afraid we must get on. In this course we are primarily concerned with Gnosticism's effect on the early church and its bishops. We are interested in how Irenaeus and Tertullian dealt with a first important heresy."

Roy acquiesced but added, "I'm just curious about why it didn't work out—if you think it was on account of its complexity, or its having so many characters—because there's a lot of good stuff in it."

Professor Morrison leaned on the lectern to gaze at Roy. "How do you mean, Train, that it didn't work out?"

"As a religion."

"But it *isn't*. It never *was* a religion. It's a mythology, a mixture of Greek, Hebrew, Oriental, and Christian philosophies. Its worship is of the self."

"I understand that," Roy said. "But Irenaeus was the bishop, and his response to the Gnostics was to burn their books. If he hadn't burned the stuff, maybe it would be our religion."

The groans in the back of the room stirred Roy's enthusiasm. "Well, why not?" he asked. "What's wrong with a super God, a confident, better-tempered one? Why not a wholly profane world, from which our only hope of escape is through the single spark we each carry on the pinnacle of our soul? I can believe that, because I've got one. It's no more fantastic than our own tradition, with God blowing the world into shape."

"Mr. Train"—Morrison sighed—"I think it will be a waste of time, yours as well as ours, to attempt to prove our ancient precepts by today's empirical methods." He frowned at Roy. "Do you understand that much of our tradition is not to be taken literally but as metaphor for the inner truth we simply lack words for?"

"I understand," Roy replied. He watched Morrison search for and find his place in his notes before adding, "But I'm not the one who said Gnosticism is dangerous. Irenaeus did."

"Yes." Professor Morrison looked up again. "We do have to get through this Gnostic material before the end of the period. If you're all with me now, perhaps we can get on."

After class, Roy walked along with me to the mailroom and while I peered in my box asked, "What do you think about that Gnostic idea of everyone carrying around his own spark, his own source of salvation?"

"For one thing," I said, "it would cut us out of a job."

"Exactly," he said brightly. "That's why we burn the infernal stuff."

After Vesper service one evening I took a stroll down Ninth Avenue. It was six o'clock and the street was full of the homeward-bound, bearing groceries and newspapers. I recognized Roy in the doorway of a vacant shop and was about to hail him when I saw a dark-haired, long-limbed girl doing exactly that.

She capered through the plodders and amblers and in the instant before she reached him her mouth broke into a great smile that made an illumination in the street. She had a pale and fine-boned face with huge, willing eyes.

They kissed. It was just a brush of the lips, but as a bystander I felt the charge; it was as if I had seen stars collide in a night sky. Arm in arm they loped off downtown, toward what I imagined to be Elysium.

Roy brought me there one winter night. It was reached by a hand-operated freight elevator, the fourth floor of an abandoned warehouse with tall, weathered windows overlooking the Christopher Street pier and a freighter docked beside it. It was an ancient, scarred place with exposed pipes and cracking plaster but transformed by its furnishings.

Rough flooring was half covered by a Navajo rug. Over a large white sofa hung an unframed canvas splashed with yellow and scarlet. Push-pinned to the wall were a dozen huge photographs taken on the docks—a pallet of grain sacks, longshoremen, derelicts, rusty shipsides awash in foul water.

The wall facing the windows had been patched, ready for painting, and was temporarily decorated with epigrams. There was a long one in Chinese characters, a couplet in Hebrew, and dozens in English, some in Roy's flamboyant hand, others in a precise, round, clearly feminine one.

It is not important what you do, read one, *but very important that you do it. M. Gandhi.* Some others I remember were *God is one's ultimate concern. Sin is a concern that is not ultimate enough. P. Tillich.* And *Be true to the dreams of thy youth. H. Melville.*

One began in Roy's hand: *When I think of the world I often imagine that God has grown bored with it and sent it spinning on its own, until I remember Thee and Me. Valentinius.* Beneath it the feminine hand had added *Ditto, though at times I'm not so sure of Thee. Mrs. Valentinius.*

There was a distinctive aroma here too. I could see a bowl of fruit and a glass jar of ground coffee on the kitchen counter, but it was more mysterious, a sweet, exotic fragrance that I sensed was the girl's. It was. I learned much later that it was called L'Heure Bleue.

As Roy brought out ice and whiskey, I said, "I don't wonder that you're sometimes among the missing."

"It's a nice place" . . . he was concentrating on filling my glass, but he smiled—"for a seminarian."

"I was wondering . . ."

"It's Joan's, but I do spend a lot of time here. Do our classmates guess?"

"No one's said anything to me."

His eyebrows soared with surprise. "I don't think Dean Tewksbury is so unworldly and I doubt he'd approve of my living arrangements." I was sitting on the sofa, and Roy had a troubled look as he took the straight chair opposite. "Both of us feel marriage is the first step to divorce, so instead we're discreet. The thing is, though, I'm getting careless. I must want to be called to account."

"I was wondering about your asking me here."

"You don't strike me as a spiller of beans." An eyebrow questioned me.

"No. I wouldn't spill anybody's beans, not if I could help it."

It was then, at the bluest moment of the twilight hour, that Joan came in. There was a sound of a key in the latch, and Roy rose and went to meet her as she came through the door. He kissed her and he took the sack of groceries she had brought and then introduced us.

Her name was Joan Tallis and as she put her notebook on a counter and hung her peacoat on a peg in the hall, she told me that she was studying law at NYU and that her class had run late.

The living room opened into the kitchen, and while Roy talked, I watched Joan. I could see her putting things in the refrigerator, taking others from the cupboards, unwrapping a slice of pale meat and seasoning it for the oven. Her hands seemed marvelously deft, and they were musical, ajingle with silver bracelets.

She was so intent on her work, slicing and stirring, bringing forth utensils and setting the table for us, that I was surprised when she spoke to me. "May I ask you a question, Ethan? I'm interested in why you chose the ministry."

"I'm a little puzzled myself," I said, "but my father's a minister. Like every preacher's kid, I mutinied. Tried to find a musical way out, but that didn't work."

Her eyes were hazel. They probed mine in a kindly way, as if to confirm a belief that men were likable beasts once you got to know them. "And now you're happy with the idea?"

"Yes. I'm not so sure the ministry is happy with me."

"What do you mean?" Roy asked. "You're a natural."

"Not according to Tewksbury. I had an interview after my psychological road test. I thought I'd done pretty well, but he tells me I'm not cut out for a pastorate."

"He's wrong," Roy said. "Surely you know that. You have sympathy and honesty and intelligence. What the hell does he want? I think he was saying there aren't enough parishes to go around.

That's true. We'll need plenty of the new evangelism to land one."

"I think the dean was telling me I'd flunked evangelism."

"Ethan," Roy said, "your chances of a parish are around ninety-three percent better than mine, and *I'm* not discouraged." As Joan passed, Roy took her hand absent-mindedly, holding her fingers for a moment before relinquishing them. "Not even with my raffish living arrangements, not even with a reputation as the class lunatic, am I discouraged." He studied me with mock imperiousness. "Would you trust me with a parish?"

"Not yet."

He smiled slowly. "But you do know what I'm doing, don't you?"

"You're trying to find your own way to faith."

Both Roy and Joan were watching me, but neither said a word.

For our supper Joan had prepared scallops of veal under a sublimely spicy sauce, and toward the end of the meal I felt close and trusted enough at this table to offer Roy some advice.

"You know something?" I said. "If you really want to leave the seminary with a ticket of approval and stand a chance for the diaconate, you ought to tone down your role as devil's advocate."

"I'm not advocating the devil," he said. "I'm asking questions I want answers to."

"In Morrison's lecture yesterday he was trying to get us to focus on Trinitarian theory, and you weren't any help, with the questions about politics."

"We can't ignore the politics. Arius lost, and he was at least as right about the Trinity as the bishops. He was making trouble for them and they were out to get him. That's what was really going on."

"But that's not going to help you when Percy Morrison sits down to write up your recommendation. He's going to remember you as the one who was always taking on the church, always biting the hand you hope is going to feed you."

Smiling, Roy nodded. "That's exactly what he'll remember."

"And you've got a lot of people still mad about the miracles controversy, your seeing them as man's work. If you deny the miracles of the past, you seem to be telling us our belief is bogus and so we're bogus."

"I have to be true to myself, Ethan. That's what my senses tell me. It's all I have to go on."

"I wonder, then, if Meach could be right. Are you in the wrong line of work?"

He shook his head. "It's the right one. I'm pretty sure of that. And if Meach doubts it, then I'm absolutely certain."

"*I'm* sure," Joan said. "There was nothing casual in finding our way here. It was no accident."

"No, it wasn't, was it." Roy smiled at her, reached to touch her hand. His eyes lingered on hers for a moment, then wandered to the window, where, under arc lights, the freighter was loading. An ambulance twirled slowly in its sling of cables as if it had dropped out of the smudged waterfront sky, then sank from sight.

"I know what I'm doing, Ethan," Roy said reflectively, paying out the words. "Or at least I know where I'm going. I don't know exactly how I'm going to get there. That may take a miracle."

Ascension Sunday fell in early April that year, and a week earlier it had been announced that the ten o'clock Eucharist service would begin with a procession to honor the visiting Bishop of Rhodesia.

The day was a warm one, and as we gathered in front of the Deanery for this event, Roy appeared. He was complaining about his academic gown, which was required for such occasions. One arm of it was inside out, and as I helped him with it, he asked, "Got a date for the procession? Can I walk with you?"

His eyes were watchful, darting this way and that. "Sure," I said. "What's up? You look full of beans today."

"Oh, the beans . . ." He was peering at the column collecting behind us. "Yes, I've been eating a lot of beans." He seemed pleased to find Meach and Fenno immediately to the rear and greeted them warmly.

Then he spoke earnestly into my ear. "Be careful in this

procession, Ethan. I hear it's some kind of test. I don't know what, exactly, but the main thing is to keep your head—and deny everything."

"What?" I laughed. "What are you talking about?"

"Keeping your head. Remember."

Across the Close two acolytes were throwing open the doors of the Good Shepherd Chapel so that we could see the great rood screen and beyond it the stone figures on the reredos shimmering in candlelight.

From within the chapel a chord sounded on the organ. Ahead of us the choir launched into "Your Glorious Temple Rising" with full voice. The cross bearer raised his cross, and we all set off after him along the flagged path.

The procession made one complete round of the Close before heading toward the chapel steps. At the crossing of two diagonal paths stood the St. Paul statue, with its semicircular stone bench and surrounding foliage, and as we approached this I was astonished to see a life-sized figure emerge from among the holly bushes.

A five-foot, inflatable doll, clad in brown robe and biretta, it hovered unsteadily over the shrubbery as though attached to an unseen hand.

A babble of surprise rippled through the procession. Behind us, Fenno's voice asked, "What in the hell is that thing? Good God!"

Bewilderment followed. The voices of the choir and then the march itself faltered. Beside me, Roy asked, "What's the matter?" Turning to look behind, he called, "What's the trouble back there?"

"It's up there." I pointed ahead to the figure, which now bounced on a bushtop and sprang upward a few feet, where it was caught by a southerly gust and wafted gently skyward.

"Where?" Roy stared ahead. "I don't see a thing."

Tilting slightly, as if the biretta sat heavily on its head, the figure passed over the chapel door, bobbed uncertainly when it reached the altitude of the steeple, and then, as if it had found its course, disappeared uptown in the direction of the Empire State Building.

Meach, still aghast, said, "Is this somebody's idea of a joke?"

Fenno was explaining, "It was one of those rubber dolls you get to sit in your car."

"Where was it, Ted?" Roy asked. "I missed it. Ethan didn't see it either, did you, Ethan?" He looked at me closely.

"No," I said. "I didn't see anything."

At the rear of the column the Rhodesian bishop was taking it stoically, as though no excess of New York would surprise him, but Dean Tewksbury's puzzlement was turning to impatience. His arm rose, signaling for advance, and we resumed our way. Our choir stilled, we straggled toward the chapel entrance in disarray.

In the aftermath of what came to be known as the Second Ascension or the Miracle of Ninth Avenue, Roy steadfastly denied he had seen it or, more to the point, staged it.

Having accepted the role of accomplice, throughout the informal investigation at the refectory round table I maintained that I had seen no ascension, but afterward I pleaded with Roy for details.

"Come on," I said, "tell me about it. Meach says you had a kid hidden in the bushes. He saw him running."

"Meach," Roy said with contempt. "Wouldn't you know he'd have some human explanation for a miracle . . . if there was one."

There was little question in anyone's mind about who was responsible for the Second Ascension, but there was some about whether it was in acceptable taste.

As it turned out, I was not the only one to deny having seen it. George Suter and even Ted Fenno soon began their own denials, and for several days the cry of "Did you see the Miracle of Ninth Avenue?" was heard in the halls along with laughter.

In his lecture on Monday, McVity paused once to ask if anyone had heard that the unusual event in the Close yesterday had been a rise in the fortunes of one St. Cyprian of Chelsea, whose sainthood, he knew for a fact, had been revoked by Pope Gregory IV.

* * *

The reward for my role in the Second Ascension came soon. We were in the refectory, lingering after the others had gone, when Roy said, "I think the dean has discovered my secret. I have a date with him tomorrow." He studied the vaulting overhead. "Last night Joan and I decided that if it makes that much difference to everyone, adding their sanction to our very satisfactory relationship—what the hell. We'll show 'em. We'll get married and go right on loving each other. So"—he sighed theatrically—"it's all settled for May twelfth, here in the chapel, so small that nobody will notice. Will you stand up for me, Ethan?"

"Roy . . ." I was overwhelmed, felt such a surprising rush of affection for him that I could scarcely speak. "Of course. I'm pleased and proud."

As promised, the wedding was small. Joan's widowed mother, a ruddy, vigorously liberal schoolteacher, had come from California. She seemed wary of Roy's silky, pinstriped delegation. This was headed by Walter Train, Roy's father. He had an anvil of a face and stood a foot taller than Roy's dreamy-eyed mother.

Roy's brother, David, was there with his shining, blond wife, Nancy. By no means least, the Trains had brought along the Bishop of Newark to preside at the ceremony.

Joan wore no veil but a circlet of daisies and a simple white dress that fell to her knees and made her look like a child. Roy also wore white—ducks and a strange wide-sleeved medieval shirt. Even more surprising to the guests, Roy and Joan had translated the marriage ceremony into the vernacular. With the help of some steamy love poetry from the Song of Solomon, they extemporaneously pledged themselves to each other and their wedding to God.

Bishop Givens was a young man for such high office. He was in his forties, and so fair of hair and skin that he had the choirboy look. However, as our voices echoed in the beautiful chapel, he seemed to expand in manner, authority, and even size.

Out on the street, as nine of us packed into a venerable Buick station wagon with the legend *Five Chimneys* fading from its wooden door, Walter Train prodded David from the driver's seat. Over family protests, he insisted, "God damn it, I know where Christopher Street is. I know this city from before you were all born."

On Tenth Avenue we sailed serenely through a red light. There was a hush among us and a protest of horns from behind. Roy looked back to see if we were pursued.

"Well," he said, "it looks as if you got away with that one, Dad, but they've got traffic lights in here now."

Nancy laughed and the tension eased, but Walter drove on, ignoring it all.

Gathered around the punch bowl in the Christopher Street loft, I could feel disapproval radiating from the Train family, and I felt it included me.

Walter Train's frame was bent, not quite filling his double-breasted suit, but his voice was a trumpet. As father questioned son about the unorthodox ceremony, the bishop fingered his collar uneasily.

"Do they teach you that here in the seminary," Walter Train was asking. "You write your own ticket any damned way you want? Does it do the job? You feel married now?"

"Absolutely," Roy said, filling a glass and offering it to Joan's mother.

"I can't believe that stuff holds up in the eyes of the church," his father insisted.

"It does," Roy said.

"The common prayer ceremony is beautiful," Joan interceded. "We didn't imagine we were improving on it, Mr. Train, but we wanted to absorb it and make it our own in some way."

"It was your idea?"

"No. It was ours."

"Good for you, Joan," Margaret Train said quietly.

Ignoring his wife, Walter Train appealed to the bishop. "What about it, Laurence? Where do you stand on rewriting God?"

The amiable young bishop in his new purple rabat was determined to make peace. "Well, as you say, Walter, there's nothing casual about our forms of worship. They have the force of the years with them, but the marriage ceremony isn't in the Bible. I don't know who wrote it, but man, surely, and if it can be made more meaningful to a couple by their putting their own stamp . . . the church has no objection."

Thus thwarted, Walter Train was soon telling Mrs. Tallis his suspicions of her congresswoman, Helen Gahagan Douglas, and I saw the bishop glance at his watch.

"Yes," he said when I inquired, "I would very much like to get back to Newark as soon as I can. There's a meeting." I volunteered for the ferry service, and twenty minutes later I was piloting the Trains' station wagon through the Holland Tunnel with the bishop beside me. When I asked about his relationship to the Train family, he took a moment to sort his thoughts.

"Margaret's father was a judge and a friend of my father's," he said. "In fact he married Margaret and Walter. It was a wedding that also took place under disapproving clouds."

"I don't understand how anyone could disapprove of Joan."

"Walter tells me she was Roy's student in Iowa, that she bewitched him, put the foolishness in his head that got him fired out there." The bishop chuckled. "And if that weren't enough mischief, got him interested in the ministry. No use for *that*. And of course she's kept Roy from going to work for him. That's his chief complaint."

"Is it a big firm?"

"Walter's no longer active—but they keep their old clients."

"*David*'s a lawyer. So he said."

"Walter wants Roy too. He thinks it will take them both to keep Train's competitive."

"Ah-h," I said. "Well, maybe Roy will come round. He may have to. The outlook from a seminary is pretty bleak this spring. Wouldn't you agree?"

Recognizing the beginning of an interview, the bishop folded his arms. "Oh, there's always room for the best of you. The church will be in a bad way if we don't find it."

"The missions?"

"No. Not necessarily the missions, but all I ever hear from postulants is that they must have a parish."

"I'm glad to hear that, because I don't feel that way at all. I'd like to find a place where I can offer some hard work in exchange for a lesson in administration. I understand the importance of it and what a thankless responsibility it must be."

"Thankless. Oh, yes," the bishop responded dreamily. "Brush fires, forever attending to the brush fires. That's perceptive of you, Ethan." He stared ahead, where red lights pulsed against the white tiles. "But surely it wasn't that, wanting to lend us a hand with administration, that brought you into the church?"

"Foreordained," I said. "My father was a Baptist minister, but then, when I was about eighteen, I was seduced."

"Seduced?" The bishop was fascinated.

"By the Anglican service. My music teacher was organist at the Episcopal church. The day I went to sing in her choir was a black one at my house."

"Good." The bishop laughed. "You're a musician."

Before we reached Diocesan House, the gothic building on Rector, just across Broad Street from the cathedral, I had learned that there had been recent bequests, two libraries of liturgical music, and that a member of the bishop's staff, a factotum with responsibility for public relations, would be leaving next month.

ll

LAURENCE Givens was a good boss, a smooth stone of a man whose polish, the parlor savvy that endeared him to the rich old ladies of Montclair and the Oranges, was merely a cover for unflinching righteousness. He saw his diocese, which embraced most of metropolitan New Jersey, in historic perspective and he was determined to write his own chapter responsibly.

He read everything—the *Tribune,* the *New Republic, Time, Scientific American,* political biographies, even the new fiction. He returned from one trip to the bookstore with a novel of Nabokov's and another by Günter Grass.

The office was a museum. One section of the lofty bookcases had been painted a brick color and illuminated to display his bibelots—pre-Columbian stelae, a Sung ossuary, an ivory tau cross, a Russian triptych—and a seventeenth-century virginal stood just within the doorway.

Even his faith was well ordered. He began the day with prayer, kneeling for ten minutes at the prie-dieu that faced his desk.

His wife, Abigail, was so mannish in looks and crusty in manner, so sharp a contrast with his own delicacy, that I wondered if he was homosexual, but I was sure he was too discreet and disciplined for this to become a factor of our relationship.

The libraries of which he had given me custody were of books, scores, and recordings, many of them rare. Both of us were soon looking forward to the daily interviews in which I would report my discoveries.

Once as I picked out a passage from an oratorio on the virginal, he came to stand behind me and follow my hesitant chords. When I finished, he turned a page to the difficult section that followed. His eyes grazed it with curiosity for half a minute, and then he sat down and played the whole with a mastery that left me flabbergasted. Back at his desk, he smoothed the pages of the catalog and gave me a wink.

In that instant I understood that I had not conned Laurence Givens into the offer of a job. He had seen me exactly as I am. Ever aware of my limitations, I can slip into another's shoes easily enough but prefer my own comfortable ones.

I had rented a room on Bleecker Street, just beyond the cathedral and a five-minute walk from Diocesan House. At ten each morning I would knock at the bishop's oak door, alert for the sound of his "Come in, Ethan. All ready for you." We would begin with the calendar, anticipating events of unusual interest and how best to announce them. I would bring drafts of press releases and the newsletter for his approval, and finally we would go over his schedule for the day, making sure he had the necessary information for each encounter.

By midsummer I had entered his confidence far enough to share in his principal concerns about the diocese. In this way I learned about St. Simon's parish. It was in Jersey City, ten miles away. It served a traditional, white, working-class neighborhood now giving way to black and Puerto Rican families. The priest there, Father Stokes, was ailing, and the parish's future was in doubt.

That same night, I made an excuse to call Roy Train. He was still searching for an acceptable job, he admitted, and was so doubtful of the outcome that he had just agreed to spend a weekend talking to his family in Morristown.

During my meeting with the bishop the next morning, I found my chance and asked whether I could tell Roy about St. Simon's.

His eyebrow arched dubiously. "Roy *Train?*"

"Seriously. He's turned down two chaplaincies, hoping for a parish."

"Fresh from the diaconate? I doubt he'll get one. It doesn't work that way."

"He knows, but he's thirty-one you know, and he thinks his experience and his capability—he's *certain* about that—lets him off the apprenticeship. If he can't find a parish soon, he'll probably go to work for his father."

"Well, that may be for the best."

"I wonder," I said. "Roy has so much to give. I'm certain he'll do something marvelous with that energy and imagination."

The bishop laughed. "That ascension . . . It put him on the map, all right, but not as a serious man."

"But he is—deadly. Showing off is a way of saying so. He's fearless. Some might feel that foolish, but I have a hunch he's a man the church ought not to pass up."

"Really? I don't sense a spirituality."

"Could you talk to him about that? I think you'd find it interesting."

The bishop sighted down his penholder, realigned it. "All right, Ethan, I'll see him, but don't get his hopes up over Saint Simon's. It's a dead end."

The day of Roy's interview was a hot one. By noon the tar was bubbling in the sidewalk cracks, as if the center of the earth had caught fire. Our determinedly residential neighborhood was hushed with the heat. Behind the hedge of the apartment house next door a sprinkler hissed fitfully. In the little park across the street one old woman sat in the shade of the dusty poplars and a dejected terrier panted beside her ankles.

Roy arrived fifteen minutes early, parking his MG between the CLERGY ONLY signs at our curb. He emerged jauntily, oblivious of the heat, in a crisp, blue clerical-collar shirt and khakis.

With time to kill, I took him on the Diocesan House tour, showing off the St. Peter chapel and the Helen Roebling dining hall with its carved overmantel as if they were my own, but his interest dwindled with every step.

In my own third-floor office he scowled at the files, the cartons of papers and books stacked along the wall, my narrow garret window. "My God, is this where you spend your time, up here in this stuffy place?"

"Yes. It's fine." I waved at a spill of parchment pages on my desk. "The work is really fascinating, Roy."

"I couldn't do it." Putting aside the Bay Psalm Book I had thrust into his hands, he said, "Tell me about *my* job. When does this priest retire?"

As I led him downstairs, I tried to trim Roy's expectations. "Saint Simon's is a lost battalion," I said, "a parish of old people who've lived in Jersey City all their lives and seen all the change they want."

Settling on a bench outside the bishop's door, Roy unfolded a map. "Can we go over there, Ethan?" He was tracing a route over the skyway. "Do you have the time?"

"I don't believe the bishop's going to offer it to you, Roy. He's puzzled, you know, about replacing Father Stokes after twenty years, but you're not his candidate. It was just my idea—and a chance for you to talk to him."

"Saint Simon's is just what I'm looking for. He'll want me there, Ethan."

"What's your family expect?"

"If I were to disappoint them, it wouldn't be the first time."

"Can David handle the office alone?"

"My father doubts it."

"You're the hustler?"

On the table in front of us lay an ankh, a looped Egyptian cross, of fine-grained dark wood, and Roy reached for it, felt its polished surface. "The old man has a plan—he's probably had it since he put himself through law school—for a stone wall of a firm that would outlast him. He thinks I'm important to that. He's right, Ethan, and he's a hard loser, wouldn't you say?"

"My father was hard to please. In fact I gave up trying, but I suspect he was no match for yours. Your father put me in mind of one of MacArthur's old soldiers, still wearing his campaign ribbons, up in the stirrup at the sound of a bugle."

Roy laughed. "He'd like that. Maybe I'll tell him."

"It's not so?"

"Joan is not so generous."

"I can understand. I wouldn't want to be on his wrong side either."

"Nor his right one." Thoughtfully he replaced the ankh. "He rarely goes to the office now. There's not much to do there, except remember when there was. His clients were contractors, men who were building roads for the state and digging their fortunes out of gravel pits."

"You mean crooks?"

His glance was amused. "The old man went to law school in Trenton. He learned the state house. He would have got an A in state house. In practice too. He found this enormous respect for the *practice*."

Behind us the door opened and the bishop stood in its frame. "Hello, Roy," he said cheerfully. "Come in, come in. Ethan tells me you're on your way to Morristown."

"Or Jersey City." Roy smiled brightly. "One way or the other."

Ignoring this, the bishop asked, "Would you like to join us, Ethan? You may have some questions too."

Roy's record from General Seminary lay open on the desk, and the bishop's freckled forehead knitted as he began to turn its pages. "You seem to have taken the short cut, transferring all this law school credit."

"I was law review—and I can't bear waste."

"But only a year of seminary. That's not much."

"I did two years of work in one," Roy assured him. "I took honors in two courses."

"Still, it's not a theological background." His thumb jabbed in the direction of Market Street. "You could walk into that office of your father's tomorrow. Your name's already on the door."

"I quit the law two years ago, Bishop."

The bishop frowned at Roy's file. "Actually you were fired, weren't you?"

Some of Roy's aplomb drained away. Straightening, he said, "I was a damned good teacher. Students couldn't get into my classes after the first hour of registration. It's not there in the vita. You'll have to take my word."

"I will. What happened?"

"I got fed up."

"With law?"

Roy studied his shoe tips and then the bishop's doubtful face. "With how it's taught and practiced. The dean and I disagreed on that. No, I was not asked back. Very painful episode."

"I see." The bishop rocked in his tufted leather chair. "Well, then, if you're in earnest about the church . . ."

"I am."

"Get yourself a curacy somewhere. You're not nearly ready for a parish. What about the prisons? Supposing I could find you something in a chaplain's office that engaged your particular talents?"

"Do you mean that Saint Simon's isn't available?"

The bishop hesitated. "No. There's going to be a vacancy there."

"Do you have many takers?"

"It's no plum."

"Which is why it appeals to me."

The bishop neatened a little pile of memoranda. "Saint Simon's is not promising ground. We have these fellows now who can mix the census and the unemployment rates in their hat and show you the future. I've seen it. The neighborhood's no longer receptive to us. In a year there's not likely to be a Saint Simon's. They sense that over there, that the parish is marked for closing. It makes for bitterness. Do you understand?"

"The more you tell me I don't want Saint Simon's, the more I do."

"Roy, there are limits to our forces. We must put them where some accomplishment is possible. We could rescue Saint Simon's once more, but it wouldn't stop the old white families from moving on, dying off. It would be romance to suppose we have any appeal for the colored and Hispanic people coming in."

In the fatalistic spread of the bishop's hands I recognized the close of the interview, but Roy did not. As the bishop rose, Roy sank farther in his chair. Cocking his head, he asked, "How can I believe in a church that's lost faith in itself?"

Lowering himself, the bishop let his bland expression give way to one of annoyance. He folded his hands and pointed the steeple of his fingers at Roy's heart. "You've got it all wrong. It's faith in you that's lacking. You're bright and flashy. I see that. But you're wholly unproved. I don't think you know what you *do* want. You're a novice in the church and it concerns me that you don't see yourself as such. How can you imagine yourself ready for a parish? Do you really have no self-doubts?"

The bishop's indignation was as real as it was rare, and Roy yielded to it. "Self-doubts?" he asked. "I'll match mine against anybody's."

"Good. They make a better case." The bishop relented. Leaning back, he studied him. "And what about your faith? Does that help with the doubts?"

"I have trouble with faith, I'm afraid."

"What brought you to the church, Roy?"

Roy's gaze went uneasily around the room and settled for a moment on his file, which the bishop had closed and moved to one side of the desk. Then he spoke. "Three years ago at Iowa, I was trying to find a platform for a speaker they didn't want on the campus. Joan told me that the Episcopal priest in Iowa City, a blind man named Tom Sewall, knew about a hall and would take me there. The two of us drove into the country along a road I knew very well.

"'Turn here by the bridge,' Tom said, surprising me that he could see at all, of course, but also that there could be a building at this deserted place. The moment we turned into the woods, a roadhouse appeared in front of us, a big one built of logs, with porches and a tumbledown dock reaching into a lake. It was abandoned but once they had rented canoes here and held country dances.

"Tom had the key and we went in. It was cold and filthy inside, but we decided it would do. Later we sat together on the steps to warm up in the sun. I began to tell this blind pastor that in bringing my speaker into town I was marking myself as a troublemaker and would possibly lose my job, but that if I didn't, I'd be letting down a lot of people who believed in me and wouldn't understand.

"Tom Sewall didn't reply at once. Instead he spoke of the beauty before us, and it *was* beautiful, the leaves in their October colors with the lake surface a mirror to them. He explained that he could see it all, not with his eyes but he'd learned how to experience beauty with a sense he'd grown to replace it. He was aware of the geese before I saw them break across the treetops, an arrow veering south.

"Tom took off his dark glasses and I looked into his eyes, expecting to find some evidence of sight, but there was none. His pupils were opaque as milk. Then he said to me, 'You must listen to that inner voice. Listen closely to be sure it speaks from beyond you, that it's not simply the voice of desire. But if it's true, then you must follow wherever it leads, even if it seems to be taking you over the brink.' Whereupon Tom Sewall folded his hands and prayed for me. He asked God to reassure me—and as we left the lake, I was sure."

The bishop inspected Roy with freshening interest and nodded. "Did you pray with him?"

"Yes. That was very strange. Prayer was not my custom."

"What kind of nourishment had you been getting from your religion?"

Roy studied a shelf of Bibles and concordances. "Not much. I was a tenderfoot at the time. Along with everyone else, I was brought up to think of religion as a fire extinguisher—emergency use only."

"Not quite everyone."

"All right . . . I'd had encounters too."

"Tell us."

"I was cynical as a schoolboy, but I had a housemaster who was a drunk and probably a pederast. When he spoke about confession, I asked about it in my smart-aleck way and so he showed me—had me down on my knees beside him, making a first confession. Later, I thought it was funny, went and made a joke out of it to tell in commons, but at the time I was frightened and moved by the experience."

"That lasted in some way?"

"A dozen years later, when my ship was sunk, I spent all of a night and part of the next day in the China Sea. The same confession came into my throat. I said it ten thousand times."

"And you were rescued." The bishop's blue eyes searched Roy's face.

"I gave thanks, yes . . . and then went on living."

"But faith still eludes you?"

Roy nodded.

"That's not so rare among clergymen as we'd like to think."

"What do they do about it—lie?"

"Some do, surely. Others search." He fixed Roy in his gaze. "Some of us find it."

Roy leaned toward him. "I will too. I want to believe in what I can't see. I want to believe in what my instinct tells me is true about God—that he is the only possible explanation of the infinite complexity and beauty and order of Creation. I want to believe that He exists and has a will that we must follow or lose our way and simply die. I want to believe that somewhere there is a concern for us beyond our own."

Laurence Givens drew back in his chair, folding his arms protectively as Roy rose before him. Barely able to contain his excitement, Roy grasped the edge of the desk to say, "Oh I *do* know what I want, Bishop. I know exactly."

Slowly, the bishop smiled. "Well, okay, Roy," he said, "maybe you *had* better go have a look at Saint Simon's."

Roy left the MG in a Jersey City parking lot and we stood for a moment looking into an empty Journal Square. Pointing out the big Loew's Theater, he said, "I remember going there. It was a sultan's palace inside, minarets and a sky with twinkling stars and some kind of luxurious fragrance that I imagined was the way it smelled in Hollywood." Now the Loew's box office was closed, its entrance chained, its marquee blank.

We walked along Bergen Avenue, past fortified storefronts, doors that opened on dark stairways. A man moved along the pavement stealthily, clutching a bagged pint bottle as if it were the last in town.

Only saloons prospered here, shadowy lairs where eerie juke box lights played on the heads and shoulders bent at the bar. Danger lay thick in the air.

We came into Foye Place with a sense of relief. In the shade of market awnings, women thumbed and sniffed the melons, counted change from their purses. There were kids everywhere, a circus of urchins in shades from tea rose to midnight. A little girl clinging to her mother's hand fastened wondering eyes on Roy.

A flight of lithe boys, bursting with laughter, zigzagged through the strollers, and in the doorway of a record shop some girls, no more than twelve years old but rouged and bangled, snapped their fingers and snaked their hips to the sound of a wailing voice.

We found St. Simon's at 27 Wayne Street, the vision of a nineteenth-century architect with the Cotswolds on his mind. Behind the palings of an iron fence there was a churchyard gone to hardpan and weeds. Within one of the arched windows, St. Simon, depicted here in stained glass, had lost his head and wore a square of plywood in its place.

"Even a halo's no protection here, Ethan," Roy said.

To the east the church was flanked by an apartment house rashed with graffiti, its entrance sheathed in galvanized steel and posted: LOITERING IN FRONT OF THIS BUILDING IS FORBIDDEN BY LAW. VIOLATORS ARE SUBJECT TO ARREST. JERSEY CITY POLICE DEPT.

Nonetheless half a dozen slim black men stood in the building's shade. They leaned against the masonry or the fenders of cars, hands in pockets.

To the west, in dramatic contrast, stood the combined parish house and rectory. It was an antebellum mansion. Six Ionic columns rose three stories to a gabled roof. The cornice was crumbling, and paint flaked from every board. The building's grace was intact yet pathetic here among its homely neighbors.

Father Stokes's housekeeper answered our ring and unlocked the back door of the church for us. Standing in the aisle of St. Simon's, I felt its chill, smelled the mustiness of worn carpet and that peculiarly melancholy odor of old varnish and tattered prayer books.

Roy was gazing at the white marble altar, the pulpit, the beams overhead. There was a rapture in his face that suggested he was dispelling the shadows, filling the pews with the people we had seen today and hearing their voices in chorus.

As though he had read my mind, Roy smiled. "I want it,

Ethan," he said. "I want this parish. I'll have it too. After a couple more talks with Laurence Givens."

Later, as we picked our way east in the belief that we were returning to the square, Roy read the street signs—Cornelison, Freemont, Van Vorst—memorizing them. He pointed out variations in the ironwork that railed the brownstone stoops. Pausing to watch the kids at their street games, he marveled at how they dissolved before a headlong truck. He waved to the motherly lookouts pillowed on their windowsills and guessed that the two automobiles under earnest reconstruction were fresh from a rustling.

Unexpectedly we emerged into a bleak plaza. It was Exchange Place and there was a tube kiosk at its north side. To the south a municipal building stood empty, ravaged by fire. Directly before us, obstructed only by a high, chain-link fence, lay the swelling, swill-fringed Hudson.

Taking my arm, Roy led me across the open space until we faced the fence. He thrust his fingers through the interstices and peered downriver. "Look, there she is, Liberty, still holding her dark torch."

The statue was surprisingly close, lording it over Ellis Island in the foreground, the tankers waiting in the roads beyond.

He pointed across the river, above the rotting Swedish and Hamburg Line docks to where the unbelievable stalagmite pinnacles of the financial district shimmered in the lowering sun. They seemed to rise from the embrace of the rivers and soar into the lavender sky.

"From here, the kids see those," he said. "Enchanted, aren't they? Carved from snow, jeweled with ice, they might be the towers of heaven. Only they aren't. Could be over here, though, *this* side of the river."

III

ROY did have several further interviews with the bishop and to my surprise convinced him that he not only understood the challenge St. Simon's presented but could respond, bringing some of the new arrivals through its old doors.

I was delighted to have Roy and Joan so near at hand. I discovered that if the traffic was not heavy, I could get from my own apartment in Newark to St. Simon's in Jersey City in just fifteen minutes.

Entering St. Simon's at ten o'clock on Roy's first Sunday morning, I could sense change. The sanctuary smelled as if it had been swept and aired. There was a tension afloat too, an anticipation and curiosity on the polished faces of the early arrivals. The parish was turning out to make judgment of its new minister.

Joan was alone in a forward pew and when I reached it she smiled and beckoned. I knelt beside her to pray for St. Simon's parish and the outcome of Roy's maiden sermon. When I had finished, I looked around and counted sixty-four communicants, half a churchful, a small white orchard. The faces were square, enduring ones, used to hardship and disappointment. I found three dark ones, all women's, grouped in a rear pew.

An old sexton touched off the altar candles while the organist, a dour little woman in black surplice and a turbulence of iron-gray hair, began the prelude.

Joan made such a contrast to the senescence. I caught a whiff of L'Heure Bleue, urbane and faintly aphrodisiac. The pale blue linen of a butterfly skirt clung to her thighs, broke over her crossed knees. Her slender hands rested there, curving subtly from narrow wrist to delicate, rose-tipped fingers. I thought them made for touching and had an instant's vision of them at erotic play, censored suddenly by a stroke of guilt and contrition, as if God Himself had looked straight into my tainted soul and made a note.

The processional, five earnest ladies and one wholly bald man in white cottas, set forth from the sacristy door and made a ragged march along the side aisle and up the main one. Roy brought up the rear, singing "Day of Wrath! O Day of Mourning!" with a heartiness that rose above the other voices.

He wore the cassock and surplice lightly, and as he mounted the altar steps the masculine energy of his body swelled beneath them. When he read the propers, his voice rose surely and there was an eagerness shining from him as though he knew he could win the communicants simply by revealing his good sense and good intentions. Beside me, Joan seemed to be seeing him for the first time.

But looking around, I saw rigid mouths, doubting eyes, scarcely a trace of welcome, and I wondered if Roy had been prejudged or if there was something about his manner, his very confidence, the undeniable elegance of his delivery, that was putting them off. In any case, Roy was oblivious. He climbed the steps to the pulpit as though arriving at a goal.

While Roy stood above us, looking out at his congregation, poised at his start, I saw Joan's eyes close in rapt, silent prayer. Her expression was pure transcendence, and the double portrait dizzied me with awe and envy.

Roy's voice was candid and easy. "I'm Roy Train, your new pastor, and I'm glad to meet you. Don't be surprised to find me on your doorstep tomorrow. From those of you I've already met, I've learned how much you all miss Father Stokes, and it's my ambition to have as many friends among you as he does."

He spread some cards on the lectern and spoke of Bob Stokes's ministry, his good works at the convalescent home, and the gratitude of troubled parishioners for his charities, but I listened in vain for the comforting sounds of response.

It was clear this was a stubborn audience. Roy glanced over them anxiously but forged on with his assurances about St. Simon's future. It was as though he were running across a rubbled field towing a kite that was indifferent to every updraft that could loft it.

He broke off in midsentence. With a puzzled expression, he looked from face to face. He collected the cards and smiled. "I see I've got my work cut out today."

Aside from an occasional cough, he might have spoken to a void. Appearing to give up entirely on the sermon he had planned, Roy hiked up his surplice and slipped the cards into the side pocket of his cassock. He glanced in Joan's and my direction with good humor and then back to the congregation, considering them thoughtfully.

"I want you to know about me," he resumed, "about what to expect of me as your pastor and what not to expect." He paused, frowned, then asked, "Do you know about the three castaways? They'd had a mishap on their way back from an ecumenical congress—a rabbi, a priest, and a Protestant minister. They'd been rowing for three days, and the Protestant was griping about doing more than his share of it, when the Catholic spied a floating bottle. The priest plucked it from the sea and uncorked it, releasing a genie into the boat with them."

Roy was clearly enjoying himself as he acted the genie's part, granting each of them a single wish. He became the rabbi, wishing himself to an address in downtown New York and immediately finding himself dining on stuffed derma at Lupowitz and Moscowitz's. Next he became the priest, successfully wishing himself to a table at Mamma Leone's.

Around us glances were exchanged, expressions thawed. The congregation seemed to hold their breath while Roy played the parson, still at the boat's oars, considering his own choice before deciding, "I wish those other guys were back here to help me row."

34

A surprised snicker broke the silence. It was followed by an outburst of laughter as, in spite of themselves, the whole audience was swept along in the mirth.

When at last it ebbed, Roy said, "So you can see I'm not going to be that kind of pastor for you. I can row well enough when I must, but I'm more of a wisher."

He nodded to the upturned, interested faces and said, "I'm going to tell you about that." He withdrew the cards, shuffled them, and read a text from St. Paul: "No longer aliens in a foreign land but fellow citizens in God's household."

For a few minutes he kept his lightheartedness, describing the discord between Jews and Gentiles at Ephesus in contemporary terms. His voice had found its listeners. It rose and fell as it grew in sureness. Roy had found his updraft.

He turned more serious over Paul's claim of Christ's victory over the feud. "He has made the two one"—Roy held the silence, let it build before releasing its weight—"broken down the enmity that stood like a dividing wall . . . made a *single* community."

Assurance ran ahead of him, clearing the way as he approached his target, the belief that in our time tolerance is the essence of Christian grace.

"Let's talk among ourselves about *neighborhood*." He said the word slowly and then repeated it. "Neighborhood. Let's talk about what the word means. See if you don't agree with me that it's the key to new life for us all. We can fill this church. I promise you that a year from now there won't be an empty pew in here, and what's more, we're going to have a good time. We're going to make a joyful noise here on Wayne Street."

In the pulpit Roy searched the faces for response and raised his eyebrows. "Do you doubt we *can* . . . or that we *shall* make such a noise?"

No one stirred, and he went on, "Or do you doubt me? Do you doubt I know how to do this? Then let me explain. We do this by trusting each other. You trust me and I trust you. We reveal ourselves. We confess what we feel, what we fear, what we truly believe . . ."

He waited as the church filled with silence, rising alarmingly

35

to waist, shoulders, neck. A man left his pew and walked out of the church. "Here, let me show you. Let me open myself to *you*. You're wondering who I am and where I've come from. I was born twenty-five miles from here. My father, as some of you remember, is a lawyer. He practiced in this county. He saw to it that I was trained as a lawyer. I pleased him—which was rare enough—by teaching in a law school."

Roy's face grew dark, as though the artifice had become a true confession and a painful one. "If you were to ask at the University of Iowa, they would tell you that I failed there. I was fired. If you were to ask my father, he'd tell you the same thing, and that I'd failed him as well as the law. But if you were to ask me, I'd say it was the other way around, that the law had failed me. I found it worked as well for wrong as it did for right. I grew impatient with it and that's what lost me my job. When I was down about that, and I was very down about it—my wife, who was my student there at the time, can tell you how down I was—it was the church that came to my help, the church that struck me as the straightest way to what's essential . . ."

A wave of discomfort was sweeping the congregation, and Roy broke off. "Well," he said, "that's why I'm here—because I believe in what we do here together. I believe in the force we can make among us. I believe it can so change events that it will save this doomed church of ours. I believe in that, and if you don't, you *will*, and so will that man who just left us. He will believe in that force and he will know what it is. Of course it is love . . . for all mankind."

Roy turned abruptly to the altar to say the Doxology, and I said aloud, "Amen!" I felt a rush of emotion, as though I had watched him swim a river and nearly drown in it but reach the far shore with such sure strokes that possibly the whole trial had been within his control. As I clasped Joan's hand, I saw she was biting her lower lip and shaking her head to keep back tears.

There were some newly glowing faces around us. Some could not take their eyes from Roy as he came down the aisle. But there were frowns too.

At the church door, turning his flock into the street, Roy was pumping hands and catching at names with all the avidness of a dark horse candidate on election eve.

Watching the last parishioner straggle down the church steps, a buoyant Roy turned to me, saying, "How was I, Ethan? How did it really go?"

"I had no idea you could get into so much trouble and still get out. You did take the hard road, didn't you?"

"I couldn't get going with the other. You saw."

"Once you got flying, you were great. They loved that joke."

He frowned. "I hadn't planned on that."

"And the confession, if that's what you call it, was very moving."

"Also spontaneous. Out she came."

"We could see straight inside, Roy. That's a gift."

There was new gleam in his eyes, as though he were getting high on victory. I said, "Of course in our pew we were predisposed, but watching these people go, I'd say you fought a draw. That's good for a first round."

"Oh, Ethan," he said, giving my arm a shake, "you're such a wet blanket. I'd hoped you'd have a good case of elation by now. We can have one hell of a time here together, you and I. Wouldn't it be grand, showing Laurence Givens how wrong he is about Saint Simon's?"

"Yes, it would."

"But? Speak up, man. What's the matter with you?"

"I saw a wall of orneriness in here this morning. I think you missed it."

"I've been seeing it all week. There's a big colored guy, a truck driver who lives up the street. He came to call yesterday. He wants to sing in the choir and he's determined about it. It won't be easy, but I know it can be done, that we can convince these old croaks what he's got isn't catching."

He had led me down the steps to the walk encircling the church to view the state of its roof. While he pointed out some loose shingles, we noticed that the organist was trying to lock the back door, her cane in the crook of her arm.

"No, I can do it," she protested when Roy offered help. She

had a cross look, and coaxing the stubborn key, she said, "The robbers are thick as flies here, always waiting their chance. They wouldn't think twice about marching in to help themselves."

"It does seem a shame, though," Roy replied, "locking up Saint Simon's like a vault. A church should be open for people when they want to come in."

She tried the door and pocketed the key, an inch of her brow puckering. "You just try that, Father. They'll have the fillings from your teeth. There's a criminal element around here and it's no good shutting your eyes to that."

Roy said, "You're right, Mrs. Gower. We'll be on the alert. This is my friend Ethan Soames"—and turning to me—"Mrs. Gower is our organist and choirmistress. As you've just heard, she does very well at both."

Nodding, I watched her lead the way toward the street, leaning into her cane.

"We were wondering, though, Mrs. Gower," Roy continued. "With only five voices, what do you do when someone's ill? Shouldn't we recruit a few more?"

"There's not many will put in the time."

At the gate Roy said, "This man Lester Moon wants to sing with you, and I promised I'd ask. He has the idea he's unwelcome."

"That doesn't surprise me, Father. He's always after us. We like our choir the way it is." Turning on the pavement to face us, she winced.

"I'm sorry," Roy said. "You're in pain."

"This hip of mine won't let me forget it."

"Are you seeing a doctor?"

Mrs. Gower shook her head. "Doctors can't do a thing."

"We must work on it, Mrs. Gower."

She surveyed her new pastor with wakening interest. "Oh, I pray, Father. I've asked His help."

"We'll ask again."

"Yes, we'll do that." Cheered some, she started up Wayne Street toward two people who had been waiting. One was a man of about seventy, with a defeated slope to his shoulders. The other was a boy, slouched against a car fender.

Mrs. Gower had gone only a few steps before turning to give some final advice. "Father Stokes was firm with that Moon. It's the only way to be."

Joan had hung bright curtains at the windows of the rectory dining room, and there was a bowl of pink cyclamen on the table. Over a lunch of borscht and black bread, Roy said, "You know what my parishioners worry about more than having colored neighbors? They worry about their kids standing on street corners with their hands in their pockets."

"And well they might," I said.

"Did you notice the boy waiting for Louise Gower? That was her grandson, Wally. I hear he gives the Gowers plenty to worry about. It was Wally who set me to thinking we need a scout troop. You follow me, Ethan?"

"Not really."

"A fifth column, inside the city walls." He held up a hand in the three-fingered salute. "That's our troop. Now you, Ethan. You'd make us one hell of a scoutmaster."

IV

I had plenty of qualms about scouting and my qualifications for leading a salient into Jersey City, but Roy overwhelmed them. Within two weeks of his proposal, I was posting handbills in the schoolyards and fixing up a troop headquarters in the basement of St. Simon's.

Seven ragged boys, including the chunky, freckled Wally Gower, turned up for the first meeting. They were alike in their suspicion of me, but they varied in skin color, just as Roy had hoped.

I told him how callow I had felt before them in my new sweat shirt and jeans. "I wonder if any'll come back."

"They'll come back," he said, "and bring some friends."

"While I was giving them the oath," I said, "one of them, and I think I know which, pinched my compass."

Roy laughed and clapped his hands. "Good for him. We'll teach the new scoutmaster a thing or two about being prepared. What did you do about it?"

"I asked for the scout who had taken my compass to return it."

Roy nodded. "That's logical."

"He didn't. Nobody said a word. Seven pair of eyes were on me, waiting for me to get mad, threaten 'em, maybe quit on 'em.

So I told whoever took it to accept it as a present. That got me a couple of good smiles. I'd just passed *their* test and maybe learned a secret."

"Which?"

"It's not scouting they're after so much as tolerance."

"Ah-h," Roy said. "You're going to be terrific at this."

Three times a week I turned up at St. Simon's, and often Roy would coax me along on his parish calls. One of the first took us into Dumont Street, where half a dozen shops stood vacant. A papered-over show window told of judo instruction inside, and what had been Allen's Pharmacy was now occupied by Mme. Zena, Fortune Teller. Louise Gower lived at number 27 and her third-floor flat was dark, its shades drawn against the steamy afternoon. I was left in the parlor with a stack of hymnals, an old Baldwin upright, and an asthmatic cat, but through the kitchen door I overheard a recital of Louise's complaints.

"It's not the kind of life you would know, Father," she summed up, "but I have a husband out of work and a grandson to look after."

"I do know, Louise." Roy was buoyant. "What I don't, I'll count on you to tell me."

She hesitated, suspecting him of smuggling humor into their interview and warning him against it. "With this hip of mine, I can't do the funerals and weddings that used to bring me in a little extra."

"Supposing we could find a spot for George."

"Whatever he could be trusted to do, he's too proud for it. He was a dispatcher on the Lackawanna, he'll tell you, and Frank Hague called him by name. No, George would rather sit in the park with the others and talk of when the trains were running. He leaves it to me to set the table . . . and on the mite the church pays me."

"We're going to get Saint Simon's solvent before long, Louise. I've got some ideas on that too."

"You'll need more than ideas to get blood from stone. The money's gone out of Jersey City, Father."

"Louise"—Roy was undaunted—"we can do whatever we want here. Don't you believe that?"

41

"I don't believe anybody's going to thank me for keeping our choir together over the years . . . for the times when I should have been home in bed."

"We're all grateful to you, Louise. We all know what Saint Simon's owes you."

As she multiplied her burdens, the scarcity of her students, the laziness of her husband, the crumbling and corruption of the community, and the torment in her joints, Roy's assurances swept in like the tide.

"We can change all that," he told her. "Come on now, Louise, give me a chance to show you how. Between us we can get the whole town singing together."

"I've been too many years in pain, Father, to expect miracles."

"But there's a reason for our pains," Roy went on in high gear. "Don't you feel that, Louise? That our pains are God's test of our worthiness? Surely you can teach me lessons in what's hard-won. God gives us the strength to deal with hardship—but we must ask for it. Shall we do that now? Shall we ask him together?"

Later, walking along Second Street, I said, "Roy, you're a whiz at counseling. Maybe that'll do it."

He glanced my way. "Do what?"

"Another call like that one, and I suspect Mr. Moon's in the choir."

"Think so, Ethan? Now *I'm* having doubts."

He paused to look into the window of a Spanish market, with its pyramids of unfamiliar tubers and spotted fruit. "You know, Ethan, sometimes when I'm trying to convince one of my poor old wretches here that Jersey City is really God's own place and all you need is a little faith and prayer to enjoy it, I can taste the snake oil in my mouth. And the sickness is real. You know what I mean?"

"Tell me."

"Louise has put in sixty years at her quarrel with the world. She's got a big investment in resentment. As you say, I can charm the boots off her." He fingered the round of his collar. "This thing's a magician's license. I can hocus-pocus her tongue, all right—but I'm not going to change her mind, not in any important way, to say nothing of her heart. I'm quite sure of that."

"It's your faith acting up again, Roy. It'll pass."

"What I'm wondering is if my faith oughtn't to be working on another level. I'm wondering if making everybody feel good is what we're really called to do."

Although Joan made no attempt to disguise her bone-bred class nor her instinctive need for privacy, she was no liability to Roy. The crustiest altar guild ladies took to her as readily as the neighborhood children, who waved and called out to her whenever she appeared on the rectory steps or set off along Wayne Street with her shopping bag.

One afternoon she took me up to the rectory's top floor, a turret on the roof with high windows all around. She had made it hers with a small painting of a couple walking under an umbrella along a Paris street, a chair, and a rough table on which she had arranged a gooseneck lamp, her tax and constitutional law texts, and a notebook.

"It's my aerie," she told me. "I'm alone up here with this terrific view of treetops and pigeon coops and gorgeous festoons of underwear, even an occasional ship's mast, but sitting down, all I see is Holmes and Brandeis." She touched her notebook, turned some pages of a poignantly fair hand.

"You really find time for reading law?"

"I'm still going to New York for my classes."

"With all the claims on a parson's wife?"

She nodded. "And as if all the claims on a parson's wife were not enough, we're having a baby."

I felt myself redden. "That accounts for it."

"For what?"

"Your looking more ravishing than ever."

She laughed and glanced down at her stomach. "In a few weeks I'll be all hump, like a camel. If you come to see me then, Ethan, I wonder what you'll think."

The thought was one of loss, as though the intimacy between us must now be forfeited, but I said, "I think that with a hump you'll be absolutely lovely."

"You're very sweet."

In the next instant we heard a door slam below and then Roy's voice calling, "Joan?" We were transfixed by the sound of footsteps mounting the stairs at a trot. In the instant before Joan turned and moved toward the doorway, we shared a private smile.

Several weeks later, as we sat at the table in the rectory kitchen congratulating ourselves on Troop Twelve's new recruits, Roy reported that the parish now counted the scouting project a success.

"I still hear a little grumbling about strange kids in the church," he said, "but even the hardshell crabs admit it's good for Saint Simon's. May Bruner was telling me that it's a gyp on a family with three daughters."

Joan, who had been smiling at our self-approval, said, "Well, it is."

"Okay," Roy said. "I was hoping you'd say that. What right do we have to deny social progress to tomorrow's womanhood, right?"

Joan laughed and straightened. "If you mean me . . ."

"Of course I do. The neighborhood kids adore you. You'd only have to open the door."

"You forget. I'm almost a mother."

"How could I forget that? Come on, Joan. You can get the girls started. We'll find somebody to fill in for you."

"You're serious about it, aren't you?" She spoke with surprising severity. "You know I have both finals and the bar coming. I should be upstairs studying right now."

"The bar exam?" I asked.

She gathered some dishes and stood very straight with them. "With the baby coming, I'm going to have to take it right away."

"Nobody *has* to take the bar," Roy said.

"I do."

There was a smoky look in Joan's eyes and I tried to become the buffer. "Joan," I said, "you're a truly amazing girl."

"Besides," Roy said, "a sensible lawyer wouldn't take the bar until he knew where he was going to practice."

"I know that," she said and left us for the kitchen.

Roy shot me a weary *Oh, women!* glance, but I resisted the alliance, calling out to Joan, "Where *do* you want to practice? Here in Jersey?"

There was no reply. Roy shrugged.

"Newark?" I smiled at the thought. "Would your father take Joan into Train's as a substitute for you?"

Roy shook his head. "It's a very chill wind from Morristown, believe me."

Joan returned from the kitchen carrying a cigarette and matchbox. Lighting up with the deliberateness of an unfamiliar act, she blew a dart of smoke over our heads. "I want to work in New York," she said.

"I'm sure you'll make some law firm very happy," I said. "And it would be really great for you, having another interest."

She fixed me in the cross hairs of her gaze. "An *interest?* The law isn't an interest. It's a profession."

"I know," I said. "I meant that having a profession *besides* the church would bring in new ideas—for both of you—add so much to your marriage."

"I don't need an *excuse* for having a profession," Joan said without forgiveness. "Do you? Would you two sit around telling yourselves that the ministry is good for a man's marriage?"

"No," I said, determined to elude the dunce cap, "but we're not having babies in a couple of months. I'm impressed . . . that's all I'm trying to say."

"What he's really trying to say," Roy put in, "only he's too polite, is that you can't do everything in this life and you do have a commitment to this parish. Being a parson's wife *is* a profession. Nobody ever told you it isn't."

"Oh, I do damned well at that," she said, "and you know I do. You also know that I haven't been studying law for three years so that I can have an *interest* but because that's what I want to do with my life."

Roy nodded while his eyes flashed a danger signal. "You want to watch out for spreading yourself thin."

"Oh, balls. I'm going to jam everything into my life I possibly can." Growing pink, she looked from one to the other of us. "What I want to know is are you for me or against me?"

"For you, of course," I said. "Both of us. A hundred and one percent."

Roy grinned at me. "You be careful or you'll have the Girl Scouts too."

During his first months at St. Simon's, Roy had discovered the Shamrock Bar on Court Street. It was a brass-rail-and-sawdust place with a high, pressed-tin ceiling and a haunting smell of moist kegs in the basement, and it pleased him to take occasional refuge there. He also liked to overcome my misgivings about meeting in its rank, raffish bowels.

Watching a middle-aged couple mounting stools at the end of the bar, I warned, "Somebody's going to recognize us."

"Not a chance," he said. "This is Sacred Heart turf, and anyway without collars we sure don't look like a couple of priests. I could pass for the Guinness salesman, and anyone can tell you're a scoutmaster, from a mile away."

But here in a Shamrock booth he was his most serious too, admitting that in spite of little victories he was impatient with progress. The stubbornness of Louise Gower over her Jim Crow choir was not only frustrating in itself, but he was coming to realize that she represented a part of the parish disposition. Reconciling St. Simon's old guard to change was going to be an endless ordeal.

Roy was ever curious about doings at Diocesan House and always asked for news. He was particularly interested in my account of our classmate Ted Fenno, who had taken a job at the denominational magazine *New Horizons*. Ted had proposed that the bishop do an article on "the new carpetbaggers," the young clergy going south for those sit-ins under church auspices. The bishop had declined.

"Why?" Roy asked. "Laurence isn't a coward. Why would he pass up the chance to put himself on the side of the angels?"

"He'd be speaking for the House."

"Would he?" Roy sipped moodily at his stout. "Well, all the better. What a chance to drag the others off the fence. Did you tell him so?"

"I don't *tell* Laurence anything. I explained about Ted, that he wants to play up the concerns of young clergy. Laurence was sympathetic to that, of course, but he's equally aware of the Southern bishops in the House. He has to work with them."

"That's bullshit."

"It isn't, Roy. He'd just delight his enemies. Ted would be the only winner."

"No need to tell me about Fenno. Religion's all politics for him now—which is why he didn't qualify for ordination." He was gazing into the mirror at the reflection of the bartender's pink, bald head bent over the evening paper. Suddenly Roy seized my sleeve to say, "But Givens is a fink not to speak out when he's got the chance."

"Would you, and get yourself in hot water for it?"

"I like hot water."

"Not that hot."

"You never know about the water until you try it, Ethan. It could be just my temperature." He drank off the shallows in his glass and waved for another. "I'd do a piece for Ted Fenno about the racism we've got up north. Think he'd like that? I'd do a piece for him on Saint Simon's."

"You'd get no thanks from Laurence, and it wouldn't help you with Louise Gower either."

"No?" He considered this and then he smiled. "I think you're wrong, Ethan. It could help a lot. Ask Ted if he's interested."

"You ask him. I don't want any part of it."

A few days later Roy told me that Ted Fenno had taken to the idea of an article on racism in the Northern church. He was already busy on a draft, which was coming easily for him. He would have it done in a couple of days.

There was trouble among my scouts. It began at the YMCA, where I had taken them swimming. A skinny colored boy named Wilson Sykes had been ducked by Wally Gower, held under water until he came up gasping. I had to separate a fierce punchout in the locker room.

Later, on his way home, Wally was ambushed. Although he got off with a broken tooth and bruises, Louise Gower was enraged. At the Wednesday vestry meeting she rose up with the fierceness of a threatened hawk to tell the story of Wally's mugging. In a voice trembling with emotion, she cried, "It's these hoodlums and it's what we get for inviting them into our church. It's no longer a safe place for any of us, I promise you that . . . and I promise you that from now on my grandson won't be going to any more scouts."

At the Shamrock, I told Roy that Wally and another of the white kids had not showed up for the Friday meeting and I'd felt a new tension between the colored and the white boys. It had been a cheerless meeting to begin with, because I had had to tell them there was no money for summer camp. I was losing my optimism about our troop.

"Well, it's an ill wind," Roy said.

"I don't know what you mean. They're all in the dumps."

"I mean about going to camp. I talked to Wally about it. He'd come back, no matter what his grandmother says, if the troop was going to Boonton."

"Well, it isn't."

"It's only a thousand bucks, Ethan. You can get it from the diocese."

"Oh, no, I can't."

"They can't spend it in a better way. Why wouldn't you speak up for us?"

"I know where Saint Simon's stands among Laurence's priorities."

He studied me. "You afraid of him, Ethan?"

"He's my boss. I'm expected to know what's feasible."

Roy's eyes became arctic but I was so sure he was acting, playing a joke, that I grinned. Whereupon Roy rose and left me. He walked rapidly through the bar toward the street, turning short of the door to toss a bill on the counter.

I reviewed everything we had said, questioning my passive attitude but in the end believing it the fit and rational one. To plead a favor, a special interest, of Laurence was distasteful to me. It was not cowardly and I was right to be stung by Roy's accusation.

After a night of these ruminations, I made up my mind to

quit and drove to Jersey City to tell Roy so. When I pushed open the office door I found him busy with an account book, but he put down his pen and said, "I'm glad you came."

"I've been thinking over what you said last night . . ."

"So have I." He wagged his head. "I was awful, wasn't I? I'm ashamed of myself. Can I say that? Will you let me off so easily?"

As I settled in the chair opposite him, I could feel my sense of injury dissolving.

"It was something else bothering me," he explained. "It wasn't the money for camp nor the bishop." He passed fingers through his hair. "It was that damned article. You were right about it, of course. It was too close to home. I'm junking it."

"Maybe you can fix it," I suggested. "Generalize it."

"Oh, Fenno had some such idea—that it could be reconceived, tied to what's going on down South." He reflected and brightened. "It *is* tempting."

At Roy's elbow lay a copy of *Newsweek,* open to the religion page and an article on the sit-ins. "You see this?" He pointed to the photograph of a Woolworth counter in Gadsden. The familiar faces of Bob Morse and Frank Le Page, alongside unknown black ones, wore the rapturous expressions of comrades in arms.

"I saw the picture," I said. "It was in the Sunday paper."

"*Everybody* saw that picture," he said. "Le Page knows how to get attention." Roy did a grand dismissing stretch and smiled. "Well, I'm somewhat cheered this morning. I figured out how we're going to take our scouts to Boonton. We're going to have a fair for 'em. We'll have the whole parish, maybe the whole blooming neighborhood, working on it."

V

ON the second Saturday of May, Roy, Joan, and I sat on the stone parapet overlooking the normally sooty churchyard, transformed for the day into a gaudy bazaar.

As Roy had promised, the whole parish, excepting Louise Gower, had taken part in the preparations, setting up the carnival games, stretching the awnings, which made a blue-and-white-striped garland along the opposite wall. Now, at eleven o'clock, the flagged court, the walks, and the pavement beyond the fence thronged with neighborhood families.

From the newspaper in his lap, Roy had been reading to us about a sit-in at Huntsville, and he asked, "Has Fenno been after you to go down on one of these plantation tours?"

"I'm on his mailing list. Why?"

"He called last night to ask if I could get away for a week."

"He knows you can't."

"He knew I'd be tempted. I really hate missing out on it, don't you?"

"It's a truly Gandhian idea. Thank God for it."

"They're really getting some voters registered," he said. "You wonder why it's taken so long—and why it's left to the ragtag of the church. Why don't you go?"

"To be quite honest, because I like my head as it is."

"Oh Ethan," Roy laughed. "You're not serious."

It was Joan who noticed Lester Moon. "Look who's come." She pointed, and I saw his gleaming, chocolate-colored dome. It floated on the pale stream of mothers and children meandering between the booths. "See how everyone's watching. Even the little kids know."

Lester paused at the fishpond to try his luck for a prize, one of the waxen, possibly edible panpipes which could be heard tootling among the children. Then he moved on to the baseball throw, where he put a coin on the counter, rolled up an immaculate white shirt sleeve, and had a try at toppling the pyramid of wooden bottles.

"Come and meet him," Roy said. "He's an original."

Lester threw a hard, fast ball and he struck the platform twice, setting the bottles rocking, but they did not fall. As we came within earshot, Lester was saying to Emily Bulford, "Them things must be *nailed* down."

"They aren't." The apprehensive Emily showed him.

"Some jinx then. You got a jinx against me. My pitch is true, but it don't work in here. How much it cost for one of them pipes?"

"They're prizes." Emily's wide eyes deflected his question to Roy.

"Hello, Lester," Roy said, putting out his hand. "You haven't met my wife—and this is Ethan Soames, who's helping us out with the scouts."

Lester acknowledged Joan and me but he ignored Roy's hand. Taking another baseball from the counter, he flipped it from palm to palm. "I was just passing and I see the crowd. I always go look what a crowd doing. I wonder I don't hear no music. No singing in here today?"

Roy pocketed his hand. "Nope. No singing today, Lester."

"Well, I am a singer." Lester's voice became richer as he spoke. "That's my gift from my daddy. He had a fine mahogany voice. He could shake the floor like an organ with that voice, and make what he say sound *deep*, like he had it straight from God." Lester laughed at his great good luck.

"We'll have you singing with us, Lester. We're working on it."

Lester sobered. "I hear them practices is still closed. They still meeting around in people's houses, ain't they—making sure they no *new* voices."

"We're getting there, Lester, believe me." Roy waved a hand at the awnings. "Now this is a benefit for our scouts. Maybe you know some of them. We're raising money to send a dozen of them off to camp in Boonton."

In Lester's eyes there was sudden nightfall. "How'd I know scouts?"

"There's some from your part of town, Lester."

He looked among the children in the churchyard and did see a colored boy and two colored girls swinging on the church gate. "Those kids grow up on a street corner. They know alleys. They know dumps. They ain't gonna be happy out there in them woods. You gonna scare 'em, with them animals moving around in the night, and get 'em a dose of ivy and a snake bite. That ain't gonna do nobody no good."

"You don't know what you're talking about—and Ethan does. He's been working with them for months."

"They've just chosen a colored patrol leader," I said, "a boy named Wilson Sykes."

Lester remained unimpressed.

"Can you understand there's a *point* to bringing kids together?" Roy asked. "Kids from different backgrounds?"

"You mean nigger kids?" Lester asked. "Say it, Mr. Preacher. Don't be afraid."

"You must see the point," Roy insisted, "in putting white kids and colored kids together on a hike. Why can't you say so?"

Lester threw the baseball, toppling two of the bottles on the stand. The third tottered, but stood. "God damn, just look at that pesky bottle, Mr. Preacher. Somebody in here's against me."

"That's close enough to a strike, isn't it, Emily? Let Mr. Moon have a pipe."

Emily smiled her relief and reached for one.

"No, man." It came out like a whipcrack. "I don't want your pipe. I don't want no favor from you."

"It wasn't a pipe I was offering."

"What was it?"

"You came to see what we were offering in here. That's what you said."

"Offer? I don't need no offer."

Roy shrugged. "What else can you do with friendship?"

This stumped him for a second. "I don't need your kind. You no friend of mine."

"How do you know that, Lester?" Joan asked, her voice cool as a stream on the blaze between the two men.

"I know." Lester's gaze challenged hers then dropped to appraise her throat and, with theatrical insolence, her swelling breasts and belly. She blushed and he smiled broadly. "I know all about you in here. I know who cleans your house and carries out your garbage. I know what you think of me." His hand darted toward her, and instinctively she drew back her arm. He laughed. "You see?"

"Don't," Roy warned.

But Joan stepped closer, opening her hands as if she had no fear of him, saying, "We're *trying* to integrate Saint Simon's. That's what Roy's saying about the scouts. Can't you please say you understand that? We're allies, Lester. We want to be your friends, if you'll only let us."

"I got only one kind of friend." His teeth gleamed as he reached toward her waist.

"I said don't do that." Roy clenched a fist.

Lester's finger jerked to Roy. "You hear that? That don't sound friendly."

"I don't like anyone putting hands on my wife. Let's not get mixed up."

"I'm not mixed up. I know just where I am. This here's the church where they don't let Lester Moon sing in the choir. Lester's that cat with the gorgeous baritone. He really *dark* but he got a voice that carries over the whole of Bergen County. I know who got the voice, man. It's you that's mixed up. Don't talk to me about no friend."

His voice trembling, Roy said, "I won't make that mistake again."

"I'm okay," Joan said to him. "I'm just fine. Don't go gallant on us." She stepped forward slightly, interposing herself between them. "You make it hard, Lester," she said to him. "Must you?"

"It's me, is it—me causing the trouble round here?"

She nodded. "Because you don't listen. You don't hear what my husband is trying to tell you—that he's trying to help."

"I don't listen? Oh, honey, you so *wrong*. I hear everything. I hear the leaves falling off the trees here and I hear every liberal-ass, hypocritical, bullshit word that's spoke here—just like what always come out of the mouths of whitey, do-good preachers that don't know *nothin'!*"

Lester's voice had been rising like a siren, wailing and hate-honed, turning all heads in the churchyard, putting an end to all other sound, and Roy was absorbing it. Feet planted, he faced Moon's attack with a resolute, icy distaste that seemed to increase the man's rage.

"You sending kids into the woods," Lester cried, "and wanting to be told you the new Abe Lincoln for it, while you shutting Negroes out of your choir and your guild and your old honky vestry."

A crowd was closing around us now, and Lester played to it. "No colored going to come to you," he thundered. "They going to *leave* you. They going to walk right out of your redneck place."

"Some of our colored people feel otherwise," Roy said, looking around for support.

Where were the girls I had seen a moment ago? Wilson Sykes was making a tail-between-legs exit at the gate. In the circle of stark faces I saw the tories, among them Louise Gower and, ironically, young Wally, who had been absent from scout meetings since Wilson had been chosen patrol leader.

"Give us a chance, Lester," Joan was pleading. "Why don't you let us show you? What possible good can it do to turn away people who are trying to be your friends?"

"You *not*. You just fucking with us. You don't *know*."

"What don't we know, Lester?" Joan asked.

54

"You don't have no *clue*—what it like to be colored—what it like to live in a darktown, raise your kids in a darktown."

"Show me, Lester," Roy said. "Why not show me?"

Lester's eyes bulged at Roy with inexpressible outrage. "No, man. You can *never* learn. You can't because you think I want your love—like some present you going to give me if I come round to your back door and you going to set it out there in a little cracked dish. No, Mr. Preach, I want you to *fear* me, 'cause fear goes in the *front* door. I know where I am when you fear me. I can deal with fear and hate—but not with that back-step love."

The circle drew closer around us, galvanizing so that I could feel its force at my back, and I heard Louise Gower's voice saying, "For the Lord's sake, will someone call the police? Look what he's doing to our flowers. This is private property and that man's trespassing."

A smile creased Moon's mouth as he asked Roy, "This your place, Mr. Preach?"

From the crowd a male voice said, "It's for people who know how to use it."

"That lets me out, don't it." Moon glanced defiantly around the crowd and took a retreating step through the flower bed. "I'm on my way—but don't let me catch no niggers hanging round your back porch, Mr. Preach, 'cause I'll be coming for 'em. I'll just come and blow my pipe." He pantomimed a fingering of the instrument he had failed to win. Whistling a bar of "Onward Christian Soldiers," he pranced gleefully toward the gate.

Roy started after him as though he might seize him, whirl him around for a brawl here in the shadow of St. Simon's steeple, and Joan's cry of "Roy!" carried a fear of that. It checked him, gave her a chance to slip an arm through his.

"Hey, Lester!" Roy called, and surprisingly Moon turned with an expression of mock attention. "You came in to wreck our fair, didn't you? Stir up some trouble?"

"Stir up some truth is what I come for."

"This door's open to you. Remember that. Whenever you want to come in."

"Gotta go now, Mr. Preach." Moon looked up the street. "I think I hear them policemen coming."

No one laughed and the group broke up gradually to gather children and belongings and to start toward home. The fair was over, but twos and threes lingered on the pavement outside, talking among themselves.

I stayed to help strike the awnings and to add the receipts, which came to a heartening nine hundred and seven dollars. Our supper together in the rectory was punctuated by long silences. We could not get the Lester Moon incident out of mind.

"Why does he do that?" Roy asked again. "Why would he refuse our help? Why would he fail to recognize an ally when he sees one? Is it stupidity and cussedness or some perverse African pride? Why can't he understand we're here to help him?"

"You weren't listening either," Joan said. "He told you that under every white clergyman's dickey beats a bigot's heart."

"Only in this case, he's wrong."

"How does *he* know that?" she asked.

Roy brooded, plucking petals from a daisy, dropping them one by one into an ashtray.

"In fact," she added, "how do *you* know that?"

"How do *I* know that?" He was doused in astonishment. "Because I abhor it. Good God, how do I know if I'm capable of murder or robbing a bank? *You* know I'm not." When she did not reply instantly, he turned to me. "And so do you."

"I don't know if it's instinctive," I said, "but prejudice is woven deep in the civilization. It must touch all of us in some way. We carry it around like the cold virus."

Roy glowered, and silence fell among us.

"But Roy . . ." Joan said, "you *do* see Lester as different . . . different from us on account of his color. Isn't that true?"

"Sure. I can't deny his skin. It's in plain view."

"Well, there you are. I think it's what Lester Moon means . . . that you can't see past his skin to the person he really is. That's why he's angry with you."

"Oh, but I *can.* That's the trouble. Right to the mule, the hate maker, the professional pain in the ass."

"Well," she said, "if you just want to make a joke of it . . ."

"No joke."

It was never easy for Roy Train to acknowledge a shortcoming, but the notion Joan had planted that Saturday night took root. On the following Monday he called me at Diocesan House to say that he had been thinking how prejudice affected all of us and to ask if I would fill in for him while he went south for a few days. He felt he owed it to the parish.

That same afternoon he came to ask the bishop's approval.

"It seems to me you've got all the sit-in you need, right in your own parish," Laurence told him. "I hear you had a row over there on Saturday. Did you get in a quarrel with some colored fellow?"

"I did," Roy said. "It's part of the reason I want to go. I want to find out something about myself—put my principles on the line. But it's for the parish too. Saint Simon's needs to see itself as part of the whole racial picture. They have the crucible down south. Don't you agree?"

"You're the pastor of a church, Roy. I don't see this as an appropriate time."

"The time is late. It's too late for words. It's too late for everything but Christian action."

The bishop sat back in his chair. "If I were a member of your parish now, and heard you'd gone off on a southern trip, I'd be puzzled—to say the least."

"For a *week,* Laurence? Ethan's going to stand in."

"Where is it you want to go?"

"Alabama."

"The Bishop of Alabama is a man named Joe Brace, an able churchman whom I greatly admire. Bishop Brace would not appreciate my sending you into his diocese without an invitation, and you're not likely to get one of those."

"So?"

The bishop gave a long sigh. "Don't misunderstand me, Roy.

I have all kinds of respect for what these Christian groups are doing in the South. They're showing great courage."

"They're showing us *up*," Roy said, "is what they're doing."

Laurence flushed and made a helpless gesture. "I can't forbid you to go." His voice was flat, lacking any trace of the amusement that usually greeted Roy's requests. "Do as you please. From everything you've said, I think it unwise. If you should decide otherwise, you're representing yourself alone, not the Newark diocese."

Roy was silent as we descended the broad front steps, but he took such long, angry strides that I had to skip to catch up with him at the curb.

"That's too bad," I said. "I'm sorry."

"It's okay." He opened the door of the MG and leaned against its roof. His eyes searched the darkening sky and found the lights of a plane as it rose from the airport.

"Maybe there's some wisdom in what Laurence says," I suggested.

"It's possible. I'll give it some thought."

"That's a good idea, Roy."

"There'll be plenty of time on the way down."

"You're *going?*"

"Of course I'm going. Can you be in the office at eight? I'll make you up a list of calls. You know the regular services and there'll be just the one sermon. I won't like missing that, but I'll get Joan to make me a tape."

VI

KNOWING that I had to match my own straightforward delivery against Roy's flamboyance, I chose for my first sermon a graphic text, the Seven Seals episode from Revelation.

On that Sunday, I stood in the pulpit of St. Simon's and told the congregation how it is not the lion whom God loves but the lamb, and what a dramatic disclosure of God's purpose that is. I dared to look into Joan's upturned face, and recognized in her attentiveness that I was aloft.

The congregation appeared pleased by the sermon, and when I stopped by the rectory, a beaming Joan took my hands and said, "You're such a joy, Ethan. I hope you know."

"Old steadfast," I said.

"We all count on you, of course. You never disappoint, but no . . ." She shook her head. "That isn't what I meant at all. You really must *not* think of yourself as some kind of dray horse. You can run beautifully. You can do anything you want to."

"Do you really think so?"

She nodded. "Anything at all."

On Monday as I came out of the church I heard a rectory window shoot up, and Joan appeared in it, waving. "Good news!" she cried.

"Roy's coming home?"

"Nothing like that." Bringing forth a page from the *New York Times,* she draped it over the sill. "I passed my bar. It's right here in the paper, seventeenth out of a hundred and eighty. How's *that* for just a girl?"

On my way back from a round of nursing homes I stopped at a liquor store in Journal Square and found a bottle of Mumm's champagne. When I brought it into the rectory kitchen, Joan cried out, "Oh, Ethan, you're too good to be true," and reached for goblets on a high shelf.

Impatient with the freezer's winter, we set ice cubes afloat in our glasses and touched rims.

"I'm so proud of you," I said. "I really am."

"Oh, come on."

"Really. I'm not just saying that. I can never get over how someone so responsive and so decorative . . . who already is all she ever needs to be, goes right on as though she weren't, and puts her brain on the line as well. I don't know why, but it starts the tears."

She laughed and said, "Maybe I shouldn't like that, but I do."

We sipped our champagne, glancing up at each other, until I asked, "Still no word from Roy?"

She shook her head. "I've left messages for him at the motel. He must go there *some*time. Not a word in three days."

"You'll hear soon."

Joan caught my furtive look at her swelling belly and she smiled. Her hands traced the imposing grade, and she went to stand in the doorway to the dining room.

Gazing at her reflection in the sideboard's wide mirror, she said, "Not all *that* decorative; I see a Saratoga trunk."

"More decorative than ever."

"Thank you, dear." Approaching, Joan planted a kiss at the corner of my mouth. There was a moment's awkwardness. The flush was still rising in my cheeks when the phone rang.

"Roy," Joan said into the receiver, "where *have* you been?"

Later, when she had hung up, a relieved Joan said, "There's been some kind of boring trouble. Roy doesn't think the man in charge knows what he's doing. The bus-in's been delayed.

60

Whatever, he says, he'll be home in a couple of days, Friday at the latest."

But Roy had not returned by Friday, and when I tried to reach him through the regional office of the Southern Christian Leadership Conference in Tully, I spoke with a Mr. Grievey, who surprised me by saying, "That man is not around."

"He must be," I said. "He was assigned to Tully by the Atlanta headquarters. A biggish fellow with curly hair, horn rims. An Episcopal priest from New Jersey."

Grievey said, "Oh, I *remember* that man, all right. I was thinking he'd gone back north."

"He hasn't," I said. "Can you reach him for us?"

"I see him, I'll tell him you're looking for him."

As I preached my second sermon and the days wore on without word from Roy, I shared Joan's concern, but I was also taking some pleasure in my role of surrogate.

I was trying to keep up with all Roy's concerns, working out his proposed budget with the finance committee and preparing an agenda for the vestry meeting. By the time I had finished with the calls and writing up the notes, it was often six o'clock. Before heading home I would stop for a word with Joan, and this invariably became an impromptu supper.

When I came into the rectory now I was likely to find Joan at her exercises, taking deep, chest-clearing inhalations and explaining that they were for the first stages of labor. Panting, turning her head, she would gasp and say, "And this is for when the contractions are getting closer and lasting longer."

She had been reading Grantley Dick Read and had found an obstetrician, a woman named Louise Meader, who had agreed to a delivery without anesthesia.

Sitting up, resting her chin on her hands, Joan told me, "The doctor says I may be early; I could have the baby any day." Frowning, she added, "You know, I don't think the idea of being a father has taken hold in Roy's mind."

"I think you'd better tell him," I said. "Leave him a message that if he's not home in twenty-four hours, he's going to miss the main event."

When she finished her exercises and went to look at the casserole in the oven, she said, "It's grand, Ethan, feeling creation take place inside you. I feel so close to God, to His big, central secret. Sometimes I feel sorry for men, missing out on it. Do you envy me?"

"No," I said, "but I enjoy sharing all this with you." This pleased her, and I went on to tell her about my fantasy that Roy would not return in time and I would be the one to drive her safely through sluggish late-evening traffic to the hospital, there to be taken as the father by the nurses and the woman with whom she shared a room. "The fantasy ends," I said, "with me sitting at the edge of the bed with your fingers sinking into the palm of my hand."

But Joan wasn't amused. Her eyes clouded as if she had felt a warning spasm. "That's just the least bit unhealthy."

The following morning when I came to open the church, I found telling scratches on the door jamb. Turning the key, I felt a difference in the release. The moment I was inside I sensed violation. It hung in the air like gas. So did a premonition that my holiday was ending and there would be a bill for it.

In the sacristy I saw that the hasp of the locker was sprung. Gingerly I opened its door. I had a moment's relief at the sight of the ewers. The ciborium was there too. Then, vertigo in full plunge, I saw the top shelf empty. The chalice was gone.

"Oh, hell," Joan said, "there'll be a stink, won't there? Someone needs to be blamed, and it's not fair, your having to deal with it."

"Maybe it is."

"What do you mean?"

"Some kind of judgment."

"Oh, pooh. If it's a judgment, it's on Roy. Damn it all, he ought to be here *now.*"

In spite of Joan's reassurances I could not shrug off my culpability. I recalled the chalice's graceful shape, chaste as an egg's, the delicate design inscribed in its hexagonal foot, then my sublime feelings when I first held it, tipped it toward the thirst that, at St. Simon's rail, was real as pain and loneliness.

Theft of so precious a charge *was* a repudiation. In someone's mind I had lost the right to it, out of weakness or the breaking of a trust, and I could feel guilt in my heart like a stone.

We had difficulty reaching Roy but found him finally at the SCLC office. From the bedroom phone Joan asked, "When are you coming home, Roy?"

"We're still waiting for the bus, the freedom bus."

"You ought to come now. We need you here."

"What's the matter?"

"Well, for one thing, somebody broke into the sacristy last night."

"And took the cup," I supplied from the kitchen extension. "They left everything else."

"They knew what they were doing," Roy said. "The cup's sterling. The rest is plate. Did you call the cops, Ethan?"

"They came and took some notes. That's about all."

"They said it was the black kids," Joan said.

"Or somebody wants to blame the black kids," Roy said. "Maybe Wally Gower, reminding us he lost out to Wilson as patrol leader."

"Louise Gower is going to love this," Joan said. "You mustn't leave Ethan to handle an angry parish"—I heard a tremolo, a small bird aflutter in Joan's throat—"while you're off adventuring."

"It isn't that."

"Oh?" she said. "Well, whatever it is, I need you, Roy. Dr. Meader says the baby could come any day now, really."

"Tomorrow. Just hold the fort till then. They're ready to come from Atlanta now and bring their own marshals. I just talked to Frank Le Page. I've waited all this time."

"We don't know anything yet," I told Louise Gower when she called to inquire.

"You don't?" she replied. "Well, there's a lot of people in this parish can make a pretty good guess. All these boys in the church running around. Their eyes are all over—you can be sure of that."

Sergeant Cormanick was proving a lackluster sleuth, quick

only to scoff at my suggestion of the pawnshops. "Nobody's going to pawn church silver, Reverend. Nobody's that dumb."

To my prodding he replied, "If you can give me the names of some kids, I'll go to work. I'll talk to your scouts. I'll get 'em down here right away, and by this afternoon I'll at least be able to tell you if it's one of them."

"No," I said. "I'd want to think that over, Sergeant. I don't like making them our suspects."

We made a dozen attempts to reach Roy again, but he did not return our calls. Late in the second day of this, a stern Joan said, "I can't imagine what's happened to Roy, Ethan, but now you must go down and get him."

VII

MY first impression of Tully, Alabama, was of a city under siege. The late-afternoon temperature was in the
nineties. A few elderly Negroes waited on benches, indifferent
to a tyrannical sun. Otherwise, the sidewalks were deserted.

Along the main street, dusty-leaved catalpas had been
trimmed to their knuckles and offered no more shade than the
stanchioned clock in front of the bank. Furniture stores alter-
nated with dry goods stores. Pickup trucks angled at the curb.
From the bed of one a thirsty hound looked forth in desolation.

The SCLC office on Eutaw Street was a storefront whose plate
glass window had been repaired by a web of friction tape.
Within, half a dozen volunteers looked up from their tasks, as
did the several children who were at a table, reading.

The field director, J. J. Grievey, was in his office. He was a
wiry, light-skinned Negro with a pelt of short hair and a narrow
mustache. As I entered, he was rising from behind a desk strewn
like a fairground with drifts of paper and Styrofoam cups. "You
wouldn't be the man?" His inflection was sharp, Northern. "You
wouldn't be our marshal?"

"Ethan Soames," I said. "We've spoken on the phone. I've
come from New Jersey to find Roy Train."

A disappointed Grievey sat down and rocked in his chair. "You see him outside?"

"No."

"Then I guess he's not here."

"Is there some mystery about him?"

"No mystery."

"How long since you've seen him?"

"We got a daily shape-up here. He was out front at noon."

"Where can I find him now?"

Grievey now seemed to come to a boil. "I tell you something, Mr. Soames. I tell you about your friend Train. He got a head on him that is too big for his good. You take him back to Jersey and it's just fine with me."

"I hope to."

"What's he like up north? People have any trouble getting along with him up there?"

I smiled in spite of myself. "Some."

"I guess they *do*. First thing he did here in Tully was go over and talk to the minister at Saint Paul's. We know those people don't want to work with us, but Train have to find that out for himself, you know, and when he *do*, he got to tell the reporters about it. 'That minister over at Saint Paul's know what's right,' Train tells 'em, 'only his people don't go along with no voter registration. Now what kind of shepherd,' he ask, 'who know the way only he don't take it because the sheep won't go?' They don't print that here in Tully but they print it over in Jackson and they print it over in Montgomery. That makes us trouble."

"Where?"

"The big cats," J.J. said. "The big cats don't like us jangling each other and calling names." He kicked a bottom drawer shut. "He want to tell *me* how to get our poor folks registered here. He supposed to take these people up to the courthouse every day and go to the window with 'em while they ask can they take the literacy test again, but Train is this lawyer, you know, and that's too slow for him. He got to tell the D.A. about it. He going to explain the Constitution to him."

Grievey shook his head in wonder. "He want to tell *me* how to run this place. Tell *me* when we are ready for the buses." As

66

Grievey brooded, his anger ebbed. "Maybe you find him up at Archibald's with the reporters. This time of day, they up there, keeping cool."

Archibald's was a few degrees more comfortable than the street but smoky from the grill, where a short-order cook was turning ribs over live coals. Beyond the counter there were five tables, and I found Roy at the farthest, talking persuasively to the burly man beside him.

"Oh, Lord," Roy said as he looked up at me, "the truant officer's here. I wasn't expecting you for a couple of days, Ethan."

He introduced me to Ralph McKenzie, a photographer for the Associated Press, and to a young woman, Ivory Childs, who worked for the *Tully Record*.

Roy had been trying to persuade McKenzie to visit a black family he had come to know, apparently in the hope that McKenzie would photograph them. But my arrival seemed to stiffen McKenzie's resistance. "You can take your friend," he said.

"I want you," Roy insisted. "I want people to see the Truaxes."

"I promised Ivory some pointers"—he turned for a lazy look at Miss Childs—on making the most of light and shadow."

Ivory Childs smiled and rolled her eyes.

Roy scowled. "Tomorrow then? In the morning?"

"On my way tomorrow, I'm afraid," McKenzie said. He was lifting a canvas shoulder bag from his chair back, taking Ivory's consenting hand in his. "I don't think Grievey's going to have the buses in at all until he gets you out of town." Departing, he added, "But that's just my opinion."

"Roy," I said, "there is no more time for Tully."

Watching the couple pass through Archibald's door into the bright street beyond, Roy said, "I cannot understand how the work of the world gets done with everybody's mind on screwing."

"Roy, you're needed at home. Now we must go to the Birmingham airport. I think you're bewitched by this place. Do you hear me?"

"I hear you." He was signaling the waitress. "Do you want some Dr. Pepper? It's not bad, once you get used to it."

"All right. I'll try a Dr. Pepper. Then we're leaving for Jersey City. If we're lucky, we'll beat the stork to your house."

"He'll wait," Roy said. "Tonight I want you to meet some friends."

"There's no time, Roy. Why don't you understand? Joan's desperate. We're all worried about you."

"Trust me, Ethan. I know what I'm doing. I'm taking you to supper in Jericho. That's darktown, where Lionel Truax lives." He looked at his watch. "First, we'll check you into the Liveoak."

"If I stay tonight, will you go home with me in the morning?"

Roy took off his glasses and polished the lenses with a paper napkin. "There's going to be a bus-in here. We've been waiting ten days for it. Some of these people have given up and gone away, but it's taking place at noon tomorrow. When it's over, I'm coming home."

It was dusk as we walked into Jericho. The air was lush with earthy smells, wood smoke, and food simmering over kerosene flames. Overhead there was a rustling of chinaberry leaves. From the windows, some already aglow with orange light, came the sound of talk and laughter.

The street was lined with two- and three-room shacks, each with its porch sagging under a cargo of cast-off refrigerators and rump-sprung sofas, each the identical hue of squash. Jerichoans lined the rails like ferry passengers, peering at the rare sight of two white men strolling here.

The Truax cottage was homely as its neighbors, but I could see a vegetable garden in back, its patch of grass bordered with marigolds. Lionel Truax, a slight Negro in a blue postman's uniform, opened the screen door to us. His eyes blinked anxiously behind rimless glasses and for a moment he seemed overwhelmed by the difficulty of presenting his family. They were gathered around a television set in a room dense with potted plants and heaped with piles of magazines and clothing.

Lucy, his spunky-looking wife, was the first to acknowledge us, looking us over carefully before saying "Hello." Will, Lionel's brother, was in a wheelchair, a homemade affair of wicker and bicycle tires. His skin was so black, it looked dusty. He wore a goatee and his sullen eyes barely grazed me.

Sophie Truax, Lionel's mother, was a woman in her seventies, gnarled as an old tree. She appeared in the kitchen doorway, clearly mistress here, to beam at Roy. "We all glad you come and bring your friend, Reverend," she said and, turning to her family, added, "You show him now."

Lionel's daughter was a slender nine-year-old, Lizzie. Her fluffy hair was center-parted, its twin shocks caught with barrettes of blue glass. Her huge eyes shone with interest in us.

The introductions were followed by an awkward silence. I broke it by saying, "We were wondering why the houses in Jericho are all the same color."

Lionel said, "It's not because we like that color. No, sir. We don't like that color at all, but it happen that a man name of Matt Cook bought a carload of yellow siding for a bargain. That was twenty years ago, and old Matt's been dead for almost as long, but if you like that color and want to take some home with you, you can still find it at the lumberyard." Lionel chuckled and nodded. "You see how one white man's careless action, one he hardly think about, reach out and touch a hundred lives here?"

Lizzie's attention had returned to the screen, where white children romped with a sheepdog, and Lionel explained, "This TV is new. It's a present to Momma, a seventy-fifth birthday present from the Newcombs, where she work, and since it come last month we just sit around and watch."

Lucy said, "Newcombs is where I *quit*. Lionel's momma work there, doin' washin' and ironin' when they need, until she too old. I work there five years ago too, which ain't long enough to get no TV."

Will said, "Newcomb own the furniture store downtown an' he get a TV cheap. Miz Newcomb think she can buy some hearts with that. Shame on us if she do."

"Wil-ll, don't you forget who quit 'em," Lucy said. "Newcombs squeezed Momma dry over thirty years an' they expectin' the same of me—to leave this place every mornin' before six to come to their house all smilin' an' give myself to their kids as if I don't have none of my own. No *sir*. When Lionel get his raise at the post office, I come home to be Lizzie's momma."

Lucy made room for us on the settle, and as we perched beside her Roy said, "Tell us, Lucy, about being a momma."

"I know all about bringin' up a colored child," she said. "I could write a book about bein' a colored mother in the South. She must teach her kids what the white man expect of 'em. A child got to be smart about that if she want to stay out of trouble. We slap 'em and we scream at 'em so's they won't make no mistake. I want my child to fear. I want her to know just how far she can go before she get hurt."

Old Sophie Truax appeared in the kitchen door again to say, "Lucy, these reverends don't want to hear about spankin' no chillun."

"Yes, we do, Mrs. Truax," Roy said. "We're here to learn everything we can about you."

"How you expect to learn about us?" It was Will's resentful voice. "You never *know* colored unless you colored. You the other side. You never goin' to pick up a telephone and hear a voice say, 'Nigger, you ain't gonna be healthy as no foreman.' You never know how that feel."

"Who said that, Will?" I asked. "Do you know?"

"That ain't half what they say when I ask for what's mine, but that don't stop me askin'. What I care for words from any white mouth. I don't even *hear* what the white man at the rubber plant say to me until five of 'em come to me in the parkin' lot an' make sure I understand about steppin' out of the way for the white man. An' they fix it so I don't have to *step* out of his way." Will gave his wheels a turn. "I gets to *ride*."

"Now don't you go on at the reverend, Will. They come to us tonight an' we gathered for thanks and good feelin'."

A segment of the news broadcast silenced our conversation. We saw the entrance of an elementary school in New Orleans, before which a crowd of white adults, largely women, had gathered. The camera closed on angry expressions, cursing mouths, hands that clenched and chopped. The people pressed forward and were kept from blocking the steps and double doors by the widespread arms of city police.

Then the camera turned toward the curb, where a colored child, a girl of about eleven, was getting from a car. Carrying her books and lunchbox, she made her way up the path at the side of a white policeman. She kept her frightened eyes upon the school door, not daring a glance at the shouting bystanders.

Lucy pointed at the screen. "You see her? *That* child know."

"She's terrified," I said.

"But she know what she terrified *of,* an' she know she goin' to live with that the rest of her life. Like my Lizzie know what come her way when she go into the white world."

"Lizzie's going to have new laws to protect her," Roy said. "A new church too. Our kids are going to know better times, Lucy."

"You a preacher," she said. "It's your business to say so."

"I sure hope you're right, Roy." Lionel turned from the screen, where the girl and her police escort were disappearing through the schoolhouse door. "That little girl's daddy must believe it or he wouldn't be lettin' her do that."

"I wish I was that little girl," Lizzie said. "You think they're going to integrate our school someday?"

"We goin' to see about that, Lizzie," Lionel replied.

"When they do, Lizzie," Roy asked her, "are you going to lead the way?"

"Sticks and stones'll break my bones," she said, "but nobody going to hurt me calling names."

"Lizzie, child," said Sophie Truax, "you don't want to go an' take all that on your little shoulders. Don't you give up your childhood for a peck o' trouble. You listen to your granny."

The kitchen table was covered with daisied oilcloth, threadbare from the rubbing of three generations of Truax elbows. As we sat around it for Sophie's supper, our faces reflecting the rich, yellow lamplight, Lucy recalled her own childhood here.

"I remember when I was a child," she said, "goin' downtown with my momma to a ol' bakery use to be on Mercer Street, an' a white woman there thought my momma was gettin' ahead of her for bein' waited on. Momma say no, she wasn't pushin' ahead, but the white woman don't like the *way* she say that, an' she slap her. Momma didn't do nothin'. She just stood there like everybody else in the bakery, pretendin' it hadn't happen. But *I* saw—and I was *scared*. Now you not goin' to believe this. I mus' been eight, nine years old, and taught never to *think* about sassin' no white person—but I kicked that white woman back."

Lucy had grown tense as she told the story, as though she were reliving the experience, but then she tossed her head and laughed. Her laughter was a release, without rancor, and we all felt it and laughed with her as she said, "Yes, I kicked her good, and oh *my*, what a fuss in that bakery. The police came and you'd have thought somebody done robbed the bank. An' you know what? When I got home, Momma gave me the floggin' of my life."

"What a relief it is, Lucy, that you can laugh about it," Roy said.

"We laugh 'cause we have to," Lucy said soberly. "We know whatever they say, whatever they do to us, we got to take it."

Beside me, Lizzie had decided that I was a friend. "I'm in the fifth," she confided, "a grade ahead of my age, and I like being with the older girls and boys. I go to Jericho schoolhouse. You passed it coming here to supper, a long house with a tin roof. I have lots of friends there and I really love my teacher, Miz Milo. She's been away to the normal school at Hattiesburg. It's Miz Milo first took me to the library up at SCLC. I go there most every afternoon and read the children's books. I see you there today. I watch Reverend Roy"—she covered a giggle with her hand—"talking with Mr. Grievey. I like Reverend Roy soon as I see him walking to the courthouse with my granny and making us proud."

Watching me nibble at the sweet, dark greens and grits on my plate, Lizzie said, "You don't have the taste for our food, do you?"

"Oh, it's good, Lizzie." I lined up another forkful. "Different, though, from what I'm used to."

"You leave Reverend Ethan be," her father said. "He not a wolf, like some I know."

"Don't worry about Lizzie and me," I said. "We've got an understanding."

"What's school like where you live, Reverend? They colored children and white together?"

"In Jersey City all kids go to the same school."

"And don't nobody insult the colored?" Lucy asked. "Nobody call 'em nigger?"

"Yes, Lucy," Roy said. "Some do."

"But we got to keep thinkin' about what we see happen at that school," Lionel said. "When we feel that pain, we got to remember it gettin' a little better every day. Maybe sometime we be well, and until then I know I can take all they got to give, and more. Most the white people in this town don't know that an' they goin' to be sur*prised*. My daddy use to say we has to *fool* the white man into thinkin' he got us beat. But you know, he fool himself. He's a fool that think colored is dumb, or think colored is lazy, or think colored is yellow."

Lionel laughed at this idea and then said, "Even if they got us in yellow houses here, they mistaken about our color. Now I'm no brave nigger, but I have no fear of that white man. Truly, he can't scare me. They some mean and stupid men here in Tully and they'd as soon hurt me as spit, but they don't scare me. They must know that they *nevah* scare me, that nothin' they can do goin' to scare me."

There was no sound around the table. Lizzie's mischievous child's face was struck with admiration for her father. Looking into it, I saw an illumination, a new knowledge that transcended her grandmother's doubts and her mother's suspicions and brought her to a belief even stronger than her father's, a *faith*, really, in the new world she would live to see.

Lionel nodded to her as if he had seen what I had. He smiled as if he had prayed for cooling rain and just heard the first roll of thunder. "Yes, Lizzie," he said, "that's why I can't wait for that ol' freedom bus to come. Maybe it come tomorrow."

VIII

THE Liveoak Motel made a forlorn crescent around an empty swimming pool, where waist-high weeds flourished. Over the registration desk a sign warned: WE ARE NOT RESPONSIBLE FOR FIRE, THEFT, OR ACCIDENT. PLEASE PROTECT YOUR PROPERTY. Its telephone booth was a rank coffin scrawled with infernal numbers and obscene proposals. But there was a wait for it, even at eight in the morning, and once in possession, Roy settled in with a mound of coins.

I hovered with a copy of the *Tully Record*. I had just read that outside agitators had made their unwelcome appearance in town—when I heard the cascade of Roy's change.

"God damn it, Frank," he was saying, "what kind of sick *is* this man? Does the Justice Department realize we've been waiting a week and a half for these guys? It's a last chance. Tully's a fizzle. What are you people thinking up there?"

He glared at the receiver. In an aside to me he said, "The marshal called in sick. You don't get sick at a time like this. Some funny business going on. Kennedy can't be that short of marshals."

"Is Frank on the line?"

"He's talking to Roland Martin. They're trying to get a substitute." Roy was listening again, frowning, then saying, "Well, supposing he doesn't? Would you come without him? You want to know what I think? I think Grievey is chickenshit. He's letting these reporters go, Frank. The AP man's leaving today. There's not going to be anybody around to cover it but the local papers."

Roy listened and then said, "But I have to go home, Frank. There's been a robbery at my church, cops and all. Why don't you just come—marshals or no marshals?"

Waiting again, Roy said to me, "It's really stupid, holding up the show while the audience starts going home." He listened again and this time his face gladdened. "Good for you, Frank. Now you guys are showing some style. I'll see you at the Greyhound station at noon. Good luck. No, I'll tell Grievey. I'll get hold of him now."

Hanging up, Roy sat for a moment staring at the telephone before he relinquished the booth. "Okay," he said. "We're going to have a bus-in today. How about that? Let's have some breakfast and then I'll tell Grievey about it. Give them a chance to set off from Atlanta."

It was quarter to nine when Roy reached J. J. Grievey at home. "It's all set, J.J.," he told him. "The bus is on its way at last. It's due in here at noon and they may not have the marshal. He got sick at the last minute."

Roy winced at Grievey's response but he replied coolly, "No, they agreed on it, Roland Martin and the other ministers. I don't believe they want any more advice."

"Mad," Roy told me with a grin as he emerged from the booth. "J.J.'s furious, but he'll get everybody out. It'll be fine."

Turning into Eutaw Street, we could see that about twenty black people had gathered outside the SCLC office, and as we parked I could feel the broadcast tension and a tuning-up of my own anxious strings.

Lionel Truax came at a trot to intercept us. He was grave with concern. "They say the bus coming in at noon but they no marshals . . . and J.J. don't like that. He want to stop that bus."

"I know," Roy said. "Is everybody turning out?"

"They call me, all right. I walk out of the post office and come down because the brigade mustering now. But you and me, we *fired*. You know that?" Behind his glasses Lionel's eyes blinked with disappointment. "J.J. say that. He say you call in the bus, and without marshals nobody going to get off and maybe we not even *get* to the Greyhound."

Roy scowled in the direction from which we had just come. "There's nobody up at the bus station. We saw two cops in a cruiser. They were half asleep. Nobody even knows about the bus."

"J.J. say they do. He say the police know. The Klan know. Everybody wants to know . . . he know. He say you going to get us all killed."

"Marshals or no marshals, we're protected by federal law," Roy said and started across the street. "Whatever these cracker cops may think of it, they're bound to enforce it."

As we approached the front door, McKenzie, smiling at the upturn in possibility, came bounding out. "J.J.'s got news for you," he said jauntily.

"I heard," Roy said. "Too bad about J.J."

"A new battle plan. I'm sticking around to see how it works."

J. J. Grievey in a polka dot shirt was surrounded by a dozen members of the sit-in brigade, a mixture of young clergy, students, and workers, evenly divided among blacks and whites.

"You going into the Greyhound *alone* now," he was instructing them. "Everybody else, all the brothers and sisters, going to be downtown making noise. We going to be parading . . ."

He took no notice of Roy as he made his way into the group, but he spoke more tersely. "Make sure you understand that this new plan is to deal with the fuckup. That's what we doing here today, we dealing with a fuckup."

"I hear I'm fired, J.J.," Roy interrupted.

As if seeing Roy for the first time, J.J. looked at him with blazing eyes. "If I could, Train, I'd put you in the closet and lock you in forever so you don't make us any more trouble here."

"I came down for a bus-in. I've been waiting over ten days for it."

"I know what you come down for, Train. You come down here

for your*self*. I'm going to see you don't go home with nothing to show for your trouble. You know what I mean?"

"No. I don't."

"I mean in the civil rights movement you are a dead man. You never cross this doorstep again. You never cross the doorstep of *any* SCLC office in this land. You don't believe me, Train? You just try-y."

"I will," Roy said. "You can count on that, and if there's any row here today, I'm going to be in on it. You can count on that too."

"If?" A muscle in J.J.'s cheek twitched. He seemed to grow by inches. "Did you say *if*?" He looked for me. "Soames, where's that car of yours?"

"In the street."

"Come on. You take me and Train here for a ride."

Grievey was first into my rented Maverick. He crouched low in the rear seat while directing us along Tully's streets. Emptied by the broiling, late-morning heat, they gave the town an abandoned look.

Turning into Boone Street, we approached the Greyhound station and saw a police cruiser with an officer drowsing at its wheel.

"Pull in here for a minute," Grievey said, and I turned into the curb several spaces behind the police car.

In the Sears parking lot were a panel truck and two pickups, drawn close to the building's wall to take advantage of its shade. Five men lounged under the metal awning of the loading platform. I saw the glint of a bottle being passed.

"Look there, Train." Grievey was peering out, catlike. "What do you see?"

He pointed out a car parked in the shade of a clump of pines. A big man in a striped shirt was removing a length of chain from its trunk. "What could that man want with a chain? Some friend of his maybe stuck in a ditch and he going to tow him out? See that undertaker, name of Wilbur Rose? What Wilbur doing with a baseball bat? Maybe he looking for a game. Maybe they going to choose up sides. Or maybe you can tell me why those men stand here drinking in the middle of this hot day? What party they maybe go to? What fraternal order you guess they belong to? Maybe they Elks? Maybe they in the Rotary Club? Or maybe Shriners? They look like they figuring how to help the crippled children, Train?"

Roy gazed balefully at the scene. "I wouldn't know," he said.

"And look here at your sleepy policeman," Grievey went on. "You figure he going to sleep on while our bus come in? Or maybe going to help our brigade boys find seats at the lunch counter, make sure nobody keep 'em waiting?"

"I think he'll keep people from getting hurt."

"Oh, yeah? He going to be keeping the peace, is he? 'Cause he a peace officer? 'Cause he wearing that uniform? You suppose he see Wilbur Rose swinging his bat? You think his eyes not so good as ours? Look over there. He must have waked up and seen Wilbur do that, cause there he go . . ."

The policeman, a ruddy-faced, handsome man with silver hair beneath his cap, had stepped into the street. He plucked the shirt free of his back and started slowly but purposefully toward Rose. Unaware he was being approached, Rose gazed across the floating layers of heat in the parking lot to where the others waited.

"He must be going to tell Wilbur to put his bat away," Grievey proposed. "Then he going to tell those men to get back to their work, lest somebody think they loitering and making some nuisance. That's what he going to do, huh, Train?"

Reaching Wilbur Rose, the policeman grasped the man's left elbow and turned him so that they faced each other. For an instant it looked like an earnest confrontation, but in the next it had turned into a playful one. Their heads bent together. A few words, then laughter, were exchanged.

The policeman moved on, crossing the street to enter the Greyhound station. A moment later he appeared in the luncheonette's window, leaning on the counter to talk to the waitress.

Roy shook his head. His voice was a whisper as he said, "I don't believe it."

"You don't believe what?" Grievey asked. "Your eyes, man?"

"The cop's going to *watch?*"

A second later Grievey said, "Soames, you drive us back now. This trip a waste of gas."

As I drove toward Eutaw Street, I glanced at Roy and found his eyes narrowed. They had darkened and they roved the street ahead. "Who do we talk to at the Justice Department?"

"You going to call somebody, Train? You going to get Bobby Kennedy on the case? You a little late, is all. That bus of yours going to be here in about a hour."

"I'll be there to meet it."

"You going to be where I say you going to be. You going to be with *me* . . . where I keep my eyes on you."

By eleven-thirty both sidewalks of Eutaw Street outside the SCLC office were crowded with Tully's Negroes. Some held placards with scrawled messages: NOT TOO LATE TO INTEGRATE! NO JIM CROW. And WE STAND TO FIGHT, SIT DOWN TO EAT. There were men from the offices, from the gin, and the rubber factory, men in overalls, hospital workers in green jumpers, a truckload of workers from the peanut co-op, and a troop of schoolchildren.

They spilled into the street, threatening to choke traffic, and indeed a car with two white men in it drove through fast, swiping at the stragglers, who leaped onto the curb, calling out "Whoo-ee!" and causing laughter and catcalls.

The twelve members of the sit-in brigade stood apart, and Grievey went among them, touching each in a benediction as he spoke. He paused longest with a big Negro in green fatigues whom they called Cooley. With his partner, a white man in clerical collar, Cooley seemed to be in command.

Grievey glanced at his watch. "Time now," he said to the twelve men. "You going to straggle after Cooley and Norman down through Jericho like you going home to lunch and you got nothing on your mind but pork roll. Then when that whistle blow at noon, you going to be all together up on Boone Street, but hanging back until you see that bus with the freedom banner

79

on it coming into the dock. Then you going to be in the station to meet it."

Grievey watched them move off before he turned to the others. There were nearly a hundred of us, and he stood on the office step to speak. "We going up into town now and make a march that going to keep everybody interested in *us*. They not going to like our marching, but we going to do it anyway. Maybe we going to get across Main Street and up Governor to the courthouse—'cause that's where we want to stand, on them courthouse steps."

Now Grievey looked at Roy, his face so intense, I thought he was about to strike him. Instead he put out a hand. When a flabbergasted Roy did not take it at once, Grievey grasped Roy's hand between both his own.

"Come on, then," Grievey said. "Let's go."

He raised an arm so that all could see, and there were cries along the line of "On, man! On!"

Following Grievey up Eutaw Street, I walked beside Roy and Lionel Truax. We turned left onto Market Street and as we approached its corner we saw some men and boys looking in our direction. Beyond them, blocking our way, stood a police car, its blue turret light winking. Traffic was stopped. Drivers were out of their cars, standing on the pavement, watching us.

As they spilled out of Market Street, our marchers were lining the curb, two and three deep, waiting for a sign to step forward and cross Market Street.

By custom, all activity in this parched town took place in slow motion. Children loitered at their play. Dogs procrastinated in their rounds. But before us men were unloading sawhorses from a truck and trundling them into a barricade at double-time.

Two policemen walked briskly toward the intersection, each restraining a leashed Doberman pinscher. Grievey seemed hypnotized by the sight.

A barrel of a man with a gold emblem on his cap was getting out of a police car, and with a hitch of his wide blue trousers, he made for us.

"Here he come," Grievey said. "Billy Beller himself coming to meet us."

Halting before us, Chief Beller said, "Hello, J.J. We been waitin' on you. What you doin' here with all your friends?"

"Right now we watching the dog show."

"You a dog lover, J.J.?"

"I love all animals—dogs, cats, even pigs, which are the hardest."

Though clearly not a bright man, Beller got the joke and nodded. "That's good, J.J. Now you just tell your boys this is the end of the line. When you go home, we'll go too."

"No," Grievey said. "I don't want to tell 'em that. They planning to march right on to the courthouse and they running a little late as it is."

Chief Beller raised a bullhorn to his mouth. "Y'all go on home 'fore you get yourselves hurt. You don't have no permit to go paradin' and these policemen here behind me got orders to see there ain't none."

"Chief," Roy said to him, "this is a peaceful demonstration. These people have a right to walk this street and to assemble on the courthouse steps."

The chief took Roy in, a slow inspection, before replying, "No, Reverend. No they don't. They don't have no such right. And so far as I know we didn't invite no outsiders down to hep us interpret our laws for us."

"It's the law of the land, Chief," Roy said. "You're interfering with my rights as a U.S. citizen."

Lionel Truax stepped off the curb then. Four policemen stood in a rank on the far curb and he took several steps toward them, clearly expecting others to follow.

Seeing Lionel go toward the barricade, trotting now, the chief cried out, "Get that boy!" and Lionel broke into a run, feinting to the left in the direction of Governor Street.

He ducked under the barricade and slowed to a trot when he realized he was alone, and saw, as we did, that the two dogs, unleashed, were streaking for him, ears back, silent, swift as arrows.

As the dogs struck, there was a gasp from the marchers like a shellburst. We watched bared fangs sink into Lionel's shirt and trousers and heard the sound of tearing fabric.

The chief had moved into the center of the street and stood now, watching the spectacle beyond the barricade. Roy walked toward him and called out, "Stop that!" He was moving one of the trestles aside when the chief cracked his hand with the butt of his bullhorn.

"You leave that sawhorse be, Reverend," Beller said. He gave the bullhorn to a young officer beside him and turned back to Roy. "Here, let's get you a special pass through these policemen to the courthouse. I see you got an interest in how we run our town. I always like to explain it to tourists comin' through so's they won't have no doubt."

The crowd was silent now as two policemen collared the dogs and pulled them away from Lionel Truax. He was rigid with fright and his clothes were torn, but there was no blood to be seen. He stood, knees bent, hands dangling. Two men in work clothes took him by the arms, and as they struggled him toward a waiting pickup truck, Lizzie Truax sprang out from the line. She was caught and held by a policeman.

"Daddy!" she cried and watched her father bundled into the front seat of the truck.

"Who are those men?" Roy asked the chief.

"They friends of that boy," Chief Beller said. "They going to look after him and see he don't get in no more trouble."

"You're responsible, Chief, if any harm comes to Lionel Truax. Remember that."

Chief Beller took hold of Roy's elbow. "Reverend, you know what you doin' here? You trespassin', is what you doin'." He gave Roy a shove that sent him staggering. "We have an uncommon respect for that collar but we don't believe it gives you no right to come buttin' into our business without bein' asked. That's trespass an' we don't take kindly to it."

"When you deny these people their rights, you're shaming all of us. This is one country."

"Where you from, Reverend? You from New York City?"

"Jersey."

"What place?"

"Jersey City."

"How'd you feel if me an' a crowd of my buddies took a bus up there an' without bein' asked we come paradin' down your street makin' a mess an' walkin' on your lawns an' bargin' in your front door to tell you you was goin' to run Jersey City the same way we run Tully?"

"I'd listen to you."

"No you wouldn't." He gave Roy another push. "You mealy-mouthed son of a bitch." Rage flashed in Beller's eyes and fired the steep flanks of his face. "You're a damned liar." He reached for Roy's shoulder as if to shake the hypocrisy from him, but Roy caught his arm and yanked him off balance.

"This is a public way," Roy said. "I'm breaking no law."

Chief Beller's anger dissolved like a passing squall. Gently, he said, "Reverend, you just plain wrong about that. What you're doin' here"—he straightened the sleeve of his starched white shirt—"is resistin' an officer." From his wide belt he unhooked a pair of handcuffs.

Tully jail was a two-story building of yellow stone. Beneath its small, high windows, rust stains leaked from the bars. In its bleak lobby, time malingered. When I could no longer endure the clock hands' weary pace, I tried to call Joan from the pay phone, and reached her at dinnertime.

"Roy's in jail?" To my relief, she laughed. "Well, you'll want a bondsman."

"There's only one and he's out of town. I think the cops sent him on a trip. He's meant to be back tonight."

"Find him, Ethan," she said. "Tell him the prisoner is going to be a father, and soon too."

"Truly?"

"It's a hunch."

"There are these false alarms," I said. "It'll be another day at least. Just hold on."

"You mean wait? Cross my legs and clench my teeth? Oh, Ethan." She began to laugh again.

"I mean that you'll be all right."

"How do you know?"

"You're a little scared. That's perfectly natural."

There was a pause before she said, "And a little angry too. I don't know if that's natural, but it'll help."

Just before midnight I reached Amos Root, the bailbondsman, at his home, and he grumpily agreed to meet me at six in the police station. I called Joan back, but there was no answer.

IX

EMERGING from the dark, clamorous tomb of Tully jail, Roy looked into my eyes without recognition. His seersucker pants were rumpled, collar and dickey wilted, hair in disarray. There was no mark on him, but he had been stunned in some way. Although he had lost his color, he stood erect, chin uptilted, shedding a luminous dignity.

His dazed eyes lingered on the armored door with its peephole into the cellway and the line of colored men waiting to enter it.

"We can go, Roy," I said. "I've got your stuff from the motel." He allowed himself to be led toward the bright, hot day outside.

He got slowly into the front seat of the Maverick, settling himself gingerly. I took my place at the wheel and locked his door. "You a little groggy? Did they do anything to you?"

It was as though my voice reached him through a wall and he struggled to understand. Eyes focusing, he shook his head. "I'm fine. When is J.J. getting out?"

I started the car and pulled away from the curb. "They're holding Grievey without bail, but there's a lawyer up at the courthouse now, trying to get him released."

"We'll go back." He reached for the door latch.

"There's a cop right behind us. Unless we drive straight to the

Birmingham airport, you'll be rearrested. The show's over, Roy. Nothing more to do here, and plenty to do at home."

At Tully's limits I watched the police car slow and turn onto the shoulder of the road, waiting to see us on our way.

"Is anyone dead?" he asked.

"No. But not everybody's accounted for."

"Lionel? The Truaxes?"

"Lionel got home at five this morning, I heard. He'd been held in a cabin out of town. But that ex-Marine hasn't turned up."

"Cooley Smith?"

"The Klan has him someplace."

"Oh, shit." He turned to look through the rear window.

"Otherwise just cuts and bruises. And we can't go back. Don't even think about it."

After a few miles I asked, "Can you talk about what went on in there?"

He thought for a while and said, "I spent all eternity in that cell. Is it really just a day gone by?"

"Eighteen hours."

He was looking out the window into swampland, where the kudzu grappled with old oaks, pulling them with slender tendrils down into the ooze. "I was alone in the cell at first, and I couldn't see anything. The window was high in the wall and there was nothing to stand on, but I could hear sounds from the street. In the distance there were shouts, full of fear, and a siren wailing, and twice, shots. I was thinking, This is all on *me*. If I had kept my fool mouth shut this morning . . . If I had not begged Frank Le Page to come . . . there would be only the sounds of people going home to their supper."

"You don't know that."

He frowned as though in pain. "Well, I do. After a night like that, I *do* know. I can't escape anything."

He began to tell about it—how, as light faded from his window, he had heard company coming, colored voices chanting a dirge as the men were herded along. Thinking he recognized the voice of a fellow marcher, James Woods, he called out to him, asking if the bus had come in and if James's brigade had taken the station.

After a long wait a voice he wasn't sure was Woods's replied, "We got the station. Some still in there when we arrested."

"I heard shooting," Roy had called. "Was anyone hurt?"

"They some hurt," the voice replied. "They some hurt for sure. They some down and getting stomped. They some dead."

"Lionel?" Roy had asked. "Is Lionel Truax all right?"

There was more silence and when he had asked a second time, several voices answered. "Lionel? Look like Lionel gone."

"Gone? What do you mean?"

"They take him and Big Cooley away in the pickup. They with the Klan now. They going to kill 'em sure. They waiting for Cooley. They don't want no nigger Marine around. We don't see them again."

The jailhouse door had clanged as more prisoners were brought in, groaning and cursing, laughing at their helplessness as they were prodded into cells, and Roy felt he had fallen into hell itself. His guilt had begun to suffocate him, closing his throat, dimming his sight. He sat on his bunk and prayed until he fell asleep.

He had awakened in a sweat. He was steeped in it, and a rancid smell rose from the thin pad of his mattress, but it was quiet in the jail and on the street. Then he heard a groan nearby, and he realized someone was in the cell with him.

Stealing across the cell, he had looked into the opposite bunk. A faint, reddish light from the corridor fell upon the bruised face of J. J. Grievey.

Roy whispered, "What have the bastards done to you?"

J.J.'s head rolled. His eyes flickered open. Gummed lips parted. "They rough me up some," he said, irony intact. "Them dogs don't like my meat. It not dark enough for 'em, but they was three cops who wasn't so fastidious. They took to discouraging me with their boots." He moved and winced with the effort. "They got hard toes. Old Billie showed up for the fun and got so interested, he missed the bus coming in."

"What happened?" Roy had asked. "Do you know?"

Grievey's answer was slow. "When they take me, we have the bus station. We not going to keep it. I know that. But for maybe an hour, any colored man don't mind the racket could go in there and wash his hands with soap."

"Is Lionel Truax alive?"

J.J. had closed his eyes in the effort to remember. "They take Lionel away. I see them do that. Those men take him away to scare us—and it scares us, all right, no matter how brave we are. But they don't want to kill nobody when the town full of strangers like it is."

"You didn't hear he was dead?"

"No." J.J. was emphatic. "They going to let him go. Lionel will come walking in. I'm sure of it."

Roy said, "Thank God."

"It can go bad. It can go bad if the man they take acts up or if Mr. Charlie get to drinking. If he get scared himself and get to thinking dead men tell no tales—then it goes bad. What I hear is they took Cooley too. Cooley too big and mean for them Klansmen."

Kneeling beside J.J.'s bunk, Roy had had a sense of deliverance, an intuition that his prayer had been answered. The touch of God's hand was as real to him as the battered body before him.

Confession rose in his throat. "J.J., I doubted you," he said. "In my pride I refused to believe the danger, even when you took me uptown and showed me men with bats and chains. Last night I believed you. Last night I heard the sounds of battle in Tully. I knew who had sent for it and got it delivered. I knew that in the morning if there was blood on the street, who'd put it there."

J.J.'s response was reflective. "You're a headstrong man. I wouldn't argue with you there. You must be a trial to that wife of yours. I pity her. But you know something? When they got done with me last night and put me in here with you, we had us a desegregated bus station uptown. There bound to be some blood on it. That's what the blood's for. Now with you and me shouting at each other all week, we got us some progress." He had laughed softly. "Roy, I'm going to tell you something. I had you pegged for a slow learner but you fool me. You learn faster than most our tourists. You okay the way you stand up to old Billie. You was *mad*. You know"—J.J. had put out a hand to find Roy's—"I believe you are part nigger."

Roy had leaned over J.J. and hugged him, wept on his chest until he realized he was hurting him.

While Roy and I were driving across Alabama to Birmingham airport, a son was being born to him. Roy's first hours in Jersey City were spent at the Medical Center and for a while father-hood hypnotized him.

As we stood at the nursery window he told me fervently, "It's miraculous. I look into that little red, squalling face and for once I feel immortal. I see it all so clearly. I understand the great truth about never-ending life. We're links in a chain leading back into the shadows of all that's passed and now forward into ages yet to come. It's stunning, Ethan. Can you look at my son there and feel any of that?"

"Some."

That afternoon I called on the new mother. Propped against three pillows, wearing a fancy negligee and rosy with happiness, she waved me into the room. The baby slept contentedly beside her while Roy at the side of the bed summed up an argument, saying, "And it's going to have meaning for all of us."

"And just junk the Walter?" Joan asked. "Your family's going to think it a bit strange, and I do too. What about you, Ethan? You're going to be godfather. How do you like calling him J.J.?"

"Surely that's a matter for you two."

"But help me explain to him, Ethan. It's such a great chance to make our peace in Morristown. I don't like Roy's family thinking I'm the wicked witch. It's not fair."

Roy was looking steadfastly at his sleeping son. "This kid's not meant to be a peace offering. He didn't come into the world to atone for my father's disappointment in me. He has no obligation whatever to the past." Roy's eyes flashed with passion and his voice rose as if he were speaking to a multitude. "I want him to have a name that rings with future hope. That's what J.J. means to me. It means tomorrow."

89

I know that Roy was sincere in his argument and yet could see it as bizarre. He was mocking himself even as he pressed it. He smiled as he thumped an emphasizing fist on the bedside table. This sent a spoon flying to the floor and woke J.J., who began to wail.

When we were coming back from Alabama, a passenger on the plane had recognized Roy from his picture. The afternoon edition of the *Atlanta Constitution* had carried a photograph of Roy's arrest by Chief Beller, along with a caption reading, "Jersey Priest Arrested in Alabama Riot."

The same picture, one that McKenzie, the AP man, had brought out with him, appeared in several papers, among them the *Newark News,* which was where Bishop Givens saw it.

McKenzie had caught in Roy's face a characteristic expression. Primarily it revealed his steamy indignation toward this arrogant fat man and his gun, but it was civilized, even beatified by a simultaneous smile of forgiveness, as if he were addressing a child in tantrum who, if dealt with humanely, would eventually come to its senses.

As I reported on my own trip to Alabama and Roy's return to the rectory at St. Simon's, the bishop kept glancing at the picture. The bold headline read: JERSEY PRIEST JAILED, ONE STILL MISSING IN ALABAMA DEMO. A syndicated story described the aftermath, the restoring of order in the town, the hospitalization and release of five injured persons, and the failure of police to locate one of the demonstrators.

"You see, Roy ignored the one thing I asked of him," the bishop said. "To go as a private citizen. That was foolish."

"I'm sure he regrets that."

"Do you realize he exceeded his authority down there too? He went against orders by bringing that bus in. Did he tell you that?"

"That was rash, and he's aware of it."

"Three days now. That man's likely dead."

"But not certainly. We have to go on praying for Cooley Smith."

"Yes, we must do that." The bishop frowned and after a moment said, "But you know, Ethan, there's a further concern. I think Roy is blind to his primary obligation. I see no sense of responsibility to his parish in all this. He seems to have that backward. The church is not his to manipulate. His insistence on doing so is undermining his ministry." He watched me for a sign of acquiescence, and when it was not immediate he ended the interview with a resolute clamp of his lips and the vow "That much will be clear to him before this day is out."

Late in the afternoon I saw Roy's MG at our curb and kept an eye out for him in the halls of Diocesan House. It was nearly dusk when he appeared, hands in his pockets, going slowly down the steps. I caught up with him as he was getting into the car.

I climbed in beside him and recognized the faraway look as a bad omen. "No peace?"

"A useful talk. That's the best I can say for it."

"It was your dragging Jersey into it. That's what bugs him."

"I didn't write that headline or the caption. Nobody asked me where I was from. I could hardly deny it if they had. Nor would I. Let Jersey look good for a change."

"He's human, you know. A little humility on your part would bring down his temperature. Can't you arrange that? Fake it, if you must?"

"I went in to see Laurence on my belly. I apologized for the story in the papers every way I knew, but it turns out the publicity *isn't* the issue. What he wants of me goes very deep, Ethan. What are we to do when every instinct, every wit we have, shouts out to march—I march, you march, everybody marches—and Laurence says, 'Wait.' There's something wrong with a church that sits on its ass while the head and the heart of the world says march. There's something wrong when your bishop tells you that thinking like that is arrogance and self-will. He even had a text for me. Peter. Think of that. 'Ye younger submit yourselves . . . that God may exalt you in due time.' That sermon is lost on me, Ethan. We can't wait for Laurence's God. He's running late."

The photograph appealed to picture editors and turned up

sporadically in papers and magazines over the next ten days. It created, as I suspect Roy had anticipated, a sanction for him, perhaps even the luster of a hero.

He received favorable mail from strangers. Ted Fenno asked him to write a piece on Tully for *New Horizons*—a follow-up on the article on racism in the church up north—and the bishop's annoyance moderated, but the publicity was no safe-conduct at St. Simon's. It seemed rather to exacerbate the parish grievance over the loss, now seen as permanent, of its Communion silver.

At Roy's suggestion, I came to the special meeting of the vestry, and found him before it, cheerful and self-assured. The onlookers were so many that the meeting had moved into the church itself. One of them, Louise Gower, was standing, hunched, hands grasping a pew back. Her voice trembled and veered uncertainly as she cried out, "Father Roy, we see you in the paper all the time but we have to call a meeting to see you here in church."

Roy smiled. "It's true, Louise. I've been away, but I'm back now."

She went on as if she had not heard. "Maybe you'll tell us why you took it upon yourself to leave and go down to Alabama and get yourself in jail. There's some of us would like to hear about that."

"Yes, I'm going to try to tell you about that, Louise."

"I've asked around the vestry. Nobody remembers your asking for leave."

"I spoke to the senior warden," Roy said. "Isn't that so, Ham?"

Hammond Walsh, a heavy man with thinning gray hair, looked concerned but nodded.

"I also asked the bishop."

"The bishop?" Louise pounced on this. "The *bishop* gave you leave?"

Roy frowned, pulled at the end of his nose. "As a private citizen." He brightened, offering her his boyish, mischievous grin. "I would have asked you too, Louise, if there had been time. I would have tried to explain why it was so important that I go—and then, even if you had said I couldn't"—Roy waited a few seconds, letting silence flood the church before he finished on a trumpet note—"I'd have gone because I was prompted by an inner voice so strong, there was no denying it."

Louise was confounded, already sinking toward her seat with a look of bafflement on her dry, white face, when she rallied, and stood, and spoke forth again. "What does your inner voice tell you about the thieving here while you were gone, Father? Does it tell you to open our church doors to all these street kids and give them the run of the place? Does it tell you to invite all the hoodlums in Jersey City to help themselves to our holy vessels?"

As though he had just won a victory, Roy was at ease. He leaned against the base of the pulpit, jingling coins in his pocket while he considered his answer. "We'll have our cup back, Louise."

"What do you mean, Father? You're going to find it now? Is that it?"

"Yes." Roy stood up straight, suddenly impatient with her. "That's it, Louise. That's what I mean. And I want your trust now." He moved down the aisle toward her, hands still in his pockets, but so resolutely that she gave way and sat down. At the end of her pew he said, "I'm going to let you in on my trip down south. I'm going to preach about it on Sunday and talk about it every chance I get, because it was an important experience for all of us. Meantime, I'll see about finding our cup too."

Although the police had decided, and the parish had come to agree, that our missing silver was well down the plunder pipeline and beyond our reach, Roy went about his own inquiry with a peculiar innocence.

Reward
The Grace of God
The gratitude of St. Simon's Parish
plus $100 in cash
for information leading to the return of their chalice.
No questions asked. Call:
Roy Train JO 7-9263

"I don't quite get this," I said, waving my copy of the *Jersey Journal*. "Do you mean to comfort the mutineers, or do you have a hunch of some kind?"

Roy had been working on the article for Fenno, and among the papers before him was a clipping with a picture of the missing Cooley Smith. His attention lingered on it.

"Not a full-grown hunch, but a place for one. If it's a wee hunch that Louise Gower is wrong about so many things that maybe she's wrong about this too, then I have a wee hunch."

I laughed.

"Well . . ." Roy shrugged. "She thinks it's one of your scouts."

"All the kids steal. I'm missing three hubcaps and my Swiss Army knife—but they wouldn't touch Communion silver. I think I'd know about that. I'd know if Wilson were lying. I could read it in his big wide eyes.

"How about Wally Gower? What do you read in his?"

"Wally occurred to me—Louise's putting him up to it—but it's too devious."

"I agree. She's not wicked and I have to remind myself of that regularly." He regarded Cooley's smiling face and turned it to the desk. "So the chances are it was one of the neighborhood amateurs with fewer scruples than most, and that the cops are right: our cup is already reminted into bogus quarters. Still, there's a chance. Yes, I do have a hunch about that. It's coming along, Ethan—a hunch maybe somebody around *knows*."

After a few days of sharing the rectory with him, Roy seemed to lose his sense of wonder and awe about his son. Some pre-dawn hours in which he had tried to console a bawling J.J. led Roy to say, "I really don't understand the force that will halt any woman in the street to admire a strange baby. I think it's the tininess that moves them in some peculiar way. Babies are actually greedy little animals, wholly self-centered, turning in any direction where there is a hope of milk or massage. They're demanding tubes, sucking at one end and leaking at the other, and yet they tap straight into the nurturing gland of women. I seem to recall some Russian proverb that a child should be brought to his father only when he can ride a horse and carry on an intelligent conversation."

"Was it your father who told you the Russian proverb?"

He smiled. "Yes, I guess that's who it was."

"But the love? Do you feel that too?"

He frowned. "Yes, of course, a whole new spark, an instinctive protectiveness of the blood, I guess, but in men it must grow, mind and heart, like a trust that thickens, gets stronger with the years."

On Sunday morning I heard it on the news. During the night, Cooley Smith's body had been found. The Alabama state police had been led by three white men to the gully where it lay. These men claimed they had been silent until now to prevent more violence. They admitted that Cooley had been shot by his captor, but in self-defense. Cooley's killer was still hospitalized, permanently crippled by a broken back.

By the time I reached Jersey City, Roy had brought in the paper and it lay rumpled on the sofa while he crouched by the television set, searching the screen for more news from Tully.

On channel after channel they were at gospel singing and guessing games. After snapping off the set, Roy said, "There's nothing more coming out; just that they've found Cooley's corpse and a white man says he shot him in self-defense. It's incredible."

"There'll be more when they have it," Joan said.

Roy shook his head. "I doubt it. We're going to see that in spite of everything the SCLC and the Civil Liberties lawyers can do, Cooley's already buried. There'll never be a trial." He riffled through the paper and held forth the account. It was in the second section, three inches at the foot of a column. "Think of it, a man dies a hero and all in a day he's forgotten."

Then Roy reached for Joan's hand, pulled her to her feet, took mine in his left, and led us both to the window. The three of us looked down into Wayne Street, with its loitering bums, its kids at play, its old woman tugging her shopping cart.

"Oh, God bless you, you ornery Cooley," Roy sang out. His face was flushed, smiling, his voice exuberant. "I scarcely knew you in this life, but enough to give you plenty of room and to speculate on what a trial you must have been to your drill sergeant. Now we pray for you, Joan, Ethan, and I, for your soul's rest and for your spirit, which is going to live here with us and remind us where we're going. For us, Cooley, you're still breaking backs."

We said amen together.

X

ROY in the pulpit seemed altered that Sunday morning, meditative, all playfulness in eclipse. He stood tall, pale, oddly chastened. He seemed to be summoning his thoughts from a great distance.

"It's strange, you know," he began, "to stand here in Saint Simon's with you and remember that less than two weeks ago I was in an Alabama jail and terrified. I was terrified because that morning I had made a phone call to a friend in Atlanta. I told him to ignore the advice of the district director and bring his bus into town. As a result of that call, I now knew that people were in jail, people were injured, people were missing . . . maybe dead. The blame was as much mine as any Klansman's.

"It was not just out of ignorance I had made that call but out of selfishness too. I had been angry with that district director. I was impatient with the waiting, with the futility of the week I had put in there. I had talked to my wife and knew that she needed me here. I knew about the theft and that I must come back at once. I had promised to come that day. And yet I wanted to *meet* that bus. I saw a way to do it.

"In my cell, my teeth began to chatter and I prayed. 'Oh, God,' I prayed, 'let Lionel live. Let Cooley live. If I have committed a wickedness in arrogance and selfishness, brought more misfortune to these poor people, let me suffer for the rest of my days, but spare them. Spare all who are innocent and in need of justice and their share of the earth.'

"I was at the bottom, what *must* be the bottom of my life. In that jail cell I fell asleep, praying to a God who I doubted could hear me and I dreamed I was in a sea, choking as waves broke over me, and then, as I gave up, sinking in ever blacker depths, astonishingly, my feet touched firmness.

"There was a brightening of my vision, like a periscope clearing the water, and I beheld a wide, smooth seascape without a horizon. Sea melted to sky and the sun burned down from a vastness of eternal space. I was overwhelmed by a sense of nothingness and futility.

"Then I saw a fleck of something at a great distance. A ship? It could not possibly sight me. Yet it grew larger, becoming the prow of a dory shimmering on a mirrored surface, its oars turning slowly, powerfully between thole pins.

"The oarsman's back, in a square-shouldered, dark jacket, was familiar. Something about the shape of his tall, graying head, the way it floated free of his task, suggested he was blind.

"As the dory reached me, drifted to my outstretched hand, I saw the oars now dragged from loops of marline. With difficulty, I clambered over the side to find the boat empty. I sat on a thwart, wringing my clothes into the bilge, feeling the sun warm on my shoulders.

"I searched the green swells on either side, but there was no one. Then I sensed a presence behind me and heard a voice, familiar, yet I could not place it.

"'Take up the oars and row,' the voice said.

"I grasped them, hefted them on the gunwales, dipped them into the water, and felt the boat make way. Rowing, I kept my eyes on the wake. It stretched astern as though drawn upon the sea with a T-square. This was odd, because my right arm is the stronger and I should have been correcting for it, but I felt constrained from turning to face the presence in the bow or indeed to watch where the bow was heading. Yet I had no doubt that my course was true, and the sureness brought a feeling of exhilaration.

"I heard the muffled clang of a sea buoy and it appeared close by, a rusting, orange frame, bearded and barnacled, swirling in the swift tide that carried me shoreward.

"Now I smelled the sweet green perfume of the land and turned to see it rising like paradise out of the sea, a still harbor embraced by an amphitheater of blue-green hills, reminding me of Pearl and Noumea and San Francisco and all the heartening landfalls of my past. I was alone in the boat."

Roy paused, grasped the pulpit's rail, and searched the faces of his galvanized congregation. "I know this morning that Cooley Smith is dead." His words poured forth irresistibly. "I hold myself to blame for that. It makes a burden I will never set down, and yet it is also the fresh spring of my faith, because Lionel Truax is alive, and that district director is alive and is my friend, and because I am alive and I know what *they* have known all along—that we cannot wait. I have made my vow to God and I will make it to you—that I will not wait for a more favorable hour. This is the hour"—he looked at his watch as though fixing it to the second—"to see beyond the color of a human being's skin.

"Ethan?" I found Roy's finger pointing at me from across the chancel. "Will you ring the bell?"

In a daze I walked into the sacristy, felt for the rope, and heaved down on it. At the first knell I heard Roy's voice saying, "You are alive too this morning and my faith tells me that some of you are ready to join me in that vow. How many? Let me see."

There was a rustling and shifting, a creaking of benches, and I looked through the sacristy door to see a congregation on its knees, the few faces not bent in prayer, stunned.

I had been so moved by Roy's performance that it seemed I had entered a strange church, a place I had never been before. I felt he had just transcended his own capabilities as preacher and priest in a remarkable way, even transcended the conflicts within his congregation. As we began the celebration of the Eucharist, I looked for signs of it.

While the communicants filed toward us, and took their places at the rail, I sought a response in their faces. Among the twenty I felt sure I would find a reflection of the incandescence

I felt, but what I saw was anxiousness and awe. I thought of people in a bus alarmed by the speed and recklessness of the driver.

I saw them whispering their dismay as they left the church and wondered if perhaps Roy's confession had done less to exonerate than indict him.

As we hung our cassocks on the vestry hooks, I noticed that Roy's face was uncharacteristically grave. He hoisted himself onto the table and sighed. "And that's the best I can do, Ethan. It didn't get to them, did it? Tell me the truth."

"If it's any consolation, I thought you were great—and so did Joan. So did all your loyals."

But he was inconsolable this morning. "My loyals? Joan tells me I should shut up."

"She doesn't feel you can change the way the parish feels overnight. That's hardly disloyalty."

"It's compromise, not loyalty. Not loyalty to me."

"What's got into you, Roy? Is it Joan's wanting a job?"

"Not a job, *no*. A job would be fine."

"What is it then? What's bothering you?"

"You've heard her. Joan wants to hire a housekeeper and have her own hairy, heavy-breathing law *career*." He gave me a baleful look. "I'm in trouble here. Just when I need to feel we're a whole, my wife and I, this crack appears between us. You know what I mean?"

"Come on, Roy. Being somebody's wife—even somebody's mother—isn't enough for a lot of intelligent, educated women these days."

"Oh, I know," he said impatiently. "I'm not blind, Ethan."

"*How* are you taking to fatherhood?"

He sighed. "That too, you know. Having a child does something unexpected to a marriage. Even before J.J. was born I could feel Joan turning inward. I could read withdrawal in her eyes, as if she had taken another lover. I guess all women when they're first pregnant get preoccupied with the life inside them, but I thought that would be temporary, just the newness of motherhood. Then the child comes along and does drive a wedge in there. From his first gasp the kid is competing for her attention."

"Roy, do you hear what you're saying?"

"Dreadful, isn't it . . . but true. J.J.'s come bawling into our intimacy—and crawled off with my carpet slippers. And now Joan wants a career too."

I was locking up the side door after the scout meeting on a Friday night a couple of weeks later when I saw a large colored man in a black skivvy shirt come uncertainly through the church gate. I recognized Lester Moon.

"Can I do something for you?"

Moon gave me a cunning look. "The preacher around?"

"He's in the rectory and he's busy tonight. What's it about?"

His smile gleamed like chrome plate. "I see all this stuff in the papers about what's going on here. I thought I come around and see for myself."

"I remember," I said. "That's why you came to the fair. We were raising money to send the boys to camp. You didn't think much of the idea."

"That's right. I don't forget."

"We just got back from Boonton, Mr. Moon. There were no snake bites, not much poison ivy, and everybody got along fine. You won't forget that?"

Moon nodded. "That's good. I'll remember that too, Soames."

Now he looked up at the lights in the parish house windows. "You know, even if the preacher is *really* busy in there, he going to want to hear what I come to say. You tell him that."

I considered for a second. "Wait here."

I found them in the rectory kitchen, Joan at the table with J.J. in her lap and Roy at the counter, a glass of beer in hand.

"Sorry to butt in."

"It's okay, Ethan. Have a beer?"

"No, thanks. Lester Moon's downstairs. I can't imagine what he's up to this time, but he wants to see you."

J.J. emitted a satisfied sigh and I realized he was dining. For a second my eyes were held by his smooth, tiny head intent on a last sip, then by Joan's gently detaching him from a luxuriant breast, revealing its bright, moist nipple.

I could feel the flash fire in my face as Roy asked, "What's the matter, Ethan? Never seen one of those before?"

Covering herself, Joan smiled. "I'm sorry. Does that embarrass you?"

I swallowed. "I didn't realize . . ."

Roy touched my arm. "Let's go see Lester."

Moon was waiting at the foot of the stairs, nodding with imperious approval.

"Ethan says you have something to tell me," Roy began.

"Maybe I do." Moon gave me a doubtful glance.

"Ethan's my partner here," Roy said. "We can go into the office."

Moon went in first. He leaned against the wall, facing us, a playful expression on his face. He began casually. "I see that picture of you in the paper, when you down south, telling off that big old sheriff. I think maybe you not all talk, like these others. I think maybe I owe you something."

"Thanks," Roy said. "That's good to hear right now. Not everybody I know thinks my trip was a success."

"When I see you lost your silver cup here, I thought, Now there's something I might be able to help the preacher with."

Silence fell upon us as Lester's implication sank in.

Roy was studying his impassive face. "You think so, Lester?" he asked. "You think you could help us with that?"

"I might."

"If what, Lester?"

"When somebody take something you have, you got to think the way a thief think. That's the only way you going to get your property back. Now if I was you, I be thinking this boy who bust in your church and take your cup, he got a couple pounds of silver under his bed and gone to a lot of trouble to get it there. Even if he got some suffering in his conscience and want you to have it back now, he don't want to risk his neck doing it. That the only neck he got. No, I doubt he give you a chance at his

neck for less than"—Moon furrowed his brow in calculation—
"five hundred dollars."

"Can you bring it in for that, Lester? Can you do it tonight?"

Lester grinned. "Oh, I'm many times a fool but not fool
enough to do that until I'm sure about those questions you ain't
never going to ask."

"Which?"

"About that boy who took it and how we going to punish him
so he don't do that bad thing again. What you going to tell the
police about a man who bring it in for you."

"We'll have to trust each other, won't we?"

"We sure will. And there's one more thing. If I was to do this,
if I was to find this boy and make him understand it was the
right thing and the safe thing to do, you understand, there
should be a little something for *me*."

There was a new hesitation between us, one in which Roy and
I exchanged a glance, my own a warning to beware. Lester
caught it and there was an edge of anger in his protest.

"Oh, no," he said, "that not my money. None of that go to me.
I want just that one thing. I want to sing for you, not when you
ready to hear me, which maybe not till next year, maybe the year
after. I'm ready *now*." His eyes were intent on Roy. "You believe
me, Mr. Preacher?"

Roy hesitated for scarcely a second before saying, "Yes, Lester.
I believe you."

At the ten-fifteen service on Sunday morning, just before the
Offertory, Roy stepped down into the nave and said in his en-
gaging, informal way, "I hope every one of you will want to share
in our Communion this morning because it's one we've been
waiting for. We will be drinking the blood of our Lord from our
own cup, the one which was lost but is now restored to us and
so the more precious."

I could see Roy's pleasure in the moment of bewildered silence, then the stirrings, the first murmurs, and the flutter of
applause.

"Yes." He beamed. "We do have reason for rejoicing and I

hope you will want to remember in your prayers of thanks the man who helped to bring it back to us. He's with us this morning."

Heads turned this way and that, discovering Lester Moon. He sat alone at the end of a pew toward the back of the church, his face grave as attention fell upon him.

In the Eucharist that followed, the chalice did seem to have taken on a marvelous radiance. As Roy tipped it from mouth to mouth along the rail, I was struck by its graceful shape, the hexagonal base with its inscription, the holy acrostic ΙΧΘΥΣ— Jesus Christ, God's Son, Our Savior—within the outline of a fish. The cup glowed as though lighted from within.

But by the close of the service, Moon had melted away, and I sensed from the puzzled expressions and the congregants' swarming sound, as they moved toward the street, that an inquiry was in the making.

On the steps, Roy pointed out the group talking earnestly in the churchyard. "Here we go, Ethan. The music."

As he led the delegation toward the office, he was reassuring Ham Walsh. "Of course I intend to, Ham. I'll tell you all I know about our good fortune."

There were eight in all, and when they were settled in the parish office Roy reported exactly what had happened on Friday night and asked me to confirm it.

"Lester brought the cup in last night," he told them. "Just as he had promised, it was no worse for its journey, and Joan and I gave it a bath and a special polishing. That's all we know and all we're meant to know."

"But you made a deal with Moon?" asked a man named Kite.

"Yes, I did. Because I wanted our cup. I agreed on absolution for the thief. We are not to know who he is."

"And some money?" Walsh asked. "How much money?"

"Five hundred dollars."

"Was that ours? Was that church money?"

"I found a private donor."

I winced inwardly when I thought of the hole that money must have made in Roy and Joan's savings.

"We're not to know who that is either?"

"No. The donor too wishes to remain anonymous. Oh, there's one more part to the bargain. Our middleman had a request to which I agreed. He's to sing in our choir."

A resentful silence was settling into the room and with sudden vehemence Roy said, "Look. The cup is back in its cupboard. It's back because of a man who has every reason to feel we've turned him away." He looked from baleful face to baleful face. "And I don't believe Lester Moon stole it or caused it to be stolen. One reason is that Lester told me so." He shook his head. "But if I'm wrong, if he did steal it, I know he *thinks* he has good reason. I know he thinks it's the only way left to make his voice heard among us."

The room had become very quiet; I could hear a tug's thin whistle from the river. "I can find reason enough to forgive him," Roy said, his voice so soft that we strained to hear it. "How about the rest of you? Think about redeeming a man simply by asking him to sing with us. I want to hear that voice, don't you? Wouldn't it make a joyful sound in your ears?"

XI

THERE was no doubt in my mind about Roy's experience in the Tully jail. He felt God had spoken directly into his ear, giving him a direction and the strength to follow it.

To me his certainty was infectious. I knew he was neither crazy nor, in any profound way, self-deluding. My admiration was the stronger for it, and those guilty weeds in my heart, the covetous feelings that had sprung into beanstalks while he was away, withered. I avoided Joan as much as I could.

When I had a glimpse of her reading on the rectory steps, J.J. dozing in a basket beside her, I would wave and pass on.

Then one afternoon I heard the jingle of her bracelets and looked up to find her sauntering into the scout office, inspecting the wilderness posters I had been push-pinning into the festering plaster.

"These are great. I'll join up if you'll take me to see the giant redwoods," she said. "You busy, Ethan? Have a minute for some pastoral counsel?"

"At least."

She took a while to settle, stretch her long, blue-jeaned legs from my captain's chair, and give me a quizzical look. "Did you know that Roy's planning to fire Louise?"

"No, not in so many words."

"What do you mean?"

"He asked if I would fill in for her in case of any trouble over the choir."

"What did you say?"

"In a pinch, yes. Of course. I could do a service."

She leaned forward, elbows on her knees, with anxiety a new tenant in her eyes. "He's lost all caution. By the time the bishop comes, he wants Lester singing in the choir, and he's so sure, you know, that he's won with him, that he has most of the parish with him, or that they'll come round, *must* come round, that he can't hear what they're telling him. I'm frightened, Ethan. Are you?"

In a reflex I shook my head. "He's always taking risks . . . always being lucky somehow."

"Not always."

"Of course Louise Gower isn't alone. It's a mistake to think so. There'll be some coming to her rescue."

"Could you tell Roy that at least?"

"Yes, I think I can do that."

I found Roy working on his article for Ted Fenno, but he cheerfully put it aside as I sat down beside him. "Look," I said, "you aren't expecting me to replace Louise permanently, are you? I have no experience in rehearsing a choir."

"Of course not," Roy said impatiently. "We do need an understudy in case she quits on us, as she's threatened to. She may refuse to play for Lester."

"Yes, she may. Are you ready for that?"

"Of course." Roy frowned and tilted back. "Why wouldn't I be?"

"Because there are a number of other people who aren't going to be happy with Lester in the choir stall."

"My God, Ethan!" he said, leaping to his feet. "We're nearly there. We've had some really great breaks. Don't you realize that? Saint Simon's is coming down the progress road. We're not going to let Louise run it into a ditch. Hell no. I'm talking to a young fellow over in Tenafly who might be willing to replace her." He walked briskly and turned to scowl at me. "You know about those who are not with us?"

The announcement of the bishop's visit, which was to be the twelfth Sunday after Trinity and the third in August, carried an additional note. The regular meeting of the vestry on Wednesday would be a closed one.

"How come?" I asked Roy. "Are you telling them that Lester's making his debut next Sunday?"

He shook his head. "That's all done. I've written a letter about it to every vestry member and one to Louise, offering to help her find another job."

"I see. Who's playing the organ?"

Roy smiled. "You're off the hook. Henry Pogue will be here on Sunday. He tells me he can even squeeze in a rehearsal beforehand."

"That's a relief. What's to happen in the closed vestry meeting?"

"I don't know. I've been asked to absent myself."

"Oh? Does that worry you?"

"No." Roy shook his head thoughtfully. "They'll want to let off steam. There's plenty, and it would only be denser if I were there. But it's absolutely right what we've done, absolutely inevitable. Don't you agree?"

"*I* do. Yes."

"And they will too . . . however painfully. Not to put too sanctimonious a light on it—as they see God's hand."

"I surely hope so, Roy."

He seemed more surprised than disappointed by my reservation.

As it turned out, the vestry met in two closed sessions on consecutive nights and the result was a brief resolution that Roy found in his mail the following Friday. He brought it into the basement office and laid it on my desk with an expression of mild surprise.

I read:

Meeting in special session on the evening of July 12, the vestry of St. Simon's Church resolved that the Reverend Roy Train absented himself from his duties to the parish without the permission of this body to which he is responsible. Moreover, that while he was absent he engaged in activities which are controversial and in some instances distasteful to members of this and other communities, that by his own admission he bears a responsibility for a riot that resulted in death, and that he has used the pulpit, which was entrusted to him in our parish, for spreading his personal political beliefs and so has broken his contract with St. Simon's Church.

This resolution was passed by a vote of seven to four, with one member abstaining. Respectfully submitted, Hammond Walsh, Senior Warden.

"Good Lord," I said. "What's this mean?"

Roy was rocking on his feet, apparently breasting the news, but there was a brightness in his eyes, circles of paleness around them. I don't think he had expected anything like this, but he clung to the insouciance that had not failed him in all the time I had known him.

"On the surface"—he was smiling as he slipped his hands into his pockets—"I'd say they've just fired me."

Over the next several days, in which we were busy preparing for the bishop's visit, Roy showed no sign of uncertainty, as though he had simply dismissed the vestry's action from his mind.

He called for volunteers to do a thorough cleaning of the church, and half a dozen women turned out with dustcloth and vacuum cleaner. I found Joan spreading a freshly laundered altar cloth and Roy on a stepladder dusting the menagerie around St. Anthony's feet.

When I asked how he had responded to the resolution, he shook his head as though it were one of those annoyances, like the head cold and the filing of the federal tax return, which have to be endured.

I insisted. "You must have done *something* about it?"

"Of course. First of all, I forgave them. That's the main thing. They really don't know what they're doing."

"But what did you *say*? Not that, surely?"

"I did send Ham a note saying that if the vestry can see, as I do, that the return of the chalice is a benediction on us all, then they must give the changes that are taking place here some time, a few months at least, to work and become our custom. Then, if they don't like it here, I'll go. But not now, because I know exactly what I'm meant to do at Saint Simon's, and by God, I'm doing it." Delighted, he shook his feather duster under my nose.

During my next regular conference with the bishop, my eye was caught by the St. Simon's letterhead. It lay alongside his pile of correspondence and had a familiar look.

Catching my eye, the bishop asked, "You've seen this?"

"If it's the vestry resolution about Roy, yes. He showed it to me."

"What's he doing about it?"

"He thinks eventually they'll see the Christian wisdom of what he's done. He's certain of it—that this is just a last outcry from the old guard, and if they'll just wait for a couple of months it will become as clear to them as it is to him now. He's asking for that."

"What do you think, Ethan?"

"Well, I was down there with him. I saw it all take place. I know he feels guilt over the death of that man. Tully was a forge for him, gave him a clear vision of what he must do."

"But, Ethan, he's lost touch with his people, don't you see?" He held the letter, weighing it. "This isn't just a little cluster of nuts. These are the responsible ones and they don't trust Roy. They believe he's lost his way, and he certainly has lost theirs."

"Can you talk to them?"

"It's not my decision, you know. It's Saint Simon's. And to be altogether honest, if I could persuade the vestry to reconsider, I wouldn't. I talked to Ham Walsh for an hour yesterday. They've had enough . . . and incidentally, you might be acceptable to Saint Simon's. Would it be of interest?"

"Bishop, Roy is my dearest friend."

"Good. I anticipated that, but I promised to ask."

"In fact, I'm beginning to feel a part of the conspiracy."

"You're hardly that . . . and you're right: I owe him an interview. You had better bring him in."

Within an hour I had brought Roy to the bishop's desk, and I watched him as he heard the bishop out. Hands clasping a knee, he was attentive and serious.

"I don't want you to leave here today under any illusions, Roy," the bishop said. "It seems to me that the best I can do for you right now is remind you that none of us have any doubt of your sincerity and even your right-mindedness, but you must also accept that there is a mutiny against you at Saint Simon's. They've come to me and said, in a way that I must accept, that they want a new pastor. They've asked me to offer them some candidates."

As I watched this sink in, expecting Roy to protest, he surprised me by nodding thoughtfully, as though it were a trivial denial, the forgoing of a picnic for a funeral.

"Yes," he said, "I can see that, all right, and I suppose it's best in the end. Perhaps it's only selfish of me, wanting to stay on and see it all come to fruit, as I know it will—as you do too." Roy looked up at the bishop with faint mischief. "But obviously I've done what I was meant to do here. And it's time, Laurence, isn't it? Time for me to move on."

The bishop was as surprised as I was, but he said, "Yes, it is, Roy. I'm glad you see it too."

At the office door, bidding Roy a sober farewell, the bishop said, "Lascelles and Aspinwall will be coming over for interviews this week. Under the circumstances you may want to scratch my visit on Sunday. We'd all understand."

"Not a chance, Laurence," Roy said. "We're counting on you. It's your first visit in years."

It struck me that Roy had managed to deceive himself, the way some people do at a time of painful loss, denying the dependency. I watched for a sign that the impact of his being fired by his parish had struck.

But during the week prior to the bishop's visit Roy appeared more vigorous and spirited than ever, as though in fact the new era of harmony at St. Simon's had arrived. He trotted through the corridors of Fairmont Hospital and the medical center, up the stairwells of the old rooming houses where our shut-ins lived, and from Mathilda Johnson's funeral to Deborah Horn's baptism, with a flexibility and an often exuberant confidence that won approval among even the grudging.

When I found Joan coming into the parish house with an armful of parcels, I paused to say, "Isn't it strange and wonderful, the way Roy's taking it, as though it's a victory for him?"

She weighed a plastic-shrouded hanger in the crook of her finger. "It is . . . astonishing. He had a talk with Bob Lascelles Monday night. That helped."

"I expect he's a sensitive man."

She looked thoughtfully into my eyes, her head at a speculative tilt. "So maybe it's not only Roy's good nature"—she smiled—"his spirit of forgiveness, but his damned perennial good luck."

After the scout meeting on Wednesday he was waiting to share the enterprises that still crowded his mind. He had arranged a businessmen's lunch to raise money for the new furnace and sent off a year's contract for the signature of the new organist, Henry Pogue.

"I'm counting on a full church for the bishop on Sunday," he said, "and for Bob Lascelles."

"He's coming?"

"Sure. I asked him to help us out as cup bearer. He was very pleased. I'd like to get Louise too. Wouldn't that be a triumph, Ethan?"

"Louise?"

"I've tried. Joan's tried. But she's sulking."

"Of course she is. You fired her."

"That score is even. I think she just wants to be coaxed. Maybe by you, Ethan. Here"—he produced a card from his shirt pocket—"I've made her an appointment over at Saint Francis's. They need an organist for the summer. Try her on that and tell her we all want her here for the bishop. The bishop wants to see her."

Louise Gower did not admit me to her apartment but let me pass the card through the door. Through the crack I could see that her hair was matted and awry and her eyes pulsed with fury.

"No," she said. "I'll come to see the bishop another time. Not while Mr. Train has our church."

"You do know he's leaving, don't you, Mrs. Gower?"

"And good riddance."

"I know he wants to make it up to you however he can. If this doesn't work out for you at Saint Francis's, he'll find you something else."

"He's so full of himself," she said. "He has no idea what he's done to other people. The damage will never be undone. You tell him that for me. I'll not set foot inside Saint Simon's again while he's pastor."

Sunday was glorious, with an indolent sun shining down from a Delftware sky into grimy Wayne Street. There was breeze enough to bring us a marshy smell from the harbor's edge. The diocesan Roadmaster arrived punctually at ten and Laurence stepped forth, pausing to acknowledge our congregation gawking from the church steps.

Joseph, the bishop's driver, entrusted me with the dressing case, and the bishop, pastoral staff in hand, set off with me across the churchyard, saying, "I'm amazed at your turnout. I counted a dozen dark faces, didn't I, side by side with your old-timers. One has to see it to believe . . ."

"Tell him," I said.

Roy was awaiting us in the sacristy. He was laughing with Bob Lascelles, a square-faced Nordic-looking fellow, as he turned to bow the bishop a welcome and to introduce Lewis Wade, the twelve-year-old colored boy just recruited as acolyte.

While I opened the case and hung the heavy vestments on our coat hooks, Roy was pulling aside the curtain to display our altar, with the guild's two tall vases of gladioli and the six tall candles in the bishop's honor.

Beyond, spectacled, lightly bearded Henry Pogue was at the organ, already intent on the Handel prelude but husbanding it until sight of the procession. Opening the door into the corridor, Roy pointed out his new choir, robed and tense against the wainscote.

"Is that Moon there?" the bishop asked.

"The big fellow just beside my wife."

As I ballooned the surplice over the bishop's head and got busy with the buttoning, he asked Roy, "How many colored families do you have now?"

"We have five on the parish register, and four Hispanics. Isn't that right, Ethan?"

"That's right," I said, laying the cope about the bishop's shoulders and fastening it. "We're coming along."

"You should be pleased with yourself, Roy."

"Oh, I am," Roy said and turned to point out to Lewis that he had missed one of the candles or it had guttered out, and sent him back to the altar with his taper.

We watched while Lewis made a second, then a third approach to the stubborn candle, until, with a kind of joint effort, it caught. Our robed, singing procession made its way up the side aisle and down the center, parting the sea of our awed congregation. In front of me, Roy's white surplice swirled around a determined stride, and the back of his neck and shoulders swelled with satisfaction.

The smooth oak of the pastoral staff felt alive in my hands as I held it aloft, crook forward, while from behind came the bishop's voice resolutely raised in "Day of Wrath, O Day of Mourning" as he brought up the end of our parade.

From the first strains of the processional hymn I had suspected that the new choir was no improvement on Louise Gower's, and though I hoped the discord was the result of unfamiliarity and would soon right itself, harmony eluded it. As the five choristers—Joan and another volunteer, two veterans, and Lester Moon—took their places in the stall, they had reached the last verse and were losing heart.

When I found my seat beside the bishop and faced them, I realized it was Lester Moon who was singing the false notes. In his determination, he was driving out the other voices. Over the organ's ledge Henry Pogue was frowning his displeasure. Joan stood beside Moon in the stall and in the moment that I caught her eyes they rolled, marbles of entreaty.

Across the chancel Roy's head was bowed toward his folded

hands, but when it bobbed up he seemed to be on the edge of laughter.

The prescribed epistle for this Sunday was from Second Corinthians, and as Roy stood at the lectern to read it, his voice filled with the resonance of Paul's language—"Such trust have we through Christ to God-ward; not that we are sufficient of ourselves to think anything as of ourselves; but our sufficiency is of God; who also hath made us able ministers of the new testament; not of the letter but of the spirit; for the letter killeth but the spirit giveth life."

The bishop spurned my helping hand as he climbed the steps to the pulpit, and from his first words it was clear his eloquence was intact. He repeated the text Roy had read, laying emphasis on our insufficiency without God.

He spoke in the most personal way of God's love, how it is both fierce and protective, allowing no falseness, no idols, and pointing out that the golden calves of our day are money and fame. These and all other concerns, even country and family, must never take priority to God. Perhaps the greatest idol of our time is self-sufficiency. It is so prized as a national virtue and yet it can so easily become pride and blind us to our need for God's help.

Throughout, Roy had seemed transfixed and when he came forward just before the Offertory to speak informally, he seemed to be still under the spell of the bishop's sermon. He first bowed his head dramatically to the bishop and then he turned to face his congregation, but for a moment he seemed speechless.

At last he said, "I know you are all as moved as I am by our bishop's presence among us. Our need is great this morning. We have wounds to heal at Saint Simon's. He knows them all and it is why he has come to us with the message that we cannot save ourselves alone, only with God's help. But I would like to add this note of my own. It is a discovery I have made here with you. It is the whereabouts of God. There is no longer a mystery of whether He exists but where. Well, He is surely in the heavens above us because He is everywhere, but He is nearest to us in our own hearts. I know that I am not a sinful creature, as Isaiah would have me, needing God's seraphim to press that live coal to my lips and cauterize me." He smacked himself on the chest. "God is here. I can hear Him, groaning for my soul. And He is there . . ." Roy's arm swept the congregation, pausing now and then as though his finger were singling out the saved, and ending his sweep at the bishop, whose concerned face broke into a smile.

"I'll be leaving soon," Roy said as he turned back to his congregation, "but you will be in very good hands if you choose Bob Lascelles as your new pastor. Wherever I go I will be thinking of you—every one." He started up the aisle, grasping the hands that were thrust forth, timidly at first, but he pulled a few of his parishioners to their feet and embraced them, apparently laughing at their surprise, but then I saw there were tears across his cheeks.

Reaching the back of the church, he cried out, "Louise? Did you come, God bless you? Is Louise Gower here?" There was a silence as everyone turned around until it was clear that she had not.

"Then Violet," Roy cried, "Violet Wilkins will stand in for Louise," and saying so, he took the hands of a large colored woman and, bringing her to her feet, wrapped his arms around her.

He went briskly up the aisle. When he reached the altar, he raised his arms to signal the resuming of the liturgy and said, "Let your light so shine before God . . ."

I had been exalted by Roy's vision, touched by joy and a clairvoyance as though I had been brought suddenly to a mountaintop and could see a great distance. The bishop too seemed moved, and I thought for a moment that Roy had so purged the community emotions that he had turned the course of events today, won himself the parish pardon.

At the closure the bishop came forward and, holding the staff aloft, blessed the congregation. I could feel that blessing. It illuminated everyone in the church. Later, when he stood with Roy at the door, taking hands and listening to the names as they came to be touched, I could believe that all the discord here had been miraculously erased.

Some faces still held a trace of the radiance. Beside me, two women shook their heads over Roy's departure and another wept as she stood before him and seemed on the point of embracing him or prostrating herself on the steps, and I was relieved when she passed on to the bishop.

But as most worshippers pressed in, they seemed disappointed to discover that the golden miter capped a short man. Beside him, Roy too was returning to human proportions.

Within ten minutes the wave of communicants had spent its force and receded, carrying with it the exhilaration and sense of possibility, leaving us beached on Saint Simon's top step.

"Well, that was fine," the bishop said. "Most impressive service. I thought your choir was a bit shaky there at first, but with some practice together I'm sure they'll do you proud."

"I do hope so," Roy said.

"And that was very moving, your valediction, if that's what we should call it." He put an arm around Roy's shoulder and gave it a fraternal squeeze.

"You think they'll remember that, Laurence?" Roy asked. "You think they'll remember that service for a while?"

The bishop was looking up Wayne Street to where the black Buick waited at the curb. Catching Joseph's eye, he signaled. "Of course they will."

"Good," Roy said. "That's what matters now."

The bishop gave him a long appraising look and said, "We oughtn't to lose you, Roy. Maybe we can find the harness that fits." He smiled at the idea. "We'll have to find a tailor for that, won't we?"

"I'm making it myself, Laurence. Someday I'll show you my harness shop."

Joan, wearing a short white linen dress, approached, and the bishop took her hand with a funereal solicitude.

"We're hoping you can stay for lunch with us, Bishop," she said.

"My dear, I'm so sorry, but I'm due in Ridgewood in a few

minutes. I have barely time to change." Seeing the car had drawn up just below us, he called, "Come and give me a hand packing robes, will you, Joseph?"

The bishop smiled and left us, his three fingers aloft in blessing and salute.

Joan, Roy, and I started down the steps toward the rectory just as Lester Moon appeared at the corner of the church. He wore an immaculate blue suit and polka dot tie and he had a fretful look.

"The new organist," he said, halting us, "he need to learn how to back up a choir."

Roy took a deep, weary breath and said, "Lester, it's your first Sunday. Wait till you put in some practice. You'll get along with Henry. He knows his stuff."

Lester frowned and then in an extraordinary burst of candor said, "Shit, I was awful. Man, I could hear myself and I knew, but I had to go on and do it, hoping I was better than I thought. I *prayed* I was."

Roy began to laugh and tears sprang from his eyes. He put an arm around Lester's shoulders and managed to say, "You weren't *that* bad."

"It's my nature," Lester confessed. "If I don't get in some door, I just beat on it louder and I shout. I never count on what happen if they let me in. But I'm going to be a *good* singer, Mr. Preach. You watch."

As Lester moved off, I saw that a woman who had been standing in the shade of the apartment house was coming toward us. She walked with difficulty, and I realized it was Louise Gower.

"Louise," Roy said amiably when she joined us. "I was looking for you. I'm glad you came for the bishop."

Her red-rimmed eyes burned at him. "I wasn't in church, Mr. Train." She shook a finger at the dark cornerstone behind us. "I won't go in—not so long as you're here trying to make us over. You won't do that, you know. Nobody can fly as you do against your people. You'll have your comeuppance, Mr. Train. Oh, you'll have a great fall."

Louise Gower limped off, leaving us speechless on the steps.

With a sigh, Joan said, "Well, there's not much left to be said, is there, except that I'm sorry for the poor woman."

We walked silently toward the rectory and lunch. Roy held the screen door open for us and as we passed he seemed to brighten. "She may be right, you know."

"About your great fall?" Joan asked gaily over her shoulder. "Don't be silly, Roy. She's a little mad, is all. You'd better come in and make us a drink."

"No. I mean she may be right that she can't change," he said, leading the way upstairs, "but she's dead wrong about the church—Louise and Laurence both. The church can change. We damned well better see that it does."

XII

DURING a regular morning session at the diocese at the end of that turbulent summer of 1961, I asked the bishop whether he had been able to think of a suitable post for Roy.

He cradled his chin in both hands. "I do hope he isn't counting on that. I meant what I said, Ethan. Roy's an exceptional man, and the church oughtn't to lose him, but for the present he's too unpredictable. Wouldn't you agree?"

"It would be a great pity not to put him to work somewhere."

"Well, he must go through a soul-searching before he's ready for another boost from me. What does he have in mind?"

I shrugged. "It seems that Bob Lascelles and his wife aren't moving in until after Labor Day. Roy's puttering around the rectory while Joan looks for work."

"Let me know what they do." The bishop took a deep breath and shook off the lowering gloom. "On the other hand, I do have a proposition for you, Ethan. Alan West at Saint Luke's in Rutherford isn't well. He's had a spotty memory since I've known him—never good with names and quite at sea without a typescript of his sermon, but such good manners it's always been rather a charming trait. He's become worse; not just names now, but in midsentence he'll forget what he intended to say. So sad.

He's barely sixty. He needs a vicar at once, and I should imagine he'd be taking Alan's place in a month. What would you say to that?"

Recovering from my astonishment, I said, "If I'm needed in Rutherford, that's where I want to go."

I found Roy in St. Simon's basement. Flashlight in hand, he was poking into a fuse box but he listened thoughtfully while I told him about Laurence's proposal that I go to Rutherford.

He gave a final twist to a splicing of wires and turned to pump my hand. "It's your call this time, Ethan. Saint Luke's is going to be just right for you—and you'll probably discover how we're failing our responsibility over there too. Good manners'll be covering for a church that forgets in midsentence what it has to say. The same all over. We're giving God a bad name. How come the world sees that and the church can't? Why is it old before its time, like Alan West?"

He left me abruptly and returned a few minutes later, saying, "That old fan over the choir's been conked out since we've been here, Ethan, but now, by golly, it's churning up a storm."

"What about you?" I asked. "What do you see ahead?"

"Indians in the woods, Ethan, skinny as the trees, and prolific. You shoot one, and two come to take his place."

"I mean what are *you* going to do?"

Roy sent some dots and dashes from the flashlight into the rafters overhead and followed the sinews of a bright cable into the darkness. "I've had an invitation. I could quit this diet of husks and enjoy some fatted calf."

"Your father?"

"My father has cancer of the colon. He wants his office to survive him. David can't handle the job on his own."

"That's a break," I was thinking that money and influence would always rescue Roy from situations that would foreclose on the rest of us. "The perfect solution."

He smiled. "You mean my future in the church is that bleak?"

"I wouldn't know about that—but saving the family law firm?"

"When I used to go there as a child, the family law firm was a place of much din, but these days it's a grim place: six rooms in a condemned building on the south side of Newark. Some old bookkeepers share it with books that no longer need keeping." He shook his head.

"Could you and David turn it around?"

"David thinks so."

"And Joan too? This might be the setting for the career she wants. You'd have a railroad."

"It does have its appeal. Some victory might be wrung from the old place. We could make it stand for a different law, take on the tatty cases from welfare and the jail. A little easier too, taking on a run-down law firm instead of the whole Episcopalian dinosaur."

"It does sound sensible," I said, "and in time all this past history will add up for you."

"Maybe. Maybe it will." He smiled. "But, Ethan, I'm a priest."

Throughout early September I was preoccupied with taking over Alan West's duties at St. Luke's. Since Alan and Sophie West were moving to a fully equipped apartment in Sarasota, the rectory came to me with most of their well-kept furniture.

When I called for news of the Trains, I reached a new number in Jersey City. "It's an old house on Freemont," Roy explained; "big, high-ceilinged rooms, very cheerful, considering, and not far from Saint Simon's."

"You commuting to Newark from there?"

"Joan's going to be doing the commuting—and not to Newark. She starts next week with Peters, Godwin, a good firm in New York. I'm staying home."

"I thought you were going to work for your old man."

"Well, instead I'll be the housekeeper," he said, "and with my hotshot working wife, I can stall a little longer. We'll get you over for dinner as soon as I've had some practice. I'll need a couple of weeks with *The Joy of Cooking*."

But a few weeks later, when I found in my mail an invitation to a Sunday afternoon party at Five Chimneys, Walter Train's house in Morristown, I assumed it was to celebrate Roy's joining the firm.

As I drove my Volkswagen Beetle along the thirty-mile route through Passaic, the Oranges, Chatham, and Madison into the fields of Morris County, I was thinking that this was a journey into affluence and a relatively unyielding past and what an irony it was that Roy had tried to travel against its traffic.

Parking on Foxhollow Road, I counted but four of the five chimneys. There were brown patches in the lawn, and the flower beds were untended. The grounds were encroached on by a recent subdivision, but the steep wood-shingled roof with its dormers and lightning rods dominated the terrain.

A vast, awninged porch swept around the house, and here Roy's sister-in-law, Nancy, a handsome, suburban blonde in a tennis dress, was supervising the caterers, who were setting up a bar and buffet. At the same time she was cautioning the two children who were disputing custody of a tricycle.

"Yes, a big bash," Nancy told me, "fifty or sixty. It's their golden anniversary. Can you imagine being married to Walter Train for fifty years? We ought to be giving Margaret a medal."

Margaret Train appeared in the doorway. Oblivious of the activity on the porch, she made her way through a cluster of rattan furniture to stand with her hands resting lightly on the balustrade and looked into the distance. When I spoke to her, I thought at first she did not remember me.

She touched back some wisps of foam-white hair and surprised me by a squeeze of hands. "Oh, Ethan, Roy's been so anxious to see you."

The foyer opened into an oval stairwell and on its wall hung the full-length portrait of a man in judge's robes. The ascetic face with piercing eyes and fastidious mouth resembled Margaret's, and I was deciding this was her father when Roy came bounding down the steps.

"Ethan, look at you!" he cried and gave me an affectionate shaking. "You're happy with Saint Luke's. I can tell."

"Have I come too early?"

"Not at all. In fact you're just in time to help me. I need to be sure I'm doing the right thing."

"Train's? You're still holding out? I thought it was all decided."

He looked out onto the porch, where his mother had bent to listen to a child's question. "Maybe it is, but I haven't been able to get it down my throat yet."

"I thought you saw a mission in it—and not much of an alternative. What's the problem?"

"One night last week I was making supper for Joan and me. I was thinking about quitting the ministry and then about how I'd got into it. It was a man named Tom Sewall, remember, who'd put the idea in my mind."

"The blind priest who sees so well."

"We hadn't spoken nor written to each other in a year, but at that moment the phone rang and from its first sound, maybe an instant before, I knew. It was Tom's voice, asking, 'Roy, how are you?' Imagine."

"I believe in ESP."

"And how about the power of prayer, Ethan?"

"That too."

"Tom said that if I came back to Iowa, he'd put me to work in his church."

"Iowa? Would you really pass up this chance, and disappoint everyone into the bargain—your father, your mother, David?"

"Well, I've been doing *that* all my life. I was thinking more of Joan." Taking my elbow, he said, "Come upstairs and listen."

We paused on the threshold of Walter Train's bedroom, whose dark furniture and heavy curtains suggested that Margaret had not shared it in recent years.

Walter was seated in a wing chair beside a casement window. He had drawn an orange dressing gown over his pajamas, as if to compensate for his own ghastly hue. In the year and a half since the wedding he had shrunk dramatically. Afternoon light seemed to pass through him as if he were so much vellum. His nose was a blade, and when his eyes were drawn to the round of my collar they flickered with resentment.

David, wearing a raveled Princeton varsity sweater, rose from a chair beside his father's to say, "Hi, Ethan."

I sensed Joan in the room and found her seated on the floor, knees drawn to her chin. Her lustrous dark hair was coiled in an old-fashioned knot, baring the white column of her neck. As our eyes met, her brooding expression became a smile.

Roy steered me toward his father, but Walter Train waved off an introduction, saying he remembered me perfectly well. Roy and I took the window seat and at my shoulder I found a framed photograph of Walter on a dock, holding up a yard-long fish. In another he sat at a restaurant table with big, pleasure-loving men.

Suddenly Walter asked me, "What do you think of your friend's getting fired over there?"

Startled by this bluntness, I looked to Roy for help. He replied with a shrug, as though to say, *Tell him whatever you like.*

"It was undeserved," I said, "but possibly, in the long run, fortunate."

Walter Train's eyes narrowed with displeasure. "This fellow used to be a fine student. He was a wonder boy on a law school faculty before he got himself into trouble out there. He finds trouble now wherever he goes, a donnybrook in Jersey City and a riot down in Alabama, a colored boy killed in it. What do you make of it, Ethan? You read any message?"

"Yes, I do. It's one of pain, all right. I think it's going to lead Roy to a productive life."

"Ready to get down to business?" Walter Train asked. "Is that priest twaddle or do you really think so?"

"I believe it."

He cocked his gaunt head. "You're his friend?"

"Yes."

"Then tell him what's good for him. That's what a friend was for when I had them. A friend is supposed to tell you the truth. I'd listen to it. This one doesn't hear the truth—not from me, he doesn't. He never has."

"Go on, Pop," Roy said. "Tell us about truth."

"Since he was a kid, no bigger than this"—Walter measured a few feet off the floor—"Roy was quicker, smarter, better than the rest. If it was hard for David, hard for anybody, even *me*, it was easy for him."

Roy groaned. "Here we go—the fishing trip."

Ignoring him, Walter addressed me. "How does a kid get that way, Ethan, thinking he can lick the world without half trying? I'm just the other way. I know I'm an average kind of guy and whatever comes my way is because of these hands, of staying up later, of getting up earlier. You know what I mean, Ethan?"

I nodded cautiously, and immediately he lost interest in me. His eyes hunted the room, fixing at last on Joan. "Well, now, it seems we've got another lawyer in the family. Something tells me you're the comer too."

Pleased, Joan said, "Thanks."

"That's pretty good, your walking over there to Peters, Godwin and getting yourself a job. I know those guys. They're a pretty foxy crowd. What are they paying you?"

She hesitated before confessing, "Twelve-five."

"That's not bad at all. That's more than we'd pay Learned Hand if he was just starting out. But you know something? They'll never make you a partner, Joanie, not if you live to be a hundred."

Her eyes brightened. "You want to bet, Mr. Train?"

Walter Train clapped his hands. Grinning, he said, "Now I like that. I like that kind of sass. No, I don't want to bet you because I won't be around to collect. But I tell you what I will do. You come to work for Train's. We'll pay you less. We'll pay you ten for a year or two until we see whether you pan out. If you do, we won't pay you any fat salary, but as a partner you'll share in the firm's income. It could be twice, three times what you'd be getting across the river. You'll want to think that over."

She nodded and looked up at Roy beside me on the window seat. "Yes, maybe we will."

"Of course," Walter said. "The both of you. You come to work for us and Roy'll come along. I don't go fishing with a bare hook."

Roy set his feet to swinging and smiled back at his father. "And I swim around the worm a couple of times before I bite it."

Walter Train's jaw worked back and forth as he pushed himself higher in the chair. "There's no hook in this, Roy." His voice had turned soft, coaxing. "You can save this firm." He held forth his skeletal hands. "I built it with these things. I built it for your mother and you two boys. I built it for all of us. You remember that."

"I do."

"Then what are you going to do about it? How long you going to keep us waiting?"

The silence was broken by Margaret Train. She appeared in the doorway, saying, "If you're coming downstairs, Walter, you'll want to get dressed. It's nearly four."

By five, the broad porch was dense with relatives and neighbors, costumed in summery pinks and yellows. They moved in slow currents toward the glider, where Walter Train, nested in pillows, whiskey in hand, held court.

Across the chatter of the throng I could hear his bray of laughter, and I saw that Laurence Givens had come. He stood with Margaret, making a book of his hands and pretending to read from it. I guessed that Laurence was reminding them that it was his father who had performed their marriage fifty years ago and that Walter's laugh had been at his own suggestion of an imminent burial.

Joan emerged from the house bearing a J.J. scrubbed and fitted out for display in apple green. I went along as she made her way toward the glider. When we arrived, Walter Train broke off a conversation and, setting his glass on the coffee table, held forth his frail arms.

"Are you sure?" Joan asked.

"Let's have him," Walter said.

An audience watched this family drama and there was no denying him. Joan put the bewildered J.J. into his grandfather's hands. Whereupon Walter drew him into his lap with such assertive confidence that the child accepted the transfer serenely, looking into Walter's waxen face with simple curiosity.

"Hello, John," Walter Train said. "It's Grandpa here. What do you think of him?" Smiling, Walter looked around the circle, then back at the child. "What about this party? Will you remember it, John?"

"His name is J.J., actually," Joan said.

He gave her a querulous glance. "Yes, I heard the joke about that. The colored cellmate of Roy's down there in the South."

"It's his Christian name—for richer, poorer."

"This fellow's John. No colored blood in this boy." Walter brought J.J.'s legs astride one of his own and, holding his hands, set him gently cantering. "He can ride. A good sense of balance there. He'll make a good lawyer."

J.J. squirmed uncomfortably, looking around for his mother, and Joan offered her hands but Walter retained him. He seemed mesmerized by the baby's face.

"My God, boy," he said earnestly to J.J., "we're the same stick. You know that? Remember me, will you do that, John? I'm your root in the ground and you're my branch. We're each of us climbing on top of the other down through the years to see what we can see, all of us standing on each other's shoulders." Walter looked around the circle of us, eyes filling with revelation. "That's why all kids like to ride up top, to get up on the old man's shoulders."

"Walter . . ." Margaret Train's mild voice quickened with alarm. "Oh *please* don't . . ."

Walter heard her and summoned strength instinctively. Holding a startled J.J. with one arm, he pushed himself erect with the other and, remarkably, rose from the swing.

Before an astonished audience he staggered slightly and then, old sinews working out of a distant memory of hoisting David and Roy to his shoulders for a promenade of this deck, he gave J.J. a great heave. J.J. cried out, arresting his course. Walter reeled, pulling the child to his chest, and there were cries all around as he fell, a great brick tower toppling into a heap, his head cracking audibly against the metal rim of the coffee table.

Restored to Joan's arms, an indignant J.J. proved to be intact, but Walter lay motionless on the porch floor, oozing blood from his temple. While David policed back the onlookers, Margaret hovered, watching a guest, Dr. Martin, feel Walter's wrist, unbutton his collar, and, after a glance at the wound, announce, "It's not deep. He'll be all right."

Margaret knelt beside her husband, cradling his head and shoulders in an arm. At her fingers' touch his eyes opened, gradually took in the scene, winced at it, and closed again.

"You're going to be all right, my dear," she assured him, allowing the doctor and David to help him to his feet. She held the door open as Walter was led into the house and then followed.

A few minutes later she returned to announce that Walter was feeling better, but she seemed relieved to find the guests making discreet departures.

"It's nothing, really," she told Roy. "Just a little touch of humiliation."

"He'll be over that soon enough," Roy replied. She smiled in response and I saw a glow of understanding pass between them.

Roy stood at the steps, cheerfully sending the last guests toward their cars, and I said, "It's never occurred to me to ask, but where does your mother stand on your future? Is she with your father on it?"

"She doesn't say much, does she? You'd hardly guess that she cares a lot about it."

"I might have. In what way?"

"Would you have guessed that she's a devout woman?"

"I might."

He nodded. "Well, it has something to do with my decision. Maybe you wouldn't have guessed *that*." Turning, he saw his mother beckoning us into the house.

We found Walter Train wearing a square dressing on his forehead. He was sitting up in bed, still in the linen wedding shirt he had worn for the party, his legs covered by a blanket. He had been opening gifts, and they lay about him on the spread. He counted us off as we filed into the room and then watched Joan take her place on the rug.

"How much does that kid weigh?" he asked.

"Twenty pounds," she told him.

"That's a whale of a lot for four months. You must be feeding him lead."

"You're a little out of shape, is all," David consoled him.

"I'm an old fool," Walter said. "Nobody's denying that." His eyes danced around our circle, confirming it. Then he turned to Margaret, who sat, hands folded, in an armchair. "Did I wreck the day for you, Peg?"

"No."

"You're used to it, after half a century."

"You shooed them all out in good time," she said. "I never like the tag end of a big party—the ones who overstay."

"I'll remember that," Walter said. His eyes strayed to Roy, who perched on the desk, chin in hand, watching him thoughtfully, then to Joan on the floor.

"What do you say, Joanie?" he asked her. "You want to practice with us? Want to start next week? What do you want to do— trusts? divorce? trial? Take your pick. You won't have a better offer."

"I know," Joan said. "I'm tempted, Mr. Train. I really am. I think you'd get a good deal, and we would too. I also think it would be quite wonderful for Roy and me to work together. I like that idea a lot, but he'll have to think so too. When I took the job in New York, we agreed it was good for both of us. It was important for me to know that I *can* practice and do damned well at it, and it was important to me that Roy know it. If I don't practice, it's because I choose not to. If I do, it's because it's better for us both, as a marriage and a family."

"Hooray," said Margaret Train. "Hooray for you, Joan."

"That leaves you with the pants," Walter said to Roy. "What are you going to do with them?"

"Joan wasn't giving away any pants. I don't think you were listening. What she's just said makes it all the harder for me. I understand her clearly enough. I understand you clearly enough. Still, it's hard. I've been praying for the right answer."

"And thinking, I hope," Walter said. "*Thinking,* for God's sake."

"That too. But I have asked God's help, and I know I'm not my own man anymore."

"Oh, Lord, that's not you talking. That's the kid again."

"That's the priest. I go where I do that best. I cannot tell you how deeply I regret causing you this agonizing pain and knowing now that I am bound to disappoint you. I want to go to Iowa and work in Tom Sewall's parish"—he turned to Joan—"if it's okay with you."

Joan waited for a few moments before saying, "Yes, it's okay with me."

Walter Train's face was gray with disappointment, and he uttered a groan. Brushing impatiently at the gifts, he sent them scattering to the floor and reached for his glass. As he gulped from it, he lost his grip, spilling whiskey down the bosom of his wedding shirt.

Margaret hovered, mopping at him with her handkerchief, and Walter said in a fading voice, "I don't understand you, Roy. In so much hot water with the church and I show you the way out. I wanted to see you take that. And you won't do that for me . . ."

"If I'm wrong, Dad"—Roy stood and took a few steps toward his father—"I'll be back here in a month, pleading with David to take me in."

"He'd be crazy to." Closing his eyes, Walter turned his head away.

It was Joan who walked me down through the darkness to where I had left my Beetle.

"That wasn't easy for you," I said, "being on the spot."

"No, it wasn't," she said. "I surprised myself too, joining up quick like that . . . but Roy's come too far since Tully jail to work for Train's. I know that. And I know Tom Sewall. There's no way of saying no to his call . . . for me either."

"Giving up that nice job?"

"Oh, there'll be a job for me. They practice law in Iowa too."

When we reached the car she stood beside it and looked up into a smudgy sky, where stars came and went. "I never expected to feel sorry for Walter Train."

"He can't bear the idea that he's fathered a clergyman, can he? For Walter, belief in God is a doubt in self, a giving-in, a giving-up, all the qualities that lose the game."

"Walter's not all fool, Ethan. He sees qualities in Roy that are out of his own dark side, the doubt and bravado that go hand in hand, the battle over the self. Roy could still lose that one."

"I'm not going to like your being so far away."

"We'll fix that somehow." Joan had been standing beside me, pale blue dress catching the starlight, but her face was dark, unreadable.

"Well," I said, "I'd better be getting along."

"Yes, I know."

Neither of us moved for a moment. She laughed gently and then I felt her hand touch mine. My mouth, aimed for her cheek, found her lips. Soft as petals, they enveloped mine long enough for me to sip, to slake a long thirst.

XIII

ARLY in 1970, after I'd been at St. Luke's for over eight years, I became briefly and inadvertently a hero of the church militant. While walking through a colored section of Newark, the scene two years earlier of fires and the stoning of firemen, I was struck in the neck by a .22-caliber bullet.

It turned out to be a fortunate wound, serious enough for a conspicuous dressing and superficial enough so that I could proceed to an interfaith meeting at the Booker T. Washington School. Here I was introduced as a casualty of the revolution in America whom God had spared.

Martin Luther King had been assassinated in April of 1968, Bobby Kennedy two months later. However tenuous the association, it was enough to put me on some panels. One of these was entitled "Ministry to the Blighted City" at Seabury House in Greenwich, Connecticut.

At the end of my performance there I heard someone say, "You're very modest, Mr. Soames, for so able a reconciler."

The voice was Midwestern, resonant as a steel guitar string. I turned and saw that I was being addressed by a smiling, square-faced man in his sixties. Below his clerical collar he wore a purple dickey and he carried a cane, a sporty, gold-banded thing of dark wood. His expression was at once worldly, playful, and compassionate. The mouth was tender, revealing an under-standing of pain.

His eyes said nothing at all, for he was blind. Gossamer-webbed pupils roved the wall behind me, and though I should have made the connection at once, I did not until we had reached the luncheon table together. A year before, Thomas Sewall had been elected Bishop of Iowa.

While we awaited the Presiding Bishop's grace, he introduced me to the clergymen around us. When we had pronounced our amens and sat down, he said, "I wish your friend Roy were here. He'd have benefited from hearing you this morning."

"Tell about the Trains, Bishop," I said. "I haven't had any recent news."

"Well, let's see. They have a daughter."

"Yes, Susan. I had an announcement of her arrival. She must be almost six by now."

Bishop Sewall had a grateful smile for the waitress as she set a luncheon plate before him. "Lovely sole," he said, passing a hand over it. "We miss that in Iowa and I make a point of being on good terms with the cook here. She does sole very well."

Although my own piece of fish had an ordinary taste, the bishop was putting his away with delight. "Yes," he said, pausing, "Roy has my old church now, Trinity, Iowa City. Being a univer-sity town, it's exciting, with all the unrest, and it won't surprise you that he's in the thick of it. Trinity's a bivouac for all the antiwar people."

"How does that sit?"

Bishop Sewall smiled. "Oh, not everyone is pleased. Roy turns up at all the meetings and opens the church to the protesters, and the university gets more anxious about student rebellion."

"In Iowa?"

"We're not so backward as you Easterners think."

"At least Roy's had his lessons in restraint."

"Learned them, Ethan?" The bishop broke and carefully but-tered a roll. "You strike me as a persuasive fellow. Do you sup-pose that as an old friend you could counsel a little of that restraint into his ear? Would it be a willing one?"

"Call him up, you mean? Out of the blue? You know, except

for Christmas cards, the birth announcement, and a very occasional letter, we've hardly been in touch."

"I think it might be more useful if you were to pay Roy a visit. Better than a call or a letter."

"I'd like that, but I could hardly come without an invitation."

"I might arrange that. I'm not too bad at the power of suggestion."

Within a week I had an invitation to come to Iowa City to preach a sermon from Trinity pulpit. The day I chose to go, May 1, was the day after President Nixon had announced that American troops were going into Cambodia. Flying west, I read that fifteen thousand people had gathered on the New Haven Green to strike Yale University.

It was Joan who met me at the Cedar Rapids airport. In the years since I had seen her, her beauty had become refined, more the maquette of her bones than her flesh. She had lost some weight. Her eyes were larger than I remembered, and when we first saw each other at the gate they shone like sun through a mist.

As we crossed the parking lot I asked, "How's Roy?"

Joan smiled. "Roy wanted to come for you." We had reached a green station wagon and she opened its tailgate for my valise. "The reason he didn't was the hope of stealing a march on me. We're on opposite sides of the war here."

"How do you mean?"

"You'll see."

We had turned south along a ribbon of road that was unfurling through fields of corn sprouts. As we skirted a barnyard where blue ceramic silos towered over hogs at their feeders, I asked, "And the kids?"

"You're going to like Susie. Quite the young lady. She's already my friend."

"And J.J.?"

She reflected. "Well, he's going through a phase. I wish Roy would find more time for him. I do the best I can, but I have a job too."

"I remember. You went with a law firm. Are you enjoying it?"

"I didn't at all. As the token woman I got scut work, updating the antitrust files, drafting wills for the clients with estates under a hundred thousand dollars, and seeing the nuts who came into the office. Everybody told me I was lucky, but I knew what kind of luck it was."

We were overtaking a tractor, which moved partly onto the shoulder as we passed. "At the coffee hour one Sunday, I was telling the president of the university about it. Gus Drinker is a parishioner and is, or at least was, Roy's friend. Gus believes in the university as a kind of sanity island in the sea getting hit by big waves from Des Moines on one side and from the new left on the other. I hadn't the least cunning in telling Gus my troubles. It never occurred to me that he had a job to offer, but on Monday I got asked around to Jessup Hall for an interview. Now I'm his assistant—legal affairs, which means finding ways to *avoid* confrontations, to keep talking."

"Great," I said, "and not the least of it, you and Roy finally working for the common cause."

"You'd think so, wouldn't you?" she said. We were crossing a narrow suspension bridge, and she glanced to the left, where a deep stream bent under a great burr oak and then disappeared into dark woods. "But you'd be wrong."

We were entering Iowa City, a turn-of-the-century town whose Victorian rooming houses and maple-shaded walks still held out against the bulldozers and transit-mix concrete trucks. The gold-domed Old Capitol building presided over the university, which sprawled along both banks of the Iowa River. On its steps a hoarse speaker was haranguing a circle of thirty students.

The town facing it appeared to be under siege. In a doorway a merchant swept shattered glass into a dustpan. Many show windows had been replaced by widths of plywood. The few that had been spared were protected by embrasures of chicken wire. NIXON SUCKS was splashed in yellow paint across the face of a clothing store. There was a smell of destruction in the air.

"We had another rampage downtown last night," Joan explained; "window smashing and firing up the trash baskets. The cops arrested a hundred kids, and thirty are still locked up.

Roy's their champ. He's been trying to raise bail all day—and from these merchants, of all people."

She slowed for a better look at the latest damage and then, turning into the Washington Street intersection, she waved to a man on the street corner and stopped at the curb.

Leaning across me, she called, "Did Roy get to you, Bob?"

He was a large man in a brown suit and he came trotting up, saying, "Oh, he found me, all right."

"How much?"

"We kicked in two hundred . . . but only for bona fide students. Not a nickel for Zachary."

Joan waved. "Thanks, Bob. Gus'll be glad to hear it."

She turned into College Street in order to point out Trinity, a green clapboard, H. H. Richardson church with a tall, steepled façade. The rectory was a block and a half away, a square white house with gingerbread along its eaves and above the porch. It faced a small park.

Since both Train children were in school, the rectory was quiet. As I unpacked my valise in the guest room I heard Joan's voice on the telephone assuring someone, "Only two hundred, and none of it for Zachary."

While Joan was driving us across town toward the jail, I asked, "Who's Zachary?"

"An organizer for SDS. There's only a few of them here but they keep a little trouble brewing, rallies every night. For most students it's better than studying for their exams, but Zach's serious. He wants to provoke a war with the university."

"Roy's for that?"

"We do differ on Zach. You'll see. I want him off the streets for a couple of days. The judge has put his bail nice and high, out of Roy's reach."

The jail, a two-story brick building, stood just beyond the courthouse, and the steep rise to it was sprinkled with students. Bearded, sandaled, and jeaned, they were gathered in groups as if for a picnic. Some were singing to the sporadic thrumming of a guitar. As we walked toward them I heard the passwords of protest from Watts and Woodstock and boisterous, self-conscious laughter.

We watched the entrance, where a cluster of students surrounded a pair of police sentries, and Roy appeared suddenly through a revolving door. I noticed that a bald spot was emerging at his crown, but as he pranced back and forth, he seemed more youthful and energetic than he had eight years ago.

From the top step he spoke to the crowd below. "We're getting everybody out now," he told them. "They'll be here with us in just a minute." To be sure, two students came through the door behind him and were greeted with cheers.

"What we should all remember about this opening of the jailhouse doors is who brought it about. It wasn't the cops. The cops like a full house here. And it wasn't the university either. No, sir. The bail for these students, who were doing nothing more than exercising their constitutional rights, was put up by the townspeople—the merchants and churchgoers of Iowa City. They paid for these bail bonds. Let's all remember that, okay?"

Behind him a stream of students issued from the door and more cheers rose. Grinning broadly, Roy trotted down the steps and came toward us.

"Ethan, you old son of a bitch. After all these years!" Extending an arm, he pulled me affectionately to his side. "I'm glad you've come. I'm glad you got here in time to see the liberation." He waved at a pair of stragglers coming down the steps to join the crowd. "If we'd left it to the university, these kids would be in for life."

"What did you mean about the churchgoers?" Joan asked. "Did you really hit up some Trinity people?"

"In a way, yes." Mischief glinted in his eyes. "There wasn't time for an every-member canvas."

"Zach? Are you getting Zach out too?"

Roy shrugged. "I didn't see how we could leave Zach behind. Zach's acting out his conscience, like everybody else."

There was a further stirring at the jailhouse door and a cry of "Hey, Zach, way to go, man!" As cheers spread through the crowd, I saw that a sullen, moon-faced youth had emerged. Long hair and a receding forehead gave him a resemblance to Benjamin Franklin.

A young woman in a gray dress had followed him out. She

had light shaggy hair and carried a briefcase. After joining Zachary on the top step, she smiled and waved, and there were more cheers.

"Where did you get the money for him?" Joan asked. "Where did you find a thousand dollars, Roy?"

"Parishioners," he said. "Our good parishioners."

"Which parishioners? What do you mean?"

"My discretionary fund."

"Oh, Roy, you didn't!"

"Oh, but I did." He sighed. Frowning, he added, "I couldn't think of a better use."

Joan shook her head angrily and turned to me. "I'm going to the office until it's time to pick up the children at school. Do you want to come?"

"Leave Ethan with me," Roy said. "We've got lots to talk about."

Joan left abruptly, heading for the station wagon, and in a moment I heard its door slam.

The woman in the gray dress was coming down the steps. She was a vigorous-looking person with a plain face and a short, muscular body. Beside her, a scowling Zachary paused in front of a policeman to give his badge a contemptuous flip. An exchange of angry words and shoves ended in the policeman's seizing Zachary's arm as if to drag him back to jail.

The woman clung to Zachary's free arm. In the next instant the crowd of about sixty students was in motion, closing like a silent wave on the struggle and sweeping us with it. Other officers emerged from the jail, one of them holding a nightstick.

A single voice broke the silence. It was a girl's and it rose like the plaintive cry of a gull: "Let him go!" It was followed by other voices. They began to chant, "Pigs! Pigs! Pigs! Let's get the pigs!"

Two of the police had seized Zachary, knocked him down, and were dragging him up the steps. In spite of his thrashing about, they had him halfway to the top, where a third officer looked on with approval. But the crowd, now in full outraged cry, surged forward with every intention of claiming Zachary for its own.

The woman began to wave back the oncoming students, and

Roy sprang out to join her. Spreading his arms, he cried out, "Not now, friends! There's a time to fight, but it's not now! They can't keep Zach if you stay where you are. Don't touch him!"

Although there was some jostling and crying-out at the back, the crowd halted, grew silent, waited as Roy turned to see that the struggle on the steps had ceased. Zachary got slowly to his feet and turned to face the police.

"Up your fat butts!" he said, and thrusting his hands into the pockets of his tattered jeans, he ambled toward the welcoming throng.

Brenda Hutton was the woman's name, and she sat beside Roy in the front seat of his battered jeep. She had the ease and heartiness of a woman who had grown up among many brothers. Her laugh was a rough, ready one. Nevertheless, I was surprised to see her touch Roy's arm.

Roy began a tour of the university at the stadium, reminding me that it was the home of a Rose Bowl team. He described the collegiate gothic medical center as the biggest teaching hospital in the country. Pointing out the glass-and-metal library of the law school, he said it was there, twelve years ago, that he had been an instructor.

"And where you met your wife," I reminded him.

Brenda Hutton showed little interest in the sightseeing until we entered the business district, where the sight of the barricaded shop windows led her to a count of remaining targets. More would fall tonight, she felt. She explained to me that a Cambodian protest had been scheduled for six o'clock.

Roy agreed that there might be more street action. "And all the fuzz will be turned out, keeping an eye on our Zach."

"Is Zach going to jump your bail?" she asked.

"I'm prepared for it," Roy replied. "I don't have any illusions about Zach. He's not an Eagle Scout. He's a radical, and I respect that. He's a true believer, and true believers are okay with me."

"And how about the parishioners who put it up?" I asked.

He scowled at me. "It's not *their* discretion. It's the rector's. I'm prepared to defend that. Everybody knows me here, Ethan. It won't surprise them."

Brenda was still enjoying Roy's response when we pulled up in front of her house, a yellow cottage on Muscatine Avenue. She hopped out at once, and to my surprise Roy did too.

"Ethan," he said. "Brenda and I have to go over some plans. Why don't you drive around town for half an hour?" He watched her unhurried progress toward her door. "There's a Jackson Pollock worth seeing at the art museum."

I did as I was told, drove the jeep through quaint streets, past rambling houses whose doorways wore a rash of mailboxes, past the Tudor- and plantation-style sororities and fraternities, past scores of students, none of whom appeared to have revolution in mind.

I saw a textbook face down in the grass and a Frisbee floating overhead. Everywhere scholars were intent on exposing a maximum of themselves to the young, May sun. Two girls, their jeans cut to breechclouts, were spreadeagled on a rooftop and a herd of boys stomped the walk below, baying at them.

As I drove, I could not escape the notion that what Roy was going over at Brenda's was Brenda herself. At one moment it seemed impossible, only some dark suspicion of my own making. How could he jeopardize the love of his exquisite wife with so coarse a woman?

In alternate moments I was sure he was doing exactly that.

I waited in front of the yellow cottage on Muscatine for ten minutes before Roy emerged from Brenda Hutton's door. He glanced furtively up and down the street before trotting down the path. With a self-satisfied smile, he climbed behind the jeep's wheel.

As he drove us toward the rectory, I asked, "Are you really screwing that woman?"

He hesitated a moment before nodding. "You wouldn't think a tough lawyer would make a good lay would you, but, Ethan, she's fantastic. A regular rodeo."

"My God, Roy," I said, "you're out of your mind."

For a while neither of us spoke. I was thinking that he had made this startling confession, with its display of gaudy male plumage, expecting that I would not only admire him for it but approve its insult to Joan.

It seemed that he had miscalculated my loyalty by a critical fraction. I think that from this moment it was vulnerable, like a heart that for the first time has skipped a beat. It also seemed as if the precipitous path he traveled had no guardrail at all.

We had stopped for a traffic light, and I asked, "What can you possibly see in her?"

"Oh, Ethan, I see plenty. For one thing, Brenda knows there's a war on. For another, she knows these students have rights. It's their university, their country, and their lives. She knows what the shouting's about."

"And you have to sanction that in her bed?"

The laughter burst from him. "Oh, come on, Ethan. Everybody needs loving. Everybody needs to give a little, get a little."

"I'm sure you're right, and that it has nothing whatever to do with your cheating on Joan."

We were approaching the College Street park, and he slowed for the rectory as if to turn in but instead drove by toward the center of town, a frown on his broad face.

As we crossed the Washington Street bridge he nodded toward the riverbank, where a couple lay on the grass, oblivious of a world beyond the interlacing of their arms and legs. "These kids know all about fucking now. They know it has to be demystified, that it's just the ultimate friendly act. Morality changes. It has to stay flexible, or it winds up in the museum with the armor and the chastity belt."

"These kids aren't married, Roy. They're not priests. They've taken no vows."

"Oh, but they have—to re-examine *every*thing they live by. They're cleaning out the attic."

"I can't believe this. It doesn't matter *how* we behave? You just shrug off the pain you cause? Is there no guilt, no sin, in the new era?"

"Of course there is." In his preoccupation he was letting other cars pass. "And there are days when I'm close to drowning in self-loathing. Do you believe me?"

"It hadn't occurred to me."

"But now, do you believe me?"

"Yes."

"I have a body that's a fully equipped inferno of temptations, and I am no less priest for it. When you have a sin to atone for, you don't want the prigs and prudes who don't know what it's like, do you? Christ, no. You want the one who knows about sin and forgiveness at first hand."

"Some license."

He laughed again but turned thoughtful to say, "Okay, it is. I'll grant you that." He was turning into a river-edged park of playgrounds and picnic groves. "Still, we should get rid of guilt altogether. It causes nothing but harm . . . constipation, hemorrhoids, and most of the suicides in the history of mankind. Think of all the poor scourged souls John Calvin turned into their graves without a taste of human love."

"You don't mean that either. We'd be out of business."

He brought the jeep to a halt at a place where children were boarding a miniature train for the journey around a circle of track. "Of all the early fathers, I like Augustine best," he said. "He can make turning the animal urge into spirit very appealing. He was such a lover of the body with that young mistress of his, and then one day picking up on Paul's mysticism—at thirty-two, mind you—and going cold turkey on the flesh."

"You've missed the moment," I said, "by several years."

He stared out on the river, where a canoe floated downstream. "But I don't want to be a mystic. While I'm in it, I want to be of this world. It's what I believe about Jesus too, that he was every inch of this world, with passions identical with mine. What a job the church has done in deballing him!" He looked at his watch and backed slowly into the road. "The Gnostics aren't so crazy, with their idea that the body's just a wrapping for the soul and doesn't matter, just self-destructs when the divine sparks go back to God."

I gave him a baleful look. "Theologically, Roy, you sound due for overhaul."

"My theology's fine. It questions and grows. It's very much alive."

On the rectory porch an angry Gus Drinker was waiting for Roy. I left them and went to find Joan, who was in the kitchen. She turned from a bowl and cookbook to introduce Susan Train.

Susan was already an elegantly female child with delicate gestures and long lashes over eyes like her mother's.

While I watched her help Joan, I could hear Drinker's voice in the hallway saying, "They're not yours to do with as you please. They're in trust, between you and every one of your parishioners."

I could not hear Roy's response, but Drinker said, "Who *did* you consult? You're supposed to get approval from the senior warden. And what does the bishop have to say about this? . . . Well, by God, he will, Roy."

A door slammed, and Joan winced at the sound.

My godson, J.J., came into the kitchen. He had grown into a handsome, sulky boy with a sensitive face. From under a shock of black hair he peered at me suspiciously. I felt he was frisking me for an overdue gift. On deciding I was empty-handed, he lost interest entirely and went upstairs.

When Roy discovered that a quarterly evaluation of J.J.'s school progress had arrived and that it was a poor one, he called him down from his room. I could hear Roy's voice in the library: "No, sir, you don't have any right to bring home such a crappy report card—a D in class behavior? What the hell does that mean? Come on, J.J., speak up. Aren't you a little ashamed of this thing?"

"No," J.J. replied. His voice was soft yet fully charged.

"Why not?" The fury rose in Roy's throat. "Come on, tell me why not."

"Lots of kids get a D in behavior."

"That's not a *reason*," Roy exploded.

"He's nine," Joan said. "Remember that he's nine."

"You don't do what the slobs do," Roy went on. "You do what's right to do."

The children were allowed to join us for supper, and I tried to get J.J. to tell me about friends and school, but he drew further into himself and left the table suddenly in midmeal.

When Joan recalled him, J.J. groaned. "Okay, okay, it's just so *boring*." Grudgingly, he asked to be excused and then trudged off to his room. Susan barely talked throughout the meal.

Later, when sounds from the campus drifted through the rectory's open windows, Roy proposed that we go see what was happening. From the top of the stairs J.J. called to ask if he could come with us.

"Not a chance, J.J.," Roy told him. "You stay in your room and make sure there's nothing more you can do to be ready for school tomorrow."

Roy and I, walking toward the center of town, could feel a tension and smell an uncertain danger on the soft night air.

On Clinton Street, which separated town and university, hundreds of students had gathered along the pipe fence that edged the campus. They were watching a dozen policemen in riot gear, each gripping a two-foot billy club by its ends. They stood in a spread rank defending the shops.

For so large a crowd, the students were curiously silent. They were watching the antics of a light-skinned Negro. In fringed trousers and feathered headband, he was trotting back and forth on the sidewalk, raising his arms like a cheerleader. "Look! Look!" he cried. "Hitler's riding high tonight. Man, I never expected to see this here in Cornville! What do we *say*?"

He was a drama student who called himself Deerslayer, Roy explained, one of several street actors who often took part in the demonstrations.

Deerslayer began to taunt the police line, calling out, "You going to get yours, you curlytails, you. Hey, oink, oink, oink!"

Then Roy saw Zachary slipping through the crowd and moved to intercept him. Catching up, he said, "Let's don't forget who it was that sprung you today, Zach. It was the merchants."

"I don't forget anything"—Zachary gave Roy a lazy glance— "including these pigs standing over there looking like they own the place. We might have to explain to them how they don't. We might have to make a real bust tonight, they keep doing that shit."

I followed Roy as he made his way through the throng toward a darkened police car that stood at the Iowa Avenue intersection. An officer sat quietly within. In the shadows beyond, a second officer stood with a tall man in shirt sleeves. Joining them, Roy introduced me to President Drinker and the campus security chief.

"If these kids go on a rampage, Father," the chief said, "you'll have a tough time making their bail tomorrow."

"There won't be a rampage if you break up your line of storm troopers. That's what's making the kids mad. Send 'em home, Chief."

Drinker said, "We all want to go home, Roy. We will when we can."

"We'd look fine, wouldn't we, going home and leaving 'em the town to trash? I see your friend Zachary out there, Father. He looks to me like he's passing out the trouble." The chief pointed. "There he goes. We've got no patience with that boy tonight. You might want to let him know."

"If they let off some steam," Roy said, "there won't be any trashing. Take my word."

"They can let off all they want," the chief said, "so long as they stay on their side of the street. I don't like these actors running out there. Next thing . . ." He looked at Drinker hopefully.

Down the line there was a surge in the crowd. Some students spilled over the fence and the chief went toward the police car, but seeing it was Deerslayer and some others in costume moving into the street to put on an act, he returned. A boy wearing an ROTC uniform strutted back and forth, and a girl carrying the bull's-eye flag of Vietnam stepped out to meet him.

"We'd better clear the street, Mr. Drinker." The chief seemed about to order this.

"Let's hold on, Henry," Drinker said. "Let 'em play it out for a few minutes."

The boy in uniform had begun to wrestle with the girl, and when he threw her to the pavement there were boos and scattered applause from the audience, more when an actor in a felt hat paid the boy in uniform some greenbacks. Then the girl rose, took up a pail of red liquid, and splashed it in puddles down the center of the street. There were cheers and laughter as the parody of blood-in-the-street continued.

Suddenly I saw Zachary's hand flash in the air. A Coke bottle flew across the street and struck one of the police. He reacted with a lunge in the direction from which it had come. A second policeman moved toward the actors still in the street, and some students spilled over the fence. There were shouts all along the line and an unintelligible warning from the police car's speaker.

Now Deerslayer sprinted across Clinton Street to place a black ball the size of a grapefruit in front of an astonished policeman, take a Zippo lighter from his pocket, and touch the flame to a wire that sprouted from the ball. Then he sprinted away, hands over his ears, and, reaching the other side of the street, turned to watch the fuse sputter, stop, fizz again, and then go out.

The crowd reacted with applause, but one policeman waggled his club and lumbered forth after the brazen Deerslayer, who immediately ducked into the crowd's protection. The students closed around him, linking arms and jeering at the policeman's sally. Then came a wave of laughter that swept back and forth in the crowd, dividing it.

The balance had swung to good nature. There were cheers and more applause for the performance. As if a curtain had come down on the show, the audience began to break up into groups and drift away, some toward the Old Capitol, where a speaker's voice could be heard, some toward the dormitories to the north or across the river.

Joan did not seem surprised that I came home alone that night; accepted that Roy had set off for a walk by himself. She was at a table in the kitchen, drafting a report for the regents on protective measures being taken at the library.

"Now you've had a look at the trouble here and seen where Roy's *at,* what do you think, Ethan? What about his backing this prickly kid against the president of the university? Gus Drinker isn't just a member of the church; he's Roy's friend. Against *me* too."

"Oh, please," I said, "don't ask me to take sides."

"But I want to know, Ethan, I'm losing my way. Instinctively I back Roy. He's always so sure, always taking the minority's cause, the weak one, the one in most trouble—only this time he's damaging a decent institution and decent people. It's going to be hard to put right in the end."

"Yes. I have the same feeling."

"Tell him, then."

"A waste of breath."

"Then what can I do?"

"I've been thinking about it, how you're both sure you're right. Maybe you are. The difference is only a couple of points on the ideological compass. Still, that's enough, isn't it, to be hard to put right in the end. I'm thinking somebody's got to give a little."

Joan gave me a wondering look. "Well, you know it won't be Roy."

"I don't believe it will."

In the silence we could hear the unhurried thrumming of a passing freight train and then the warning of its air horn.

Joan said, "Ethan, you know what I think of that? I think it stinks. My principles are just as fine as Roy's. Why should I have to turn them in? Why should I be the one who always pays with *my* beliefs and now *my* job?"

"Joan, dear, that isn't what I said."

"Yes, it is."

"Then it isn't what I meant."

"The hell it isn't," she said and turned back to her report for the regents.

The next morning I woke to household sounds, the children's voices as they breakfasted in the kitchen below, Joan's as she shushed their cries and consoled their complaints, then the hum of a dishwasher and the tinkling score of a television cartoon.

I came downstairs to find Roy talking to someone in the living room. He beckoned to me and I entered quietly to find that his guest was the Right Reverend Thomas Sewall, Bishop of Iowa. He had been speaking, his hands clasped around the gold-banded cane, but he paused, aware of me though I had made no sound.

"Hello, Ethan," the bishop said. "I hear you've come to share your knowledge of the battlefields with us. That's good news."

"Thank you, Bishop. I don't think it's much surprise to you, my being here, and I'm grateful for whatever you had to do with my visit."

"It's all Roy's doing, Ethan." His mouth had a pleasurable tilt, as if some joke had occurred to him and when he had it just right he would tell it. "I gave him an account of what you told us at Seabury House and he couldn't wait to get you here. He likes to keep things lively here at Trinity and"—he shook his cane in Roy's direction—"there are those who believe that on occasion he overdoes it."

Roy had been enjoying the bishop's mild scolding, looking pleased with himself as he spun himself to and fro on the piano stool. "While life doth last," he said, "I'm rector at Trinity and the fund is to be used at the rector's discretion. That's my understanding."

"*With* your discretion, as well as *at* it, Roy. That's how a discretionary fund is to be used. If you've dug into it imprudently, you'd better replace it, and quickly too."

"No imprudence, Tom," Roy said. "Risky, maybe, but prudent. I want everybody at Trinity to join in saying that it's more important to have the kids free, able to shout and sing and march their outrage at the war, than for us to replace our gutters and downspouts. I want the discretionary fund to say so and I want the person who prefers new gutters and downspouts to stand up so that we can see who it is."

"Ethan"—Bishop Sewall appealed to me with outstretched hand—"help me out. He's a daredevil, your friend. Can we coax him away from the brink?"

"If anyone can, you can, Bishop."

Roy said, "I'm here, Tom. You can tell me directly. I'll do as you tell me, of course. But I know you won't ask me to act against my conscience. Which is why"—Roy smiled—"I not only respect you, but love you."

The bishop laughed. "How much did you use? Gus tells me it was the better part of a thousand dollars."

"Gus is right."

"I know a lady in Des Moines who'd like to donate a thousand dollars to your bail fund. What shall I tell her, Roy?"

"Tell her thanks. We'll need it soon. Tomorrow maybe, but not today."

Outside the rectory the bishop was about to enter the black Plymouth in which he had been driven from Diocesan House in Des Moines. Before he did so, he faced down College Street, where crimson paint had been splashed across the white sandstone façade of the public library.

"It's sad," the bishop observed, "war's ravage in this pretty town. It's like going to see a friend and finding him laid up in bandages."

"They're a good sign, Tom," Roy said. "If we don't deny the illness, the patient's going to recover."

Thoughtfully the bishop slipped into the Plymouth's front seat and, nodding, closed its door.

Grasping the window edge, Roy asked, "Forgive me?"

"Sure." The bishop took Roy's hand in his. "I did that on the way over." He searched for me. "Ethan, do you think your friend here is a little crazy? Is he in for a fall?"

My impulse, even with Roy beside me, was to say the truth, that I thought he was. But I could not. My tongue would not move. Then I was reminded of an incident of years ago.

"I was once in a waiting room, some twenty stories up in a New York office building," I said. "A man was washing the windows. I could see him on the ledge, carrying his pail and squeegee as he moved from one window to the next, swishing away the soot, leaving each pane immaculate.

"I was intrigued by the way he used his safety belt. Moving to a new window, he would clip one end to a cleat beyond him. As he swung to the next sill, he would vanish for an instant behind the masonry. When he reappeared, he attached the loose end of the belt and went to work. He did it repeatedly until he saw me watching. Then, to my horror, I saw him unhook both ends. They were swinging in the wind as he prepared to move on. He stepped out of sight—and was gone. I leaped from my chair and ran to the window just as he appeared in it, winking as he hooked himself up."

The bishop laughed and reached for my hand. "You speak in parables, Ethan. I like that one. Perhaps it's the only way we can get our windows washed."

XIV

ALONE, I walked along a ravaged Clinton Street past
new plywood barricades, red-daubed granite, and pud-
dled shards, wondering what could heal this wounded community. What could a minister say to reconcile its determined
adversaries? What could console this transient generation that
felt so betrayed by the university, the custodian of their spiritual
well-being, or console the university, which saw before it a generation possessed?

A sermon could try. When I found that the lesson for May 3
was Acts 18, the story of Paul's propagating the new faith in a
hostile world, I felt a mystical assist that sent me into the Trinity
pulpit with a heart full of evangelical gumption.

I remember looking out upon a surprisingly full congregation. Students in their jeans, beards, ponytails, and granny
glasses had taken the back pews or stood warily near the door.
Faculty, stiff-spined and country-checked, reigned over the forward pews. The womenfolk, thin-lipped from raising families
on stingy, assistant professors' paychecks, bright-eyed from ac-
quaintance with Emily Dickinson and a recollection of Fiesole,
seemed to welcome me. I found Gus Drinker, his slim, vivid wife
beside him. He looked paler, more drawn, than he had on Friday.

Across the chancel, Roy's gaze was prodding, as though to say *Here they are, Ethan. Tell 'em the truth. Back me up. Maybe they'll believe it from you.*

I began by describing Paul's mission, his journeying across the civilized world to tell the Jews of the Diaspora about this wonderful new Man and His revolutionary ideas. Then I imagined what he must have felt as he realized his message was causing riots. He had been flogged for it and jailed at Philippi. But as Paul despaired of teaching Jews that Jesus was Christ, he had another vision, in Corinth. God came to him in the night and said, "Be not afraid but speak, and hold not thy peace for I am with thee . . . for I have much people in this city."

I could see the assent in Roy's face and feel a chill from the congregation, but I was not finished. I went on to tell the sequel at Ephesus, how the riot there among the silversmiths was quelled by a man whom Luke does not even name. He was simply the town clerk, but he took advantage of a moment when the crowd was hoarse from shouting to remind the people how lucky they were to be living under a government that permitted such demonstrations and provided a legal way to settle grievances. Mobs and rash acts, he pointed out, flouted their great gift of civilization. Whereupon, according to Luke, the uproar ceased and Paul called unto him the disciples and embraced them.

Gus Drinker looked pleased. He thanked me at the door, and then, best of all, Joan came along with an absolving hug. Roy, however, was furious. "That's bullshit, you know," he told me over lunch. "I hope you didn't come all this way from New Jersey to tell my kids to put their trust in the law."

His bad temper was not reserved only for me; he snapped at the children and overruled Joan's plan for a picnic at Lake McBride.

The next day as we stalked the riverbank he was still punishing me for my sermon. "The students know that kind of hypocrisy when they smell it. You're talking about a law that locks them up when they say what's on their minds."

"I came to do what I could to bring your people together, Roy. Isn't that what you wanted?"

"You can't do it by lying to these kids," he replied. "They're right about the war. It's wicked. They want to say so and nobody listens. Do you think somebody's listening in the courtrooms? Read the papers. Breaking glass, though, that gets heard. Gus Drinker hears that. Even Nixon hears that through his ear-plugs."

"I thought you respected Gus. I thought he was your friend."

"Oh, Gus isn't evil. He does the best he can, but he's in the system. He answers to the legislature. He's all forty watts of the light from the middle-class intelligence."

"You're turning away from *all* your friends, Roy."

"Nope. I'm *counting* them."

"Tom Sewall?"

"Most certainly."

"You turned him away. I heard you do it. He came to help you yesterday and you refused him."

"Tom knew I wouldn't take his money. He knows I like trouble and trouble likes me. He came over to bring me his sanction. If you didn't see that, you're the blind one."

"And Joan?"

Roy massaged the bridge of his nose. "Joan and I are okay. We do quarrel, as you've seen, and sometimes I react with naughtiness. That's my way, as you know well enough."

"It's no joke. You're steering straight for the falls."

"Oh, shut up, Ethan. I don't need advice from an old hen. Neither does Joan."

"Are you punishing her, Roy, for being on the wrong side of the argument?"

"Oh, my . . ." He seemed stunned. "I do hope not." He turned to scowl at the swift current that swirled around clumps of willows, baring their roots, and spoke deliberately. "Joan's a little confused again, over whether she can be the parson's wife and herself too. She has to work that out every couple of years, but she does. She needs to be somebody in her own right. She needs to prove herself somewhere else. I understand that. Women have such a need to compete with us now, to keep their self-respect. That's why she needs this job . . . but you know I have needs too. I need to be loved for what I believe in."

"And that's a sanction for Brenda?"

Roy smiled. "The flesh is weak. It's also unimportant."

"I can't imagine Joan will think it's unimportant, nor that she'll put up with what she doesn't like. She won't *like* sharing you with Brenda. You're kidding yourself."

Roy grasped my wrist in what started as an affectionate gesture but tightened as if he were bent on cutting off the circulation. "Brenda turns me on. We came together making bail for the kids. There was understanding. You know what I mean? You have to do something about that unless you're a chicken."

"That's how temptation always speaks."

"Oh, shit." He turned away. "What's happened to you, Ethan?"

"Disillusion," I said. "I can't help you. I'm going home." We had paused in the middle of the footbridge and were looking down onto the heaving back of the river and the dam of uprooted trees it had swept against the piers. Some students ran past us in a clatter, and I felt the bridge sway underfoot.

"Tonight?" he asked.

"There's a flight at six. I'll see if I can get on."

"I'll drive you."

"I can get the limousine."

"Or Joan. Joan'll take you."

We walked on silently, and as we began to climb the hill leading up toward the Old Capitol building, we noticed that a demonstration was starting there. Students were coming from all directions, some at a trot, dodging around the slower ones. There was a confusion of voices, a shouting distorted by amplifiers, and a vast murmur in the air. It seemed resonant with bewilderment and fear.

Roy caught at the arm of a girl hurrying by. "What is it, Lindy?"

"They've killed some students," she said, panting.

"Who did?"

"The National Guard. In Ohio."

"Killed?" Roy whispered in fervent disbelief. "Oh, Jesus, no."

In front of the Old Capitol a crowd was multiplying, and we stood at its edge to watch Zach. At the top of the steps and already hoarse, he was repeating a litany: "They've turned the guns on us—they've turned the guns on us now." He held up a clenched fist, and the answering shouts echoed from the building walls. Behind him the SDS speakers, heads banded in black, waited their turns at the microphone.

Off to the right there was an outcry, and we saw the crowd parting for the university president.

"Gus," Roy murmured, "you're in for trouble."

As he tried to climb the Old Capitol steps, the students refused to let him pass, and from above Zach called out, "Here's Gus come to talk to us. I bet he'll say, 'Go back to class and study for exams.' Do we want to hear from Gus?"

There were a few shouts of "Hell, no!" and then laughter as the president was pitched from one rejecting pair of hands to another. The rhetoric resumed, fractured and irritating as it squawked from the amplifiers but with a strong, steady pulse.

As though by arrangement there were only two campus police cars visible. They had driven up to the walk at the north end of the campus, and I could see only four uniformed men, standing uneasily on the fringe of the crowd.

Now there were cries and a scurrying at the north edge, where a fragment had broken off to harass the departing Gus Drinker.

"Jessup, Jessup, Jessup Hall," they chanted, and the sound bounced like a volley ball among outstretched hands. Students were running past Gus toward the administration building, pushing aside a security officer to burst its locked doors and disappear within.

"Here we go." Roy stood on tiptoe, watching. "This'll get the show started."

"You want to see them wreck this place?"

He gave me a puzzled look. "The building? Why the hell not? It's *their* turn to speak."

Windows were being opened now and a shower of index cards and correspondence fluttered upon the throng below.

"The cops can't just stand by . . ."

"They'd better today," he said, "if they know what's good for them."

"Making a mess of the offices. There's no sense in it."

"Some kids are dead in Ohio, Ethan. You're not listening to the speakers."

"I hear perfectly well, but this doesn't avenge them. Good God, what's happened to you? The Guardsmen are no different from the rest of us. They don't know what they're doing. They must be forgiven."

Roy's eyes flashed with contempt, and I had a momentary vision of two middle-aged ministers grappling in the midst of a student demonstration.

There was an outcry to our right, and we turned to see that a heavier rain had begun to fall from the windows of Jessup Hall. Ribbons of adding-machine tape were followed by a downpour of trays, files, and a wastebasket. The cheering crowd scattered as a wooden file splintered on the sidewalk, and then the window itself, shattered from within by a chair leg, came down in a shower of glass.

Two students appeared swinging an office Underwood and managed to tumble it over the sill. It struck the steps below with a great crunch that momentarily silenced the crowd, as though in the crushing of its intimate springs and jigs some language unspoken, some life, had just perished. A sound rose from many throats at once. It was an awesome cry for more.

"A-Day has come," Roy said.

"What's that?"

"All spring they've been wanting to bust the armory." Roy was glancing about searching faces. He called out to a tall blond boy in overalls, "Peace—pass it on, Dave!" He began to move through the crowd swiftly now, seeking friends. Finding a familiar-looking girl, he said, "Peace—pass it on, Deb!"

He explained to me, "It's a plan. We have a brigade of monitors who try to handle the big busts. The SDS has been eyeing the armory all spring. They'll get there today." He touched the neckband of his T-shirt. "I'm going to put on a collar. You want to stay, Ethan? Want to give us a hand?"

"I'll stay."

I stood alone in the doorway of MacLean Hall, watching the students as they came from classroom and dormitory to flood the new grass around the Old Capitol. They were spectators, and as the speakers grew hoarse and incomprehensible, they seemed to grow bored with them. The crowd ebbed, drifted on.

Roy appeared beside me. He had added a clerical collar to his outfit of T-shirt and shorts and made a curious figure as he studied the crowd.

"I think it's fizzling," I said.

"They're winding up. Waiting for dark."

Indeed, the sky to the east was deepening, bringing the dusk and with it a rise in excitement, a sense that the waiting was nearly over. As the oratory flared, the crowd came pressing back, an incoming tide.

At the foot of the Old Capitol's columns, two speakers were calling for draft cards, and several appeared, held high as they passed from fingertip to fingertip forward and up the steps to be put to the flame. The chanting began: "Hell, no, we won't go! Hell, no, we won't go!"

I followed Roy as he trotted down the hill toward the factorylike brick building of the Memorial Union. Among the students flowing through its entrance were several who wore white armbands. In the lobby, the information desk, the box office, and the newsstand were closed, but students were rendezvousing here, huddling in groups, deciding what to do.

In front of the closed elevator doors stood a long table. A sign raised above it read MONITORS FOR PEACE. A dozen students and several clergymen clustered around it, consulting pages of typed instructions.

Halting abruptly, Roy said, "Well, look who's come."

It was Joan. Wearing a dark, businesslike dress, she was tying a white band around a clergyman's arm.

"Hello," Roy said as we joined her. "What brings you here?"

She looked at him evenly. "The news from Ohio."

"Is there anything new? Is it all true?"

"There are four kids dead at Kent State," she said. "It's just been confirmed. No one knows how it started, but apparently the Ohio National Guard had live ammunition and got nervous and fired at the kids. Chalk up a big victory for the Guard. I can't get over the idea that it was a game to them, as it is with most of these kids here, playing at being radicals, playing at being soldiers. They thought it was a kind of party."

"It's not a game here. Not now."

"I know."

"Gus coming too?"

"Gus has plenty to do where he is," she said.

"I guess he does." Roy took an armband from the basket on the table and tied it around my arm, then turned to speak to a pair of students who were leaving for their posts on the campus.

"Keep the peace," he said, raising two fingers in the sign. "Remember, keep smiling. Let 'em pass."

Joan took an armband from the basket and tied it around Roy's arm. "Did you hear about the buses?" she asked.

"Nope."

"Two busloads of some kind of militia are up in City Park."

Roy reflected, then offered her an armband. "Do you want this?"

"Yes," she said, "I do."

Outside, dusk had fallen. Lights were appearing through the new foliage outlining the highway along the river, and as we approached the Iowa Avenue bridge we could see that half a dozen students sat yoga style or lay sprawled in the Highway 6 intersection. A police cruiser stood by, having staked out the roadblock with purple flares. The traffic, studded with livestock trucks and milk tankers, was choked as far as we could see. A pair of monitors moved along the column, talking to the drivers.

While we stood watching the shadows lengthen on the river's opposite bank, imagining sinister preparations for battle there, I said, "Whatever the outcome, it isn't *all* bad."

"What do you mean?" Roy asked.

"I mean you two, your being together, and knowing it."

"At the moment," he said, "I'm not counting on anything."

"I am," Joan said.

"Oh?" he asked. "What are you so sure of?"

"This morning I told Gus Drinker to look around for a new legal assistant."

We watched some lights blinking high on the bluff, and then Roy said, "I hope you feel good about that."

"It was my decision, if that's what you mean." she said. "I did have some friendly advice."

After a moment Roy said, "It would be useful to know if those buses are still in City Park and who's on them."

"I'll go," she said. "They're more likely to let me through."

"Okay," Roy said.

We watched her cross the bridge, saw a policeman bar her way. She appeared to turn back to our side of the bridge but then slipped quickly into the darkness at the railing. A second later I caught sight of her armband. She was moving up the opposite bank toward City Park.

Roy and I walked south until we came to the Burlington Avenue bridge, and here Roy talked our way past a pair of policemen so that we were able to cross the highway and climb the palisade beyond. From the summit we looked down on the dark river as it swept beneath the three bridges toward the pillow of mist at the powerhouse falls.

Hillcrest dormitory rose behind us and we climbed to its top floor, where a campus policeman admitted us to the student lounge. Its big windows commanded a panorama of the east campus, which rose from the opposite riverbank past great playing fields flanked by the student union and the library to the Old Capitol, whose frosted columns and gilded dome shimmered under floodlights.

At a short-wave transmitter, a woman operator was calling in reports from police outposts, over-ing and roger-ing them in self-conscious militarese, anxiety manifest in the half moons darkening her blue shirt.

Gus Drinker leaned against the Coke machine, talking to a short, simian man with a gold badge attached to the shirt of his brown-and-beige uniform. He was saying, "You can count on it, Gus. They've been instructed, every damned one. We're just making a show, is all—just reminding the kids where they are."

"They know where they are, Oscar." Gus waved toward the window, through which we could see the swarming pathways. "Look!"

Glancing at us, both men seemed annoyed by the interruption, but Gus put out a hand for Roy's and introduced Oscar Titus, the Johnson County sheriff. Titus gave us an impatient nod, but the university president smiled and surprised me by saying, "We could use one of those visions now, Father."

"We've brought you one, Gus," Roy said. "All five thousand of those kids over there are on their way to the armory. I hope you're thinking about that."

Titus said, "We'll be looking out for the armory, Father."

"Tonight, I think you'd better be looking out for the kids," Roy replied. "They're going to want to help themselves to about a dozen of those Springfield rifles in the racks. They'll want to carry 'em down to the bridge and pitch 'em in the river. I hope you're going to let 'em."

The sheriff laughed. "That's government property, Father."

Roy scowled at him. "As guns they're worthless. You know that. But the kids want 'em. For God's sake, give 'em to them. They'll be of some use at the bottom of the Iowa River."

Titus, still smiling, shook his head. "Save your breath, Father. We're not opening up the armory so that students can play in there. There's explosives and weapons, you know. People sure to get hurt. How would that look in the papers? Come on, Father. We're busy here."

"Who did you bring to town, Sheriff? Who came in those buses? Where are they from?"

"Deputies," Titus said. "We've brought 'em down from Linn County."

"Two busloads? Where would you get two busloads of deputies in an afternoon? It's the Guard, isn't it?" He appealed to Gus. "Don't put the Guard out there."

Gus reflected, but the sheriff glared at Roy. "I know you, Father Train. I know what you want to see here tonight."

"Is the Guard in town, Sheriff?"

"My deputies, all properly sworn. They're here to protect these students."

"Protect them?" Roy asked. "From what?"

"From harm—harm to themselves, harm to others."

"Are they carrying guns?"

The sheriff declined to answer. "Let me give you some advice,

Father. Stay out of the way. If you want to help us, don't go marching with the troublemakers out there. They'll cool down and nobody'll get hurt."

"I'll be praying you're right," Roy said.

"Good. Keep it up," the sheriff said, beckoning to the officer who had admitted us. "Arthur, will you show these gentlemen the way out?"

From the riverbank we could see that the mass of students surrounding the Old Capitol was taking animal shape. The emotion that had been building throughout the day had catalyzed these thousands of figures into a single one and energized it. A head swung slowly across the steps; behind it a thick body coiled around the building, and its tail trailed away in shadows beyond.

Its writhing motion was lighted here and there by bursts of torchlight, and we could hear the cries. A chant of "Rot-see, must go!" was picked up by a drumbeat. "Rot-see, must go!" *Boom-boom.*

When we tried to cross the footbridge, a policeman waved us away. Roy turned into the darkness, following the river upstream to the narrow span of the railroad bridge. I was alarmed to find myself leaping from tie to tie over the rushing water. When I caught up with him at the far end, he was confronting a sentry.

"Clergy," Roy was saying. "We're clergy and we have urgent business up the hill."

"Nobody can cross the river, Reverend." He was young, courteous, a probationer, but he was resolute, his billy club a closed gate. "I'm sorry, but I can't let anybody pass either way."

We heard a voice from the walkway below the trestle and, looking down, saw Joan, armband gleaming.

"Did you see anything in the park?" Roy called.

"It's got to be the Guard," she said. "I counted sixty men."

Roy looked thoughtfully at the sentry and then said, "I'm sorry about this, but I have my orders too." Crouching, he sprang, catching the man at his waist so that he tripped backward over the track and tumbled down the bank.

We were away before he cried out, scampering through a

grove of pines while Joan went on with her report. "I didn't see arms, but they're carrying packs and wearing those space hats. I followed them for a while. They were coming down Riverside, single file."

"Toward the field house," Roy said, "and the armory."

We halted in a grove of trees, momentarily hypnotized by the sight of the torchlit parade coming through the darkness toward us. There was a sound of a window shattering somewhere up the hill, and a drum beat out a funeral cadence while the body of marchers swayed and fattened, gathering in the onlookers and coming on across the slope of campus toward the riverbank.

Zach was at its head in black cap, fist raised. Beside him, Deerslayer, naked but for his shorts and black headband, dark skin glowing with sweat, jigged and flapped the yellow-starred flag of the Vietcong. Around him, a dozen fists pumped toward the charged sky.

Roy watched them pass and then fell in, waving, calling someone by name, then dropping back to repeat it, letting him know he was here. Joan and I followed.

As the van entered the broad approach to the Iowa Avenue bridge, we could see that three state troopers waited there, big men in campaign hats, trying to look casual, as though it were just a good-natured ball-game crowd, but they were stiffening as they watched the parade's approach.

Under the traffic light at the far side, the dozen students of the roadblock were standing, waving encouragement, when the militia appeared. They came at double-time, a file of a dozen men, from behind the impacted traffic, street lights glinting on their bubble headgear.

When they had formed a phalanx across the far end of the bridge, the chanting of the parade—"Rot-see, must go! Rot-see, must go!"—wavered, and the van hesitated.

"The fool sheriff," Roy said, "is going to try to stop us here."

The head of the parade was only inching forward now, the chanting replaced by shrill cries of "Pigs! Pigs! Go home, pigs!"

The line of militia stood at ease, hands clasped behind their backs, shoe sole to shoe sole, a fence from one rail to the other.

Their capsuled heads gave them an astral look, put their humanity in doubt.

No rifles or small arms could be seen, but each carried a knapsack, a green pouch slung from a shoulder strap. It was big enough to contain a small weapon, tear gas, or Mace.

"This is Sheriff Titus speaking." The voice came from a loudspeaker on the nearest police car. "We are acting under orders from Governor Ray. There is a curfew in effect. Students must return to their quarters. You may not cross the Iowa River until eight A.M. no matter where you live. If you're over there, you will have to spend the night in the east side dormitories."

There was a moment's silence, followed by a girl's strident cry: "Pigs! Pigs! Fuck all pigs!" And in the same moment Deerslayer dashed across the intervening space to snatch at one of the green pouches. He was caught by two of the militia.

Deerslayer's captured cry, "Come ON!" drew forth two more marauders and one, a wild-haired girl, pulled a knapsack from the back of a struggling militiaman. Opening it, she held up the contents, a hero sandwich and a crimson can of Coke.

There were cheers. The comic relief brought forth a surge of good nature, and beside me Roy said, "I take it back. Titus is no fool. He only looks like one. That's brilliant. It's farce. They love it." He clapped his hands.

The crowd surged forward now, through the line, which yielded with surprising ease, the militia allowing themselves to be danced against the bridge railings. For an instant exuberance filled the night.

But now a second line of defense appeared. Three firemen, booted, helmeted, appeared at the edge of the footwalk, hugging the brass nozzle of a hose. Seeing them, the march, now only paces from the west shore, uttered a rollicking sound, that of a holiday throng debarking at a vacation island.

They had begun to run toward the outstretched arms of the roadblock when the firehose burst forth with a stream like a ram, staggering students against one another, thundering on the drumhead, plastering Deerslayer and his flag, sending a girl sprawling in its wash, and provoking cries of outrage.

The parade's van was backing away, pressing against the forward thrust of the march. One of the roadblockers was seen crouched over the hose and stabbing at it as two troopers ran to seize him.

He was pulled clear but not before he had punctured it twice, leaving behind a pair of fountains that distracted the firemen at the nozzle. Another and then another roadblocker pierced the troopers' cordon. One, astonishingly, had found a hatchet and left a welling gash in the firehose.

As the stream at the nozzle languished, spilled away, a great shout went up. There was an excited thumping of the drum as the parade surged forward, turning into Riverside Drive and setting off toward Grand Avenue and the field house at its summit.

"I want to get to the armory before they do," Roy said, and Joan and I trotted after him, following a path through a ravine, then higher along flights of steps onto a terrace in front of the field house. Every window of the huge building was dark, but as we tried its doors, finding them barred and chained, a pair of men came toward us, shining a flashlight beam on each of us in turn.

"There's a curfew," a voice challenged. "You're not allowed here."

"Can you hear that?" Roy asked. The parade's clamor was rising toward us, the drumbeat now accompanied by a horn, four blasts to underline "Rot-see, must go!"

"Tell them about the curfew," Roy said. "They'll be here in a couple of minutes."

The light went out.

"Is the armory open?" Roy asked.

"Open, Father?" The voice had turned respectful.

"If it isn't," Roy said moving off, "we'll have to open it."

Roy began to trot through the darkness toward the armory entrance at the far end of the building, but he stopped suddenly, crying out, "Who's there?"

Peering into the shadows on our right, we saw glints like fireflies.

Roy asked the silence again, "Who's there? Speak up."

The Melrose Avenue street lights were reflecting on Plexiglas domes. There were dark shapes too, restless with waiting. A flashlight lit our faces, and a voice asked, "Where'd you come from, Father? Down at the river?"

"What's going on?" Roy asked. "What are you doing here?"

"Waiting for them."

A file of uniformed men stood along the wall and under the rounded arch of the armory itself, where its doors, wide enough to receive a truck, were firmly shut.

"Can you open those doors?" Roy asked. "Have you got the key? Let's save them the trouble."

"We can't do that, Father. There's government property inside, guns in the lockers, ammunition, pyrotechnics."

"Good. Can you open the door?"

"No, I can't. I wouldn't if I could. I don't have the authority to do that."

"Get it," Roy said. "Get it before it's too late."

There were lights behind us and, turning, we saw that the parade's forerunners, a police motorcycle and a jeep, its searchlight probing the roadside, had emerged from Grand Avenue.

A moment later the parade appeared. Shambling drunkenly, it seemed to gather itself and then plunge into the parking field, setting an errant course for the armory doors.

There was an infinity of students. In the sporadic torchlight they looked three-quarters naked. Their random cries spun together, wove into a chorus, and then into a profound, awesome shout of triumph.

As it rose around us, the armory wall and the whole parking field suddenly went bright as noonday, cutting off the shout as though with a knife. From the crenelated battlement overhead, three floodlights bathed the façade and the ramp, where a score of helmeted militiamen stood like statues.

The army of students confronted this reception in silence. Two militiamen guarded the armory doors. The others were spaced evenly along the front of the building, each with the same bold spread of legs. From each shoulder hung a businesslike M-1.

"The dumb son of a bitch," Roy said. "I knew it."

165

Deerslayer broke the interlude, running forth with his Viet-cong flag streaming. He sprinted along the wall, whooping eerily, causing the sentries to shy. He went dancing up the ramp toward the armory doors, then scurried back to the cover of the crowd, where some laughter erupted and then shouting.

The drum began to beat and some stones, gravel from under-foot, rattled against the armory doors like the rain's first patter before the thunderstorm.

A first torch flew overhead to land at the foot of the doors. Instantly a sentry stooped and flung it back. It landed in the clearing between the ramp and the surging front rank of the crowd. As it sputtered, a second torch landed alongside and several figures ran forth to add fuel.

Zach made a circuit of the mounting bonfire and climbed the ramp. He called out in his hoarse voice, "We've come to bury our dead tonight!"

"Right on! Right on!"

"Who's going to help?"

The wild-haired girl came to stand beside him, raising her fist as she shouted, "Whose side are you on?"

I was surprised to find an anxious-faced Gus Drinker stand-ing with us, scarcely recognizable now in khakis and shirt with rolled sleeves. Roy was saying to him, "For God's sake, Gus, can't you call these guys off? Can't we open the armory?"

"No," Drinker said, "we can't. I've been trying for an hour. The governor tells me it's just a few hoodlums. I wish he could see this."

The SDS sound crew was dragging an amplifier up the ramp, and the first chords of a guitar twanged out on the night, start-ing a chorus of "Freedom! Freedom!"

"Will you *speak* to them, Gus?" Roy asked. At Drinker's nod, Roy walked toward the ramp, where the girl was bawling into the microphone, "What do we say to the army? What do we say to the war?"

Roy interrupted the circle of waiting speakers behind her to speak to Zach. The bonfire, now consuming planks from a fence and a camp chair, was sending aloft a spark shower, and in its light I could see Zach refusing him. Deerslayer dramatized this with a war dance, waving the flag in Roy's face, but Roy was persisting.

Holding up a single finger, Roy was shouting, "One minute! One minute!" He made a comic figure in his big boots, long, hairy shanks, and tattered shorts topped by the dickey and round collar, but at the same time a heroic one. He was pressing them, calling in his debt.

In the next instant Roy had the microphone and was holding up both arms for attention. As the din abated he cried out, "I'm with you. Anybody knows me, knows that. We all want the army out of here."

There was some spotty cheering.

". . . the Guard off the campus. Now! The governor doesn't understand that. We want to send him a message tonight that he won't forget, a message that says this is our place and not the Guard's. They're the ones who have no business here."

In front of me a flash went off, and I saw a photographer crouched there, winding in a new frame.

"Did you see that?" I asked Joan. "I think he's made the papers again."

"Yes," she said. "He does know his minute."

"But before we do," Roy went on, "let's hear what Gus Drinker has to say. He's here with us." Roy pointed him out, hands in his pockets, grave as a mourner. "Will you listen to Gus?"

There was a confused cry from the back, where people could not see what was going on. Someone in front shouted, "Yes," and Gus took uncertain steps to join Roy on the ramp but when he was recognized, the president coming to thwart them again, there was a groan of protest.

Deerslayer menaced him with his flag. Shouts of "No!" grew into a clamor. When he accepted the microphone and tried to speak, saying, "We all know what's happened in Ohio today . . ." it was lost beneath the outcry.

Gus Drinker made an appeal with outstretched arms. He cringed as he was struck by pebbles and then a blood bomb, a flying sack that exploded on his chest, staining his shirt red, then another full in the face. When two sentries rushed to protect him, he allowed himself to be led away to a rising chorus of boos.

The chant "Rot-see, must go! Rot-see, must go!" resumed.

Now Zach and the others scuffled around Roy, trying to wrest the microphone from his hand, but he clung to it, dodging and straight-arming them, shouting, "All right, now we've brought the war to our place. We're all at war tonight—and some of us may die in it. Is that what we want—war and death?"

There were cries of disappointment and disapproval. "Go home to Jesus!" and "Tell it to Spiro!" they called out to him. Roy's voice rose to meet that of the crowd. "If you're against war and death," he cried out, "pray for peace now! Pray for peace! Will any of you pray with me to stop the war? Will you pray it to yourselves now? Will you pray it out loud with me? Please, God, stop this war!"

He put the microphone in his pocket and, spreading his arms wide, shouted again, "Please, God, stop this war!" and then again until a few voices joined in. The third time, there was a small chorus with him.

Three of the speakers closed on him and as Zach tried to take the microphone from his pocket, Roy retrieved it, tried to speak into it, but finding it dead, tossed it away.

Roy began to shout, "Believe in the power of prayer for Christ's sake. You want power? Is that what you want—power to change the world? Power over these guns? Then pray—and God will give it to you!"

The SDS speakers were struggling over the microphone, which squawked and thunked, but Roy's voice carried over its sounds.

"I'm going to open my church," he called out. "If you follow me there now, we'll pray together for power. We'll pray together until we get it. We'll open every church in town and fill them with people praying for the power of peace. Who'll come with me?" He looked around the crowd. "Will you?"

From the rear of the crowd came a confusion of shouts, but the front line stood immobilized. Behind Roy the struggle among the speakers had ceased. Even Zach, clutching the microphone to his chest, seemed to hold his breath.

It was Deerslayer, still waving his flag, who made the first move. He took a step toward Roy and said matter-of-factly,

"Come on, then." Falling in beside Roy, he set forth. Together, they walked into the crowd.

Immediately Zach's voice resumed speaking, as though what we had just witnessed was a trivial interruption. But the crowd was parting for Roy, and as Joan and I followed him and the waving banner, others joined in, making a thin file that snaked back through the crowd.

A drum was coming along, and it began to beat out a brash, military cadence. The column, with Roy at its head, drew clear of the demonstration and became a parade of sixty or seventy persons counting out the cadence. Then a girl's voice began to sing, thin and unsure, but gathering to itself a ragged but joyous chorus: "Onward Christian soldiers, marching as to war . . ."

Glancing at Joan, I saw that her eyes too swam in tears.

The band that followed Roy up Washington Street would not have filled Trinity Church, but its departure seemed to turn the tide of the demonstration.

As though the brute will had been cloven, the group was dividing into lesser ones. Behind us I could hear an assortment of new rallying cries. On the bridge, the troopers made way for us, and I heard the shouts of "Drinker's house!" and "Downtown!"

When I caught up with Roy, I said, "You may not have stopped the war but you busted up this battle."

Roy grinned. "When they wouldn't hear Gus, I got mad."

Joan had run ahead to open the church. As we reached the public library on College Street, I could see her framed in the doorway.

Roy was welcoming the marchers in, encouraging the uncertain ones toward the front pews, when we heard a shout of "Look!"

There was a new light in the sky, and everyone going into church now turned to see what was happening. At the foot of the hill, the Rhetoric Building was going up like Vesuvius, shooting sparks, turning the town into a momentarily gorgeous, magenta inferno. Magnetized, we all left the church and began to walk toward it.

XV

Ayear later, in early June of 1971, I returned to Iowa City
on a mission. As the white barns in their green cornfields
rose up to meet the plane's lowering wheels, I could feel my
ticket. It had been bought by my diocese and it weighed against
my ribs.

I was recalling the morning when we had stood against a
rope to view the smoldering ruin of the Rhetoric Building. It
lay in its coffin, a charred martyr of excess. Under the eyes of
a fireman, an instructor was sorting through the sheaves of
scorched pages from a file.

There was revulsion on the faces of bystanders, but even as
we all shared in that we sensed a correctional purpose to this
pyre, the kind of awful crisis that is necessary to recovery.

That morning's *Daily Iowan* had printed a photograph of Roy,
in his peculiar costume of hiking boots, cut-off jeans, dickey,
and round collar, pleading with the crowd at the armory. It
became a symbol of the swinging hinge of community feeling,
the moment when the university began to heal its war wounds.
That night Roy won back all the credit he had lost in the pre-
ceding year.

What I had not known until Laurence Givens invited me to

Newark for lunch was how far Roy's redemption had gone.

"It doesn't surprise me that Roy's become something of a hero out there," Laurence was saying. "He's a magnet. He draws attention and sometimes it's favorable. You know him better than anyone—Joan excepted, I daresay. Has he really grown up, Ethan? Has he turned into an oak while my back's been turned?"

"He has some oaken qualities . . ." I sensed my words were being weighed and I chose them carefully. "Courage. A nose for injustice. An ear for hypocrisy. And he puts more weight on them than most of us."

"But what, Ethan? Not quite solid? Still erratic? That tendency toward the extreme?"

"Bishop, you know Roy's nature perfectly well, but the Iowa experience has vindicated him. I don't know anything quite like vindication for bringing out a man's judiciousness."

The bishop was cutting a spear of asparagus into three equal lengths and he nodded in agreement. "What do you think he would do with wider responsibilities?"

"Grow with them."

"What would you think of Roy"—the bishop's bright blue eyes searched my face—"as Bishop of Iowa?"

I laughed.

"Yes, it is far-fetched, but you know it's a possibility. Tom Sewall is sixty-eight. He's so brave about it, you don't notice, but his health is poor. The Parkinson's is pronounced. It's hard for him to walk, even to sit for any time. He's in constant pain. He must retire soon. He wants a coadjutor to come in with him and carry the burden."

"He's thinking of Roy?"

"I don't suppose Tom Sewall believes there is any more likelihood of it than you or I. The heroism in campus battles may impress some laity but it cuts precious little ice with the clergy there. There's not a liberal among them. It's a diocese of small-town parishes, all conservative, all Republican. Hard to imagine they'd go for Roy at all. Tom knows that perfectly well."

"But he's proposing him?"

The bishop nodded. "He's one of four candidates. A gesture perhaps, an approval for Roy, who's going to need all of that he can get to have any sort of future there among the orthodox. It's also a tweak for the House of Bishops, me in particular and Joe Brace, who hasn't forgotten Roy's visit to Alabama. Tom has his own mischievous streak."

"If nobody votes for him it won't be much of a tweak."

Laurence Givens examined the length of asparagus on his fork. "I think it would be a mistake to write him off too quickly. Tom's a beloved man. His clergy will certainly weigh his feelings about a successor. And I'm not fool enough now to underestimate Roy Train, particularly a new one. Men do change, take on spiritual strength. Has that happened to Roy? What sort of bishop *would* he make?"

In a rush of candor I said, "When I was with Roy last, the question that kept rising in my mind was whether you can keep faith with God when you break it with your wife."

"Really?" The bishop sat back in his chair and folded his hands. "Well, that's not so uncommon as we'd like to believe, but it's hardly an asset in a candidate for Holy Office, is it? What was this? An infatuation?"

"A woman he'd been working with in the peace movement. A lawyer. They'd become very close."

"And you're sure about it?"

"He told me. I met her."

The bishop sat frowning at his glass. "I don't know exactly what to do about that"—he took a sip of the wine—"except propose that you go out to Iowa for a week or so and see what's going on."

Immediately I was overwhelmed by misgivings about having revealed this privileged information. In my eagerness to be honest and accurate, I had stumbled into a bed of muck. I felt as soiled by it as if I had been a party to the adultery. In the week between my betraying Roy and my boarding the plane, I had tried and failed repeatedly to wash it away.

We bounced on the runway of the Cedar Rapids airport. As our velocity spent itself and we turned toward the terminal, I was hoping it would be Joan come to meet me.

Roy was at the gate, a little heavier but boyish as ever. He did a little jig when he caught sight of me, and as we reached each other, he embraced me and took my bag.

Walking toward the jeep, he said, "Joan wanted to come too, but she had to go over to the school. They wanted to talk to one of us. I won, on the grounds that with this dog-and-pony show I'm in, I wouldn't be seeing so much of you."

"Campaigning? Is that what you're doing?"

"As if I were running for the Senate, stumping the parishes around the state, Ankenny to Waterloo. Bean suppers and the United Thank Offering. Hard on the stomach and the corners of the mouth, but actually I love it."

"You sound like a hopeful candidate."

"I am—in spite of the odds."

"What are they?"

"One in ten. One in fifty. What does it matter? Making book and picking winners is God's business. All I have to do is run."

"You want the job?"

We had turned onto the familiar two-lane road to Iowa City, and he drove along swiftly, swinging out to pass a tractor and slower cars. "What I have to do, I can do better from the cathedral. That's all, really, except that Tom would like me for coadjutor."

"He thinks your chances are better than one in fifty?"

Roy shrugged. "Tom knows his clergy. They're Anglicans, every one. Not my kind of guys."

"The laity then?"

"I don't worry about it. I'm running on faith."

"That God wants you for Bishop of Iowa?"

He smiled. "We'll have to see about that."

"What sort of God is that, Roy, who wants you to run for bishop? Is that the one within you?"

We drove in silence for at least a mile, and I thought he was not going to reply. Then he said, "I'm sure God is different for each of us, and that doesn't matter so long as we believe. What does matter is that He, or She, be of high quality and wholly yours. Then you do the miracles. Maybe not mountains. Moving the Adirondacks would be abusing the easement. But a good-sized hill. Easy."

"Your oarsman? The man who came for you in the boat?"

Roy shook his head. "Not remotely human. Not substance but idea. Inscrutable. Ineffable. No more possibility of our grasping God's nature, to say nothing of finding the words to describe it, than there is of a mosquito's conceiving the nature of his, I mean her, victim. Less. A mosquito probably *smells* something delicious. Maybe she could describe that to a friend, and maybe tell about your neck too, as a vast, succulent landing field, everywhere a spring of lovely red Burgundy. But with our measly five senses we can't know a thing about God."

We were following the river into Iowa City, passing students on their bicycles, clumps of them waiting at street corners for a bus.

"And Brenda?" I asked. "Are you still seeing her?"

Roy scowled at me. "You know, you're getting to be a Pecksniff, Ethan. Beware. It's a trap."

"It concerns me, Roy. It worries me that it doesn't worry you."

"That's true. It doesn't . . . because the flesh doesn't *matter.* It's just the tinder, the kindling wood that gets the real caring started, the lasting spiritual fire."

"You have a lasting fire with Brenda?"

He gave a hopeless shake of his head. "Come on, Ethan, try to understand. Brenda's a political woman. She sees Christianity as politics, Jesus as a political leader, a superb one. He ran for Messiah as an outlandish, scarcely credible candidate, and He won with the biggest plurality ever. That's a pragmatic approach to religion, I admit, but it's historically true and there's nothing wrong with getting God elected. I believe in that too."

"I thought it was pure faith you counted on, not politics."

"Both," he said. "You have to have them both to get where you're going. From the beginning, when I thought the idea was just a joke, Brenda took my running seriously, reminding me that races don't always go to the favorites and that even losing could be good for me."

We had reached the center of town, where students were

crowding the entrance to the bookstore with armfuls of their old texts and bearing away packing cartons. Roy's ambition came as no surprise, but I could scarcely believe his welcoming the manipulations of Brenda Hutton, his blindness to the damage he was doing to his wife and children, nor how he had muddled it all with misguided belief. On the drive from the airport all the guilt I had brought along had melted away. I did have a mission here.

As we passed Trinity Church, Roy was describing the other candidates, "The clergy's choice and all-round favorite is Paul Hershey. He's a conservative from Saint John's, Toledo. Then there's Bill Krueger from Saint Thomas's in Little Rock. He's progressive enough to take the moderates. Charles Forward is from Saint Paul's, Wheeling, another conservative, more so than Hershey. He'll have the High Churchers—but then Brenda goes on to show how I can run behind them all during the race and then take 'em in the stretch. Brenda talked me up to a woman who happens to be on the bishop's nominating committee. So when I told them what a poor risk I was, Mae Showers spoke up. 'Mr. Train,' she said, 'we all know who you are and what to expect of you. Your candidacy is needed. This, if you like, is a call.'"

"That was when you agreed?"

"I was standing in the Trinity Church choir when this fierce old woman spoke to me as if she didn't expect an argument. The idea wasn't crazy at all. Doors, cathedral doors, were swinging open. I did have to run."

I heard Joan's voice when Roy and I were mounting the rectory steps. It came from behind the fig tree and impatiens that screened an ell of the porch. She was sitting on a slatted wooden swing, hands clasped, speaking earnestly to her son. Beside her, ten-year-old J.J. stared at the empty glass in his hand and picked with a thumbnail at its decorative border.

J.J. saw us first and jumped up. "I don't know," he cried. "Anyway, she's a dirty liar. I wasn't at any *movie*." He glared at us, his delicate child's face coarsening with resentment. Then he ran as if escaping from a trap, calling back, "She blames me for everything. She's always getting me in trouble. She's an old bitch."

"What a welcome," Joan said unhappily. Putting out both arms, she gave me a distracted kiss. "I'm sorry, Ethan."

"You didn't make out too well at school?" Roy asked.

Joan picked up the empty glass. "I'll tell you how it went at school. It seems that during the noon recess J.J. took off on his bike and didn't come back for two hours. He missed his science and math classes, and when Nancy Singer asked where he'd been, he told her he'd been here."

"And he hadn't?" Roy asked.

Joan shook her head. "I'm not happy about *that*, not one little bit. I guess he was downtown at the movies. A teacher thinks she saw him with a bunch of boys coming out of the Astro, which he was just denying."

"Maybe it was another kid," Roy suggested. "Maybe the teacher does have it in for him."

"Oh, Roy, don't say that. Nancy Singer isn't a petty woman. He sasses her and she does ride him for it, but not vindictively. She's not out to *get* J.J.—but she needs our help with him."

"We do our best."

"We do? Then it's your turn."

Roy's eyes rose toward the rectory's upper floor. "Okay," he said reluctantly.

Watching him go, Joan called after him, "Talk to him, Roy. Get him to tell you." But Roy did not acknowledge this and soon we heard his voice rising somewhere within the house.

"Poor J.J. isn't doing well at school, and Roy's impatient with him," Joan explained. "He expects so much and at the same time doesn't give him any attention until there's a crisis." There were wails above us and Joan shuddered.

I said, "I was hoping you'd come to meet me. I'm feeling a little guilty about the visit. I want to explain."

"What about it?"

"I have an assignment. Laurence wants to know about Roy and his chances of getting elected."

"That's easy. They're about the same as that camel's getting

176

through the eye of a needle. Tell Laurence so and then stay for the convention. It's only ten days off."

"I could. My deacon's standing in, and there's no Communion on Sunday."

"Good. And you know what J.J. could use right now?" She glanced upward, where all was silence. "A first class godfather."

When I had settled in my room, I went back down the hallway to J.J.'s door, behind which he was drowning his troubles in rock music. I tapped, then tried the knob, to find it locked. "It's Ethan," I called. "I have something for you, J.J."

When he opened the door, he looked me over suspiciously but seeing that I was bearing a gift, admitted me. He unwrapped it quickly and seemed disappointed to find it was merely a harmonica, though it was a gleaming chrome one I had found in the cutlery shop at LaGuardia.

J.J. sounded a few chords, then frowned.

"Give it here," I said and found I could blow my way up the scale. After some fumbling, I was able to recall the opening bars of "Yankee Doodle," which brought the slightest smile to his face. "Kids used to play these a lot," I said. "I guess they're out of style now."

"They sure are."

"I had a friend who could play Beethoven on his."

When I returned his harmonica, J.J. climbed onto his bed. "You going to hang around a while, Ethan?" he asked.

I folded my arms and leaned against the door jamb. "Do you wish I wouldn't?"

"I don't care."

"Was the movie any good?" There was a fortifying of J.J.'s face, but I insisted. "The one at the Astro."

"It's *Big Jake*, but I didn't see it."

"Weren't you there?" When again he didn't reply, I said, "I'm just curious. I'm not going to rat on you, J.J. I'm just exercising my godfather rights."

He put the harmonica to his mouth, blew, and then sucked back a chord.

"That's the half-tone," I said. "You get a half-tone when you inhale."

"I was up at Ehbe's, the record shop," he said. "They had the new Neil Young. They just got it in." His face darkened, as if he already regretted the confidence. I did not press my luck further.

Dropping the harmonica on a shelf, J.J. reached beyond to the stereo and turned up the volume.

I nodded at the textbooks on his desk. "What are you doing for school tomorrow, J.J.? Do you have to read something? Write something?"

"I did it. It was easy."

"That's good. I'm glad the work's easy for you."

"Boring too."

"A lot of it is," I said. "I'll see you later."

The next day I went along with Joan while she did some errands. As we sat waiting in the parking lot of the Longfellow School and Joan spoke of how the election absorbed Roy, seemed to draw him ever farther from her and the children, I gave in to my own temptation and decided that she ought to know the truth.

"Have you spoken to Laurence yet?" she asked.

"I told him he needn't worry, that Roy thinks he has a chance but really doesn't. The clergy want a conservative bishop, and they see him as a likable, slightly loony radical."

"No, there's not much ground for his optimism."

"I'm worried, though."

"Really? What about?"

I looked into her dear face with its faintly amused and curious expression. She turned to watch the schoolhouse door, which had opened to release a romp of sixth-graders. I thought, I cannot say this. The words will not pass my lips.

A teacher in a gray skirt caught at a passing child, held his hand long enough to speak to him, and I thought this must be Nancy Singer, for the child, released, now coming down the steps, was J.J.

"Because Roy's unfaithful to you," I said.

As J.J. spotted the car and came trotting toward us, Joan did not take her eyes from him. "Is it Brenda?" she asked.

"Yes. Did you know about it?"

"Not in words. Nobody's said them. I haven't said them to myself." She opened the rear door for J.J. "But I guess I did *know.*"

Minutes later, Susan hopped down the steps and climbed in beside J.J. On the way home, Joan spoke to the children, asking what they had done in school, but once she touched my knee and said, "Thanks, Ethan."

Later, I was stricken to think how I had risked my friendship with Roy and to suspect that my affection for Joan had triggered it. I kept the sense of betrayal at bay by telling myself I had done Roy a necessary if painful service. He must not risk his great marriage further nor continue to see Brenda unless he was making a joke of presenting himself as a candidate for a bishop of the Episcopal church. Now I had to tell him what I had done.

At five-thirty I heard the jeep come into the drive and his voice calling cheerfully that he was home from the hustings. But by the time I got downstairs a few minutes later, he had left. He had told Joan that he had work to do, and she guessed I would find him in his office at the parish house.

I walked slowly down College Street in the soft spring evening. Shafts of lavender and gold from a lingering sun played on the children swinging and crying out to each other in the park and on students loading a canoe onto a car rack. The beauty of it only deepened my foreboding.

The parish house was open and I went along the corridor to the rector's office. Its door was unlocked but Roy was not there. A framed photograph of Joan stood on his desk. Smiling from beneath the brim of a ribboned straw hat, she looked on the disorder of his books and papers, the typewriter with half a page of sermon notes.

The telephone startled me. It rang persistently for a minute, but I did not answer it. I was sure that Roy was with Brenda.

Some low lights were on in the parish house lounge, but it

was empty, as was the corridor leading into the church. I passed the coatracks, the stacked metal chairs, and paused to look at the Christian education pamphlets in the rack and to read the notices on the bulletin board of a pancake supper and an organ recital.

I pushed on the swinging door that opened from the narthex into the nave and saw that the church was dark except for the last gray light of evening falling from the clerestory and the narrow windows into the churchyard. It was still as the center of the earth.

As my eyes became accustomed to the shadows I saw that a figure knelt at the altar rail. I took a step forward and the door banged behind me, but the figure did not stir. Head bowed, hands folded, he seemed carved from stone.

When I realized it was Roy, I slipped back out the door, closing it softly, and left the church.

Roy turned up for supper in an exuberant mood without evidence of his meditations. He talked about his trip to Waterloo earlier; how an old woman had said to him, "You don't look like a bishop to me but I don't put much store in looks. It's the sound of a man's voice that tells who he is, and I like the way you talk. I'd come to hear you preach."

The best news, though, was about his principal rival. "Paul Hershey made a big hit while he was here last week," he said, slicing another piece of the pork, "but nobody noticed that Jean wasn't having a good time. She has a family-counseling practice in Ohio, but it turns out she'd need a license here. She found she can't get one without a degree. Brenda doesn't think she'll come."

The name that Roy had dropped so casually into his account seemed to resonate and give off a sulfurous smell at the table, but he took no notice and went on. "If Paul drops out, I'll have a damned good chance. Better get on the bandwagon, Ethan, before the crowd."

I did not go with him to Ankenny the next day, but he returned at six, a little drunk on his campaign elixir, to tell us at supper how he had won new friends in the farm communities, ridden a combine, and planted a quarter acre of seed corn.

I asked him to come for a stroll with me and we set off into a town that had been emptied by the graduation exercises. Our footsteps sounded in empty streets.

Peering at me, Roy asked, "What is it, Ethan? You're a tower of disapproval tonight."

"I'm working up my courage, Roy. I have some things to tell you and none of them are pleasant."

"Oh?"

"You know that Laurence sent me out. He's very curious about what's going on here."

"What are you telling him?"

"That you're a very dark horse."

"Not so dark now. If Hershey drops out, I'll have an even chance against Krueger. Laurence had better not write me off. Nothing he can do about it anyway"—he smiled but was partly in earnest—"if God wants me to have the diocese."

We were alone in the street and I knew the moment had come. All doubts, all qualms vanished as I put a hand on his sleeve and halted us on the street corner.

"I don't know if you mean it, if you truly believe that God is with you now, but it's not true. You've been seduced. This woman has convinced you that you have a chance to be bishop when you don't. You seem to have lost all judgment, Roy. But that's not the worst of it. You're cracking yourself in half. You've poisoned your marriage. I asked you last year and I ask again. How can you do that to Joan? How can you do that to yourself?"

Roy backed away in dismay.

"Joan knows now. I've told her." I said it in a whisper, but it echoed all around us in the street. "Joan is my friend too, and I cannot possibly share in deceiving her, any more than I can tell you less than the truth."

We stood facing each other without saying a word. Three students passed, eyeing us curiously. Then Roy took my arm and started walking slowly up the street. "I wouldn't have done that to you, you know, no matter how wrongheaded I thought you were."

"Roy, you cannot offer yourself as a candidate for bishop of the diocese from the center of an infidelity. For God's sake, I'm trying to help you. You must not go on seeing Brenda. You must talk it out with Joan. You know I'm telling you what's right and what you must do."

"But you *don't* know!" he shouted to the sky. "You don't know enough to interfere. You don't know enough to pass judgment. Who the hell do you think you are? Brenda's not a replacement for Joan. Brenda's my strategist and she's essential to me. Jesus, Ethan, you don't know anything about marriage."

"What should I know?"

"That there are times when you go on instinct, what *feels* right . . . not how it might *look*."

"Can you tell that to Joan?"

"Ethan, Ethan," he said, his voice softening, "you've got so much to learn about love." Ahead of us there was a glow from the lights of the hospital on the far side of the river, reminding me of the night we had watched the flames of the Rhetoric Building light the sky. "But stick around. You will. I know you will."

It is customary for the candidates in an election for bishop coadjutor to await the results at home, but as the day of the special convention approached, Roy spoke of attending. He said, "As a member of the Iowa clergy I've got a vote and I'm going to use it."

He expected that on that Thursday morning of June 17 we would go to Des Moines together. But on the day before, Joan, while doing the family laundry, discovered a small envelope in J.J.'s pants. Within it were five rose-colored capsules.

"I have no idea," I said when Joan showed them to me. "Would they give him medicine at school?"

"Cold remedy," Roy said. "One of those antihistamines. Did you ask him?"

"I'm going to," she said, "as soon as he gets home."

When J.J. was confronted with the crumpled envelope and its five capsules, he seemed puzzled and then resentful. Resolutely he said, "I don't know what they are."

"But where did you find them?" his mother asked. "How did they get into your pocket?"

"They were in my locker."

"And you just put them in your pocket? You didn't ask anyone? You didn't show them to a teacher?"

"I was going to. I just forgot."

Returning from a meeting with convention delegates at Trinity, Roy had a harried look. When Joan asked him what he was going to do about J.J. and the capsules, he replied, "You know, Joan, I can't really deal with it tonight. Gus Drinker tells me I'm queering my chances by turning up at the convention. I want to get some other opinions."

When we were at supper, tensions layered the dining room, kept us quiet through the meal, and erupted in a quarrel between J.J. and Susan over the size of their desserts. Irritably, Roy sent them from the table.

Several times he went to answer the telephone and after one of these calls he said he had decided to spend the night with Tom Sewall. Saying he would see us in Des Moines in the morning, he drove off.

With the children now quiet under the spell of television, Joan and I sat on the rectory porch. She was in the slatted swing, rocking it slowly, touching her sandaled toes to the deck. It was in both our minds that Roy was with Brenda.

"What time should we start in the morning?" I asked.

Joan shook her head. "I want to clear up the rosy capsule mystery if I can. First thing I'm going to talk to Nancy Singer."

I was thinking how alone and vulnerable she was that night, swinging back and forth in the encroaching dusk, melancholy eating her spirit. I yearned to be able to restore her. I imagined myself rising from the deck chair where I sprawled, going to her on the swing, touching her hands, and holding her in my arms, reassuring her that my own love was stronger than ever. But I did not.

After an awkward good-night kiss, I went off to my guest room bed in great confusion. I lay there, miles from the envelope of sleep, thinking how my love for Joan was the essence of my relationship with both Trains. It was the energy that ran between all three of us. Roy was as aware of it as Joan, and it was as innocent as it was strong, because we were friends. We were both priests and Christian friends. That was a double harness for desire.

Nevertheless, I was having a fantasy in which I tiptoed along the quiet hallway to try her bedroom door and to talk in whispers at the edge of her bed until I was invited in. As I slipped toward the erotic dream, I heard the soft turning of the doorknob, a rustling, and saw a whiteness.

Beside my bed a real Joan asked, "Hello—are you awake?"

"Of course," I whispered.

"May I come in?"

She shivered, nestled beside me, and I took her into my arms, wrapping her in warmth, and heard her sigh with satisfaction. After a long time I dared to kiss her, felt her lips soft against mine, taking their shape. With my fingers I traced her forehead, eyelids, the bridge of her nose, telling myself this was Joan lying beside me, the dream of over a decade now a truth, frightening me as though I had emerged in the middle of a myth, fulfilling the oracle's words to beware the wish lest it be fulfilled.

I thought of Roy too and wondered what he would think if he knew that here at home his wife lay sighing in the consolation of his best friend's arms.

My hand fell away from her warm flesh but she reassured me with a light touch to my chin and, so emboldened, I stroked the lattice of her back, felt her buttocks firm under the batiste of her nightgown, but I was too awed by this collision of dream and reality to feel the hoped-for eagerness of my loins.

Fear scampered along my spine, devouring every carnal sprout until Joan drove it away. With a courtesan's touch, loving, desirous, she coaxed, beckoned forth my hiding beast, and as midnight chimes tolled in a distant campus tower, I entered her triumphantly, gorgeously, sank my whole being in her willing body.

Waking from the sweetness, feeling her leg's tangency to mine, hearing her breath, feeling it soft on my shoulder, some strands of hair falling all along my upper arm, I heard a distant warning like the qualm a passenger feels at the ship's first languorous roll as it sets into the sea.

This woman beside me, no longer aspired to but familiar, accessible, and in some way mine now, was going to require, in the morning's bright light, a commitment. It was up to me now and I knew I must not falter.

"Awake?" I whispered.

"Yes."

"What are you thinking?"

"That was lovely."

"Yes," I said. "What else? Are you wondering what we do now?"

"No."

"I was . . . about how you were going to like Rutherford."

"Oh, Ethan." She began to laugh.

"I'm serious. There are good schools."

Her hand, smelling faintly of L'Heure Bleue, covered my mouth. "You are a darling," she whispered into my ear, "but a hopelessly crazy one."

I was afloat, magically, precariously, over an abyss, sensing that in the next instant whatever was supporting me would give way. I dared to ask, "Why?"

She sighed. "Other loves," she said.

"Yours?"

"No. Yours."

"I have none."

"The church, for one."

"All right, but she's a forgiving one."

"Roy, for another. You couldn't lose that love, could you?"

After a moment I admitted, "No."

"We'll have troubles enough with just this hour." Her fingers touched my lips before she slipped away.

Alone again, I fell into troubled sleep, a dream in which I was tumbling down a rock face, grasping at roots and crumbling shale, ever faster toward that same abyss. I woke to a reality as terrifying as the dream.

For more than ten years I had believed in an inaccessible

Joan, a Joan who, if she were miraculously mine, even briefly, would make my life heroic. The discovery that I could possess her and it would change nothing, that I was the same man shorn of that illusion, had shattered me. I was no longer sure what was real or false.

I could see a dark vein in my life begun with a first envy of her. Was that as innocent as I had supposed? Could I have done otherwise? Now I gathered in the depth and the many layers of my betrayal. Even as I let Roy remind me of the need to be on familiar terms with wrongdoing, I knew that I was damaged in my core. My soul was sick.

I got out of bed and, like a child, knelt at its side to ask God for His forgiveness, His mercy, His strength and direction.

In the morning I rented a car and set off alone for Des Moines. Driving the interstate through a quilting of blue-black fields with their sprouts of new corn, I hurried. As I watched for police cars in the mirror, the needle of the speedometer touched seventy-five and then eighty. Atonement lay ahead. I needed Roy's presence and his hand.

Booths promoting denominational publications and societies made a midway of the Fort Des Moines Hotel's second floor, and here in the throng's midst I had a glimpse of Roy's thinning crown.

He was in a ring of delegates surrounding the table of the Iowa Council on Christian Youth. I took in its aggressive display. Overhead a bannerlike sign read: AT THIS MOMENT THE AVERAGE AGE OF ACTIVE IOWA EPISCOPALIANS IS—and a screen projected 57 in electric numerals of a vivid green. On both sides placards read: THE YOUNG WANT TO KNOW ABOUT LIVING. ARE WE WITH IT? ARE WE TALKING THEIR LANGUAGE?

Behind the desk Brenda Hutton, looking more utilitarian than I remembered her, was passing out questionnaires, and she thrust one into my hands before recognizing me.

She withdrew it, then relented. "Keep it, Reverend," she said tartly, "only don't fill it out. We don't want Jersey in our survey."

Roy turned from another conversation to say, "I'm glad you got here. Where's Joan?"

"She was going to school. She wanted to talk to someone about those capsules."

"But she's coming?"

"I don't know," I said.

Roy was perplexed. Then, sensing my discomfort, he peered at me closely. Perhaps I only imagined it but he seemed in that instant to see into the depth of my heart and read it perceptively. There was a squint to his eyes and half a smile on his mouth. I felt a relief.

"She'll get here," he said.

There was an exclamation around the Youth Council table and I saw that the average age had risen to fifty-eight. As Brenda began to explain how the age meter worked, Roy drew me away.

"Was that some kind of joke?" I asked. "About my not filling out her questionnaire?"

"She has a sharp tongue when she's thwarted, but it's me she's pissed off at." He frowned at the table, where Brenda was talking earnestly to an elderly priest. "I found her tacking up that poster of me, the one in front of the armory. Can you imagine?"

"She's determined. I'll give her that."

"And never knows where to stop." Roy shook his head. "It takes one to know one. I don't need any more ballyhoo. It's getting serious now." He bounced on the balls of his feet. "Tell me what you think, Ethan. Would I be a mistake? What kind of bishop *would* I make?"

I know he intended this facetiously, but I said, "I think you'd be a good one," and I was wholly, fervently sincere. "I've had my doubts, as you know, but today I have none. I think you'll make a lot of people angry before you're through, but it'll be worth it."

"Good," Roy said. "That's good. Why today?"

I took a deep breath. "I've had my own night in the sea."

From beneath his heavy brows Roy's brown eyes searched my face. He nodded. "And someone came for you?"

"Yes."

* * *

187

I tried to call Joan from the hotel, but the rectory number did not answer, and as I backed out of the phone booth I nearly collided with the Bishop of Iowa. He was moving across the lobby alone, swinging his gold-banded cane, and I stepped back to let him pass. He paused and, not quite locating me, asked, "Is that Ethan Soames?"

"Yes, Bishop," I said.

"I'm on my way up to my room, Ethan. Will you come along with me?"

Riding up in the elevator, the bishop was smiling, nodding agreeably as he told me, "Well, it's official. Did you hear? We've just had a very gracious telegram from Paul Hershey, telling us he's withdrawing his name."

The bishop led the way onto the thirteenth floor of the hotel, saying, "No, I can't say I'm displeased, though we're all quite stunned. There'd been a rumor, you know, but then nothing came of it. At this late hour we're in some disarray, I'm afraid."

"It should mean a better chance for Roy."

"Ah . . ." He smiled at his cane as it explored the corridor ahead of us. "You wouldn't think our early fathers had much to do with Roy's chances today, would you? But they do, Ethan. They have their resurrection every time we elect a bishop in Iowa. In their hearts our priests are still High Church. We're keepers of the flame and we keep it guttering in spite of all the drafts from the world outside. They're fond enough of Roy, but they have difficulty visualizing him at Diocesan House. You can't blame them, really."

The door to the bishop's suite stood open on a gathering of clergymen, twenty or more. It was hot in the room, and many were peeling out of their jackets while two of them struggled with windows. Conversation died away as Bishop Sewall entered.

"It is warm in here, isn't it," the bishop said as he settled into a chair. "Please make yourselves as comfortable as you can. Perhaps we will be able to share our views very quickly."

The bishop's chaplain was first to speak. "Paul Hershey has asked me to apologize to you for his procrastination and to say he feels we'll be better served by Charles Forward. He wants you all to know that he believes a younger man is preferable, that Chuck is full of vigor, and at the same time he's old prayer book."

There was a murmuring and the bishop asked, "What do we think of Paul's suggestion? Some of you know Forward. Is he your man?"

A voice at the far side of the room said, "He was at Virginia with me. Chuck's a serious man."

"One can easily see," the bishop said, "why Paul regards him so highly. You don't suppose—what an insidious thought—that Paul was running interference for him?"

A voice said, "That did occur to some of us, Bishop."

"But you were too generous to say so?" The bishop smiled. "Well, this is a time for candor. I know many of you admire Chuck Forward. Are there similar feelings for Bill Krueger?"

"Chuck Forward has integrity," said a bearded priest. "He's dedicated to our traditions. He knows the value of our rituals. We can't ask for better credentials."

Bishop Sewall raised his hand to forestall further tribute to Forward. "Should I take it, then, that we don't want to give further thought to our evangelicals?"

An embarrassed silence filled the room. Understanding passed like a collection plate from face to face. A voice said, "We all know Roy Train, Bishop. He's a wonder boy."

"But is anyone going to vote for him?" the bishop asked.

A voice in the back said, "I love Roy Train, Bishop. He tells us a lot of truth. There are times when I think he has a touch of the divine fire in him . . . but you know we'll never vote for him. He's a troublemaker. Wherever he goes, there's damage. That's not forgotten."

The bishop conceded, "Yes, it's true, Henry. I'm not urging Roy Train on you. I agree it would be foolish to ignore the record, but now the field is changed I want to be sure we don't slight anyone. What damage did you have in mind?"

"We all know he was fired from his parish in Jersey City. He got his congregation angry with him and in the middle of it went off to Alabama. He got in another quarrel down there and fouled up the bus-in. A man named Cooley Smith was killed."

"Ethan?" the bishop asked. "Are you here?"

"I'm here, Bishop," I said. "I'm Ethan Soames, rector of Saint Luke's, Rutherford, New Jersey, and I'm Roy's friend. I was at seminary with him and I liked him from the moment I first saw him. I worked with Roy at Saint Simon's, and what you say about him is all true. There was a lot of trouble there, but he didn't bring it. He found it there. Every urban problem was on Saint Simon's doorstep, made worse by a changing neighborhood. Saint Simon's was marked for closing when Roy went there, but it's open today, a live mission to live need. I was in Alabama with him too, and you're right again about his getting into trouble there, but even the angriest felt in the end that he had acted with courage."

A tall, white-haired priest with dark-hollowed eyes asked resonantly, "Mr. Soames, from what you know of Roy Train, would you trust him with your diocese?"

"If it wanted new vision, new vigor."

"But would you vote for him?"

"Without a question."

There was a brief silence, broken by Bishop Sewall. "I would like to say this in Roy's behalf—that from what I can make out, he is more interested in the future of our church than in its past. He appeals to young people in a very realistic way. I think that's a consideration in our election today, and if I have a further service to perform for you it's this. If Roy became my coadjutor, I would be here for as long as the good God feels it necessary to see an orderly, reasonably decorous succession."

The bishop rose and said, "But in the end we must each vote the urging of our own conscience. God bless you all." His hand trembled in the blessing.

The councils and the caucuses had broken up and were spilling into the corridors. As I searched the jostling stream of delegates for Roy I could feel new uncertainty and tension in the air. Grave faces gave way to lively ones. Voices were high and urgent. A little bedlam was loose among us.

I squeezed into an elevator and was spewed out into a lobby

that surged with unpredictable tides and undertows. Although I looked everywhere, I did not find Roy until a quarter to three, fifteen minutes before the balloting was to begin.

It was to take place in St. Paul's, which at that hour was still relatively empty. As I walked down the center aisle, my footsteps echoing on the stones, I saw him. He was kneeling at the baptistry altar.

I sat in the nearest pew and soon he came to sit beside me, smiling and saying, "You know, I think it's going to be okay."

"What's going to be okay?"

"The outcome. However it goes. I have this understanding now. Do you want to pray with me for a minute?"

We knelt together in the pew. I asked forgiveness for myself, and for Roy I asked guidance.

The sounds of the resuming session, a shuffling and snatches of amplified conversations, rose behind us, and we stood and found the delegates assembling in their pews. A voice was calling for the tellers to report to their captains.

Just within the main door at the back of the church I saw Joan. She wore a dark blue dress with a white collar. The sight of her, dark hair brushed to a gloss, face pale, ethereal in the smoky light, pierced me, a cold blade of remorse.

The feel of her body clung to my hands and I could not purge my memory of the moment it had absorbed me. I wished it were not so and prayed once more for God's forgiveness.

She came toward us at a steady, confident pace. Her beauty, poignant as ever, had taken the shape of my own capacity for betrayal. My instinct was to escape, and in fact I was taking a couple of retreating steps when she called, "Ethan, don't go."

As she reached us I looked into her eyes and found them glowing with understanding. They seemed to say that she was a partner in all my pain and confusion. I had no idea what allowed her to contain and master these feelings, but I knew it was not lack of concern.

The balloting was begun in a businesslike way. The chairman, a dignified lawyer from Dubuque, read the telegram from Paul Hershey and then accepted a motion that nominating speeches be dispensed with. He ordered the ballots to be passed out to the delegates, and as this was begun, he read the names of the remaining three candidates.

Roy moved to the most obscure pew and, Joan between us, we sat down there. It was in the shadows at the back of the church but we had a view of the long table set up in front of the pulpit, where the ballots were to be counted. Up front, waiting there, was Brenda Hutton.

Once marked, the ballots were passed to the end of each pew, where they were gathered in baskets and brought forward to be sorted and counted. While this was proceeding, I saw that Bishop Sewall had taken the chair at the far side of the altar. His collar gleamed, immaculate against the purple, and surprisingly he held his crook loosely between his knees. His head bowed slightly as if he might be constructing the scene in his mind from its tense whispers and hurrying footsteps.

The counting and recounting was under way at the table. As the three piles of ballots grew, I could see that the one nearest me lagged behind the others. I noticed Brenda frown as she touched it, and guessed it was Roy's. When the last ballot had arrived and the final count taken, the near pile had risen but I did not think it had attained the level of the other two.

The head teller wrote the results on a card. A whispered conference took place around it before he carried it up to the chairman's podium on the altar's top step. The silence in the church was complete while the chairman frowned at the card. Then, instead of reading the result into the microphone, he crossed the altar and spoke into Bishop Sewall's ear.

The chairman returned to his podium and for a moment nothing happened. It was as if the bishop was unclear as to how to proceed. Then he rose slowly and, using his crook to feel the way before him, went to the center of the altar and came down its steps, gathering momentum as he came.

He hesitated at the mouth of the aisle and then started down it as though he were heading for the entrance door. When he reached the last pew, he paused, tapped it twice, and turned in, brushing people's knees as they did their best to make way for him.

Bishop Sewall kept coming until he reached us. With a wide smile he held forth his crook. Roy rose. Roy faced him with glistening eyes, then closed them to grasp the crook beneath his bishop's hand.

XVI

HOME again in Rutherford, hustling to catch up with parish work, I found that the Iowa experience had the quality of a dream. Joan's glistening hazel eyes, so ardent about life even as it failed her, haunted me, as did that radiance in Roy's face when he grasped the outthrust bishop's crook. However, it was my unfinished godfatherly business that prompted a call to Iowa City.

Joan answered the rectory phone. "They turned out to be red zingers," she told me. "Speed. J.J. did have a story to tell about them. He didn't tell it at once for fear we'd make him give up his music, but it seems that all the kids have been taking pills. J.J. says he's been popping those things for months. He told Nancy Singer they helped him do his homework and kept him from being bored in class. He'd taken some money from the house and done some shoplifting to pay for them. Imagine, Ethan, *our* child. It's not going to be easy, getting J.J. off them, but there are methods, and I'm learning them—at the hospital and the prison, where they have programs for dealing with addiction."

"Is Roy taking it seriously now?"

"Very."

"Then the future's not entirely black, is it?"

There was a moment's hesitation before she said, "Oh, Ethan, don't Pollyanna me."

"I'm being realistic. There's so much hope in what you've just said, hope for you and Roy as well as J.J."

"I guess that's true. In fact I'm beginning to see the disaster as beyond J.J., beyond us. It's everywhere. You have no idea of the kinds of drugs these kids are taking—not just pink pills either. And some are even younger than J.J. It's really frightening."

"Maybe there's a way to turn poor J.J.'s trouble into a blessing. Pull out the stops. Maybe you can help more than J.J."

"Maybe. Maybe I can."

"You can do anything you choose."

"Some days."

"Did J.J. say anything about a "Rhapsody in Blue" record?"

"You gave him that? Yes, he was playing it yesterday. I wondered."

"Tell him I'm having my troubles with the Grateful Dead, but I'm trying."

"Oh, I love you, Ethan."

A month later, Joan astonished me by turning up in my office in Rutherford. With her dark hair cut smartly short, wearing a sleek raccoon coat, she looked happier and younger than when I had seen her last.

She shone in my reflected delight, and as we hugged each other, I asked, "How come? Can you stay a while? Can I give you tea? Can I show you my house?"

"I was hoping for both," she said, "and I want to tell you about Diocesan House in Des Moines. We moved in last week and it's quite wonderful—Frank Lloyd Wright's idea of how an oatmeal tycoon should live, but very adaptable to a bishop."

My rectory had been built and furnished by my predecessor, Alan West, and his wife, Sophie. I had always thought of it as a primrose in the weedy garden of Rutherford suburbia, but Joan, once inside, raised a critical eyebrow.

"It's a pretty enough house." Her eyes lingered on the Currier and Ives prints and soapstone fire-starter. "But I was hoping to find you in here."

"It's true, I'm not wild about knotty pine but I've got so I hardly see it."

It was five months since I had last seen Joan. Passing time had diluted the guilt I felt when I thought of her visit to my bed. When some daytime sight or sound reminded me of her, I remembered our lovemaking as a fantasy. In the night, on waking from a dream perhaps, I could relive that hour with pleasure. Knowing it was as much a part of Joan's secret experience as my own made it glow like a pearl.

Entering my bedroom with its view of St. Luke's steeple, a bright sun drawing a tree's shadow across my candlewick bedspread, I felt a stirring of that nighttime pleasure and a tension too in knowing it was not to be acknowledged. I was relieved to find that Mrs. Corwin, the housekeeper, had tidied up.

Admiring the four-poster, Joan sat upon it and put out her hands to try the mattress. Smiling, she said, "You're an attractive man. You must have plenty of opportunity."

I blushed and recovered. "Saint Luke's has its share of matchmakers and divorcées."

"Any lucky enough to be invited up here?"

"A few."

"I worry over whether someone loves you as you deserve."

"Whatever, no one has become a habit."

She cocked her head. "Why is that? Do you punish yourself?"

"Some. You think I shouldn't?"

"Not to excess, surely."

"You don't have a scourge?"

"Not like yours. Not nearly so large and itchy." She looked at the toes of her Cossack boots, tapped them together, and then gazed at me quizzically. "I don't think you know the womanly secret."

"I'm sure I don't."

"We're not so different. Our flesh has a will too. We need to be loved. We starve without that and we can't bear its antithesis, which isn't hate, you know, but being ignored."

In the moment's silence I almost reached for her hand, which still lay invitingly on the bedspread only a foot from mine, but when she spoke again the impulse withered.

"Do you know what I mean, Ethan? What's *your* need?"

"There are times when the idea of having a woman is overwhelming, but just any woman would be far worse than none at all."

"And you never come across the one who will do?"

"Yes. I have. She's unavailable."

Joan blushed, sighed, and as she rose and turned toward the door, gave me a cryptic smile.

In the kitchen with its seagull tiles gleaming in the afternoon light, I made tea and we sat on opposite sides of the counter while Joan made friends with Ambrose, my good gray cat, and told me what had brought her to New York, and from there to New Jersey.

She had spent three days in Harlem at a hospital youth center and she had called on half a dozen foundations, asking funds for her drug program in Des Moines. She had given it a nickname, Hoist, which had stuck. She had rented an old house near diocesan headquarters and installed a clinic for the treatment of young addicts. It was staffed and was treating patients. The high schools were welcoming her educational program.

"And is it better between you and Roy?" I asked.

She thought for a moment and said, "Yes, it is. You were right about that. Roy thinks Hoist is wonderful. He's making it into a diocesan project." Her face brightened with the pleasure of insight. "It's extraordinary how Roy is drawn to accomplished women. Any woman who can do something well fascinates him, not because he likes the competition, not *that*, but because she's running as free as he is. I think that makes her a sexual challenge. But then comes the ambivalence." She laughed. "He isn't wild about having one of them in the house."

On my doorstep Joan looked full of new hope, and she seemed grateful to me for it. Her farewell was a warm smack of a kiss. When she was a couple of steps away she turned back to say, "And listen, Ethan, don't ever have any regrets about us. I couldn't bear that."

"I promise."

* * *

Just before Christmas of 1971 I had another call from Joan. She was in New York again. Her plan of going home had been thwarted by the storm that was snarling air traffic in the Midwest and had closed the Des Moines airport. She was going to stay until morning and would welcome my advice about something. Was there any chance of my coming in for dinner?

The ladies of the altar guild were counting on my help in setting up the crèche in the baptistry, but I made my excuses. As I was changing into my good suit I heard a winter storm warning on the news and decided against driving into town.

When I boarded the bus, snow was falling, and once we were on the skyway it grew heavy, choking the traffic, so we were an hour late into the terminal. Cabs were not to be had, and I took the subway to Seventy-seventh Street, then walked along deserted sidewalks through a fierce wind and mounting drifts to an address on Madison Avenue, a new apartment house.

I took an elevator to the penthouse. Joan, answering the door, looked at me in surprise. "I tried to reach you and say not to come. The storm's getting much worse. We won't find any restaurants open . . . but come in and help me. I was just looking in the cupboard for something to open."

She had borrowed the apartment from a man named Waldrop. He was with the Rockefeller Foundation, which had just agreed to help fund her program. The Waldrops had left earlier in the day for Barbados. Through a huge sheet of glass we could see lighted towers aswirl in curtains of snow. Horns and wheels were still as the storm settled in, muffling the city in its huge white tent.

Exploring the Waldrops' kitchen, Joan told of how successful the former addicts were proving as therapists. "It's that they've found a way out. I think it's working, Ethan, and I've just talked two foundations into funding us. We can buy the house now, hire some new people, reach out to the whole state with an education course. I'm really terribly excited about the way it's going."

"Just as we'd hoped."

She had been on the point of opening the refrigerator door,

but she paused, somewhat crestfallen, a question in her wide, hazel eyes. "Well, not quite," she said.

"Roy?"

"Roy's coming to New York for the quarterly meeting next month and figured he could see the foundations while he's here. But there were a dozen possibilities, all of them chancy. Waldrop was going to be away and I knew it couldn't wait. We had quite a quarrel over it. Can you believe that, Ethan?"

"That he wants to take Hoist away from you?"

"Lest it—you know—turn my sweet submissive head."

"I don't believe that."

"Well, something's wrong. He wants Hoist woven into his diocesan outreach. That's okay, but what he means by that is whatever isn't *his* idea about Hoist is disloyalty. The friction grows, becomes a presence in the house, sits down with us at meals, climbs into the car with us, like a guest of mine who's overstayed his welcome."

"Your having some public attention is new to him. He'll get over it."

"I don't think he will. Roy doesn't get used to what he doesn't like. He makes it a cause for his own disloyalties."

"Infidelities?"

"Oh, I don't know." She sighed. "And I don't want to know. I have such a callus on that part of my heart, I scarcely feel anything there anymore." Whereupon she opened the refrigerator and stooped to peer into the shelves. "Oh, good," she said. "Guinea hens. I feel sure Malcolm Waldrop would want us to have them."

Watching Joan's hands at work now rinsing lettuce, hearing the jingle of her bracelets, I was floating back to Christopher Street and the night I first coveted her, thinking what a magical life it is that takes its sweet time with so improbable a wish but then grants it.

I was so enchanted with this sense of a past recaptured that I touched her arm. Joan looked up, smiled as if she had expected that, and when my fingers encircled her wrist just above the bracelets she gave a final blot to the leaves and sighed. Then she turned and faced me with her questioning smile and, slipping her arms beneath mine, laid her head on my chest.

For the longest time we stayed so, listening to the drumming of our hearts.

"What are you thinking?" I asked.

"Oh, Ethan, what are we to do? *You're* my counselor. Tell me."

"What do you want to do?"

"Talk forever. Tell you all my troubles."

"We'll do that."

"I hadn't counted on this, though." She was looking at the window, where the snow beat with determined fury at our warmth. "What kind of fate sends this our way?"

"The driven snow?"

Pulling away, Joan tossed her head. There was a trace of mischief in her eyes, but as she turned down the flame under a casserole her face became serious. "I don't want to cause you suffering, Ethan."

"You can't, dear Joan. Nothing you can do or not do."

"That's not true, you know."

"In my whole life I've never been happier than I am now. Nothing can change that."

She thought and then reached for a bottle of wine, handing it to me with a corkscrew. "But I know how the guilt gets to you. You were gray with it that morning in Iowa. I thought you might die of self-hatred on the way to Des Moines."

"I recovered. And it never reached you."

"Of course it did. And the worst of it was being your temptation."

"Did you have any remorse that morning?"

"Not much, which is surprising, because I have a pretty strong sense of morality."

"How *did* you feel?"

"As if I'd been swimming in a clear, green sea. What do you make of that?"

"Happiness."

I lit four candles on the dining room table while Joan set out our plates side by side so that we could face the great window and watch the swirling dance of the blizzard against it.

"Tell me about us," she said at last. "When are we okay and when are we not? What is sinfulness? Is it this—what we're thinking about now?"

"No."

"What is then—just the fucking?" She said the word with a laundering candor.

"Well," I said on a long breath, "the fucking *is* a sin. That's in the book and there's no denying it. But . . ."

Joan filled my glass and her own. "Go on. But what, Ethan?"

"To be alive is to feel strong emotions, and loving someone is the strongest. It can't be evil. It *can* be the opposite. I'm certain that virtue, in the sense of sticking to the old rules, is changing. All things must. What's right and what's wrong is more flexible now, more difficult to grasp, but no less Christian. I'm sure of it."

Chin in hand, she studied me. "That's Roy talking."

"That's me talking."

"Then you've come—I was going to say fallen—quite a way since last summer."

"That's true."

"As a priest"—she edged forward on her chair, warming to her inquiry—"you condone certain sins in your own behavior?"

"My vows can't change my humanity. I have to deal with my desires. Denial is no longer a solution."

"But as a *Christian?*"

"Oh, the Golden Rule still holds. There's no room for a humanist argument there. How am I doing unto Roy? How do I reckon with the Decalogue? Well, I can't. Even thinking about such perfidy is against the old law. I'm a man and a priest in the twentieth century, and I think Christ's truth allows me some leeway in those Mosaic prohibitions."

"Do you preach that?"

"From the pulpit? Hardly?"

"Couldn't we just say that we're asking forgiveness in advance for the wickedness we intend? We know it's wicked—and not the least of it is that you're settling an old score with Roy too."

"Am I?"

She nodded. "As surely as I am."

"You're making it hard for me."

"It's hard to be super-honest with each other, but I want us to be. That's important. I want you to know about my fury with Roy."

"His having other women?"

Joan shrugged. "They're part of the message that tells me I'm dispensable, that I'm getting in his way, that he can get along just as well without me."

"I'm sure Roy knows in his heart that he can't."

She shook her head. "He used to know that, Ethan, but he doesn't anymore."

"What changed him?"

"His mission's got the better of him. This is a frightful thing to say, but Roy no longer knows where he stops and God begins."

The storm had quieted and Joan rose to go to the window and look out over a still, white city, ghostly and deserted under a phosphorescence from the skies.

When I went to stand beside her she asked, without turning, "Will you stay with me?"

"Yes."

"But you mustn't suffer. We love each other tonight. I need to be cared about and wanted—enough to last a while."

Beside me, Joan slept, her breath soft against my shoulder. By moving my hand half an inch I could touch her warm flesh. The smell of it—moist, perfumed, musky—was overwhelming, rising in my nostrils like a sweet, suffocating mist.

Through the curtains light was emerging, enough for me to see that the hands of my watch stood at a few minutes past six and that Joan's face on the pillow was a study in peace. In the soundness of her sleep, all care had vanished and she was herself as a child, an exquisite adolescent at play in an old dream of expectancy.

It flitted through my mind that I might reach out my hand, that it would be no unkindness to wake her into a real embrace and prove my love again with lips and hands and the storm of wanting her.

Then I heard a distant sound, some sigh of machinery, perhaps a rising elevator. In the growing light now revealing the shapes of bureau, lamp, and telephone, I felt a warning, a finger's touch that grew into an arm of injunction. A sac of qualms burst within me, flooding the vessels of my body, setting them pulsing with reproach and loathing, shrinking me into myself.

To survive, I had to be out of this bed and this place. I needed to be alone. Here I would smother within the minute.

As I stood at the mirror putting a comb through my hair, Joan woke. "Going?" she asked.

"I think the storm's over, and I have a service at nine."

"Come here," she said, rising on an elbow, blinking away sleep. "Sit down for a minute." I sat beside her on the bed and she looked into my face. "Oh, hell, you've gone gray again. I'm so sorry."

"I can't help it."

"I know."

"I'll get over it. You take getting used to. Will you be back soon?"

"Maybe."

"You'll let me know?"

"Yes." The kiss was tender but shadowed, short-changed. "I'll let you know."

Her eyes, the knitting of her brow, her smile, showed her concern for me as she watched me leave.

It was late June before I heard from Joan again. She wrote to say that she would be spending the next week in Washington, helping to prepare testimony for a House committee on the nation's health.

I took it as a query of my intentions. After several of my messages had gone unanswered, I reached her at a Washington number. She was far busier than she had expected to be but she agreed to have dinner with me the following Wednesday. I reserved a room at the Mayflower. On an upsurge of purpose, I asked for a good one with a double bed.

Joan had suggested a restaurant on Q Street called the Mandarin. Waiting for her, I was buoyant. I felt youthful and sure of myself.

She was half an hour late. I was in the foyer looking out when she arrived. The car was an inconspicuous gray one from a government agency pool. She stood for a minute talking to the driver before turning to enter the restaurant.

We settled in the booth I had reserved and took some time for reacquaintance. Under a businesslike gray suit she wore a white silk blouse, and only one bracelet circled her wrist. I felt a new sureness in the way she leaned back against the red leather banquette, arms folded, taking me in with affectionate curiosity.

She seemed comfortable and knowledgeable here. Already she had a little of the federal mannerism, a distraction, as if her thoughts lingered on some business of the day. It was this air that drew me to the point as soon as we had ordered our meal.

I touched her hand. She smiled in response and I took my courage from that.

"When we were together in New York," I began, "you were pretty gloomy about you and Roy."

Joan's eyes slipped away, went roving among the tables before she said, "The prospects haven't changed much, but I have. I'm grateful to you for that, Ethan. I'm feeling much better about myself."

"We didn't talk about the possibility of a divorce, but you must have thought of it."

"Of course."

"What would be its effect on Roy?"

"He'd be shaken." She weighed her water glass. "But he'd survive. Roy's always self-contained, self-propelled, and there are always women rushing forth to look after him."

"So far as I can discover, no bishop has ever gone through a divorce procedure. What would be the effect on the church? How would the diocese take it?"

"Oh, Roy will find a way to make them like it. You know that."

"It'll be more agonizing than you and I can possibly imagine, but I have the patience to wait—if it takes a dozen years."

Joan was unprepared. Surprise widened her eyes. Concern tautened her forehead. "Oh, Ethan," she said softly. Her neck bent to a sympathetic angle, telling me all.

"I'd be such a disappointment to you." She took my hands in hers, looked into my eyes, and I dissolved. "Trust me to know that . . . and protect yourself. You're too dear for me to hurt you."

"Why?" I pleaded. I wanted reasons to rub into the new wound of my disappointment. "Tell me why."

She watched as drink and food were set before us. "Because I know what I'm doing with my life now. I'm here to help with testimony for the HEW hearing next week. My days are full and so am I. I feel good about myself in a way I haven't in years."

"But that doesn't explain why. Is there something I don't know? Have you met someone here?"

She looked evasive. Her nod was barely perceptible, but it was like the slamming of a great door. "Oh, Ethan," she said, "spare us, please."

I did as she asked. I spoke with unexpected fervor about the break-in at the Democratic National Committee headquarters and speculated on the possibility that the scandal might cause Nixon's defeat, feeling that if at any moment I paused, I would weep before her.

I had raised my hopes cautiously on the way to Washington. They had become a fabulous structure, a pagoda rising from the Potomac's bank. Now, the next day, as I stood in line at a ticket window in Union Station, it lay about me, so much wreckage on a deserted fairground.

The morning was a rainy one. Low clouds hung over the Maryland tidelands, and as I stared into them from the train window, I knew that I was turning back to a life as predictable as that of Ambrose, my old gray cat.

I was thinking of the inevitability of it too—how it had been only illusion that I might borrow some of Roy Train's galactic course and make it my own.

The illusion itself began to seem less a bad thing than an enchantment. It was as welcome as it had been temporary. Possibility, I thought, is what exalts life, is the wine of it, and a blessing for which to be most grateful.

By the time the train reached Newark, I had restored one old loyalty, several old convictions, and felt a rising of spirits. On the street I found the sun coming out.

XVII

M Y parish duties in Rutherford were routine and predictable, but a few weeks after my return from Washington, concern for a member of St. Luke's congregation took me to the West Coast.

I had not anticipated a California with slums, yet I was entering a neighborhood of littered alleys and derelict rooming houses. Were it not for the insistent, smoggy sun, Venice could have been Newark.

Number 1106 Columbine was three-storied, as dilapidated as its neighbors, but distinguished by a coat of fluorescent lavender paint. At the lower windows shades were drawn.

Over the doorbell there was a crayoned sign, RAINBOW SPIRITUAL CENTER, and on the mailbox a list of names, overlaid with deletions and additions like the growth rings of a tree. Among the more recent, I found D. Cooper.

I rang and rang. When at last the door opened I faced a narrow, rumpled youth in torn undershirt and jeans. His eyes were glazed and irritable, as though I had awakened him.

"Hello," I said. "I'm looking for Dorsey Cooper. Does she live here?"

He weighed the question while taking in my clothing, the

rental car at the curb, my being alone. "No," he said, starting to close the door. "Nobody of that name."

"Wait," I said, "it's right here on the door. Look. She gets mail here. I'm her minister from back east. I've come to see how she's getting on."

He studied the name. "Oh, yeah. She's not here anymore. She went away."

"Where? She must have left a forwarding address."

He shook his head. "She just took off . . . like a bird." He closed the door firmly and I heard the lock turn.

Every sense told me that Dorsey was inside the lavender house. I parked up the block in front of a Mexican restaurant, where a single tree cast its shade on the baking pavement. From here I could see the entrance to 1106 Columbine and note that not everyone was turned away.

In the course of the afternoon I saw a large Hispanic woman with two children admitted, then several pale, pregnant girls waddling awkwardly, a miniature Indian holy man, dark pate gleaming, wearing dhoti and sandals, and then a Nordic giant in sailor pants and T-shirt. There was a tattoo on his left forearm.

It was almost dusk when Dorsey came out the door. She was carrying a laundry bag and her red hair was bound up in a blue bandana. She was barefoot and so skinny in her long cotton dress that I scarcely recognized her.

When she drew abreast of the car, I called, "Dorsey?" but she seemed not to hear. It was as though her own inner music silenced the world around her.

At my second call she paused, turned slowly, and looked into my face without expression. There was a dreaminess in her eyes altogether alien to the spirited girl I had known.

"I've come to see you, Dorsey," I said. "Could we talk for a minute?"

Recognizing me, her face darkened. She shook her head. "No. There's nothing to say."

"There's so much, Dorsey. Give me a chance, will you?"

"You've come from my mom, Father Ethan. You've come to get me."

"She'll come herself, if you'll let her."

"I'm not coming home. Not in a million years. My mom thinks I'll have to, now she's stopped sending me money, but I . . . I can find work."

"She wants you to know that she loves you."

Dorsey denied this with a sullen expression that brought vividly to mind the child of ten, adorned in the rosiest, most exquisite innocence, from which a vixen could spring, her every adolescent hormone in full rebellion.

I remembered going with her mother to Dorsey's school. Miss Morse shook her head over a string of C's and D's and told us, "She's such a quick child—bright, really—but I don't know what to do with Dorsey. When she gets a low mark or doesn't win some game, she's sure it's someone else's fault. She's so angry at any thwarting. It was the gym teacher's telling her she must come in from the playground that caused the incident. No, I *saw* her. Dorsey struck her deliberately. She sees herself as judge, not just of *her* actions but of those around her. She simply can't grasp the idea of another authority."

"It's awfully hard," Jessica Cooper murmured, "for Dorsey, without her father."

"Oh, there's a dozen children of single parents in the class," said Miss Morse, "but Dorsey's grudge is so deep. She can work up this passion for anyone who gives her approval, and then at the slightest criticism she's on fire with indignation. It roars in her like a blast furnace." She cocked her head at Jessica. "I thought perhaps if we could work together . . ."

Jessica looked doubtful. "Well," she said. "Sometimes, from what Dorsey tells me . . . about that gym teacher, I wonder if she isn't more right than wrong."

"Oh, dear . . ." Lucy Morse gave me a helpless look.

The recollection dissolved into a mature Dorsey standing a few feet from me, looking up an empty Venice street. "I'm sorry you came all this way," she said. "I have to go."

But in fact she didn't move. She stood rooted to the pavement, and I pressed this small advantage.

"Why don't you get in here for a minute?" I proposed. "It's air-conditioned. I won't keep you, Dorsey."

Warily she came closer. When I held the door for her, she sat on the edge of the seat, then pulled her bare, soiled feet inside and closed the door after her. She smiled. "It is cooler in here."

"You look a little thin, Dorsey. Are you getting enough to eat?"

"Oh, sure. It's my diet."

"What kind of diet?"

"Oh, you know, sprouts, tofu, herb tea. It's very healthy and I can get it on food stamps."

"I see . . . and save the money for drugs."

Frowning, Dorsey looked away. She watched someone emerge from the door at 1106 and come up the street. It was the man with the tattoo, and she sank lower as he passed.

"Is it marijuana?" I insisted, waited. "Something else? What do you take?"

"Don't ask that, Father Ethan."

"I'm sorry, Dorsey, but I must. We trust you, your mother and I, but we know that when you're on dope you can't take care of yourself. We're scared about it. Can you tell me the truth?"

"The truth . . ." She turned the idea languidly in her mind. "If you want to get to the truth about yourself and the universe, you have to make yourself really open—open to others, open to inner peace. That's the main thing."

"Whatever drugs do for openness, they can destroy you too."

"Not if you know them. They're nothing like alcohol. Alcohol is what's ruined so many people. I *have* done bad things to myself, but I don't anymore."

"Will you tell me about it?"

She shook her head. "You'll tell Mom. She'll get it all mixed up and come make trouble."

"This is between us. I won't try to help unless you ask me."

"I need to find a job that isn't waiting tables. I really hate waiting tables." She looked at the lavender house in a pained way. "I have friends who give me money, only that makes me feel helpless too."

"Is there someone you love here?"

Her sorrow seemed to deepen and she lowered her head.

"But it isn't working out?"

"I don't *know.*" There was self-pity in her voice. "I can't tell.

It's my fault, really. I always want to own somebody, and that's wrong, I know. I can't help it."

"There's someone you don't own?"

"We're meant to share. We can't *own*. It's crazy to think we can."

"But not wicked. It's very human, not wanting to share someone you love."

She shook her head. "You wouldn't understand the things we believe."

"I might," I said. "I'd like to try." I waited a while and then asked, "What do you do with yourself, Dorsey? How do you spend your days?"

"I help out with the group sessions and I work in the kitchen. There's nine of us. I meditate a lot. And I study."

"What do you study?"

"The ways to enlightenment." She looked into the garden of the Mexican restaurant, where a family was sitting down around a picnic table. "I'm not stupid, you know. I'll find some kind of job that's useful and helps people, where they'll let me use my head, and someday I'm going to get my degree."

"Good for you. In what?"

"I don't know. Religion, maybe."

"Religion . . . Well, that would make some news in Rutherford, New Jersey. Wouldn't that be something, Dorsey?"

"I don't even like to think about Rutherford."

This suppressing of her past recalled an evening when Jessica Cooper summoned me to the police station. Dorsey was in juvenile hall, charged with possession of a controlled substance. Pale with fright, yet without remorse, Dorsey told us that when the police came to break up the party they had let most of the kids go but had brought her in for sassing them.

When Jessica asked how she had come to be at a party of seniors, she fumed at the complaining neighbors. "They could have called *us*. We'd have turned the music down. That was mean."

"The neighbors have a right to their sleep," Jessica told Dorsey as we led her toward the car. "And with the boy's parents away, you were just asking for trouble."

"But those cops have no right to come busting into people's houses in the first place, or taking me to jail. I'm just a kid."

When she was seventeen, Dorsey ran away, leaving a note on her bureau that she had joined the mission of the Reverend Sun Myung Moon. Jessica was stupefied with worry. When a week went by without word from Dorsey, I tried to find her through a locator. She had left traces in the settlements at Roanoke and Tulsa, but a whole year passed before I had evidence that, after a quarrel with the leader of the settlement at Phoenix, she had left the movement altogether.

It was August of 1969, the summer of those bloody killings in California by the drug-crazed followers of Charles Manson, and I read their names in the newspaper accounts fearful of what I might find.

When at last Jessica had a letter from Dorsey saying that she was living with friends in Los Angeles but in need of money, we were hugely relieved. "I want you to leave me alone, now," Dorsey had ended her letter. "I need to get my head straight and that means I don't want anything to do with my past life."

Now, with Dorsey beside me in the car, I felt that for the first time I had found leverage and if I was firm enough to provide the authority she both rebelled against and sought, I could turn her life into some useful direction.

"Tell me how you feel about the drugs, Dorsey," I said. "Does it occur to you they may harm you in a way you'll be sorry for? Do you ever think of them as self-indulgence?"

"Oh, no, not that at all." She looked at her folded hands. "Pleasure, maybe. There's a spiritual pleasure in feeling one— in *being* one—with the cosmic consciousness. But you have to be really open to that. I mean, in the kind of civilization we're forced into, you have to have some kind of springboard—you know what I mean?—to get free of the inhibitions, the strait-jacket our society puts us in."

"But you'll be in another straitjacket, Dorsey, one you can never escape. Do you think you can just leave your drugs behind?"

"When I want to."

"A friend of mine in Des Moines has started a program to

treat teen-age addicts, twenty of them, each one lost, written off by the state's Department of Corrections like a bad debt. In eight months she's got half of them back in school or working. She uses a kind of reality therapy. She's found a way for them to face the truth: that they've given in to a power greater than any they have and there's only one slim chance to win their life back."

Beside me, Dorsey was silent, but I could sense an alertness.

"Do you know what that chance is?" I asked.

"Yes."

"What is it, Dorsey?"

"A force greater than their own."

"Do you know what kind?"

"Spiritual."

"That's right," I said. "You do know."

"I know a lot of things. I'm not dumb."

"Okay," I said. "Do you know what you want from life? What it will be like for you in ten years? What kind of woman do you want to be at thirty?"

She smiled, made a helpless gesture. "I don't know. Should I?"

"Do you see yourself with a family, maybe? With a husband and children to love?"

"I see myself with everyone to love."

"What exactly does that mean?"

"It means dissolving my ego, freeing myself from the trap of self so I can reach satori."

"What is that? What does satori mean to you, Dorsey?"

"It's what I said before. Love . . . without any ego in it. Not wanting anything *back* from it. You know?"

"Oh, yes, Dorsey. Of course I do. That's my line, didn't you know?" We stared at each other for a couple of seconds and then simultaneously we smiled.

"You know," I said, "if you wanted me to, I might be able to help you find a job. The one I have in mind wouldn't pay much, but it would be useful and they'd let you use your head certainly. You'd have to leave here, though."

"I'm not going home," she said.

"Would you go to Des Moines?"

"Would I like Des Moines?"

"Some do," I said.

From the Rose Café, a block from the Venice boardwalk, I called Joan Train in Des Moines. When I started to explain my predicament, she said, "But Dorsey sounds just the girl for you, Ethan. Don't you blow it, now."

"Seriously, are you still recruiting young people with a drug history for Hoist?"

"It depends."

"She's packed a lot of rebellion and a little Zen into her twenty years. Along the way she's picked up some kind of mystic grab bag and survived on its contents. She could be ready to make some order there now. Could you find any work for her?"

"I might. We've just taken another house, for intensive care. She could stay there, for a while anyway, until we see how she works out."

"I think if she's put to work Dorsey'll be okay, but there's a certain risk. I'm not saying there isn't."

"Send Dorsey on. Tell me what flight."

XVIII

IN the midst of the Advent season of 1972, Bishop Sewall suffered a stroke, and although he responded to treatment, his doctors insisted on a salubrious climate. He submitted his resignation, moved to a mountaintop near Taos, New Mexico, and entrusted the Iowa diocese to his coadjutor.

Early in 1973 I found an article in *The Episcopalian* about Roy's reopening of the Davenport cathedral. Alongside a picture of a pale, twin-spired building with gracefully arched, flamboyant windows, there was an account of its closing in 1952, when the diocesan headquarters moved from the Mississippi River town of Davenport to the state capital at Des Moines.

"The new Bishop of Iowa," I read, "the Rt. Rev. Royal Train, has renovated the structure and, on March 10, will preach an inaugural sermon from its pulpit. Its subject is to be 'What's New in Christianity.'"

A few weeks later I was startled to see, on a back page of the *Times,* the headline BISHOP LIKENS CHURCH TO SINKING RAFT, WOULD MODIFY TEN COMMANDMENTS.

According to the story, Roy's cathedral sermon had described traditional Christianity as requiring a leap of blind faith, "one that has left many intelligent people feeling derelict, as if floating out to sea on a foundering raft.

"What's new," he had gone on to say, "is a church welcoming the human mind back to the altar. What's new is a concept of Jesus who sees the big sins not as private but as social ones, the corporate sins of war and prejudice."

A further account of the sermon appeared in the religion section of *Time* magazine. When a reporter had asked him if he really intended junking the Ten Commandments, Roy had replied, "Not all. I'm not condoning murder surely, but all good and evil is relative. Making love to a woman who is not your wife is less evil than putting people in jail because they disagree with you."

I guessed that this was a deliberate provocation, that Roy's itch was upon him. Just when I was wondering how soon my bishop would react, he called me.

"Are you in touch with Roy?" Laurence Givens asked.

"I haven't heard from him in months."

"What's got into him? I've been assuring everybody the responsibility out there has sobered him. It seems I'm wrong. Some of the Southern bishops are angry. They're determined to shut him up. This kind of careless sensationalism can't be going down well in his own diocese either."

"He told me he was going to put his diocese on the map."

"Lord!" Laurence said. "I can't believe he has the kind of support out there to get away with this stuff. I'd like to know. Can you find out? Could you possibly go out there and see him, Ethan—remind him that tongue of his speaks for all of us?"

"I think so, Bishop." I turned the pages of a crowded calendar. "I could get away for a day anyway."

"How soon, Ethan? I need to tell Joe Brace we're moving."

"The early part of next week is possible."

"Good. Let me know."

It was Susan Train, now nine, who answered the telephone, saying "Diocesan House" in a businesslike voice. Her mother was away, she said, gone to Washington to help with a drug bill, but her father was in his study. He was meeting with some men from the reformatory at Anamosa, but she felt it would be all right to interrupt.

"You want to come out for a visit?" Roy's voice was querulous, as though the lapse in our companionship was a failure of mine.

"If that's okay. I could come out Sunday afternoon, if I won't be any trouble."

"Of course you won't."

"Will Joan be back?"

"Maybe. If she knows you're coming. I'll tell her. What's up, Ethan?"

"Well, I want to see you both; that's the main thing. But I have a mission too. You can guess it."

"The flak? Last Sunday's sermon?"

"You must be getting a lot."

"Some. But you'd be surprised how much of the response is favorable."

"I'll be bringing some that isn't."

"Yours?"

"Laurence's, for one."

"Laurence is jealous. Nobody comes to hear him preach, and besides, he wasn't listening. The people who are angry simply missed the point. It was about who Jesus really is."

"Joe Brace missed the point. He and some of the Southern bishops say you're losing your grip. Any chance of that?"

"What do you think?"

"By the time these things are reported in the paper, they do seem incautious. I worry about you."

"Come and see. Come and hear me preach in the cathedral on Sunday."

"I have my own service, Roy. I'll be out in the late afternoon. Don't bother to meet me; I'll find my way."

From the airport gate I took a taxi to Diocesan House, the two-story mansion, designed in 1936 by Frank Lloyd Wright, that Joan had mentioned to me. Its leaded windows were brightly lighted and thrown open to an early dusk. From them came amplified blare of rock and roll music. Alighting, I felt the beat through my shoe soles. Peering through a window into the paneled living room, I saw four youths in jeans, T-shirts, expressions of suffering, bent over their instruments, long hair threshing.

They stood in a pool of extension cords whose streams ran across a pale Chinese rug to the room's electric outlets. An audience of three watched from a chintz-covered sofa. There was a tall boy, whose mop of dark hair fell to his eyebrows, and two girls, one large and black, the other pale, emaciated, with yellow hair that appeared wet. All three were transfixed.

I recognized the swaggering guitarist, so absorbed with his fingering, as my godson, the twelve-year-old J.J. Train.

The bell was not answered, but the front door opened to my touch. After I had set down my valise, I crossed the vestibule to look into a large gallery that had been made into the diocesan office. Its several desks and banks of metal files stood deserted, stark under an institutional fluorescence.

A glass-enclosed terrace lay beyond, and by the light from the kitchen windows I saw a long table partly set for a meal. As I watched, a young girl in white painter's overalls appeared, carrying a platter. Her long-legged stride put me instantly in mind of her mother. It was Susan.

"Hi," I said. "I wouldn't have recognized you, Susan, you've grown so."

She came toward me, smiling, putting out a tentative hand. "Ethan. Did you just get here?"

"This minute." I leaned to kiss her. "What's that din?"

"The Weathermen? They're rehearsing. They have a gig tonight, the first they've ever been paid for. They'll be done soon. I promised the neighbors."

A shadow crossed the window light. "Is that your mother?"

Susan shook her head. "She didn't come." There was a plaintive strain in her voice that again reminded me of Joan. As she began to set plates around the table she added, "Daddy thought she might."

"She's been away for a while?"

"Since the end of February."

"Good Lord, what's she doing there?"

"They like her, I guess. She has an office. You can see the Capitol from her window. Mummy wants me to come and stay with her over spring vacation.

"She isn't coming home before then?"

Susan widened her big dark eyes and gave a shrug. "This council where she works is trying to get a bill passed. It takes an unbelievably long time."

I nodded toward the kitchen. "Is that your father?"

"No." She had begun to anchor paper napkins with the table silver against a teasing, southerly breeze. "It's Dorsey. She's making the casserole."

"Dorsey *Cooper*? She's *here*?"

"Sure."

"For supper?"

"Oh, Dorsey lives with us now. She's practically one of the family."

Dorsey, smiling brightly at my surprise, appeared in the doorway. She was drying her hands on a towel. "Hi, Ethan," she said. She wore a brief red jersey, and her neatly combed bright, rust-colored hair fell to bare shoulders. As she leaned to put a kiss on my cheek, I wondered if the sparkle in her eyes was part defiance.

"I work at the hostel, just up the street," she explained. "I'm doing some of Joan's stuff while she's away and being big sister here."

Susan willingly offered herself for Dorsey's demonstrative embrace and added, "We're cooking supper tonight. I hope you like vegetarian."

"I'm going to love vegetarian," I said.

In the kitchen, watching Dorsey lop the greens from a bunch of carrots, I asked, "What sort of work is it you do at the hostel?"

"Counseling, mostly, but I'm keeping up with the field work too. I try to get out there. We have people trouping the state, showing our film and talking to school kids. We go wherever they'll have us."

"If you're going to make a career of counseling, won't you need a degree in social work?"

"I could get one"—she was slicing the carrots into slender rods and arranging them in fans on a white platter—"if I was going that route, but actually I'm thinking of another."

"Which?"

"Remember my wanting to take a religion course? Roy's been encouraging me."

"Here? Do they have a religion department at Drake or at Ames?"

"Actually, I was thinking of seminary." Dorsey gave me a sidewise look in time to catch new astonishment in my face, and laughed. "Oh, Ethan, you don't know the half of it. You were right about a lot of things here. I know what I want now."

"What's that, Dorsey?"

She was shaking her head cryptically as Roy appeared through a swinging door. "If anybody else calls," he announced, "I've left town." Seeing me, he embraced me and danced me across the kitchen linoleum through the swinging door into the dining room, where sounds of the Weathermen pummeled the walls. There, he spoke into my ear: "So much to tell you . . . have to stay a week."

He seized my valise and led me upstairs and into a guest room. I hung up a pair of trousers and carried my toilet kit into the bathroom.

"No Joan?" I asked.

"Joan's AWOL," he announced as he sat on the bed, "and her absence is a big disappointment, I know. Well, it's no news to you. You were down there visiting the hotshot lobbyist having her independence day. So I've had to bring Dorsey in here to look after the kids. It's more than just the times. She's punishing us. I don't know what to make of it, really."

"I can tell you something about it," I said. "It's one of the reasons I came."

"Oh, yeah? Let's get a drink first," he said, rising, and I followed him down the broad stairway of Diocesan House. As we passed the living room, we encountered a blast from the electronic organ, and Roy winced, hurrying me toward the kitchen, where Dorsey and Susan were taking earthenware from an oven.

Roy, taking two glasses from a cupboard, said, "You'll be amazed, Ethan, what these kids can do with pinto beans and cottage cheese. You'll swear you're eating lamb and there won't be a sliver of animal flesh in the whole elegant collation. We're

all going to live to be a hundred and ten, like those Vilcabam-
bians in Ecuador!" Waving at the display on the counter, he
ducked into the refrigerator for ice and soda. "Such an openness to possibility now. Don't you find that? We were always con-
fined by the damned customs."

Following him out the kitchen door, I said, "Well, *you* weren't."

He closed the door of his study behind us, shutting out some
of the rehearsal's insistence, and from a desk drawer produced
a bottle of vodka. The next minute, while I was sipping
the strong drink he had made me, the telephone on his desk
rang. He eyed it suspiciously, ignoring three appeals before answering.

"Speaking," he said and listened for a minute. Shifting in his
chair, he protested, "No, no. I asked if they could not have faith
in an earthly Jesus who used doors and had sexual longings like
the rest of us. *I* didn't say that about the heavy kissing. I was
quoting Philip." He laughed, took a gulp from his glass. "The
point is His being human, His being of *this* world, the one we
know with all its real, human problems, and that's where the
church has to work."

He hung up, frowning at the instrument.

"Somebody missed the point?"

He gave a dismissing shake of his head. "These guys are earn-
ing a living. I can never tell if they'll help deliver the message
or boomerang it. It's a gamble. I generally take it."

The telephone rang again and this time he let it ring, motion-
ing me to follow him. We carried our glasses through the diocesan office and out its door. At the shadowy end of the terrace
we found a pair of wicker chairs and settled in them to peer into
the dusk where a lawn sloped toward the budding orchard beyond.

At this distance the music relented and for a few minutes we
listened, caught up, beating out the rhythm with toe and hand.

"What was the sermon about? Jesus kissing whom?"

"About the earthly Christ, Jesus as man. But of course they'll
remember only the footnote about the kissing."

"What footnote?"

"Really? You don't know what they're finding in these caves, Ethan? All this stuff the church was burning fifteen hundred years ago?"

"Dead Sea scrolls?"

"The scrolls, yes, but now these gospels they've found in Egypt. Philip's tells just how stuck Jesus was on Mary Magdalene. 'The woman who knows all,' he called her. He thought her visions were even better than Peter's. He not only made her a disciple; he singled her out for special teaching. It's not clear what that special teaching was exactly, but he did kiss her on the mouth so frequently that the other disciples complained about it. 'Why do you love her more than us' they asked him." Roy laughed. "And Philip tells us his typically Jesus answer: 'Why do I not love you as I love her?'"

"Good Lord, Roy . . ."

"What's the matter?"

"How can I explain *this* to Laurence?"

"Tell him I'm skywriting. Tell him I'm okay and I'm writing this message in the sky over Iowa, one letter at a time. I'm not finished yet."

"He won't find that reassuring."

"Tell him it'll make sense when it's finished." He was watching Dorsey bent over a lantern on the supper table, coaxing its mantle to a bright, white light.

"Look, Ethan." Dorsey's cheek, chin, and shoulder were dramatically highlighted, the rest of her in shadow. "It's like that painting, you know the one?"

"No."

"In the Louvre. Mary Magdalene." He laughed again. "Oh, the powers of suggestion."

The music ceased suddenly, leaving us in blessed stillness. You could have heard the flutter of moth wings, and it was a moment before a daunted creation resumed its own sounds.

Dorsey was gathering the children, nine in all, around the supper table, and as we went to meet them Roy explained that three were patients from the Hoist program, a few of whom she regularly invited here for supper.

J.J., now nearly man-size, was effusively glad to see me, swaggering some before his friends when I congratulated him on the rehearsal.

"I had no idea," I told him, "you'd become a performing artist."

Delighted, J.J. asked, "You really into progressive rock, Ethan?"

"I think I could *grow* to like it."

"Come hear us tonight then. We're playing our first gig."

"We'll see." I sat beside Roy at one end of the table.

At the opposite end Dorsey was acting as hostess, drawing out the kids on plans for their appearance, which, I gathered, was to take place at a nearby shopping mall in an hour's time.

Again I was struck by the change in her appearance and behavior since I had seen her in Venice. The lassitude, the resentful downturn of mouth, had been replaced by a glowing enterprise. A tanktop sheathed the swell of breasts like a red tulip and in the lamplight her skin was a rich cream.

Roy was still watching Dorsey and J.J. beside her. "My son's having his first big crush," he observed.

"She worries me, Roy," I said. "I feel responsible."

"For Dorsey? But she's a joy, Ethan. We couldn't do without her."

"She's driven her own mother to despair."

"She's an angel. I keep forgetting you sent her to us. But see how J.J. dotes on her. She talked him down off his limb when even Joan couldn't reach him. This band was her idea. She got them this engagement—fifty bucks, can you imagine, for an hour of that noise?"

"She's really useful in Hoist?"

"Of course. Dorsey's having lived through the drug experience is what makes her so valuable to the rest of us. Only an exaddict knows the way out of the maze. I think we should ordain a few." Roy clapped his hands in delight. "Now that would start a flurry in the old pigeon coop."

"Don't even think of it. And is it *wise*, having her here at all, with Joan away?"

"The looks? For the Pecksniffs? Oh, Ethan! Besides, J.J. wouldn't stand for her going."

"He'll get over it."

"Do you ever get over your first big crush? *I* haven't. I was fourteen and she was maybe twenty, Dorsey's age. Her name was Mary and she was blond, the daughter of a Navy officer who'd rented the house next to ours at Falmouth. One night she took me skinny-dipping. She went into the sea first, and I can still see her coming out. She ran toward me across the beach, dripping and naked in the moonlight. 'Feel the duckbumps,' she said, and I did. It was such *pain,* Ethan, not having the least idea what to do next." Roy laughed. "The thought still floods me with sweet anguish."

At eight the Weathermen and their camp followers left us, bundling their instruments into a van and driving off, Dorsey at the wheel. With the house quiet, Roy ignored the stacked dishes, poured us each a brandy, and led the way back to the chairs on the terrace.

When we were settled, I said, "I think you must persuade Joan to come back, Roy, before you get yourself into more trouble."

"I'm afraid that's not so easy." Roy sighed. "What she's up to in Washington is more important to her."

"The Brenda episode is still painful. She can't forget that."

"And she's determined that I don't either. But you know that's not the illness. A symptom, maybe. That's all."

"Tell me about the illness."

He sat for a moment staring into a soft black sky seeded with stars. "My job is the center of my life. Without it I'd vanish, so much mist in the morning sun."

"Yes. It does have to do with that, with what you see as your mission."

"Well, I refuse to give it any such pious name." He waved a dismissing hand. "Let's say my *concern.* My concern, yes, and it's not only that I'd vanish without that but I'm dispensable to it. I can be replaced and I will be if I fail it, neglect it in any way. It's a very delicate bargain I've made with it. Joan was part of that bargain."

"But Joan has no quarrel with your concern, not in itself."

"Oh, but she does, Ethan. Whatever she tells you, I know. These days she has her own."

Roy had finished his drink, and though I had not, I followed him into the kitchen and was surprised to find Dorsey busy at the counter.

"What happened?" Roy asked. "Concert cancel out?"

"No." She faced us solemnly. "They're not playing until nine-thirty, and I thought I could clean up here while I wait." I noticed she wore three narrow, silver bracelets that chimed softly as she loaded the dishwasher.

While Roy refilled his glass, Dorsey said, "If you drink that stuff you won't sleep well. In the morning you'll grouch at the kids."

"Brandy's what you do with an old friend," Roy replied. "It takes precedence over tomorrow's cares. Want any help with the cleanup?"

She shook her head. "I'm going to read Mark." Putting away the brandy bottle, she added, "I'll go for the kids at eleven."

From the terrace we watched a nearly full moon rise out of the misty treetops at the bottom of the garden.

"Dorsey's reading the Gospels?"

Roy was lighting a cigar and he puffed at the flame of a kitchen match until the end glowed red in the darkness. "I've given her some things to study."

"What things?"

"Bonhoeffer, Tillich, Martin Luther King. She's curious about theology, and she takes to it. It's strange how much she knows by instinct. No philosophy at all, but she wades right into Kier-kegaard, and by God, *argues* with him."

"To please you, do you think?"

"For starters, maybe, but she has a clear idea of herself now, a goal."

"What goal?"

"Seminary."

"That's crazy," I said.

Whether it was the cognac or my sense of a failing mission, I spent a wakeful night. Weariness had sent me to bed at ten-thirty but I was kept waiting at sleep's threshold. I heard the van leave and return with Susan and J.J. Later, as the house quieted, there were voices, Roy's and Dorsey's, soft yet urgent, rising at the edge of my consciousness, the opening and closing of doors, and swift, surreptitious footfalls in the hallway. A sense of dislocation, of the serpent lying beneath the innocent-looking stone, led me from one nightmare to another.

The morning was a bright one. I woke to birdsong and the clatter of normality, cars in the driveway, voices, kitchen sounds. It was nearly nine by the time I had dressed and paused at the head of the stairwell. The door of the master bedroom was open, and Roy in crisp white shirt and striped cotton trousers stood at the bureau, reflectively combing his thinning, gray-tinged curls.

Catching sight of me in the mirror, he brightened, turned a shining, fresh face to me. "You sleep okay, Ethan?"

"Some."

"It's going to be a gorgeous day. Why not stick around? Come out to Spirit Lake with me. Meet some real Americans."

"I've got to get back."

"Why the hurry?" he asked.

"A funeral," I said. "There's a man in Rutherford who never liked to be kept waiting. I'd stall him now, though, if I thought I could talk some sense into you."

"I hear you perfectly, Ethan." Roy was groping in the closet, where a few of Joan's dresses hung alongside his suits. "You can tell Laurence that."

"What about heeding me?"

Donning a jacket, he pointed to a copy of the *Des Moines Register* that lay folded on the bedside table. "Sit down for a minute. Read the paper."

Sitting on the edge of the broad, unmade bed was a surprising sensation. Beneath my buttocks there was a stirring, as though I rode some vast, soft-fleshed, thin-skinned animal.

"What *is* this?"

"A water bed. Get yourself one and you'll never have another wakeful moment."

Probing it, I said, "I'd be terrified . . . of drowning."

Roy laughed. "The story's on page two."

When I lifted the folded newspaper, I uncovered a cluster of three silver bracelets. The sight so dismayed me that I had difficulty in concentrating on the article in my lap. It was headlined: BISHOP TELLS OF CHRIST'S LOVE AFFAIR.

Below, I read:

Citing recent discoveries of Gospels suppressed in a second-century heresy hunt, the Rt. Rev. Royal Train, Episcopal Bishop of Iowa, told a full cathedral congregation yesterday that the humanizing of Jesus is an important step in understanding the new church's mission in the world.

According to these early gospels, Mary Magdalene was a follower whom Jesus often kissed on the mouth, thereby offending other disciples, Peter in particular. Mary in turn was outspoken in her opinion of Peter as a man who "hates the female race."

Bishop Train pointed out that this credibly human episode of Jesus' life had been denied us for fifteen hundred years by a church obsessed with "doing its laundry." He went on to say that the notion of a kissing Jesus was important to our understanding of His actual feelings about flesh and spirit and the true sins of our own times.

"Well," I said to Roy, "this isn't going to console Laurence or get you any fan mail from Bishop Brace."

"The papers have got into the habit of making news out of my Sunday homilies." He shrugged, looked at his watch. "My first appointment's in ten minutes. Shall we get some breakfast?"

Following Roy downstairs, I was wondering if it was possible that the bracelets were Joan's—if the housekeeping were such here that nothing was ever put away or if perhaps Roy had them at his bedside purposely as an augury of her return.

One of the diocesan secretaries was already at her desk, typing, and Dorsey had driven the children to school. Their breakfast dishes had been cleared from the dining room table, and ours lay waiting, eggs and coffee smoking on a sideboard warmer.

Roy filled his cup. "You might tell Laurence this. Tell him there is nothing careless in what I'm saying here. Tell him I'm bringing more people into the church than I'm turning away.

We have seventy-two parishes now, and thirty-one thousand communicants, up two percent over last year. What I'm saying needs to be said, in spite of Joe Brace."

"And what about your marriage?"

"It's none of his business."

"It is mine, Roy. I can't bear to see you and Joan drift apart like this when I know that underneath the quarreling and disappointment the love is big as a house, and the need even bigger."

Roy looked out the window to where a man carrying a pruning hook appraised an apple tree. "She doesn't believe in me anymore." He shook his head. "Without the believing . . ."

"Joan believes as much as she ever did, but she feels *you've* changed, that you've got an idea of yourself as prophet. You hear God speaking to you so directly that you're always right, and whoever disagrees is wrong. She feels you're a little drunk on that voice you hear and it leaves no place for her."

"Is that what she says?"

"What's important is what *you* say."

"I say it's bullshit, of course. I'm no different from what I ever was—older maybe, wiser, more sure of what I have to do here. It's Joan who's changed, Joan who's gone to Washington and wants a career in the government. I can't stop her."

"You can. If you love her."

He was watching the man lop a branch from the tree.

"Do you?" I asked.

"In my dreams, in my bones, I do."

"Why can't you convince her of that?"

"You'd think a woman like Joan wouldn't need convincing. You'd think her instincts would tell her so."

"If I were to see Joan, could I give her a message from you?"

"Yes," Roy said. "Tell her I want her to come home."

"Haven't you said that?"

"Not in so many words."

"I'll tell her—and leave the dreams and bones part to you."

As I left Diocesan House, Dorsey appeared on the doorstep. She put out both hands for mine, and there were three bracelets on her wrist.

"When you get home, will you do something for me, Ethan?" she asked.

"Call your mother?"

"If you like. That isn't what I meant."

"What was?"

She brightened. "Will you pray for me?"

"Of course."

"Ask God to keep on showing me His way."

It was six and the shadowy little bar of the Watergate was dense with federal bureaucracy, but I saw a hand wave from a corner table. Joan had combed her hair straight back and fastened it with a silver clip. It gave her fair-skinned face, with its fine care lines at the eyes, a serene dignity.

While the waiter was getting our drinks, she spoke warmly of her work and how it seemed forever multiplying before her. "We're preparing a bill," she said, "that can't possibly get to Congress before May. Next fall is more like it."

Joan's hazel eyes strayed among the tables, where heads bent to their confidences and a woman's laughter rose above the babble. "I've found an apartment in an old building on H Street, and life here ain't bad."

"You're missed at home."

Joan nodded. Eyes widening, she looked away.

"The kids seem to be getting along all right," I went on, "but they're just making do until you come home."

"Well, of course I think of them all the time," she said. "Susan's coming for a visit during her April vacation. I think she'll like it. If she does, perhaps she'll come back in the summer for good. She'll be going into fifth grade in the fall. There's a good school nearby; I went to look at it this morning."

"And J.J.?"

"He's very loyal to his father."

"Nothing wrong with that."

Joan looked into my eyes with sudden, combustible indignation. Then she sighed. "No, nothing wrong with that. He should hang in there. They need each other."

"I thought Roy was drinking more than usual. Is it something to worry about?"

"Yes, it is. His drinking is serious, and a pretty accurate barometer of the weather within."

"And doesn't that have to do with your being away?"

She seemed uncertain but in the end shook her head. "It starts as self-indulgence and ends as punishment. It doesn't punish the world half so well as it does me. A drunk's best girl is his trigger. What he really wants out of her is another ride on the roller coaster of rejection and forgiveness. I'm afraid Roy's got to handle the drink himself. Maybe Dorsey can help."

"Whose idea *was* it, having Dorsey stay on?"

"When you sent Dorsey to us, J.J. was in more trouble, trouble at school, and then he was caught breaking into a house with another boy—but Dorsey took him on and it was quite wonderful to see him change. All at once he was interested in school and tomorrow. It wasn't easy for me, as you can imagine, to admit that."

"But filling your shoes now? She makes no bones about that."

Joan laughed. "Dorsey's all up front, as she'd say. I don't see anything devious about her. She's full of love. I think that's true, and it makes her a fine counselor. We talk on the telephone almost every day about the kids and about Hoist. We get along very well." Joan put her chin in her hand. "I find it hard to dislike her. Does that surprise you?"

"Well, it does, because it seemed to me that it wasn't only J.J. who was taken with Dorsey."

"Yes, Roy too." Joan frowned at her glass, raised it, and drank its dregs. "I don't dwell on it."

"But you accept it?"

Joan nodded. "I must."

We ordered second drinks and when they came, Joan said, "We once talked about how a divorce would affect Roy."

"It was in another connection."

She nodded and our eyes met in an instant's mourning. "And what do you think now, Ethan?"

"I think of shambles. In the light of Roy's latest utterances on the new morality, I think of a diocese in uproar. I think of Roy himself coming apart. His dependency on you is greater than you think."

"In my kind of therapy you learn how to do the unimaginable. It's only when you knock out the dependency that a patient can really confront himself—learn to stand."

"He's in a lot of trouble now with these fearless sermons of his. There's a big move on against him."

"Brace you mean? He's nothing new."

"Many others. Laurence sent me out to warn Roy. The Southerners want a crackdown at the General Convention. There's a resolution making the rounds. They have a dozen signatures."

"I can believe a dozen. Roy thrives on a dozen adversaries. But the moderates won't turn on Roy, not even a divorced Roy. They're dismayed by what he says, but at heart they love him for saying what they don't dare to say . . . and he has Tom too. Tom is always there to protect him."

"Tom's a sick man, Joan. He may not be able to come to Saint Louis."

Joan sipped her drink, conceded with a nod. "Laurence, then. Laurence Givens won't want a hanging."

"Every time Laurence sees Roy's name in the paper, a hanging is less abhorrent to him."

Joan shrugged.

"Joan, it's like watching some terrible collision take place in slow motion. It's so unnecessary. If one of you would only speak. Dumb male pride ties down Roy's tongue. He loves you, Joan."

"Oh, in his way, yes. But the years have made me skeptical. It will always be in *his* way."

"He'd change it. He's a man in despair for lack of you."

"I wish it were so simple. I wish it were just a bad connection."

"But you *do* love him. Why isn't it so simple?"

"Yes, of course I love him. I love the Roy I married, the wild man who dreamed of fixing what was wrong with the world, but he no longer exists. Maybe he never did. Maybe I imagined him. Anyway, we change. He changes. I change. We're ships drawing close, passing, then no longer in sight of each other. Sometimes I wonder when the moment came in which I could no longer change my course. I think it was when I realized that I was expendable."

"You're not. That's what I've come to tell you. 'Tell Joan I want her to come home,' he said, 'because I love her. In my dreams and in my bones I do.'"

"Well, you know something, Ethan? It's sad to say, but it's too late. For me, it's simply too late."

Her gaze drifted off, and then she was waving. I turned to see that a man at the end of the bar was smiling at us expectantly. He was a plain-looking fellow in his late fifties, carrying a brief-case and umbrella.

"It's a friend named Henry Cross," Joan said. "He's taking me to dinner. Please join us if you like."

"No," I said, "I'd better be getting along."

XIX

A few weeks before the opening of the General Convention of 1974, Roy called to ask if I would go to St. Louis as his scout, discover what I could about support that was likely to rally around him and any intelligence of the opposition, in particular the maneuvers of his old adversary, Bishop Brace, who was known to be mounting a campaign against Roy among the Southern bishops. I promised to do what I could.

The site of the convention, the Chase Plaza, was a tiered wedding cake of a hotel that rose up from an entire city block of St. Louis, a bastion of affluence on the border between the city's wealth and poverty.

I had been installed there for a day when my phone rang. "I'm in 804." It was Roy's voice, taut as a banjo string. "I just checked in. What's the news, Ethan?"

"It's not great, but Laurence is still hopeful."

"Did you get to Holy Joe?"

"For a minute. Long enough to say you were willing to make your peace with the clericus."

"Only, they'd prefer my neck?"

"Bishop Brace likes you personally, Roy."

"He does not."

"He says he does. He says that damn it all everybody *likes* you, but while you're out telling the world that our rites have no meaning he can't bring himself to ordain another deacon or celebrate another Eucharist, and you aren't going to change your ways with a slap on the wrist. He is determined, Roy. He leaves no room for argument."

"I'll have one for him."

"He won't listen to it," I said. "It's important for you to be reasonable now, to appear a little contrite. If you can possibly bring yourself to it, offer them a concession. Then maybe Laurence can arrange for you to sit down and talk with them."

"Does Laurence say he can?"

I sighed. "He says that without it, the clericus is deaf to you. Brace wants to bring formal charges before the convention."

"I'll bet he does. And what's Laurence think of that as an idea?"

"He's opposed, of course, but he sees one advantage to it. They'd stick to theology. There'd be no dirty laundry on the line."

"It's not dirty laundry. It's my *life* . . . and I'm not ashamed of any of it. The shame is all theirs."

"He was talking about Dorsey and her taking Orders. She's a liability. You can't afford it, Roy."

For a few seconds he breathed at me.

"Have you eaten?" I asked.

"Breakfast. In Des Moines."

"I'll meet you in the lobby."

Roy and I stood at the side entrance of the Chase Plaza, looking up a street of expensive shops that halted at the wall of warehouses and tenements to the east.

"Last night they mugged a man here," I said; "a Mr. McHenry from Rochester, New York. He stepped out for a lungful of air, and a couple of guys stomped him and took his wallet. He's lucky to be alive."

Roy nodded. "It's hard to know the battlefields. They're underfoot before you know it."

Opposite, red-and-white-striped awnings shaded the windows

of a pancake house, and when we were settled in one of its booths with buckwheats before us, Roy asked, "Is Laurence really *our* man?"

"You know Laurence as well as I do. He's incapable of deception."

"But as a matter of loyalty—is Laurence's with me or with the Dixie clericus?"

"Laurence sees himself as arbitrator, a healer of differences. He's as anxious to save your neck as the church's face. If they aren't the same thing, they coincide."

"How much does he know about Joan?"

"Joan? Everything. I've been very candid."

"Is he as candid with Joe Brace?"

I shrugged, shook my head. "Joan's leaving you isn't the issue."

"Oh?" He looked at me skeptically over a forkful of pancake. "Bishops have been guilty of every crime that's conceivable, plus a few that are not, but in the history of Christendom there's never been one with a divorce."

"It hasn't been mentioned and I don't believe it will be. Divorce is a commonplace, even in Alabama, but Dorsey is not. Dorsey's a scandal, and that has to concern you."

He nodded solemnly. "I'm concerned for her."

"For God's sake, it isn't her precious career on the line. She's a mixed-up kid."

"Ethan, sometimes I envy the clarity with which she sees the world."

"You forget. I've known Dorsey since she was a child. There's a little fist of resentment in her against every kind of authority."

He shrugged. "She resents disapproval. The world always disapproves of its emancipated. Dorsey's a natural Christian. Children recognize it at once. So do junkies, sick people. Last week I took her up Tom Sewall's mountain in New Mexico. He saw a fledgling saint in her."

"The Dixie clericus sees your little tootsie in her. It sees that in proposing her for Holy Orders you've lost all discretion. Is it true?"

234

"Not yet."

"Then tell them so. That's all it will take to sit you down with them."

Broad chin cradled in a hand, Roy brooded. "It isn't just Dorsey, you know. We've got a whole generation of truants out there looking for a decent set of values, trying to find a home for their vagrant love of God. It could be the church. We must see to that, you and I."

"Getting Dorsey into a cassock isn't the only solution. There's a plausible ministry in blue jeans, and you'd be the first to tell me so."

He sipped his coffee and set the cup down with a clatter. "You're right there, of course, but as usual the clergy's the loser."

"Give it time. Right now there isn't a commission on ministry that would endorse her . . . unless it's in your own diocese."

He shook his head. "A little resistance there too. I've heard from two members."

"Tell me, Roy, what does go on in Iowa? When you launch one of these rockets from the cathedral pulpit, what do your people do?"

"It's amazing what they do." He looked around with mock furtiveness and whispered, "This is classified, naturally, but I've done a little demographic survey and I know these things. A typical Iowa Episcopalian is a woman in her fifties. She's better off, better educated, more sophisticated than the average, and as you rightly guess, my people *are* conservative. Nobody beats them at resisting change. So of course they don't stand up and cheer my sermons, but they sure come out to hear them. I fill every pew."

"And they don't complain? They don't object when they see the stories in the papers?"

He gave a dismissing shake of his head. "It's the Iowa aberration, the occasional flouting of what's expected. Every now and then it turns conservative ears to what some liberal Democrat is saying about the world beyond our two rivers, and then even the Republicans defy their instincts and send Dick Clark and John Culver to the Senate. It's passion, Ethan. They know passion when they hear it, and they hunger for it. When I tell them that my sermons are meant to startle Christians out of lip service and make them *think* about their religion, they do. They take the notion home, right into the house with the roast and the Sunday *Register*."

"You must get *some* complaints."

"Everybody knows I took the shutters off the Davenport cathedral and put it back in business and then brought national attention to it. They love that—to be known nationally for something other than tall corn."

"And in the end?"

"In the end?" He smiled. "How will it all end? In the final judgment?"

"No, no. Not that, please." I looked at my watch. "Just Dorsey."

"Oh, well . . ." He leaned against the dimpled upholstery of the banquette. "Clearly the time is not right for her vows."

"Let me tell Bishop Brace."

"Isn't there an advantage to holding that in my hand? If I'm to sit down with the clericus and give it my course in contemporary theology and still pick up my passport, wouldn't it be better to wait until then to concede on Dorsey?"

"Roy, my dear deluded friend, you are in with the lions and you are naked."

He laughed. "Never. Not in a month of Alabama Sundays. But go ahead, Ethan. You can tell Joe Brace that Iowa has shelved all plans for the ordaining of its hippies."

On the street again we walked eastward, in the direction of the river. Beyond the hotel the neighborhood looked like the scene of a recent battle, and at hand the windows displayed antiques and expensive dresses. Roy paused before one that at first appeared empty. A slim tree trunk emerged from a six-inch hole in the floor and disappeared through the ceiling. Then I realized that it was embraced by the thick, intricately patterned body of a snake.

"What is this place?" I asked. "A taxidermist's?"

"No, no, Ethan. Watch."

He tapped the window and to my horror the snake writhed

slightly, as if dreaming of prey, and moved a fraction of an inch up the tree trunk.

"God save us," I said. "Let's get back inside that hotel."

I found Roy later in the crowd around the registration desks at the ballroom entrance. He was moving happily among the booths of the publishers and outfitters, gathering pamphlets and greeting people as though he were campaigning.

"They're rounding up the committee now," I said. "They seemed eager about it, willing to leave the floor of the opening session for you."

"That's fine," Roy replied. "Where do we go?"

"A conference room." I held out the slip on which Laurence had written: "Wyaconda Room, mezzanine, 2:00 P.M."

Roy nodded. "I'm ready. I've just had good news, Ethan. Tom's coming. He'll be here by Friday in case the clericus is in full cry by then."

We were expecting a cool but forbearing reception in which even the crossest of the Southern bishops would have an outstretched hand for Roy and an invitation to draw a chair up to their table.

So we were unprepared for the scene awaiting us in the Wyaconda Room. When I entered, my first thought was that we had come to the wrong place. The twelve bishops of the theology committee were seated at the far side of a long table. They made a tableau that brought sharply to my mind the Last Supper.

Bishop Doncaster of Connecticut, the chairman, was at the center, and I recognized Bishops Brace, Warren, Grandin, Tyson, Finch, and, at the far left, Laurence Givens. Several rows of folding chairs faced the table and held an audience of about twenty clergymen, most showing their purple.

I never expected to see Roy confounded, but in the sudden silence that greeted our appearance I watched his eyes sweep from one grim face to another. As though struck in the heart, he went rigid.

The smooth, resonant voice of Bishop Doncaster broke the tension in the room by announcing Roy's arrival. "The Bishop

237

of Iowa," he said. "We've been awaiting you, sir. You'll find a place down front."

I followed Roy to the first row and noticed that a typescript lay in each vacant seat. While Bishop Doncaster called the meeting to order, I held my copy and listened to the chairman's statement that this was a special session of the Presiding Bishop's standing committee on theology, called together this afternoon at the request of the Bishop of Alabama.

It was only when I saw that Roy was not listening but giving his attention to the stapled pages in his lap, his eyes widening, that I turned to my own and read:

Right Reverend Fathers in God:

We the undersigned bishops of the Protestant Episcopal Church in the United States of America have been increasingly distressed by the behavior of a member of our own holy and consecrated fellowship, the Right Reverend Bishop of Iowa.

His every utterance seems to repudiate the vows he took at his ordination, pledging himself to drive away erroneous and strange doctrine.

In repudiating our Lord's virgin birth and the doctrine of the blessed Trinity, the bodily Resurrection, in denying that our creeds contain articles of faith at all, he has confused and divided our clergy and communicants.

Although any man may question certain basic principles of our religion and retain his moral character, that man is most surely not a Christian.

Therefore we undersigned bishops offer this presentment of charges against Bishop Royal D. Train under Article VIII of our Constitution and under Canons 53 and 56 of the General Convention. To wit:
1. Holding and teaching publicly a doctrine contrary to that held by the church.
2. Violations of the Canons of the General Convention.
3. Violation of his ordination vows.
4. Conduct unbecoming a clergyman.

Holding that our faith is our most precious heritage, we urgently request that this Committee on Theology request of Bishop Train a public repudiation of his divergent views. Should

he fail to comply, we urge the Committee to endorse this presentment of charges and forward it to the Presiding Bishop, rec-
ommending a trial for heresy, and if he be found guilty, deprived
of his bishopric.

Respectfully submitted . . .

While I read this extraordinary document I became aware
that Bishop Brace was now standing, reading it aloud in his rich,
round-cornered baritone, giving it the ring of Scripture as he
put it into the form of a motion. Before he sat down, it was
seconded by another Southern voice, but Roy's hand was in the
air, gesturing urgently.

Recognizing him, Bishop Doncaster warned, "The committee
asks you to limit your response to twelve minutes, Bishop Train."
He glanced at his watch. "We will want to hear other views from
this assembly. Also, we must ask you to avoid discussion of theology."

"Twelve"—the first sound of Roy's penetrating voice caromed
off the walls of the low-ceilinged room—"twelve minutes. Let
me take the first of them to say that what I asked of this committee was an opportunity to speak informally with my accusers.
I wanted to explain the undercurrents of the resistance to my
views, so I am, to say the least, surprised to find myself in the
dock here and given twelve minutes to refute this"—Roy held
out the presentment between his thumb and forefinger as
though it were infectious—"this bad joke, which, incidentally,
looks like the work of twelve medieval lawyers. I will certainly
not be bound by it. My dear friends and reverend fathers
in God, I know what my rights are and I will exercise every
one."

He frowned at the first page. "You know these are the very
charges on which the fourth-century bishops nailed Arius,
which gives you an idea of how far we've traveled in sixteen
hundred years. Anyway, point one. Yes, my friends, I will tell
you exactly what I believe and what I preach. I preach a Christianity centered on a real, historical, political, and virile Jesus, a
vigorous man with a message for us, never truer than in this
hour when it is the last hope of our civilization. I do not believe

nor do I preach the emasculated, spaced-out version who passes through walls and cannot laugh or love in the way that you and I can laugh and love.

"I do believe in a Christianity that is a constant search for God in all things and all beings, and in the Christian paradox that while God is in all places and you must search for Him everywhere, you will find Him only here . . ." Roy tapped his chest.

"Bishop Train," Doncaster interrupted, "I must rule you out of order. You have been asked to avoid discussion of theology. Please confine yourself to the motion."

Roy glared at him. "That's what I'm doing. I'm saying that I have not preached a word that violates the doctrine of our church or my ordination vows."

Now Bishop Brace leaned forward and spoke to Roy as though in confidence. "We haven't the time today, Roy, nor, to tell you the truth, the patience for this kind of superficiality."

Roy's eyes blazed at him. "God damn it, you do!" he roared. "You will all sit here and listen to me until midnight while I answer these vicious, false charges you've brought against me. As a lawyer, I know my rights here."

Roy's voice rose over the murmur of protest. "As a theologian, I know that my every utterance has been within the bounds of doctrinal orthodoxy as laid down by the pastoral letters of this House."

Bishop Doncaster began to rap on the table with his knuckles, reddening as he repeated, "Order, order . . ."

Roy's indignation only flamed the more. "I have never denied the virgin birth of Jesus Christ. What I *have* said is that biblical evidence and common sense suggest that Joseph was his natural father. Nor have I disputed what our founders meant by the doctrine of the Trinity, but the Trinitarian concept is *not* Holy Scripture. It was arrived at in the fourth century by two hundred and fifty bishops who were trying to settle a dispute between Arius and Alexander . . . and neither Jesus nor the Apostles ever heard of it."

There were cries of "Out of order! No theology!" and Bishop Doncaster banged at the table with a prayer book.

"The job before us all," Roy continued, "is to revise some of the ancient solutions to the problem of God's nature. We must bring them into line with sixteen centuries of advance in human knowledge."

The chairman and several bishops were on their feet, making a phalanx of protest. "Sit down, sit down!" they cried, waving their arms at him while Bishop Doncaster thumped away at the table with his prayer book.

At the height of this clamor I was aware of a banging on the door, as if someone had come to complain of the noise. It was insistent, rising in urgency until it silenced the room.

Relieved by the lull, Bishop Doncaster called out to the chaplain who was acting as master at arms, "Stephen, see who that is, will you?"

The chaplain unlocked and opened the door upon a short, thick man in blue denim work clothes. He had the lustrous black hair and angular features of an American Indian. He scowled at the assembly of clergymen, ducked out of sight, and reappeared, pushing a wheelchair in which rode the anxious-faced Bishop Emeritus of Iowa, Tom Sewall.

As he rolled toward the front of the room, Bishop Sewall's birdlike, white-wisped head nodded slightly, as though he were absorbing the scene through his sixth sense. His expression turned to one of understanding and relief.

"Welcome to you, Tom," said Bishop Doncaster. "We had no idea you were coming to join us."

Bishop Sewall spoke softly to the Indian, who brought the wheelchair into the front row and retreated to the rear. Everyone, Roy included, resumed his seat and watched Tom Sewall straighten the blanket covering his lap.

Folding his trembling hands upon it, Tom Sewall spoke in his slender reed of a voice. "Thank you for allowing me in to your meeting. From what I could hear at the door"—he smiled—"I was about to miss some exciting times." He waited. There was no sound in the room. "May I go on?"

Bishop Doncaster said, "The chair recognizes Bishop Sewall."

"Thank you," Tom said. "I do have something to say to you

all and I'm afraid it won't keep." His head bobbed right and left. Beside me, Roy leaned forward to peer at Tom Sewall's face, which was as pale as a winter moon.

Raising his hands as sensors, Bishop Sewall asked, "How many of us are here? Are we about thirty-five?"

"Yes, Tom," Bishop Doncaster replied. "That's about it."

"Thirty-six." It was Laurence Givens, who had just counted the house.

"Good," said Tom Sewall. "Thank you, Laurence. Well, you may wonder why I've come down from my mountaintop today. I had sworn to remain there until God summons me, hoping thereby to suggest to Him a sense of my direction. You may think I have come down in order to give a hand to my friend Roy Train. Do make a noise for me, will you, Roy?"

"I'm here, Bishop."

Tom Sewall's face was luminous for a moment. "I think you would scarcely believe me if I were to deny that, so I surely won't, but perhaps you will also believe that my love for Bishop Train is not my first reason for coming here to join you. May I have a copy of the document you're considering?" He opened his hand, and Bishop Dunlap of Kansas, who sat beside him, laid his copy of the presentment on Tom Sewall's palm.

"Oh, yes, yes," Tom Sewall said, balancing the typescript on the cradle of his fingertips. "This is why I came. I've always wanted to feel the power of one of these things. I never could believe it, but, by golly, it's no disappointment, is it. Feeling is believing. When you get to be my age you don't encounter many surprises, but this is one, finding that after all this time, ever since the temple priests heard their first mutterings, it has so keen an edge—such keen *edges*. It must be as old as man's belief in a power beyond his own."

Tom returned the presentment to Russell Dunlap gingerly. "We haven't seen one of them lately, not outside the glass case where we keep the crossbow and the guillotine. No, I never imagined I'd see one in use." He sat for a moment, meditating, and the room throbbed with silence.

"I wonder if it would be a good idea before you vote on this motion to have a good look at the canonical provisions for the heresy trial of a bishop. They are the same canons that convicted Galileo for maintaining that the earth revolved around the sun. We might also consider whether we in the Anglican communion can afford a chastising of one of us for speaking his mind. However angry you may be at our Iowa maverick, you must admit he's right that we are living in the twentieth century and cannot hold back the falling of its leaves. What would a heresy trial reported in our newspapers tell the world about the state of Christianity—a truth?

"What do we say to a generation which has learned in its classrooms and laboratories that its intelligence is its greatest gift from God and they suspend it at their peril, particularly at a church door? I think we must respect that, even among ourselves, or we are doomed."

Bishop Sewall brought his hands together as though for prayer, and his head dropped over them. There was a rustling in the room as some of us followed suit, but in the next moment a whispering brought my head up to see that he had slumped forward and his hands had fallen to his lap.

The Indian appeared beside him and bent to his ear, and Roy touched my knee as he walked over to crouch at the wheelchair's arm. "Tom?" he asked. "Are you all right?"

Slowly, the old bishop's head rose and nodded. "Just bushed," he said. "I'd better go for a lie-down. Harry?"

Roy stepped aside as the Indian turned the chair and wheeled it toward the door. Short of it, he swiveled the bishop around to face us.

In a clear voice Tom Sewall said, "Is there someone here who would make a motion to defer the presentment of charges against Bishop Train, long enough to be sure it is his head that will fall to it, and not our own?"

At the table, Bishop Doncaster rose uncertainly to reply. "There is already a motion on the floor, Tom. Will those present agree to consider the motion of the Bishop Emeritus of Iowa in place of the motion already placed before them? If so, is there a second?"

There were several cries of "Second!"

Before the chairman could call the question, Tom Sewall

raised his hand and said, "God bless you all, my dear brothers." As the words left his mouth he wilted again, and the Indian turned the chair toward the door, which was swung open before him, and the bishop was gone, leaving the room in silence.

After a moment Bishop Doncaster said, "Will all those in favor of the substitute motion please rise?"

At first there was no sound, but then a slow shuffling was heard as, one by one, the bishops rose and twenty-two of them were standing.

An escalator bore a file of us from the mezzanine to the floor below, where the House of Bishops was still in session. Laurence Givens had picked his way along to the step just behind us, and now he leaned forward and with a tentative smile said, "Well, that wasn't half bad now, was it Roy? Were you expecting Tom?"

Roy shook his head. "Not until Friday."

We watched our slow descent in a wall of mirrors. "Well, you must be very pleased at the outcome," Laurence went on, putting a light hand on Roy's shoulder. "Couldn't have worked out better for you."

Roy did not brighten. "It was Tom's victory today," he said. "But it was just a skirmish. The Dixies are still after my hide. I'm not kidding myself."

"If I were you, Roy, I'd count my Southern blessings. They know you're being looked after. Don't push your luck."

"I'm glad you think it will hold, Laurence."

Laurence smiled. "I'll pray that it does."

"Thanks," Roy said. "Did you tell Joe Brace I'm getting a divorce?"

Laurence hesitated. "That was very difficult for me."

"I'm sure it was," Roy said.

"You do understand?"

"Don't worry. You saved me the trouble."

The theology committee swelled the House of Bishops assembled in the Khorassan Ballroom, so I found a place in the gallery at the left and listened to an argument in favor of creating a new diocese of Southern California. At the same time I followed the spread of news from our meeting. Once Roy had

244

taken his seat, other bishops were finding the occasion to pass by and offer a congratulatory handshake. He seemed to brighten now, laughing at a remark that had been whispered in his ear.

Then I noticed that the Indian stood at the ballroom entrance. A chaplain who had been stationed there moved swiftly along the side aisle and up the platform steps to the Presiding Bishop's side.

At once, Bishop Richard Houghton rose, interrupting the debate on the floor to say "I must share with you the news that Bishop Sewall has had an attack of some sort. The chaplain tells me that our dear Tom suffered a fainting spell in the elevator and he has not yet revived. He's been taken to Mercy Hospital, which is not far from the hotel. I propose that we adjourn until eight tonight so that we can pray for his deliverance and safe-keeping."

Bowing his head, Bishop Houghton led the prayer.

XX

IN the lobby a smell of cataclysm hung in the air. Clergy and laity with startled eyes clustered in twos and threes, talking softly. I noticed that a woman in a blue beret stood beside the revolving door at the entrance. She was weeping, face buried in her hands. It was only as she drew them away that I had a glimpse of stoplight red hair and bounded toward her.

"Dorsey," I said taking her arm, "what in God's name are you doing here?"

She shook her head in despair. "I dreamed it all," she said, sobbing; "my coming into this big hotel where I've never been before in my whole life, and seeing Tom carried by me on this stretcher, passing so close that I could reach out and touch him . . . and feeling him *cold*. Oh Ethan, Tom was dead."

"It's only an attack. He has fainting spells all the time. They've taken him to the hospital to get him over it—but you're not meant to be here, Dorsey. Believe me, you could not have chosen a worse time."

"I know!" She nodded vigorously. "But Roy needs me. I *had* to come."

"The kindest, most loving thing you can do for Roy is to leave here at once. Don't try to see him. Will you do that for

him, Dorsey? Roy's in deep trouble here and much of it has to
do—"

"With me," she grieved. "I know. They think I'm some kind
of groupie." She looked from cluster to cluster of sober clergymen. "Well, I can't care what people think—so long as it's right
in my heart."

"But it mustn't be right in your heart, not when Roy's in danger. You put him in danger by being here—even being seen with
me." I glanced about, sure I would find Roy loping toward us at
any minute, and drew her into the shadows beyond the newsstand. "Where did you leave your car?"

She poked into a drawstring purse for a Kleenex. "I came on
Trailways."

"All right, will you go to the terminal now? Will you catch the
next bus back to Des Moines?"

She shook her head deliberately, setting the luminous hair
swirling in a way I had known since Dorsey's adolescence, that
flaunting of her intransigence, a warning of those reserves of
stubbornness which stood ready to parade before the House of
Bishops. "I have to see him," she said.

I drew my room key from a pocket and put it in her hand.
"Go to my room, 713, and stay until someone comes for you. It
will be Roy or me. If you're hungry or thirsty, call room service,
but don't come out for any reason. I'll find him for you. Do you
understand?"

Dorsey closed her child's fingers over the key. "Thank you,
Ethan . . . dear Ethan." She put a kiss on my cheek and went
swiftly toward the elevators.

In the waiting room outside the intensive care unit at Mercy
Hospital there were five bishops. Two read their Bibles. Two
stood talking by a window. Roy leaned against the counter of an
office where three nurses sorted patient information from a bat-
tery of electronic screens.

"It's a big one," Roy told me gravely; "a serious heart attack.
But Tom's alive and his condition is stable. We're welcome to
whatever comfort we find there, but I think his chances are slim,

Ethan. We won't know for a while. Meantime, no news is good news."

"I'll bank on that," I said. "Did you know Dorsey was coming?"

Roy shook his head without expression. "Where is she?"

"In my room at the Chase. She won't go until she sees you. Can you run over and tell her she must?"

"Yes. I'd better do that."

There was a note pad on the counter and I wrote the room number on it. "Be careful," I said.

As he folded the slip of paper into a vest pocket, one of the nurses spoke to him. "You can see him for a minute now, Bishop Train. Dr. Fletcher said it will be all right."

She pointed out a door across the waiting room and with a certain awe I watched it open for Roy and close behind him.

I had read most of a back issue of *National Geographic* before I inquired. "No," the nurse said, "Bishop Train isn't with Bishop Sewall. He stayed only a few minutes. He would have left the unit by the east entrance, into the corridor."

Outside it was dusk and I could not find a taxi, but I went at a run, threading my way through the evening traffic that crawled along the streets and the boulevard through Forest Park, arriving back at the Chase Plaza as darkness fell on the city.

A key to 713 was in my box and I found the room empty. There was a tray with the remains of tea and a sandwich. The bedspread was much rumpled, and a wadded Kleenex lay on the night table.

No one answered Roy's phone, but I went up to the eighth floor anyway and found his door ajar. Peering in, I saw a chambermaid straightening the bed cover.

"Hello," I said. "Is there anyone . . . home?"

"No. Just straightening up."

I looked toward the bath. "You're sure?"

"There's no one here. They've gone."

I visited the hotel's coffee shop and its several bars. There was no sign of them. I stood beside the doorman in his hunting pink, and when an empty taxi appeared I got into it and returned to Mercy Hospital.

In the waiting room outside the intensive care unit the vigil was being kept, but the faces were new ones. I recognized only that of a Bishop Drury.

"No." He shook his head. "I haven't seen Roy in some time."

"*Was* he here? Did he come back?"

"I saw him about an hour ago. Perhaps more. He was in that little chapel on the ground floor."

With its bare altar, the chapel was determinedly ecumenical and very still. Then I saw Roy. He was in the second pew, a shadow against the wall, his grizzled head sunk to his chest.

When I sat beside him he did not move. His hands were folded, his eyes closed. At first a finger quivered and then he emerged. A moment later he gave a deep sigh. "Hello, Ethan," he said.

"Are you all right?"

"Yes, of course." He leaned against the back of the pew and lay his arm upon it, one hand on my shoulder.

"I've been to the hotel. No sign of Dorsey anywhere."

"Dorsey's on her way home."

"You're sure?"

"Yes."

"Well, that's a relief."

Roy began shaking his head, at first in denial, then in wonder. "Dorsey has this really metaphysical sense of my . . . She seems to know just when I need my booster shot."

"Hardly the appropriate moment for *that*."

His eyes rounded in amazement. "For believing in me? Oh, Ethan, appropriate it is. Critical is more like it."

In the morning when I left my room for breakfast it was twenty minutes past seven and the hotel seemed exceptionally quiet. An empty elevator arrived for me and turned me out into a deserted mezzanine. As I walked along in the direction of the coffee shop, I was thinking how strange it was to be under the same roof with nearly a thousand fellow churchmen and to feel so entirely alone.

Downstairs, on the bulletin board outside the ballroom the typed report of Bishop Sewall's 8:00 P.M. condition had been replaced by a hand-inscribed card. It read: "Bishop Thomas Rogers Sewall passed quietly into the hands of God at eighteen minutes past three this morning. *Requiescat in Pace.*"

Many of the laity had deserted the House of Deputies meeting to swell the morning session of the House of Bishops. They streamed in to fill the seats around me in the observation section and, when these were taken, to stand against the ballroom walls. There was a suppressed anxiety in the whispers and the rustle people made in finding their places.

At exactly nine, Presiding Bishop Houghton stood at the podium and said, "Our beloved friend and brother the Right Reverend Thomas Rogers Sewall has left us this morning. Let us be silent together now and pray for his everlasting life in the grace of God."

A minute or so later the P.B. brought the silence to a close by announcing that at three o'clock there would be a requiem for Bishop Sewall at St. Mark's Church. He looked at the agenda waiting on his lectern, then at his watch.

"As you know, there is much for us to do this morning and we must move on to it, in spite of the burden of grief we share today. Surely we have lost the gentlest of our fellows, a man whose afflictions seemed to open his heart to the world and who taught us the nature of acceptance and compassion. If there was ever a saint among us . . ."

The P.B. heaved a great sigh and was adjusting his glasses for a look at the first item of business when Roy's voice was heard rising from somewhere at the back.

"Mr. Chairman!" he cried. Now I saw him making his way across a row to the center aisle. His hair and suit were rumpled and his arm waved for recognition, but the P.B. ignored him. "Bishop Houghton!" he insisted and came resolutely forward.

With obvious reluctance, the chair peered over the top of his glasses, saying, "The chair recognizes the Bishop of Iowa."

Roy took the steps to the platform at a trot and arrived beside the P.B. at the podium. "I want to add a few words to our farewell," he said, looking down upon the sixty bishops of his church. "Tom Sewall was my friend and I cannot let him leave us without saying what I know to be the truth about him. He would want me to do that."

Bishop Houghton had sat down to one side of the podium, but his head was cocked at Roy, his brow gathering anxiously.

"The truth about him," Roy said, "has nothing to do with acceptance. He hurt in every joint and organ and the pain did not soothe nor humble him. It never became easier to bear. He did not thank God, as you may want to believe, for his blindness nor those mean kinks in his spine nor the paralysis of his legs. These were the scourges of God, and sometimes he would cry out in fury at Him, Why me?

"My dear brothers, you must know that Tom Sewall was really not an amiable man. If you saw a lamb, you were deceived. Don't be mistaken about his saintliness. It lay in the alchemy he worked on his emotions. He yearned for the color and shape of the world that you and I know. His heart was full of outrage that they were denied him, and if you thought otherwise, you missed the point of his laughter and his love. It was anger— exorcised.

"Tom Sewall persuaded me to join the ministry fifteen years ago because he saw that I was angry too. Whenever I had a chance to make my peace, he urged me against it. Tom will always be telling me to go on saying what I believe—"

The P.B. rose now and took a step toward the podium, intent on reclaiming it, but Roy hurried on, saying, "Oh, yes, I *do* believe in resurrection. I believe in Tom Sewall's resurrection. I am saying good-bye to him this morning, but he is going to be alive and well in me—and, by God, in you too. That's a promise."

Nudging Roy aside, the P.B. said, "Our thanks to the Bishop of Iowa."

Descending the steps, Roy plunged into an agitated audience. As though by a squall, its surface was lashed in turbulence. A few hands reached forth for his, but most of the bishops shunned him as if what he had might be catching. Across the assembly arms were going up, and Bishop Brace was already on his feet.

Recognized, he said, "I feel very strongly that the remarks we have just heard from the Bishop of Iowa are in extremely poor taste on this occasion. I find them offensive to the memory of a very dear friend and I will venture further to say that Bishop Train will come to regret them. I move they be stricken from the record of this meeting."

Roy, who was making his way across a back row toward his seat, paused to cry out, "I will not regret them, my dear brother, or anything else I've ever said."

Clearly Roy would have added a great many more words had not the sound of the P.B.'s gavel begun to fall like stones from the amplifiers, along with his authoritative voice, calling, "Order, order . . . The chair rules both the motion and the discussion out of order."

St. Mark's, a replica of an English country church, lay in the Westmoreland Place enclosure of banklike Tudor and Norman houses opposite the hotel entrance. A stream of clergymen had been filing across the street, and by three o'clock there were only a few seats left.

"In here," Roy said, urging me ahead of him into the last pew. "Whatever the P.B. has to say about Tom is going to rile me, and you'll be happier if I don't make a spectacle of myself."

Sure enough, Bishop Houghton launched his eulogy from a parable in John. He reminded us of how Jesus had restored the blind man's sight with those poultices of dust and His own spit and told him that He had come into the world to give sight to the blind and to blind those who could see. Finally He had turned to the skeptical Pharisees to equate blindness with sinlessness and explain it was God's mark, the manifestation of humility.

Beside me, Roy squirmed. "What utter bullshit," he muttered. "That isn't what Jesus meant at all. He meant don't ever think that because you're luckier than the next man, you're any better. Nobody *wants* to be blind. Does he think he can convince us we do?"

"Don't listen," I whispered. "You've said your eulogy. Everybody heard it. Now it's their turn. This is for the survivors."

"You're right, Ethan," he said, patting my knee. "Squabbling over the corpse is offensive. Tom wouldn't care for it." Folding his arms, he gave his attention to Bishop Houghton's closing words. Then he turned and said into my ear, "But he would want us to prepare for the resurrection."

"Whose?"

"The presentment's."

I frowned my disbelief. "Not possible, Roy." I found Bishop Brace in the third row, his face uptilted in an expression of purest beatitude. "Look at him. Not now, while we're singing the requiems."

"You're a good fellow," he whispered, "but so naïve. Joe Brace came to Saint Louis to punish me. He won't be put off. He's not the patient man to wait three years for another General Convention. He'll want his presentment on the floor of the House before adjournment on Sunday."

"He's not half so foolish. Tom made it clear the publicity would be devastating. Don't even imagine it, Roy."

From a pocket Roy drew forth a note written on Chase Plaza stationery and held it for me to read:

Dear Roy,

I am as aware as anyone on earth of your devotion to Tom, and this is primarily a note of sympathy for your loss today. I'm sure it is greater than that of any single one of us and I can understand your remarks of this morning in that light. Nevertheless, some of my fellow members of the theology committee were made uncomfortable by them. I have tried to ease their minds and been partially successful, but I will need you to complete the job. I suggest you give us an hour to talk among ourselves this evening and then join us at nine, prepared for some reconciling of views on what is seemly behavior in a bishop of our church.

Earnestly, Laurence

"All right," I said. "That's a reasonable request. Do it. Surprise them with a little flexibility. They've agreed to forgive and forget today, in Tom's name. If *you* don't, they have every right to think you're crazy."

Roy's eyes had gone to the altar of St. Mark's, where twelve candle flames burnished a brass cross. His wide jaw was set. "But I am, Ethan," he said gravely.

The committee on theology met this time in a small room, the John C. Frémont Suite, on the hotel's third floor, in a desire to limit attendance and create a mood of informality. At nine, when we appeared at the door, I was admitted only at Roy's insistence.

The members sat around a long table, with Bishop Doncaster at one end and, opposite, the grave, Solomon-like eminence of the Presiding Bishop himself.

From my seat beside the entrance I watched Roy take the chair saved for him at the table while Bishop Doncaster thanked him for joining them.

"These are not to be formal proceedings at all, Roy," he assured him, "but rather a recognition that we who are most responsible and most concerned for the good health and good name of the Episcopal church are going to fulfill Bishop Sewall's last wishes, execute his last will and testament, so to speak, make certain we are all agreed on the details.

"Laurence has been making a good case for you," Bishop Doncaster went on, "going over all the theological points you've made and showing us how, in your own view, they are not in violation of your vows, or even our constitution, just as you have maintained."

Roy, unprepared for so conciliatory an overture, took some time in lowering his guard, in looking around the circle of faces, before he leaned back in his chair and smiled.

"I'm not sure what I'm meant to do here, but I can affirm what Laurence has said. I agree in every way with each of our Christian principles. I am only pleading that all who are curious about faith and belief be encouraged to bring their full intelligence to bear on the doctrine, to ask it every question that occurs to them and test it against whatever is significant in their experience."

Although Bishop Brace appeared to be falling asleep, a warble of approval made its way around the table, ending at Bishop Houghton, who observed, "What Roy has been saying here re-

254

minds me of the favorable aftermath of Vatican Two and the clear indication that a free and open discussion of our time-honored beliefs, if entered upon in good heart, can have a positive effect on us all."

Encouraged, Roy urged the committee to read the article in the *American Scholar* about recent translations of the Dead Sea scrolls. He asked if they had read the accounts about the discovery in Egypt of what appeared to be authentic gospels. The theory went that they had been suppressed during the fourth century. There were so many new lights, he said, coming to bear on the truth about the historic Jesus. "And they can only enhance," he concluded, "only strengthen, His power to guide us."

It seemed as if the meeting's business had been completed, with Roy, astonishingly, the victor, when I noticed that Bishop Brace, who had been silent throughout, had roused himself. He was gazing at Roy stoically.

Brace's smooth voice came gliding so quietly into a lull that it was a moment before Roy was alerted. "There is one point we haven't yet settled," he said. "It's Article Eight of our constitution, and it does seem to me that, before we break up here, we might make sure we agree on the meaning of 'conduct unbecoming a clergyman.' I know what I mean by it."

Roy crossed his arms on the table. "Why don't you tell us, Joe?"

"I'd say that seemly behavior in a bishop involves respect for all the sacraments of our church, the Sacrament of Marriage in particular—deed as well as word. What do you say to that, Roy?"

Roy smiled. "I'd say it's none of your business."

Bishop Houghton murmured his disapproval, and immediately Bishop Brace leaned toward Roy and said, "If this were a formal session, Roy, and you gave us an answer like that, I would call it an admission of guilt."

"Of what?" Roy demanded.

"You know very well what we're talking about," Brace replied. "Do you want me to say it?"

"Yes. I want to hear the accusation, Joe. Don't be shy."

"Is your wife divorcing you, Roy?"

Roy turned to look into Laurence's unblinking gaze, then back

255

at Bishop Brace. "Yes. That's hardly an immoral act on my part."

"The grounds for her action are. I won't argue the point with you. If you can't see it yourself as a breaking of our Holy Vows or a fouling of the sacrament itself, God help you."

"Oh, Joe," Roy whispered, "I'm so glad you said that. I might have taken the advice of the well-meaning friends who urged me to ignore the false charges in that presentment of yours. Listen, my indiscretions are my own to carry. I don't want your help with them. God alone can help me with their burden, and I don't want a delousing and scrubdown here tonight. I want my accusers to understand that they have no monopoly on right and holiness and are no more immune from hypocrisy than the rest of us.

"Now, I know what I'm doing here. I came to remind myself that I'm still part of God's action. That's all I need to know about doctrine. He who does the work of the Father will know it. I know what my faith tells me. It tells me that I am going to respond formally to your charges against me. Get that present-ment out of your pocket, Joe. Let's make it official. Let's write it into the minutes. Pursuant to Canon Fifty-six, Section Four of the General Convention, I demand an investigation of all these allegations against me in a public trial."

On Sunday morning, the convention's final one, Roy and I met for breakfast in the hotel dining room. He was neatly shaved and wore a fresh collar, but his face was haggard.

"I've been up since four," he explained, "revising the petition and then trying to get it duplicated. At six o'clock on a Sunday morning you can get anything you want in this hotel, except a public stenographer. Well, I got a copy."

"The P.B. has one, Roy. Why do you want others?"

He took a slow sip of coffee and, setting down his cup, said darkly, "In case he doesn't *do* anything about it before noon. I haven't heard a word."

"I've brought it," I said.

"Oh?" He was momentarily suspicious. "You've seen him?"

"I was summoned at eleven last night."

"To the P.B.'s?"

"He's appointing a committee, and he wants to announce that today in a way that will satisfy concerned parties but not go public with it. He needs to know beforehand that you'll accept its judgment."

Roy looked at me warily and stretched his neck backward to stare up at the ceiling. "Hardly," he said at last.

"Come on. You know as well as I do it's the only possible course. You're really not going out on the street with it."

"Don't, Ethan. Don't tell me what I may or may not do. Not this morning."

"Ask me, Roy. The important question."

His attention strayed around the room, his mouth like a sulky child's. "Okay. Who's going to be on the committee? Joe Brace?"

"No—but to keep it fair all around there'll have to be a couple of Southerners, one from the clericus, one a liberal, a couple of your choice, and the rest as impartial as he can find."

"Under who, Ethan? Who's the chair?"

"Laurence."

"Laurence!" Roy said the name in dismay, as though it really hadn't occurred to him. "He's always there, damn it, my old albatross. Will I ever know if he's my friend or not? What do you think?"

"I don't think he sees it that way. He's after the truth."

"One man's truth . . ." After a long silence Roy pushed his chair away from the table. "Well, I'll find out this time."

XXI

ON a bitterly cold evening just after the New Year of 1975, Roy telephoned to say that his divorce had been swift and astringent, like a dreaded operation that, once performed, was simply a new seam in you and a little less painful each day. He was coming at me headlong, though, his speech superheated and faintly slurred, so that it crossed my mind he had been drinking.

"I've got a job for you, Ethan. A wedding."

"Whose?"

"Mine. Advancement, too—best man to vicar."

"In Iowa? Davenport?"

"Well, no, actually. Not the cathedral. Instinct cautions. It's hardly the time for pageantry here."

"How hot *is* the water in Iowa?"

"I do have a small insurgency in the backyard. It's not entirely my paranoia that reveals Joe Brace's long arm reaching all the way from Alabama. He wants the Givens committee to believe I'm losing my diocese."

"Which is actually loyal?"

"The majority of my people here are like my own kids. They love me in spite of my warts . . . maybe *for* my warts."

"But tolerant of so hasty a remarriage?"

"I'm getting some nasty letters. There's always a Louise Gower rising out of the bushes to shake an umbrella at me, but I'm not going to let her stand in . . . the way."

"Whose way?"

Roy hesitated, laughed. "You old watchdog, Ethan. You're going to do this for me, aren't you? Marry us in your church?"

"I'm going to have to explain it to Laurence," I said. "But okay. When is all this?"

"Soon. I want to be an old married man by convention time in September. How about early next month—the fifth or sixth?"

"All right," I said. "Nothing going on here on the sixth."

As I wrote *Roy Train–Dorsey Cooper Wedding* into the book for four P.M., Thursday, February 6, I was overcome by a sense of loss. The hero in Roy had once seemed immune from the attrition of the years, but what a beating it had taken lately. What a farce he was making of his promise.

Did the embracing of that young body refund his own youth? When the loving was done, what could they possibly have to say to each other? And worst of all, he didn't seem in the least aware of collapse, making the loss less his than mine.

Laurence had his misgivings. Within an hour of my call, he was standing against my bookshelves, steaming disapproval. "I can understand how your affection for Roy might lead you to sanction this marriage, but I think that might appear as diocesan approval. He's in a lot of hot water. Doesn't he realize that?"

"He sees it as politics, his Southern foes conspiring to nail him at the General Convention. He says all's well in Iowa. Standing room only at the cathedral on Sunday."

"They must come for the spectacle, which I hear is a sorry one. He's drinking, loses his thread in the middle of a sermon. And now this girl. They're living together quite openly."

"Marriage may be of some help there."

"Very unwise, I think, for you to perform the ceremony. I certainly couldn't condone it, Ethan, in any church of this diocese. Imagine the reaction at the convention. We mustn't forget that marriage is a Holy Sacrament, nor join in turning it into a joke. Whatever our church has become, it's no justice of the peace. If Roy must have a legal marriage, let him go to a court, but he's a long chalk from the sanction of his church."

I put off the call for several days but in the end got up my courage.

"You know I'd do anything for you, Roy," I told him, "but it seems a wedding is the exception. It slays me to disappoint you like this, but Laurence is firm. Not in his diocese."

"Joe Brace has whispered," Roy said darkly, "into another willing ear."

"Not mine," I said. "And in fairness to Laurence, there's nothing personal involved. He cares about the meaning of marriage within the church. I can't argue with that, Roy."

There was a long silence on the line, and when Roy spoke again there was a January chill to his voice. "I think you're telling me there's something trivial about my marrying Dorsey, something back-door."

"Roy, you're my best friend in this world. Whoever you love, I love—but at the same time I cannot act contrary to what I sense are the best interests of the church."

"You disappoint me."

"There are a dozen different ways you can get married."

"I know them all. I wanted yours."

"I'm sorry, Roy. Maybe after the convention, when the trouble has died down."

"Oh, shit," he said.

"I'll do anything else. I'll stand up for you again. I'll give the bride away. I'll dance until sunrise . . ." But I found I was talking into a dial tone.

Oh, what a sting in that disconnection! I told myself that the spurning click and the deaf humming in the line that followed were only the sounds of his despair. Nevertheless, Roy's petulance, his indifference to my obligations, remained unforgivable. When the weeks wore on without a word of apology, when I heard that Roy had dealt effectively with the outcries over his divorce and that he and Dorsey had promptly married in a Chicago church, I concluded that our fifteen-year friendship had ended in an absurd and yet wholly tragic mishap.

It was not quite so. In late February I was pulled out of a deep sleep by a loud and insistent ringing of my telephone. A transatlantic operator asked for me, and then I heard someone say, "Ethan?" It was a familiar voice, a woman's, distorted by vast distance and primitive transmission. "It's Dorsey, Ethan. Can you hear me?"

"Where are you? You sound as if you're on the moon."

"Egypt," she said. "Luxor, Egypt."

"What in heaven's name are you doing there?"

"It's our wedding trip. Didn't Roy tell you?"

"No."

"I wouldn't bother you if we weren't in trouble, but Roy's lost. He's been gone for three days, and I'm frightened. I think something's happened to him."

"Is he drinking?"

"It's not *that*. Our car broke down in the desert and he went to this village for help. He never came back."

"Did you call the police?"

"They've searched everywhere. They claim nobody ever saw him."

"Well, he can't just have disappeared, Dorsey."

"But he *has*. Wild things happen here. With these children carrying guns, it's like the war's still on. And the spell. I mean the ancient past is such a force, you begin to think the dead are stronger than the living. There's this curse we heard about in Cairo—the Jesus curse."

"There's no such thing, I promise you."

"We *saw* it, on the wall of a tomb. And I know this sounds crazy, but it has something to do with Roy's being lost."

"Do you think the police are giving you the runaround?"

"They sure don't believe me. They think we're just crazy tourists and I'm making it up when I tell them Roy's a bishop."

"Maybe that part's a blessing. It would mean a lot of sensational stuff in the papers."

"I don't care what's in the papers. I want to find him."

"There must be an American consul there. Explain that you want help with the police but not scandalous publicity. The papers could do anything with a story like this."

"Can you come, Ethan, and help?"

"They'll find Roy, Dorsey. I don't even have a passport."

"Please. Roy needs you here. He'd want you to come and help me."

"Do you know that Roy and I had a difference over the wedding?"

"Of course I know. He worried about it. He talked about it in Cairo."

"What did he say?"

"That he loves you. He sent you a postcard about it from the Coptic Museum."

"It's five in the morning here, Dorsey. When the passport office opens, I'll call them and see what they can do."

"Tell me when you're coming. Send me a cable at the Luxor Hotel."

I was numbed by a dozen hours of air travel and stepped onto the soil of Upper Egypt with a head full of bubbles. I was not sure whether I was dreaming the Luxor airport or actually straggling toward it in a file of passengers.

It stood in a sun-baked clearing of the lush canefields and palm groves of the upper Nile Valley. Taxis and buses waited on the far side of a high metal fence posted with Arabic warnings.

The building was ocher-colored, a rotunda with a pair of blunt wings, defended by a score of boyish soldiers in thick khaki and sweat-stained berets. Odd-looking, probably Russian-made, automatic weapons swung from their shoulders.

Inside, the guides and drivers waited, calling out to us in sharp, incomprehensible voices and holding cards aloft—Cook's, Misr, Savoy, Mina Palace. Over the swarm of porters I saw the torch of Dorsey's hair. Although she had cut it boyishly short, African sun had brought forth its full coppery brilliance.

Seeing Dorsey in the midst of this foreignness was the first assurance of my own reality. Even at fifteen yards her need was apparent, her broad face pale with anxiety. An urgency of my own, the closing of the broken circuit of affection with Roy, swept me toward her. I found myself embracing Dorsey as if hers were my own blood.

"Ethan," she wept into my ear, "thank the good Lord for bringing you."

We waited for my luggage in the little café. It was crowded with olive-skinned Arabs in their galabiyahs and layered with the perfumed smoke of their cigarettes, but we found a table. I asked, "There's still no news of Roy?"

"None." Dorsey was biting her lip, barely holding back the tears. "And the worst of it is, they think I'm making it up. That's what the Egyptian police think, and the American consul isn't all that much better. They think Roy and I had some kind of quarrel and he's run out on me. Maybe they'll take *you* seriously."

"I'm sure we can make them understand," I said. "Tell me what you were doing in the desert."

"We were on our way back from Nag Hammadi. We'd rented a little Morris car here and driven down that morning. We had this incredible run of luck, finding this guide who took us into the cave where the gospels were supposed to be hidden, finding these Coptic inscriptions on the wall, and then, right across the Nile, this unbelievable Miami Beach kind of hotel all ready for us. Roy couldn't wait. He decided we should come get our stuff here and return the same night. So we took this short cut."

"Into the desert?"

She nodded. "The guide showed us on the map how the road cuts across the big loop the Nile makes between Luxor and Nag Hammadi. It's not a regular road but it was supposed to be passable. He said so."

"But you got stuck on it?"

"Yes." She strangled momentarily on the recollection. "We could see the village and we started walking toward it, but when the dogs came he sent me back to the car. He said I should run the heater to keep warm and he'd come for me, but that was the last I saw of him. I waited in the car until dawn, when three Arabs came along in a truck. I tried to make them understand that I had to go to the village, but when I got into the cab with them . . ." She began to weep.

263

"They harmed you?"

"They scared me to death. I didn't know where they were taking me. It turned out to be the police in Nag Hammadi, and *they* decided I was smuggling something in or out of the country. It was hopeless trying to explain what Roy was doing here."

"I'm not quite clear on that either."

"He wanted to see the place where the Saint Pachomius monks had buried the Gnostic gospels. The police, of course, had never heard of them."

"I have. Roy's been telling me since we were in seminary how Irenaeus had them burned because they threatened the power of the priests. But he's no archeologist. He doesn't read Coptic."

"He's been reading them as they were translated, and just a couple of months ago he came across the Jesus curse. That really fascinated him."

"I don't know it."

"'Cursed is everyone who shall trade in my words'—something like that—Jesus' own warning in the Apocryphon of John."

"What's the connection?"

Dorsey frowned with the difficulty of explaining. "Before we even got here, Roy saw one between the curse and the way the gospels came to light. From the beginning there was a lot of trading in them. The curator of the Coptic Museum in Cairo told us how it took so long to release them. They were discovered in 1945. Thirty years it's taken, and as many intrigues. Everybody who touched them suffered in some way."

"But what did he expect to find in Nag Hammadi?"

"He wanted to find out what happened to Hassan, the farmer who broke open the pot and took the first money for one of the books. It was only a couple of Egyptian pounds. He was really cheated, but he got involved in a murder and then went crazy. Roy thought he was being led to some truth about the man. He said that. Some hand was guiding him."

A porter with my valise was beckoning to us, and we followed him from the terminal toward the line of taxis. The town of Luxor was eight miles away and we drove toward it through fields where the willowy cane was being harvested and loaded onto wagons. Mud-colored native houses clustered on the bank of an irrigation canal. Old, rag-swaddled fellahin stared at us from a bridge rail. A boy, his short legs flying from the flanks of a galloping donkey, waved to us.

Luxor had a festive look, with its shopfronts festooned in vivid-colored fabrics and shining metalware. The Luxor Hotel was a fortresslike brown-stone structure facing the temple grounds, where groves of ancient columns and the single obelisk of Ramses II soared into a brilliant sky. Beyond the temple I could see the eternal, olive-colored flow of the Nile.

The hotel grounds were carpeted with beds of crimson cannas. Under one of the yellow umbrellas two businessmen sat at a table. While I was paying off the taxi, one of them, a slender fellow in a blue suit, came to meet us.

Dorsey introduced Quincy Tuck of the American consulate. He promptly sent my valise inside and drew us off to his table to meet Lieutenant Boulis of the tourist police.

Boulis wore slacks and sport shirt. He put forth a plump hand, and his pleasure-loving face smiled an all-Egyptian welcome and glowed with reassurance.

"Here in Upper Egypt we have very little serious crime. A few thieves, you know. Pickpockets. Our people are simple. Also, we are many police here. We have most fine intelligence. So not to concern yourself that harm comes to Mr. Train in this way . . . only that some misunderstanding or accident can have happen."

Dorsey scowled at him. "You've been saying that for over a week now. You keep telling me there's nothing to worry about, but you haven't found a trace of my husband."

Lieutenant Boulis smiled back affably. "In every small village we have our ear. This one where you last see Mr. Train walking is no exception. The station at Nag Hammadi has made full inquiry and we know he did not reach Al Saqi. So we make daily searches of the desert all around. We know from our long experience Mr. Train will come forth. There will be an explanation. We look now in hotels. There are many here in Luxor, in Aswan, in Cairo."

Watching him skeptically, Dorsey sank lower in the basket chair.

"Tell me, Father," Tuck said to me, "are you here on behalf of the church?"

"Oh, not at all," I replied. "I'm very unofficial, just an old friend of Bishop Train, come on my own to do whatever I can to help. In fact I was hoping there won't be undue fuss about this in the papers. At home Bishop Train is the center of some controversy, and lurid stories of any sort could be useful to his enemies."

"I understand," Tuck replied. "The soft pedal is preferred. That's in favor here too. The Egyptians are putting great store by President Sadat's visit to Washington next week"—he waved at the empty tables in the Luxor's garden—"and possibilities for American tourism. Don't want to give an impression of Egypt as a dangerous place."

From the chair's depths, Dorsey snorted her disgust. She was glaring at me. "I could care less about the pussyfooting," she said. "I want to *find* Roy. Maybe if the papers get hold of it, they'll make a stink and then the police will *have* to find him."

As Dorsey and I made our way through modern Luxor, we found a town of stalls, one-story shops teeming with boys and young men, all calling out to us, "Hello, hello," offering some unnecessary object or unwanted service. At the center we found dusty Karnak Square, where a busload of passengers waited stoically for a driver.

Palm and eucalyptus trees shaded clusters of turbaned Arabs squatting on their heels, smoking and watching the comings and goings at the Central Police Station. This was a two-story building with blue shutters. Its steps were flanked by sentry boxes and a pair of signs in English, one reading, DEAR TOURIST, THE LUXOR POLICE IS AT YOUR SERVICE; the other, DEAR TOURIST, IF YOU HAVE ANY PROBLEM CALL 82350, 82461.

The two guards who sprang at us were not half so friendly, but after a contentious exchange between themselves they led us past a room, where a man clutching some bolts of cloth was being slapped repeatedly, and into the presence of an officer.

He wore a khaki sweater with blue epaulettes bearing the police eagle, and when he looked up, I recognized the familiar curves of self-indulgence.

Captain Salah welcomed us cordially to his dungeonlike office with its rummage-sale furniture and ordered tea by a clapping of his gold-ringed hands. This appeared instantly, steaming glasses borne by an Arab with a thug's face. We sipped its syrupy sweetness while President Sadat looked down upon us sternly from his frame on the dirty, pea-green wall.

Captain Salah asked to look at my passport and did so quickly, nodding and returning it while he explained that as yet the search parties had found nothing but they would continue until Bishop Train was found. The whole of Quena district was on alert.

While we talked he continued his work, signing sheaves of identification papers, each with its set of fingerprints. Everyone in the district is kept track of in this way, he explained, for work permits, for every imaginable purpose—one more reason that Upper Egypt was so free of crime.

"It is puzzling to me, personally," Captain Salah told us, "that this drags on . . . seven days is it?"

"Eight," Dorsey corrected him.

"Well, I am relieved now," he said, turning to me, "to be sure of the bishop's intentions here. You see, we knew him only as Mr. Train, who drank many whiskeys at the hotel and showed an impatience with our telephone system. He first came to our attention just before he seems to have disappeared, through an accident of his motor car. It was not serious, but it took place at ten o'clock in the morning."

"It was the cab driver's fault," Dorsey said. "He had plenty of room to get over."

"Yes, I am aware that the bishop is an innocent person, and yet police in this country must take care for everything—for espionage, perhaps, or narcotics, or the traffic in our antiquities."

"I told you it wasn't any of that," Dorsey said.

But Captain Salah was growing alert to a commotion in the

corridor. His visored cap was snatched from a desk drawer and clapped on his head. He was at attention when a senior officer, a short, fierce-eyed man with a bristle of mustache, burst through the doorway. His cotton tunic bore richly embroidered epaulettes, and he was followed by a retinue of aides.

When the salutes had been exchanged, more chairs were drawn around Captain Salah's desk and a pair of scribes in dirty galabiyahs were instructed in vehement Arabic punctuated by jabs of the officer's thumb.

Only when this was done were we presented to General Samil, chief of the Quena district. After the arrival of another round of tea, he uncovered a waxy bald head, polished his thick-rimmed glasses, and explained that he had taken a special interest in this case.

"Given the bishop's interest in antiquities," he said, "it is my belief he will be found in one of our many excavations. This is always a danger of the desert. A Canadian girl disappeared in this way just a year ago. An amateur at archeology, she had entered a narrow burial passage and become lodged in one of its turns. It is why our searches are intensified from Nag Hammadi. We will soon have news from there."

Later, as Captain Salah escorted us to the door of the station, he assured us, "You must not worry. Everyone in Egypt looks out for our visitors. Anyone will come to help you."

"What happened," Dorsey asked, "to that Canadian girl?"

"Ah-h." His hands opened heavenward. "Too bad. An unfortunate recollection."

"She died?" I asked.

He nodded. "Of thirst and starvation. She had cried out and no one heard, but she had paper and pencil and she wrote letters to her family. Her body had been partly eaten by the jackals."

At noon, Dorsey and I set out in a rented Volkswagen, following a two-lane concrete road northward, downstream along the green east bank of the Nile. The river was broad here as any I had seen, and nearly empty of traffic. A couple of feluccas, with their striped, shark-fin sails, idled in midstream, and against the west bank a departing ferry looked no bigger than a raisin.

Beside me, Dorsey was noticeably silent. In her gray eyes lay a smokiness that recalled the episode at the Rutherford jail.

"Well," I said, "the police may be slow getting started, but they do seem to be on the job now, wouldn't you say?"

There was a wait before she said, "Oh, they make me so *mad*, with their goofy caps and big-shot gold braid. I'd sure hate to be a woman in this country. They don't listen to me at all. It's like I'm a child who has to be humored. Did you notice?"

"I guess they don't know quite what to make of Americans."

"Americans?" She sat up straight. "They don't have any trouble with you. He was telling you about the Canadian girl who got eaten by the jackals and pretending I didn't exist. You don't have any trouble fitting right in with that either."

"With what, Dorsey?"

"With the idea I'm some kind of second-rate person who doesn't *deserve* to be taken seriously, some kind of sleazy hippie who isn't qualified to care about Roy. Well, I *do*. I love him and I'm going to find him, in spite of everybody."

"I know better than anyone how far you've come and just how you must be feeling. I've got a lot of respect for you, Dorsey. That's one reason I'm here."

We rode in silence for a while. "Yes," she said at last. "I believe you, Ethan. I'm sorry. It's just that I feel so helpless." She brightened immediately, pointing out the scene of the accident.

Near the entrance to the Temple of Karnak the traffic had swelled, and with customary impatience Roy had swung out to pass a cart and collided with a taxi. During the dispute, the onlookers had taken the taxi driver's side, raising fists and shouting in a menacing way.

The arrival of police only heightened the din, so Dorsey, huddled in the Morris, feared for Roy's safety. However, he was grinning as if it were a farce he was playing out for her entertainment.

Roy silenced the crowd by reaching for his wallet. Drawing forth a note, he presented it to the driver, and everyone watched the man consider it, then look more carefully at his damaged fender. When the driver frowned, Roy added a second note.

This brought forth smiles all around, scattered applause, and in a few minutes they were on their way.

To the east there was a view of Karnak's awesome pylon, and I was impaled by the thought that a thousand years before the birth of Christ this same hewed stone was soaring up from the desert to dumbfound Thebes' visitors. The notion of Dorsey and me passing in its shadow in this instant, this tick of a clock that told the millennia, sent me freefalling in eternity.

We followed the Nile's east bank along its great detour. It is as if the river has suddenly decided to leave its northward path and flow directly into the Red Sea. It digresses so for sixty miles. Then, at Qus, where a sugar mill smudges a brilliantly pale sky with its thick smoke, the river has a change of mind. Recalling its original intention, it begins a slow turn through Qena to find its old course at Nag Hammadi and resume its way toward the Mediterranean.

Just before two, we reached El Qasr, the mud-brick village that lies a few miles short of Nag Hammadi. It was clustered around a small mosque whose rocketlike minaret was crowned by the crescent moon of Islam. We stopped here, as Roy and Dorsey had, to find the ruin of the St. Pachomius monastery, the first in Christendom and presumably the source of the red earthenware jar and its thirteen gospels.

While we gazed at the monastery's ruin, weed-grown steps, and scattered columns, Dorsey told me in an emotionally precarious voice how Roy had prayed here and how the boy Omar had appeared on his bicycle. He had worn a brown stocking cap and a blue-and-white-striped galabiyah, and his impudent brown face grinned as he had asked, in comprehensible English, if they wanted a guide.

Yes, Omar had told them, he knew the cave; it was near Hamra Dum. The boy's eyes had danced. "Boom, boom!" he had cried and pantomimed the firing of a rifle.

"A range?" Roy had asked him. "Target practice?"

Omar had laughed and nodded his stocking-capped head. "Target practice, but I will keep you safe. Twenty-five pounds for me is very cheap. I will hide my bicycle and come with you now."

Today there was no sign of Omar. We stopped at the market-place so that Dorsey could inquire. With her red hair and blue jeans, she must have been an unusual sight here as she asked for Omar among the solemn women and their watchful children. No one understood her.

As we left El Qasr, the Jabal al Tarif appeared suddenly, rising from its bed of green feathered palms in a soaring battlement of pink stone, tiered and time-carved into towers and spires, buttressed at its base with heaps of talus. In its flank, caves appeared, pairs of deep-set eyes peering out at our approach.

To reach it we turned up a grass-grown lane and parked in the grove where Omar had brought Roy and Dorsey. We had to descend into a gully choked with underbrush, then up its far side onto the banks of loose sand and gravel.

"*Sabakkh*" Omar had called this stuff underfoot, explaining how it was used in his village for fertilizer. It was here, within a few yards of where we stood, that the red earthenware jar had been discovered. A goat path climbed the Jabal's foot, and above us we could make out steps scaling its sheer face toward the bright dome of the heavens.

Dorsey went ahead of me, climbing as though possessed. The sun was still hot, and I had to pause to get my breath, losing sight of her and then finding her again, far above me, still climbing steadily.

I caught up with her on a parapet that formed the lip of a cave. Below, I had glimpses of the meandering Nile. The sail of a felucca passed magically through silvery palms. The pharaonic colonnade at Dendera stood at the horizon. Directly across the river the smelter of an aluminum plant was surrounded by its forest of steel scarecrows. Its company town was dominated by a stucco monolith oddly reminiscent of Miami Beach.

Dorsey glanced at me for encouragement and peered apprehensively into the mouth of the cave. Producing a small, red flashlight from her purse, she led the way through rubble into a fetid and chilling darkness. The weak beam touched a harp of rib bones. Something moved, and she cried out as it skittered farther up the passage.

She played the light along the seamed and shaling walls until she found the inscriptions, broken panels of crude but well-preserved Coptic script, some of it still accentuated with red dye.

"Standing here," Dorsey said, "Roy decided we had to come back. He needed a flash camera to take pictures and a better light to go farther up the cave."

Taking the flashlight from her, I shone it around, finding more panels of the script. "What did he think they were?"

"Some message carved by the Saint Pachomius monks—maybe about their act of sealing up these gospels in a jar and burying them here, who they hoped might find them and look after them. But the odd thing was that Omar, this little Arab kid, seemed to know what Roy was talking about. When Roy asked if he'd heard of a man called Hassan, Omar nodded. His name was Mohammed Ali al Hassan, he said, and he told his story pretty much as we had heard it in Cairo."

I followed Dorsey out onto the parapet, where she pointed out the loess bank at the foot of the Jabal al Tarif. "He'd been digging there for fertilizer when he struck the olla with his mattock. Omar told how Hassan had cracked it open, hoping for some treasure, and when he found just old books he kicked them in his anger, but at the end of the day he put them in his saddlebag and took them home."

"Is this man alive?" I asked.

"Omar wasn't sure. There were so many stories, and he didn't know which to believe. It was known that Hassan had murdered someone, and most people in the village say he died of his wickedness, a vicious, raving old man. There are a few, though, who say he is a Sufi, a holy mystic, and still lives."

"Oh, my," I said. "This is what got Roy excited and put him on the trail. Did the boy offer to help?"

"At that moment Omar became distracted. He stepped out here to listen. Then we heard it too, the sound of gunfire." Dorsey paused now, listening as if she might hear the sound again, but there was only the distant baying of a dog. "Omar had turned serious, and he hurried us down the path to where we had left the Morris. He seemed relieved when we reached the main road and joined the traffic crossing the Nile bridge into Nag Hammadi."

Across the river a lowering sun gleamed on the towers of the hydroelectric plant that surrounded the white hotel like a forest.

"That's the place where you planned to stay?"

Dorsey nodded. "Omar showed us the way there, up the west bank to the Aluminium Hotel, and waited while we took a room and bought a bottle of Egyptian gin from the bartender. Then, on our map he pointed out the red line that went straight across the desert to Luxor and showed us where this road left town."

"But Roy couldn't get more out of him about Hassan?"

"He kept asking, but Omar didn't seem to hear. Then, as Roy was paying him for the day, Omar smiled. He turned crafty and smart-alecky, as he had been at first. He said that if Roy would give him *another* twenty-five pounds, he would look for Hassan. It was such an obvious swindle that we all laughed, but after a minute Roy gave him the money."

Dorsey and I decided to drive, as she and Roy had done, from the Jabal al Tarif to the Aluminium Hotel. As we crossed the Nile bridge into Nag Hammadi, we heard the shrilling of an air horn and we were caught behind the crossing gate that was lowered for the passing of the Aswan-Cairo express. While we waited in the halted traffic behind a great wheezing diesel truck, its bed stacked with aluminum ingots, and a tiny donkey straining at his load of sacked sugar, Dorsey cried out, "Look, Ethan, for God's sake! Here he comes!"

Weaving through the line was a boy on a bicycle. He wore a stocking cap and blue-striped galabiyah. Grinning and waving, he came to a halt at Dorsey's window.

"Omar, we looked for you," she said.

"Hello, yes." The boy said. "You must go to the police now." He pointed out the radio antenna rising over the rooftops of the town. "He waits."

Major Hany, the chief of detectives, seemed to be expecting

us. "Yes," he said, clapping his hands for tea, "perhaps there is news for you now. We cannot be certain as yet."

Our patience was tested by Major Hany's accounting for his excellent English. In fact, he told us, he had read much of our literature at his university in Alexandria. He had grown particularly fond of Defoe and Sterne. Of our own Americans he knew and admired Arthur Miller, T. S. Eliot, and Harold Robbins.

"Please," Dorsey said. "Has my husband been found?"

"A man has been found at Al Saqi," Major Hany said. "He is thought to be American but he does not speak and there is no identification on him. An ambulance is ordered."

"Can you take us there?" she asked. "We want to go right now."

"We will go directly, but first it is necessary to obtain permissions. The road you traveled is restricted. Also we must requisition a police car. While we are waiting, please tell how you happened to enter the desert."

"We were told the road was passable. We could see on the map that it was more direct—and that is the way my husband does things."

Major Hany rolled his eyes. "We have admiration for your American ways, but in this case they were unwise. What was your husband's urgency? What was he doing here? This is hardly tourist's Egypt."

"We came to see the cave at Jabal al Tarif." When Hany showed no sign of recognition, she added, "Where the Gnostic gospels were found."

Major Hany frowned and shook his head.

"Really?" Dorsey asked, "You don't know about them? It's a famous discovery here. How we know the name of your town. Thirty years ago a man called Hassan found them."

"Ah-h." Comprehension broke like sunrise on Major Hany's intelligent face. "Of course. The farmer of El Qasr. I had forgotten about the holy books, but his is a most well-known case." He smiled. "A crime like your Chicago."

"In Luxor," I said, "we were told there is no serious crime in Egypt."

274

"I am sorry to disagree"—Major Hany sighed—"but we are kept busy enough. In villages at the other side of the Nile live many outlaws. The feud is a way of life there. When we police must enter these villages, we say good-bye to our friends with much feeling."

Hands behind his head, he rocked beneath the gaze of the ubiquitous President Sadat. "This fellow Hassan committed a most bloody crime. His father, a watchman, had been killed at his post by a marauder from the neighboring village of Hamra Dum, and the mother in her grief instructed the two sons to keep their mattocks sharp for this man, known as Ahmed Isma-il. When he did appear in the village of El Qasr, the word was passed. Hassan and his brother, Kalifah, seized him, took him to a field outside the village. There they cut off Ahmed's limbs while he lived and in the ancient act of vengeance cut his heart from his breast and devoured it between them."

Seeing that Dorsey was shaken by this account, he went on cautiously. "All this is undeniable fact which emerged in the investigation and testimony at the trial, yet neither brother was convicted. Kalifah was murdered in turn by members of the Isma-il family, and Hassan was acquitted because of"—Major Hany made a spiral at his temple—"peculiar behavior. The judge decided he had been possessed by an evil spirit and so lay beyond man's jurisdiction."

"Bishop Train had just learned something about this man," I said. "He hoped to find him and wanted to return to Nag Hammadi that very night."

"Hopeless," Major Hany said. "If Hassan lives, he would be of great age and, one may presume, have a head full of maggots."

The clock on Major Hany's wall seemed to have stopped, and Dorsey rose to look from the window for the promised police car.

"I am so interested in America," Major Hany said. "Tell me about the custom of your divorce. Does a man have grounds for this when a wife fails to provide him with children?"

"No," I said. "The lack of children would be regarded as a shared misfortune."

"Ah-h." Although baffled, he nodded acceptance. "And a woman? Could she divorce her husband for contracting a sexual disease?"

"Good Lord." I turned to Dorsey, but her back was turned. "She can have a divorce if the parting of his hair displeases her."

The major stared at me skeptically. "And that is Christian?"

"Not exactly," I said, "but it is humane, and we're for that."

From the window Dorsey asked, "Is this it—the jeep?"

Dorsey and I sat in the rear of the army jeep as it passed the barricade at the outskirts of Nag Hammadi and set off on the gravel road she and Roy had taken south.

She recalled that it had been about six o'clock, with the day's heat moderating. Roy had been in high spirits, pointing out how the golden haze that lay upon the desert was becoming a vast purple-and-orange sea.

Roy had seemed drunk with discovery and anticipation, delighted with whatever ancient grandeur would next be revealed to them. The road became rockier, challenging the Morris's springs, and there was no sign of human life. As the sun sank, approached the desert's rim, lakelike shadows appeared in the hollows.

The track was becoming less distinct, but Roy discovered the five masts like a mooring of golden boats on the horizon. It was just to the east of their direction, Dendera, he decided, the columns I had seen from the Jabal. They had come about half the distance to Luxor.

At that moment they heard a new sound in the Morris's thrumming, one that grew into a thump which could not be ignored. Stopping, they found a rear tire gone nearly flat, and when Roy looked into the trunk he found that the spare was missing.

They ate some cheese and biscuits they had brought from Luxor and washed them down with the gin and then decided to drive forward on the flat tire. They had gone less than a half mile when the rim ground to the rocks, bending and dragging them to a halt.

Off to the right they made out a dark fringe that could be

trees and a wadi. As they watched, a column of smoke rose from it, straight as a pencil into the evening sky.

Dorsey was wearing rope-soled espadrilles that she had bought in Cairo. They were already frayed, and Roy thought the sharp stones of the desert floor would shred them entirely.

"They'll do," Dorsey assured him as they made ready to walk.

Roy offered her the gin bottle, and when she declined, he smiled and raised it with Anubis' toast: "To the dark river of the night and the sun toward which it flows." He drank from its neck and pocketed it, and they set off.

When they were about half a mile from the village, so that they could make out thirty or so houses gathered in the wadi and camels tethered under its clump of palms, but no human figures, they saw something moving toward them. At first it came errantly and then straight at them. Closing, it became three dogs, running swiftly. All had slender snouts and skeletal bodies like whippets. Two were a mottled yellow and the third was a rusty black, so short-haired that he looked shaved.

The animals halted a few yards from them. The two yellows huddled behind the black one, which crouched, ears laid flat. Dorsey hung back, praying aloud, "Oh, God, please help us," but Roy kept on, hand extended toward the trembling black, saying, "He's all right. He's just come out to say hello, haven't you, fella?"

The black dog gave an instant's warning, a snarl that bared brown fangs, and then sprang, seizing Roy's extended hand in his jaws.

"Son of a bitch!" Roy cried, pounding the writhing body with his knee until he had freed his hand. Then, surprisingly, the dog slunk off, long tail drooping.

The skin of Roy's wrist had been torn, but there was little blood flowing. Roy sucked at the wound, spitting and keeping an eye on the dogs. The black one had settled on his haunches, sphinxlike, to watch them.

When Roy told Dorsey that she must go back to the car, she had refused, insisted on coming with him, but he pointed out that her shoes would hold them both back and that it was going to be cold.

"There's a heater in the car," he had told her. "Don't worry about using up the gas. Stay as warm as you can." He waited until she had started back. When Dorsey was almost to the car, she turned once more to find night dropping across the desert like the folds of a great curtain, and she watched Roy disappear into it, walking toward the village, the dogs at his heels.

XXII

THERE were chickens pecking at the dried dung cakes stacked along the wall. At the back, where strips of dirty fabric hung from a line, a man lay on a bamboo cot. He was covered with a blanket. His hair was matted and his jaw was stubbled with gray, so at first I thought this wasn't Roy at all.

But Dorsey was already beside him, saying, "Oh, my poor darling, what have they done to you?" Her fingers touched his forehead and the filthy poultice that swathed his right hand.

"Hot," she said, taking her eyes from his face. "What have they done to him?"

Major Hany shrugged.

"How soon will the ambulance come?"

"Presently," Major Hany said. He had been talking with the old woman who reported that Roy had been found in the mosque this morning. He was there when the first villagers had gone for worship. Although he was an astonishing sight to them, they had not disturbed him because he was in the position of prayer. Later in the day he was found to be unconscious.

From the rooftop we had a view not only of the village of Al Saqi but of the infinite Libyan desert beyond. Several dust clouds approached, raising our hopes, but they became trucks laden with workers or with oil drums, and all passed on.

"Why can't we get a helicopter?" Dorsey asked.

"We would like helicopters," Major Hany replied, "but ours is a very poor country."

We were startled by Roy's voice and turned to find that his eyes had fluttered open and he was smiling weakly. "Hello, darling," he murmured, raising his left hand in feeble salute. "You've come, haven't you? You've both come. I knew you'd come for me."

"Oh, yes, my dear." Dorsey knelt at his side, kissed him gingerly. "Are you okay, Roy?"

"I knew"—Roy frowned at her—"you wouldn't marry that guy. You didn't marry him after all, did you?"

Dorsey took a moment to absorb his mistake but did not flinch from it. "No, of course I didn't."

"How do you feel, Roy?" I asked. "Going to be all right?"

His eyes blinked slowly. "Mm-m. Think so."

"Were you drugged?"

Squeezing his eyes shut, he waggled his head. "Slow clearing."

"Where were you? Can you tell us? Were you lost?"

He smiled. "Found, Ethan. I've been found. It's so easy. You just give in, and then you're found."

"Who found you, Roy?"

He looked up at me hazily, troubled with focus, but his eyes were filling with wonder. "*He* did."

"Who, Roy?"

"He found *me*." Roy was drifting off. "Isn't that strange?"

The ambulance was army equipment, a camouflaged, Russian-made truck fitted with four berths. The attendant put Roy into a lower one, allowing Dorsey and me to sit with him. As we started across the desert toward Luxor, Roy was still unconscious, and although he was strapped to the litter, his head rolled drunkenly, so we took turns holding him.

We could feel him shivering, and the lurching and slamming of the ride was further outrage to him. I hammered on the window of the cab, shouting for the driver to slow down, but he went all the faster.

When we reached the Nile road at El Qurna, our way became blessedly smoother. Rousing, Roy said that his hand pained him.

"It's all right," I said. "We'll be at the hospital in a few minutes. They'll fix you up. You'll be fine."

"Just take it easy now," Dorsey urged.

"What was I telling you?" Roy asked.

"Where you've been," I said. "Were you in the desert?"

"When you left me," Dorsey asked, "did you get to the village? Can you remember that?"

Roy's eyes screwed shut as he struggled to recall. Yes, he could remember entering the village, how a child's face had appeared in a doorway and vanished but no one had come out to meet him. Then he had discovered a truck in the square. To his surprise it was an old Model A Ford.

Now Roy's recollection opened further. He had gone looking for the driver and come upon three Arabs at their supper but could not make them understand his need to go back for Dorsey. For bond, he offered his money, his watch, and the remains of the gin. Then, as he was climbing into the truck, he was struck on the head.

His hand went to the swelling above his left ear. The memory returned of waking in a closed room with no idea of how much time had passed. It was a dark, foul place, and an old Arab sat watching him, puffing at a water pipe. There was also a boy in the room who spoke some English. He told Roy he had been mistaken for an Israeli soldier but he was in good hands now. He would soon feel better. He was the old man's guest. He had been expected.

Roy was able to explain that he had left his wife on the road and was relieved when the boy left to find her. With his hawk's face and skin like an elephant's, the old Arab was fearsome-looking, and a foul smell issued from the folds of his robe, but he nodded and smiled as he came to sit beside Roy. His fingers tried the lump on Roy's head and he peered at the wound on his wrist.

The old man brought a basin of steaming water, added some medicine, and put the wrist to soak. Then he urged Roy to try his water pipe and in fact Roy's pain did ease under this treatment and he slept a while, waking to find the boy had returned. The Morris was empty, he said, but Roy should not fear. Occasional vehicles passed, and one would have taken his wife to Nag Hammadi.

Roy's account was interrupted by the impatient wail of our siren and soon we stopped short at the rear entrance of the Luxor Hospital. As he was trundled away on a rubber-tired cart, Roy waved his bandaged hand.

Dr. Foud was mild-looking. He wore an embroidered brown silk shirt, and the stethoscope collaring him was the only mark of his profession. He picked his way across the visitors' room to look from one to the other of us, rubbing his hands.

"What sort of animal was it?" he asked.

I said, "A village dog."

"Did you see it? Did it behave in any unusual way?"

"It was wicked-looking," Dorsey replied. "Lean and mean. Only my husband would have put out a hand to it."

"We asked in the village today," I said. "They knew of no sick dogs."

"Let us hope so," Dr. Foud said. "And how long ago was he exposed?"

"Eight days," Dorsey said. "No, nine now. Is that all right?"

Dr. Foud nodded. "Well, we will look after your husband to-night, and perhaps in the morning we can tell you something more definite."

Luxor Hospital is a two-story, white, colonial building with galleries and gray shuttered windows opening onto El Nil Street and its procession of white-booted poinciana trees. Opposite, on the green Nile bank, men were mending sails. At the Pyramids Nile Cruise Co. dock, boys were hosing down the decks of a rose-hulled steamer and there was a cheerful sound in the golden air, a jingle of bells, the snap of a calèche-driver's whip and the clip-clop dance of a bony horse's hooves.

In the hospital office we were told that Roy's room was number 7 on the second floor. We could hear his voice as we approached. He was hopping about the room in his loose, knee-length gown, resisting the pleas of a lovely Egyptian nurse to eat his breakfast. When she appealed to us, Roy seized the untouched tray from his nightstand and, thrusting it into her hands, sent her from the room.

Walking about, he seemed pale and tense. "I couldn't sleep," he explained. "When I lie down I feel dizzy. I've been up most of the night."

"Didn't they give you something?" Dorsey asked. "They must have Nembutal, even in Egypt."

"I'm full of the stuff," Roy said. "I'm on the serum, the vaccine, and two kinds of tranquilizer." He frowned at his right hand, which was swathed in a fresh dressing. "The swelling's down, but it tingles, as if it's still soaking in that red bath—and I feel so *gloomy*."

"You didn't finish the story," I said. "Do you think you could get back in bed and tell us a little more?"

He was undecided. His reddened eyes flitted this way and that, and he complained of a dry throat. No, he didn't want a drink either, but he allowed Dorsey to lead him to the bed and settle him on it.

It was difficult for Roy to re-enter the time of his captivity in Al Saqi; it was as though he were trying to recover a lost dream. When I asked who his host was, however, Roy's attention focused. He seemed surprised that I had not guessed. The man was Hassan.

"He told you so?" I asked.

Roy said that he had suspected it from the first. All doubt had vanished as the boy translated the old man's story about a curse that had fallen upon him as a young man, how it had resulted from his coming on an ancient olla. There had been a Coptic cross on the seal of its mouth, and standing over it, Hassan had wondered if in smashing the jar he would release a genie. Then he had struck the blow that changed his life.

Roy dwelt, fascinated, on these details, as though he were seeing them now with his own eyes—how, as the olla had shattered, a genie did rise from it, a golden cloud, particles catching fire, sparks that danced before Hassan's eyes, but when he had dared to look among the shards he had found only old books. He had kicked them away in anger and at the day's end packed them into saddlebags, intending to burn them and so destroy their force.

But that had been the night on which Hassan and his brother had avenged their father's murder. Next day he had no sooner gone to work in the canefield than he had felt in his chest the beating of a second heart. He grew faint and could not lift his mattock. The screams of the murderer, Ahmed Isma-il, filled his ears, so that when the police came to question him about the man's death he could not hear what they asked. This was many years ago, and yet the second heart still woke him each night and warned him not to leave the village.

Roy's account was interrupted by a fit of coughing, and Dorsey held him, trying to contain the wracking of his chest and shoulders. He asked for water and she poured a glass from the carafe on the bureau. Taking the glass anxiously from her hands, he raised it to his lips and instantly rejected it, spilling the water and complaining, "It's *cold*. It's *ice* water."

"No, it isn't," Dorsey pleaded. "Feel. It's lukewarm."

Denying it, shivering, Roy allowed Dorsey to pull the bed-clothes up to cover him, but she had no sooner done so than he sprang from the bed to move about the room as though looking for something. Pulling back one of the shutters, he gazed across the Nile into the Valley of the Kings, the tiered corniche with the necropolis in its embrace.

"How does the doctor think you're getting along, Roy?" I asked.

"He wants to send me to Cairo," Roy replied.

Dr. Foud met us under the trees of the courtyard. There was a circle of metal chairs there that had been used in a staff conference just finished. We turned down his offer of a cigarette and watched him light one.

"We believe Bishop Train should go to Cairo today. We are concerned that he may be too ill for us to care for. Will you persuade him?"

"How ill?" I asked.

Dr. Foud made an uncertain balance of his hands. "Incubation for rabies is several weeks. If Bishop Train should have had the misfortune to meet a rabid animal, we would still be in good time. But, as you see, he is agitated. He complains of a sore throat and this thirst which he cannot satisfy. He has a little fever, and his pupils are dilated. Not good. It is possible these symptoms come from the vaccine . . . Still, I am a bit nervous. We are not equipped here."

"What might happen to him?" Dorsey asked.

"He could grow worse," said Dr. Foud. "Light would become painful. As rabies virus travels through the nervous system, it destroys tissue. It is drawn to the larynx in particular, and so we see the spasm and drooling. It is inability to swallow."

"How is it cured?" Dorsey asked evenly.

"If a patient has contracted rabies, there is no cure."

"None here," she said. "No cure here in Luxor, you mean?"

Dr. Foud shook his head. "Nowhere on earth."

"We're going to take you to Cairo, darling," Dorsey told Roy. "You're not to worry about the trip. They'll make you very comfortable."

Roy pushed himself higher in the bed. "Why?"

"You'll have the best of care at the rabies clinic. It's just a precaution, Roy."

"Does the doctor think I have rabies?"

"Maybe," she replied.

He considered that, his gaze drifting toward the gallery and its view of western Thebes. "No," he said, "I don't want to go."

"I think we'd better trust Dr. Foud," I said.

"I can't leave Luxor," Roy said. "There's more to do here, you know. We'll get a dependable car and drive back to Al Saqi. I want you to see that guy."

"But we've got to get you well first. That's the main thing."

"I'll go back to Al Saqi with you, Roy," Dorsey said. She sat at the foot of Roy's bed, one hand on his knee, as if even now she trusted in his prescience.

In the corridor outside I said to Dorsey, "We'll have to follow the doctor's advice. Roy's in no condition to decide."

"He's decided, Ethan," she said. "We'd never get him to Cairo without doping him up, and we haven't any right to do that."

"What will you tell Dr. Foud?"

"That we're getting a second opinion." She was searching in her shoulder bag. "I've got Quincy Tuck's number in Cairo. We'll get somebody to come up from the American hospital."

She hurried off to make the call, and when she returned to Roy's room it was with the news that an American doctor would come to examine him tomorrow. Meantime, there was no thought of moving him.

Roy seemed momentarily relieved but he soon turned irritable, complaining of his itching skin and a dryness in his throat. At suppertime he refused his meal and for half an hour stared fixedly at the ceiling. Then his mouth began to work. He chewed and swallowed and spoke of being hungry.

When the nurse returned and tried to spoon some mashed vegetables between his lips, he shook his head violently and began to retch. Dr. Foud was called, and he bent over Roy to explore his neck and arms with his fingers and to put a stethoscope to his chest.

Beckoning us from the room, Dr. Foud said, "I'm afraid there is no longer a question. This spasm which the bishop endures is what we have most dreaded."

Although he urged us to go to the hotel for some rest, Roy was in such discomfort that we could not leave him. He croaked and swallowed painfully, from time to time whispering to himself, "Yes, I see. I see what it means."

Mercifully, he dozed, and then, just before midnight, he stirred and asked to have the light on so that he could see us both, and pillows propped behind him. His eyes looked drunk with pain, and yet there was a serenity to his voice, as though he spoke from the midst of a dream more vivid and real for him than his hospital room.

He told of a vision the old man had had. It was about a person who would come bringing him a truth that would make his peace with Allah. This person's face had appeared in the vision, but he had been unable to recall it until he saw Roy's. It was the same.

Now Roy asked Hassan if he knew that the beating was that of Isma-il's heart, the one he had eaten in the night of his re-

286

venge, and Hassan had shrugged. The man had killed his father. A Muslim man's strength lay in the honor of his family.

This was the beginning of Roy's understanding. He asked what Hassan had done with the books, and the old man replied that his mother had used some pages from them to start her fire but that a Christian priest had come to see them and prevented her from burning the rest. It was this priest who had brought Hassan a few pounds for the old books.

Roy explained that one of these Coptic books had been smuggled out of Egypt and sold for ten thousand dollars, and the others had been seized and suppressed by the government. He told how, for twenty-five years, they had brought more pain than riches to all who had touched them, fulfilling a curse of Jesus that had been contained among them.

Now Roy told Hassan that his vision had foretold a truth. He, Roy, had brought the answer to his prayer. It was a question. Could he forgive his father's murderer now? If he could, the beating of his second heart would cease forever.

Roy began to weary, his voice fading as he remembered Hassan's response: that it was too late, that these were not his ways, and that he was too old and sick to change.

"I told him it was not too late," Roy murmured. "I told Hassan he must do it now, must tell me so, that he forgives this man and his son and his grandson . . ." Roy's weariness overcame him. His eyelids fluttered and closed.

"Could he understand you?" I asked.

Roy's voice was a whisper. "They have a word for it—*samah*. Hassan said he would repeat it many times a day, until he knew"—Roy smiled—"if I were a true or a false prophet."

Roy said no more, and we realized he had fallen asleep. As Dorsey and I turned to each other, I looked for the reflection of my own skepticism, but her face was wholly credulous, eyes wide with revelation, as if she had just heard the Sermon on the Mount.

In the morning Dr. Butterworth arrived from the American University Hospital in Cairo to take Roy into the examining room. We were heartened by his flinty New England voice and amiable manner. As he talked with Dr. Foud in the garden, he seemed to be prescribing a treatment.

But when we were called to join them, Dr. Butterworth said, "I know you're hoping I'll disagree with Dr. Foud's diagnosis. I'm sorry to say that I can't. Bishop Train has rabies. It is already acute, too advanced for us to offer any hope but a miraculous one."

"Can we take him to the clinic in Cairo?" Dorsey asked.

The doctor shrugged. "The patient must be treated during the incubation phase. Once that is passed, there is nothing to be done." He was held for an instant by the resolve in Dorsey's eyes, but shook his head. "He's hypersensitive. A trip to Cairo would be a useless agony for him. Dr. Foud and I agree that the bishop is better off here."

Far from breaking down at the news, Dorsey seemed strengthened by it. I had expected her to want comforting, but as she drifted away from me, it seemed that she was willing herself to stand straight. I watched her leave the hospital and start along the promenade toward the hotel.

The temple grounds were deserted at this hour, and I sat for a while in the forecourt, where a dozen slender columns with their papyrus-bud capitals cast long shadows on the baked earth as they had each evening since the Nineteenth Dynasty of the pharaohs.

I was thinking about Roy's life ending here in this unexpected place and found I could not believe it. I had always conceived of Roy as more durable than I. I felt sure that like some d'Artagnan he only seemed to be in death's corner and would still overcome his mortal odds.

Dorsey was at our table in the nearly deserted dining room of the Luxor. Although conversation was impossible, we sat together quietly, thinking of Roy. She scarcely touched her meal, but there was a high color in her face and quickness in her eyes.

Setting down her coffee cup, she said, "You know, I don't believe them. I don't believe those doctors know what they're talking about, either of them. I have this strong feeling Roy's going to get well. He's going to fool them with his faith. He will, Ethan."

"Wouldn't that be a wonderful miracle, Dorsey," I said. "We mustn't count on it, though. I'm afraid we'll have to be ready to accept Roy's leaving us."

"Well, I'm not ready," she said with a flash of her old rebelliousness. "I'm not ready for that."

When we returned to the hospital in the morning we found room 7 empty. It was swept clean and its bed made up with crisp linen and plumped pillows. The sight struck us speechless. Dorsey ran toward the office and it was some time before I discovered her. She was beckoning me from the door of room 23, the last on the floor.

"He's here," she told me. "It's quieter and they've made it dark for him . . . but he's worse, Ethan."

The shades had been drawn and a screen placed across the inch or so of open window. The nurse hovered, trying to keep a sheet over his writhing body. His damp, disheveled hair gave him a wild look, but he recognized me. As he propped himself up, I saw that saliva oozed from the corners of his mouth.

When he asked for a drink, the nurse left, presumably to bring him one. When she did not reappear, Dorsey brought him a cupful from the cooler in the corridor, and Roy took it fearfully. He took a sip, then snorted it through his nose, and, flinging it away, dove beneath the sheet.

Dorsey knelt at his bedside. When she touched him with her folded hands, he recoiled as if she had scalded him. I stood at the opposite side and asked, "Roy, do you think you can pray with me?"

He nodded and brought his hands together. His lips formed the words of the Lord's Prayer and gradually his voice became audible, joining Dorsey's and mine. We had reached the words "Lead us not into temptation" when he was taken by a spasm of coughing. It split the closeness of the room with its croupy echo. It was the sound of a dog's yelp.

That night I found the Coptic church on a narrow street beyond the police station. A porter sweeping the chancel insisted on giving me a guided tour and receiving a tip before he took me to the priest. He was in the rectory with friends, watching a soccer match on television.

The priest had no English, but he understood my five Egyptian pounds and I left with a pyx. As I passed again through the sanctuary I saw Dorsey's head bent over a pew back, and I waited for her on the steps.

Watching the passage of dolorous camels with their bone-weary gait, spunky, dust-covered mules pulling carts with strange cargos, the boys calling to me, "Change? Change money?" I felt sure I was afloat in a dream from which I would soon wake to find myself at home in Rutherford with a sermon to prepare for tomorrow.

When she came through the church door, Dorsey seemed refreshed. We walked toward the hotel, and she said, "I asked for strength and God has given it. He's taking Roy to Him now, and we mustn't grieve for ourselves. That's so hard, isn't it, but we have to remember that it's His will. And He's given me the strength through Roy. Isn't that a wonderful legacy, Ethan?"

We arrived at the hospital at eight the next morning. As I lit the candles on his nightstand and set out the Communion vessels, I watched the working of Roy's mouth and the drooling at its corners, wondering if there was any possibility of his taking the wine.

After putting the ribbon stole around my neck, I stood beside him and began, "Almighty God, look on this your servant, Roy, lying in great weakness, and comfort him with the promise of life everlasting . . ." It seemed to me that his fevered eyes were without recognition, but as I reached the consecration, said the words, "For on the night in which He was betrayed He took bread," I felt his eyes upon me, becoming aware.

I broke the wafer between my fingers, and he began to respond, repeating the familiar words, ". . . this is my body which is given for you . . ."

I placed a quarter of the wafer between his drooling lips. We watched him struggle to take it, then weep as it emerged in crumbs at the corners of his mouth.

Raising the little chalice, I went on, "Drink ye all of this for this is the blood of the New Testament which is shed for you," and the words echoed from Roy's lips. "The blood of Christ," we said in unison, "the cup of salvation."

"Let me . . ." Across the bed, Dorsey held forth her hands, and after a second's hesitation I passed her the chalice. I watched her lean over him, bring it to his wet mouth. Roy's eyes widened with fright as he looked into hers, then drooped in submission. His parting lips sipped. His mouth swelled slightly and then his throat fluttered once, twice, and he smiled at her.

He fell into peaceful sleep. Although the darkened room was stifling, his breath came regularly. As the afternoon wore on we took turns at his bedside, and I was alone with him when he wakened. His eyes seemed clearer and the tortured grimace was giving way to gentleness.

He seemed surprised to find me here. "Ethan, I'm so glad." There was a fleeting puzzlement. "Joan? Is she here too?"

"It's Dorsey, Roy. She's just down the hall, getting some air."

"Of course. I meant Dorsey. And it is close in here. Do you want to open those shades, Ethan?"

"The light won't bother you?"

"No."

I opened the shades and the shutters beyond, admitting the purple dusk and a refreshing, desert coolness. As I sat down again, I found him staring, perplexed, at his loins, where an erection had raised the sheet. "Look at hope here," he said. "How eternal she is."

"You *are* feeling better."

"Oh, yes, I am." His voice was rapturous. "I feel quite wonderful. So full of joy. If only we could have gone back to Al Saqi together. That would have made it complete, wouldn't it? I wanted you to meet that man."

"Maybe we will."

"Not much of a healer though." A bright moth of irony flitted across his gaze and he smiled. "But then, who's perfect? You don't have to be an all-round holy man to be holy." He waggled his head slowly. "You couldn't doubt him, Ethan. If you saw him, you'd know he was the man whose mattock had brought down the curse of Jesus. Be sure to tell Laurence, Ethan. Take him back a souvenir."

"I will. I don't know what he'll make of it."

"Tell him. Tell him for me what to make of it. Tell him I found an old hermit who had fallen under God's curse and that I threw him the lifeline. Tell him there is a Jesus curse and it falls on those who stand between God's knowledge and man's. It's what makes the priesthood such a dangerous profession."

Roy closed his eyes as if he were going to rest a while, but I felt a bleak and sudden wind blowing up from the abyss, and I knew that my friend was dead.

I knew, as I had at the start of our friendship, that he was neither a fool nor a clown but a serious man who had to come to faith in his own way. He believed that all he needed to guide him was that spark he carried, God's imprint. I could not be sure how much I had come to share in that belief but certainly I admired it.

In the world's sense, Roy had lost his way tragically. It was that immoderate self of his that had taken him astray, lost him Joan, the sustaining human love that mattered most to him. But now it seemed to me that Roy's essence was less his selfishness than a great reach beyond his own frailties, limitations, and possibilities.

It seemed to me he ought to have been better rewarded for that, and maybe he had been. He was ever surer of the faith he'd sought. It had sustained him in these last hours, bringing him through an agonizing ordeal, as if he could no longer be reached through his flesh—as if to prove again that the body really doesn't matter. Maybe it only seemed a painful death. Maybe to Roy it had been euphoric. It was only what *he* felt and perceived that mattered.

As I knelt at Roy's bedside I felt a kind of emptiness, painful as Roy's thirst, and the prayer came to my lips like cool water to them. "I am the Resurrection and the Life," I said. "He that believeth in Me, though he were dead, yet shall he live. Receive thy servant Roy into the arms of thy mercy . . . and the blessed rest of everlasting peace."

* * *

Dorsey was on the gallery, staring at the dark flow of the Nile. "I think it's over," I said. "I've sent for Dr. Foud."

"Oh, Ethan—why didn't you call me?" she cried, and flew down the hallway.

I waited on the gallery until I saw Dr. Foud arrive on his bicycle, locking it carefully to the rack before entering the hospital. When I reached room 23 Dr. Foud was closing his bag, but he stood for a moment at the bedside, hypnotized by Roy's upturned face. All pain gone, it had become benign, marblelike.

"It is a mercy, you know," he said. "We can all be grateful that he has left us without the need to suffer further."

"He didn't suffer." Dorsey spoke proudly, possessively from the foot of Roy's bed.

"Oh, dear lady . . ."

"My husband told me he had not suffered at all. He was full of joy."

"Yes, of course," Dr. Foud said. "Why don't you go along to your hotel and get some rest? If you will come by in the morning, we can see to the details."

Dorsey and I walked slowly along the promenade, watching the green light of a ferry crossing to the Nile's far side. "They're going to believe him, now," she said. "That's the miracle. Roy was a prophet, Ethan. I feel so strongly that he was telling God's truth, and while he lived nobody understood that. They're going to understand him now. Roy's going to *live*."

"Yes, Dorsey," I said. "I have a feeling he will."

EPILOGUE

IT is two and a half years now since Roy's death and it has
taken me all of that time to set down this recollection of him.
In the course of it I have seen Dorsey's prophecy come partly
true.

Wherever clergymen gather, sooner or later Roy's name will
emerge. Everyone seems to have a Roy Train anecdote, and
some are scurrilous. Someone will say, But you know Roy Train
was right about this or that. We're *doing* that now. It was the new
Presiding Bishop, young Arthur Griswold from the diocese of
Washington, whom I overheard saying, "Well, you know, when
all's said and done, if we hadn't *had* a Roy Train we'd have had
to invent one."

For me, of course, Roy was a good deal more. He was another
part, a wished-for extension, of myself. When I try to describe
that part, I say that he lived as honestly and fearlessly as he could
and in the end did little more harm than the rest of us.

Joan, who is married again and living in Virginia, might not
agree, but I suspect she would. J.J., whom I see from time to
time, calls his band the Resurrection, which surely would have
pleased his father.

What I remember most vividly about Roy is how even on the
threshold of death he was full of joy and hope for the future,

as if he knew something I did not. To my surprise, a belief has rooted in some fertile corner of my soul that all Roy told Dorsey and me about his experience in the desert was essentially true.

Roy's idea of virtue stays with me too—love, forgiveness, tolerance, as the functions of a whole society, which the church must struggle toward constantly, however difficult and remote the possibility of arrival. It is the struggle, not the victory, nor the failure either, that counts, and that is what he left me for a faith.

ABOUT THE AUTHOR

John Leggett is the author of four previous novels—*Wilder Stone, The Gloucester Branch, Who Took the Gold Away?*, and *Gulliver House*—and *Ross and Tom*, the critically acclaimed double biography of Ross Lockridge and Thomas Heggen. Since 1970 he has been the director of the Iowa Writers' Workshop. When he is not in Iowa, he lives in Manchester, Massachusetts, and Napa, California.